ARNOLD   MAR   2010

P9-CFO-758

RECEIVED

JUL 0 9

CALAVERAS COUNTY
LIBRARY

P.I. on a
Hot Tin Roof

Also by Julie Smith

TALBA WALLIS MYSTERIES
Louisiana Hotshot
Louisiana Bigshot
Louisiana Lament

SKIP LANGDON MYSTERIES
New Orleans Mourning
The Axeman's Jazz
Jazz Funeral
New Orleans Beat
House of Blues
The Kindness of Strangers
Crescent City Kill
82 Desire
Mean Woman Blues

REBECCA SCHWARTZ MYSTERIES
Dead in the Water
Death Turns a Trick
Tourist Trap
The Sourdough Wars
Other People's Skeletons

PAUL MCDONALD MYSTERIES
True-Life Adventure
Huckleberry Fiend

P.I. on a Hot Tin Roof

A Talba Wallis Novel

JULIE SMITH

A Tom Doherty Associates Book New York

This is a work of fiction. All the characters and events portrayed in this novel
are either fictitious or are used fictitiously.

P.I. ON A HOT TIN ROOF

Copyright © 2005 by Julie Smith

All rights reserved, including the right to reproduce this book, or portions thereof, in any form.

This book is printed on acid-free paper.

A Forge Book
Published by Tom Doherty Associates, LLC
175 Fifth Avenue
New York, NY 10010

www.tor.com

Forge® is a registered trademark of Tom Doherty Associates, LLC.

Library of Congress Cataloging-in-Publication Data

Smith, Julie, 1944–
P.I. on a Hot Tin Roof / Julie Smith.
    p.   cm.
"A Tom Doherty Associates book."
ISBN 0-765-31255-7
EAN 978-0-765-31255-6
1. Wallis, Talba (Fictitious character)—Fiction.   2. Women private investigators—Louisiana—New
Orleans—Fiction.   3. Justice, Administration of—Corrupt practices—Fiction.   4. Judges—Crimes
against—Fiction.   5. African American women—Fiction.   6. New Orleans (La.)—Fiction.   7. Women
poets—Fiction.   I. Title: Private investigator on a hot tin roof.   II. Title.

PS3569.M537553P15   2005
813'.54—dc22
2004061962

Printed in the United States of America

0 9 8 7 6 5 4 3 2

To my superlative editor, Win Blevins,
and the ever-inspiring Meredith Blevins—
two dear and talented people

Acknowledgments and Author's Note

Though this story takes place in the parallel universe of Talba Wal-lis's New Orleans, I've tried, as always, to make it as realistic as possible, something I find I can never do without a platoon of kind in-formers, coconspirators, and accomplices. Working with them is always not only a huge help, but a great delight—it's such a pleasure to hear smart people talk about what they know.

All my thanks to Debra Allen, Glen Pitre, Mary Howell, Sam Dal-ton, Kathy Perry, Joe Delery, retired Captain Linda Buczek (NOPD), Grant Smith, Greg Herren, Ray Ladouceur, George Terrebonne, Laura Lippman, Steve Sidwell (for some of Buddy Champagne's choicer ex-pressions); and, as always, my husband, Lee Pryor (for a thousand things). All mistakes herein are mine and not theirs.

This book is a work of fiction, yet one thing it describes is very real indeed—the sad decline of Louisiana's shrimping industry. We're also a state famous for our colorful judges, and some have been convicted—or at least accused—of most of Buddy Champagne's crimes and misdeeds. But no one judge, to my knowledge, has been so much as suspected of all of them. Buddy's misbehavior is truly a composite, and to the extent that the character of Buddy himself was inspired by anybody, it's a fictional character. I confess that, like Talba Wallis, I found he reminded me of Big Daddy in the Tennessee Williams play from which I borrowed my title.

P.I. on a
Hot Tin Roof

The Day They Busted Big Chief Alabama Bandana
by the Baroness de Pontalba

It was just eleven days
Before the meanest Mardi Gras in fifty years—
The time we had that shootin' up near Josephine Street
At the Muses Parade
And then a reveler died at the Endymion Ball
Reachin' for a pair o' beads—
The long pearls, I like to hope.
(The Superdome folks said wasn't nothin' *wrong with that*
*   platform—*
She should never *been standin' on that chair.)*

Could *be right.*

And that was just the start of things.
Next thing, they had to close the river—
(Little boat hit a big one.)
And all the cruise ships takin' all the locals out
Who was fleein' the city for Mardi Gras

Couldn't leave

And everybody got sent home with they money back
And all the people comin' in for Carnival
Ended up in Gulfport, Mississippi
'Stead of takin' off they shirts for beads
(The long pearls, I like to hope)

Down on Bourbon Street.

And then a whole front of thunderstorms
Closed down Lundi Gras
At the river,
And the Zulu King and Queen
Arrived at the Spanish Plaza by automobile
'Stead of their traditional pleasure barge

(Though Rex braved the river)

And all day Fat Tuesday the rain come down
In little squalls
That kept some of the toughest Indian gangs drinkin'
Inside Ernie K-Doe's Mother-In-Law Lounge,
Lest they get they feathers ruffled
Or worse yet, they spankin' new museum-quality suits
Waterlogged
And worse for wear.

But none o' that ain't happened yet

P.I. on a Hot Tin Roof

On that perfect February Sat'day
When the Poison Oleanders
Played they songs and calls out behind the Old Mint.
And inside, they had a bead workshop for little kids,
Which Big Chief Alabama Bandana single-handedly
Presided over
Before he played his gig,
His first in three years, due to a little slip that
Cost him precious time up in Angola prison.

(It could happen to anyone)

And Big Chief Alabama had on his new suit,
The one he'd made for that Mardi Gras he missed so long
   ago,
When they took him away,
Which normally he'd'a saved for
The Big Day itself,

But he just couldn't wait.

Well, the chief played a beautiful *gig.*
Played his fool heart out,
Inspired like he was 'cause he was home at last and
It was Carnival time
And his mouthpiece was there in the crowd,
An angel to him 'cause she
Got him out on a technicality
(And that was also her name),
Though she was known to some
As the toughest white bitch
In Orleans Parish,

And proud of *it.*

After that, the other brothers in the gang
Gotta go somewhere
And Big Chief Alabama's got all the paraphernalia
From the bead workshop,
So his lawyer say,
"Look, I'll run ya home."

And she goes and gets her car from that parkin' lot
Over on Elysian Fields
And they be loadin' up the car with all the bead stuff
And Alabama's gorgeous purple head dress,
Which he'd removed to do the heavy liftin'
And some drunk fool come through and
Run into both of 'em and knock 'em down.
They drop what they loadin'
And when they look down,
They's a crack pipe on the ground
Along with all the beads and feathers
And his lawyer's big black tote bag.

And two white po-lice be hangin' on the corner.

Two cops from the same Po-lice department that
Not so long before had busted two well-known artists,
(One a teacher at the New Orleans Center for the Creative
  Arts)
Down by the Santa Fe Restaurant
For walkin' while gay—
And they spent four whole days in Orleans Parish Prison,
Fendin' off insults and advances from the
Very ones that put 'em in there.

Now THAT ain' right!
Well, them same two white po-lice come runnin'.

P.I. on a Hot Tin Roof

Help the chief up,
Dust off the lawyer chick
And see that pipe.

So they happen to look in the front seat of the car

And they see somethin' green
In a plastic bag, which they claim *is pot,*
Which, if it is, makes it okay
To search the rest of the car
And they say *they find*
Two big fat rocks o' crack cocaine
In the trunk with Alabama's kiddy workshop stuff,
Even though Big Chief Alabama was at the time
A member in good standing
Of Narcotics Anonymous
And his angel and mouthpiece and lawyer-chick
Was a member in good standing
Of the Louisiana State Bar
(Though that *don't necessarily mean nothin')—*
And they know *that rock's a plant.*
'Cause somebody don' like somebody—
But that *don' mean nothin'.*
And both *they skinny asses end up in Central Lockup.*

Now ain't that *a bitch?*
No wonder nothin' else went right that year.

CHAPTER ONE

It was one of those robot voices, a male one: "You have a collect call from Orleans Parish Prison."

Uh-uh. She didn't.

Talba Wallis was already crying and she didn't need any more grief, but she didn't give it a thought. This one wasn't for her. She got those calls about every three months. Something happened to people's dialing fingers in Central Lockup, maybe from the drugs or alcohol that got them in there in the first place. She clicked off her cell phone and went back to chopping onions. Her mama, Miz Clara, was slow-cooking ribs in the oven, and Talba was making potato salad for a family meal: Her brother Corey, his wife Michelle, and the adorable Sophia Pontalba (partially named for her aunt, and now talking a blue streak) were coming over soon. Talba still had to make greens, too—her way, not Miz Clara's. Her mother was inclined to cook them for hours, with lots of pork. Talba and Michelle liked them just barely wilted. Dessert was king cake, a present from one of Miz Clara's housecleaning clients, so no worries there.

She had time, if she put her mind to it.

By the time the phone rang again, she had the salad together and had begun washing the greens. The same voice again. She sighed. May as well tell the poor bastard he had the wrong number. She reached for the phone, nearly tripping over two cats currently trying to wrap themselves around her legs to get her mind off her cooking and on their dinner. She waited for the prisoner's name.

"Talba, it's Angie. I need you."

Angie? Angela Valentino? Angie was about as likely to be in Central Lockup as Sister Helen Prejean. Angie neither relieved herself on the street nor smoked pot in public. She avoided bar fights and had no domestic partner to chase with a cleaver. She was a lawyer in good standing. What the hell was this?

"Angie, hang on; I've got to dry my hands." Talba set the phone down for a moment and found a paper towel. "What the hell did you do?"

"Listen, I'm not the problem, they popped Alabama, too—planted drugs on us."

Big Chief Alabama Bandana, one of Angie's most celebrated clients, a musician and Mardi Gras personality famous for his drug problem.

Somebody *could* have planted drugs on him—or maybe that was just what Angie wanted to believe. "But . . . but . . . your parents . . . ," Talba said. She couldn't figure out why Angie was calling her instead of them. Talba's boss was Angela's father, Eddie Valentino, one of the best-connected people in town. If anyone could spring his daughter, Eddie could.

"They went to the Gulf Coast for the weekend. Dad's got his cell phone off."

I'll just bet he has, Talba thought. Eddie was nothing if not discreet, but you didn't have to be a genius to figure out that the Gulf Coast had an aphrodisiac effect on his wife, Audrey. He took her there whenever he could and was always unavailable until they got back.

"You know what it's like in Central Lockup? God forbid you should ever find out. You get access to a phone, but no phone book. You can only call numbers you know by heart."

"Oh. Maybe that's why I get so many wrong numbers." Talba heard herself babbling, aware that she was in shock.

Angie said, "Huh? Listen, it doesn't matter. You've got to get us out of here."

"Obviously. Where do I start?"

"We've got to find a judge who'll set bond on a Saturday night."

"Give me a name and I'll call it."

"No, let my lawyer do it. Jimmy Houlihan. Problem is, I don't know his home number. See if he's in the book, will you?"

"*Your* lawyer? Lawyers have lawyers?"

"Jimmy's a friend."

Uh-huh, Talba thought. *Ex-boyfriend.* Fingers shaking, she looked him up. "Not here—only his office. But I could call his answering service. Or better yet, let me go online. I can't call you back, right?"

"No, but I can call you next time the phone's free."

"Forget it. You've made contact—I'll do the rest. You okay, by the way?"

"I'm making lots of new friends, none of them deputies. No problem, I'll live. I'm just worried about Al."

"Want me to call his family?"

"You can try, but I don't know his number by heart. His real name's Albert Brazil; he might be in the phone book."

"Okay, I'll take it from here. Hang in there, okay?"

"Thanks." Talba heard the relief in her voice. "Listen, one last thing. Tell Jimmy it can't be Buddy Champagne."

"What can't be?"

"The judge. Anybody but Buddy. Whatever happens, not Buddy. Even if we have to spend a week in jail."

"Got it. Not Buddy."

When Talba put down the phone, she noticed that her palm was damp, along with her temples. Whew. This was a blow.

Well, so much for Michelle's health-food greens. She went in search of Miz Clara, who was taking a preprandial snooze, secure in the knowledge that her daughter had dinner under control. "Mama? Can you wake up?"

Miz Clara started. She was wearing a pair of old sweats and a T-shirt, the kind of thing she wore to work; no wig, and she probably wouldn't put one on, either—this was just family. "Sandra, whassup, for heaven's sake? I jus' barely drop off and you come in here shakin' me like somethin' on fire." She called her daughter a different name from the one Talba called herself, and thereon hung a tale—no one in the family ever mentioned Talba's birth name, which was neither San-dra nor Talba.

"Mama, Angie's in jail."

"*Angie?* What she do, insult a judge?"

"Says she was framed. Listen, I've got to get her out. The potato salad's done; you mind fixing the greens?"

Miz Clara looked at her watch. "Take two hours to make greens—I got thirty minutes."

"Mama, it doesn't. Just put them in a steamer for awhile."

"Mmph."

"Michelle likes them that way."

"She would." Michelle came from a much fancier family than the Wallises ever thought about being.

Talba could feel the minutes ticking away. Every second she wasn't working on the problem was a second Angie and Alabama would have to spend in jail. "Go on," Miz Clara said. "Do what ya gotta do. I'll feed ya rats." Cats, she meant. Blanche and Koko were more her cats than Talba's.

First, Talba thought, the musician's family. An Albert Brazil was listed on Villere Street. That would be him. Most Mardi Gras Indians lived in Tremé. A woman answered. "Mrs. Brazil?"

"Ain' no Miz Brazil."

"I'm looking for the family of Albert Brazil."

The woman's voice changed. "Somethin' happen to Albert? Yeah, I'm Miz Brazil." *Just not legally*, Talba thought.

"Listen, Albert's fine. But there's been a mix-up, and I'm working on it. I work with his lawyer, Angela Valentino. . . ."

"Oh, Lord, don't tell me he in jail again!"

"Not for long, if I can help it."

"Who you? Why you callin' 'steada Miss Angela? I ain' know who you is."

"My name's Talba Wallis. I'm a P.I. who works with her father, Eddie Valentino. We do a lot of work for Angie's firm."

"Well, why ain't Miss Angela callin'?"

"She's—uh—" Something told Talba to dissemble. "We're both working on it. She's trying to get a judge to set bond. Asked me to call you; set your mind at ease."

"Swear to God, this the last time! Albert done swore on the Big Book he clean, he stayin' clean. He barely out of jail, and now he back in. You get him out, tell him he better not come home."

Talba knew she shouldn't give out any more information than she had to, but she wanted to ease the woman's pain if she could. "Angela says the drugs were planted."

"Oh, yeah! Uh-huh. That what he always say. They all say that; don't you know nothin'?" She hung up in a fury, leaving Talba with uncomfortable nigglings. Everybody in jail said they were framed. She was well aware of that. She knew Angie well enough to know she wasn't a druggie, but surely the lawyer was being naïve where the Chief was concerned. Talba was inclined to agree with the self-styled Mrs. Brazil—there were probably very few innocent people moldering in Central Lockup.

Finding Jimmy Houlihan's number was a piece of cake, given Talba's computer skills. And after no more than twelve or thirteen rings, a man answered. "Mr. Houlihan?" Talba asked.

"Jimmy? You want Jimmy?" The man sounded as if he wasn't sure he'd heard correctly. In the background she could hear the buzz of conversation, the clinking of glasses, and two different kinds of loud music, one involving drums. "Think he went to the parade."

Talba thanked him and hung up, surmising that since Houlihan lived on St. Charles Avenue itself—the main artery of almost every parade of Carnival—a parade party was in progress. Technically speaking, it wasn't the first weekend of parades—Krewe Du Vieux had rolled the weekend before in the French Quarter.

But it was the second day of the twelve days of almost constant parading that mesmerized the city while paralyzing its traffic every year at this time. The only break would come on the following Monday. Otherwise, there would be at least two parades a day in New Orleans itself, plus many more in the suburbs until Ash Wednesday. No one who lived on St. Charles or near it escaped entertaining. People with college-age children found themselves running impromptu dormitories and soup kitchens; those with out-of-town friends who had the price of airline tickets became instant B&B proprietors; and anyone who was left who knew anyone at all pretty much held open house—whether they wanted to or not.

Since it was only the second day, spirits would be high; nobody'd yet be burned out. No wonder you couldn't hear yourself think at the Houlihan house. Talba was going to have to pay the lawyer a visit, and that wasn't going to be easy, given the traffic. Still, she knew she could do it if she followed Eddie Valentino's Foolproof Carnival Driving Formula, which involved staying on I-10 whenever she could and avoiding Magazine and Prytania as if they were St. Charles itself—in other words, sticking to the lake side of the parade route. (It got more complicated the night of the Endymion Parade, which rolled in another neighborhood entirely, but there were ways, and Eddie knew them.)

Talba followed the Valentino blueprint, ending up on Baronne and wondering where she was going to park. But as it turned out, she needn't have—many of Central City's most enterprising entrepreneurs had set up temporary lots at twenty dollars a spot. This had to be a place where they just couldn't wait for Mardi Gras to come around. It was a dicey neighborhood, the kind where, on a normal night, you might not be all that surprised to find a car window broken or a lock smashed when you returned. Talba figured that tonight the twenty dollars not only paid for the spot, but ought to cover protection as well. Best of both worlds, she thought, admiring capitalism in action, and, despite herself, catching the festive feeling of the neighborhood. Carnival might be a pain, but once you broke down and gave in to it, it sucked you in like a purple, green, and gold patch of quicksand. She certainly hoped Jimmy Houlihan was a good enough friend of Angie's to resist the irresistible.

The Houlihan house was overrun. It was a big brick edifice with columns, decked out with Mardi Gras garlands that failed to make a good showing against the red brick, but a Mardi Gras wreath on the white door took up the slack. The door was open now, and the porch was jammed with white people, glasses and go-cups in their hands. A pale guy in a pinstriped shirt, obviously thinking Talba didn't belong, asked if he could help her.

"Happy Mardi Gras," she said. "Jimmy said to pop by if I could."

He planted a big one on her. "Happy Mardi Gras," he rejoined. "Bar's inside."

Talba grinned at him, dying to wipe off the slobbery kiss, but thinking it might be rude. "Jimmy around?"

He shrugged. "Saw him awhile ago. Look for a Mardi Gras rugby shirt."

She checked out the crowd. Half the men in the crowd wore green, gold, and purple shirts. "Thanks a lot."

She left him guffawing, obviously having had a beer or two, and made her way inside the house. A woman in jeans, smooth hair in one of those neat pageboys favored in this neck of the woods, spotted her and snaked her way through the crush, probably wondering if Talba was someone off the streets, attracted by the crowd. Talba waved as if she knew her. "Hiii! You must be Patsy Houlihan." She'd found the name on an opera Web site. "I'm Talba Wallis."

"Oh, uh, hi. Uh. Talba. You must work with Jimmy." She looked a little confused.

Good. Talba must have guessed right. "I'm a client." She let it hang there awkwardly, forcing the other woman to make some kind of move.

"Well. Let's get you a drink." She turned, expecting Talba to follow her to the bar, which Talba did.

The bartender was African-American, like Talba herself, wearing a white waiter's jacket. "Just water, please."

The guy didn't smile at her, didn't seem to be enjoying his work. She tried Patsy again. "I was hoping to say hello to Jimmy."

Patsy swiveled her head. "Oh. Jimmy. He may have gone out to the street."

Better fess up, Talba decided. "Actually, I'm kind of a client by proxy. I've got an emergency, but unfortunately I don't know Jimmy by sight."

The white woman's features froze. She was one of those bird-like, gym rat types whose day was probably all about getting her fingers and toes painted. The kind who had a garage that opened with a remote and never parked on the street for fear of getting mugged. She might not be a racist, but Talba had a feeling this was the first time an African-American who wasn't on staff had ever been to one of her parties. And she wasn't adjusting any too quickly.

Talba had a feeling mentioning Angie's name wasn't the way to go. "I'm a P.I.," she said. "My firm works with his firm." It might even be true. Eddie'd been around so long he'd probably worked with every lawyer in town at some point.

"But I . . . but it's Mardi Gras!" In some other context it might have

23

sounded shallow, but in New Orleans, everything stops for Mardi Gras. Talba could grasp Patsy's displeasure. This was like appearing at someone's house on Christmas morning.

She was almost out of ideas, but at that moment a man in a Mardi Gras rugby shirt danced up. "Hey, darlin', you're missing the parade." He put a well-shaped hand on Patsy's shoulders, and was rewarded with a scathing look.

"Jimmy?" Talba said, before Patsy could recover. *Can this marriage be saved?* she thought.

The man removed his hand from his wife's shoulder and offered it to Talba. "I don't believe I've had the pleasure."

There were a lot of different ways you could say that phrase. This man said it gently, sincerely, as if, despite its stiffness, it came naturally to him. Talba saw that he was tall, with good shoulders and a big chest. He had silky brown hair—quintessential white-dude hair—and small, stylish spectacles; one of those pinkish Irish faces; a rounded nose, but an oval face, an open one. An attractive man, someone Angie could be friends with.

She gave him a broad smile. "Sorry to barge in like this. One of your clients asked me to get in touch, but when I called . . ."

"Oh, God, no telling who answered the phone."

"It was someone who didn't seem to know where you were." She glanced nervously at Patsy. "I wouldn't have come, but your client's got a sort of emergency."

He laughed. "Don't tell me he called from Central Lockup."

Talba lifted a wry eyebrow. "Guess it's happened before."

Houlihan seemed to be uncomfortably aware that his wife was taking in every word, and doing a slow burn at the same time.

"Patsy, you go on and have fun. Let me see what I can do for this lady."

Patsy drifted away, apparently determined to keep up appearances, but Talba surmised that her house at Mardi Gras had the same rules as an exclusive men's club—no business was to be transacted on the premises.

Talba smelled a spat in the making. She felt sorry for him. "It's Angela Valentino," she said.

"Geddouttahere!"

"She was with Al Brazil when they got popped. You know, Chief of the Poison Oleanders?"

"Sure. Everybody knows Big Chief Alabama. By reputation, anyhow. What happened?"

"She says somebody planted drugs on the Chief."

"That Angie. What a little Pollyanna."

Talba was getting impatient. "I work with her dad, so she called me. Said to get you to get a judge to set bond for both of them."

He nodded. "I can do that. Hey, no problem whatsoever. We got a couple judges soakin' up the suds right out on the porch."

"Well, one thing. She said anybody but Buddy Champagne."

This time he was the one speaking eyebrow language. "Well, that do make it harder."

"Champagne's here?"

Houlihan shrugged. "He's a neighbor. Easiest thing in the world to set it up."

"Loosely translated, she said she'd rather rot in jail."

He laughed. The judges weren't the only ones soaking up suds. "Hey, you're a pretty sharp cookie. Who are you, anyway?"

"Talba Wallis. I work with Angie's dad. He was away, so she called me."

His face clouded. "But why didn't she just call me directly?"

"They don't give you a phone book and she didn't have your number memorized."

"Well . . . she used to." She could see the regret in his face and thought that anyone married to Patsy Houlihan could be forgiven for having a wandering eye. "Angie's really in jail? Little Angie?"

"Last I looked, little Angie could take ten men about your size." It was true, though it had a great deal more to do with attitude than Angie's own size—she was a perfect size eight, maybe even a six.

"Woo. 'Tain't it the truth." Houlihan sighed. "Okay, let me go do the honors. Make yourself at home. I'll find you when it's done."

"Shouldn't be hard." Talba waved at the sea of white faces. "I kind of stick out in this crowd."

"Yeah, well," he muttered, "Patsy's in charge of the guest list." He melted into the melee. If he and Angie had been an item once, he seemed nostalgic for old times.

25

Making herself at home was a good trick, Talba thought, when your hostess hates you, but she set about making friends with the sour bartender. "Long night, huh?"

The man sighed. "Long as a piece of balin' wire."

"I heard that," she said, rolling her eyes. Evidently she wasn't the only one who had her differences with Patsy.

"Sure you wouldn't like a little something in that water?"

Talba handed him her glass. "Little more ice, maybe. I've got to be alert—got to go bail someone out in a while."

"I'm sure sorry to hear that."

Talba raised her freshened glass. "Happy Mardi Gras," she said.

CHAPTER TWO

She went outside to watch the parade, thinking maybe Patsy wouldn't mind her presence so much if she wasn't in the house proper, what with the silver and everything. She wished she'd changed, but the hostess had on jeans, too. Why should she feel underdressed?

It seemed hours, but it was probably only about twenty-five minutes before Houlihan sought her out again. "Mission accomplished. Nearly had to throw Ken Friedland in the shower to get him sober enough to make the call, but it got done. Buddy'd sure have been a lot easier."

"Thanks."

"Listen—Ken was pissed that he had to work. Wouldn't release Angie on her own recognizance. Sorry."

Talba was unsure what he meant. "You mean he wouldn't set bond?"

"That much he would do. Reluctantly. It's five thousand dollars for Angie, but he doubled it for the chief. That's fifteen hundred to a bail bondsman—can you swing it?"

"The important thing's to get Angie out. She can worry about Al."

"Listen, let me help you."

Talba thought nervously of Patsy. "Naah," she said regretfully. "We'll be fine."

"You sure?" But he looked relieved.

"Really."

"Well, there's one thing. Judges can set bond, but they don't really have any clout with the sheriff. Every prisoner brings in so much revenue per day; so nobody gets out before midnight the day they're arrested. That's the rumor, anyhow."

"Damn!"

"You ever done this before?"

Talba shook her head.

"Go to Harry Nicasio. He won't cheat you."

"An honest bail bondsman. What a concept."

He laughed again. "You're a piece of work, you know that?"

"That's what Eddie says. Angie's dad."

His eyes took on a faraway look. "Never met Eddie."

"You've got to be the only one in New Orleans." She figured Jimmy just didn't remember him—everybody'd run into Eddie at one time or another.

"Good luck to you," he said, and touched her shoulder.

She made her way out to the street, crossing the avenue between floats, retrieved her car, and drove, first to an ATM, then to the West Broad Street office of Harry Nicasio, whose male, skinny, black assistant took her cash and walked her over to Central Lockup, where she waited six hours for Angie to be processed, first into the system, then out of it.

As usual, the lawyer wore black. Black T-shirt and black jeans, practically guaranteed to stand up to anything, even a night in jail. But for once, the elegant Angie managed to look disheveled.

Without a word, she went for a hug and held on tight for a while. Finally, Talba ventured, "You okay?"

Angie bit her lip. "Pride's hurt, that's all. Jesus! That's an experience no one should have."

"You've got to be hungry."

The lawyer ignored her. "How about Al? Jimmy get him out?"

"His bond's been set, but I couldn't get the cash. It's a thousand dollars. Can you?"

"Shit! Who keeps that kind of money around? What are we going to do? We can't wait for the banks to open; he'll have to spend the rest of the weekend in jail."

"ATM?"

"Yeah. Maybe. I've got a gold card—I think I can get eight hundred dollars, and I've got about a hundred fifty in my purse. Do you have another fifty?"

"Yeah. Just. Same deal with me—I could only get four hundred, but I had a couple of hundred bucks, and a hundred of that went for your bail. I can give you the fifty, and still buy you breakfast." Talba looked at her watch. "But, Angie, it's three A.M. It'll take hours to process him—believe me, I know. Why don't you go home and get some sleep and we'll do it first thing tomorrow."

"I can't leave him."

Talba had enough sense not to argue. "Okay, okay. Where's your car?"

"They made me leave it parked on Esplanade, near the old Mint— that's where we got picked up. Al was playing a gig there. Just get me there and I'll take care of the rest. You've done enough for one night."

Talba sighed. There was nothing she'd rather do than go home, but she felt like Angie did—she couldn't really leave a friend in trouble. "Look. I'll go with you to get the money and post the bond. But you don't have to wait for Al—he's got a wife. Or something. She can go get him."

"I don't trust her."

Talba sighed again. But the way Angie stumbled when she tried to walk, teared up every five minutes or so, and kept absolutely silent told her the lawyer simply wasn't up to it. She was in shock, too disoriented to function. In the end, they posted the bond, and finally went by Brazil's house to alert his wife and give her taxi fare to go get him. By then it was almost five, and Angie was so far gone she'd stopped speaking entirely. Her eyes had receded into sockets deep as potholes.

Not good, Talba thought, *very not good,* and wondered what to do to help. Just take her home and tuck her in, maybe. Stay with her in case she woke up hysterical. But sometime on the drive home, Angie breathed, "Talba?" in a mousy voice, very different from her normal commanding contralto. "Is a hamburger possible?"

Yes! Talba thought. *The fever broke.* "La Peniche ought to be jumping about now."

The lawyer winced.

29

"Okay, okay, we'll get a burger to go."

She drove to the Faubourg Marigny hangout and found a parking place. "I'll just be a minute."

"No. I don't want to stay in the car alone."

"Come with me, then."

Zombie-like, Angie opened the car door.

"Sure you can walk?"

"Of course I can walk. I was in jail, not a war." She was definitely bouncing back. And somehow, the cheerful atmosphere and good smells of the restaurant had such a salubrious effect that she agreed to sit down and order, "like normal people," as she put it.

Talba ordered a full breakfast, but Angie stuck with the hamburger plan, and wolfed it, washing it down with a bourbon and water. "Want to tell me what happened?" Talba asked, between bites of grits and scrambled eggs. She was getting a second wind herself.

"Somebody planted drugs in my car."

"It wasn't locked?"

"Sure it was locked. They opened it with a slim jim or something."

"Angie," she said gently. "Al's got a history. I know you want to believe in him and all, but do you realize how unlikely that sounds?"

"No, listen. They couldn't search without probable cause, right? Here's what they did. One of them came running down the street, ran into us, knocked a bunch of stuff out of our hands, and dropped a crack pipe on the sidewalk. These two cops just happened to appear out of nowhere, saw the pipe, and just casually looked in the front window, where there just happened to be pot on the front seat. Then they found rock in the trunk, and threw us up against the car before we knew what was happening. Listen, if I did have pot, would I leave it on the seat of my car?"

"How do you know the guy dropped the pipe? It could have been Al's, right? He must have had it in something he was carrying."

Angie set down her glass, now about two-thirds empty. Her face was taking on a lot more color. "Talba. I saw the guy drop it. Anyway, the pipe's not the point—it was just a prop. The point is, there was pot in plain sight in my car. And the cops were there way too fast. It just doesn't add up."

You're dreaming, Talba thought. "You know how much juice it would take to get two cops to do something like that? And why would anyone care? Alabama might be a Big Chief, but he's just not that big a fish."

"They didn't want him. It's not even a good arrest—the judge'll throw it right out. They wanted me. That's why I'm such a wreck. You think a little thing like a night in jail could turn the meanest white bitch in town into a zombie? He depended on me, and this is what happens!"

"Somehow I get the feeling I'm missing something."

"You know what? I'm going to die if I don't get to bed soon. Let me tell you tomorrow, okay? I've got to make sure LaKeisha gets Al out, get hold of Dad . . . I think we need a meeting. You doing anything tomorrow?"

Talba had a date with her boyfriend, Darryl Boucree, who'd had his daughter Saturday night. She hadn't seen him in days. "Nope. Totally free," she said. "What time you want to meet?"

"I can't call Mom and Dad back from the Gulf Coast, and anyway I wouldn't want to. You know what a good mood Dad's always in when he gets back."

"Uh-huh. And think I know why."

"Yeah. Works for Mom, too. I don't know why, but it never seems to have that effect on me. But let's let them have their little honeymoon, shall we? And maybe meet tomorrow night? Somewhere besides their house—the last thing we need's Mom's input."

Talba could hardly think of a worse idea—Audrey in mother bear mode might involve firebombs. "Sure," she said. She could at least spend the day with Darryl. His daughter, Raisa, would still be there, so sex was out, but she figured Eddie needed it a lot more than she did. She could live with the schedule change. "How about this? What if I call Eddie and say you and I have an emergency—get him to meet me at the office?"

"Perfect."

Eddie found the call from Ms. Wallis, as he invariably called his young associate, on his home voice mail, and he didn't feel good about it. He phoned her back: "What's so important it can't wait till tomorrow?"

"Eddie, it's Angie's deal," she said. "I just called so you could kill the messenger and still keep your family intact."

He sighed, feeling still less good about it. "Why don't y'all come over for dinner?"

"Angie said no. Because of Audrey." So it directly involved his daughter. He was now feeling downright anxious.

"Well, let's at least make it a bar. I got a feeling I'm gonna need a drink. And Angie knows all the bartenders."

So they agreed to meet after dinner at the Touché Bar in the French Quarter, which was technically part of the Royal Orleans Hotel, though it had a separate entrance and none of the guests would probably be caught dead in it. It was strictly a hangout for locals, but you could go in the back for privacy if too many friends and neighbors were bellying up. Eddie'd picked it because the Quarter was convenient for the two women, and the hotel was just about the only place there he could be sure he'd find parking.

He got himself a beer and engaged a couple of drunken lawyers and a besotted judge in inane conversation until his daughter appeared. She didn't look good. As usual, she was dressed in black, and it emphasized the circles under her eyes. "You're starting to look like your old man," he said. "Ms. Wallis swears she can gauge my mood by the color of my eye bags. Yours are looking kind of inky."

"Well, yours are kind of rosy, Dad. Good weekend?"

She was trying for lightness, but he could see the tension in her face. "Yeah, great," he said without enthusiasm. "Way too long ago. Whatcha drinkin'?"

She didn't hesitate. "Bourbon and water."

Ms. Wallis popped in the open door and sneaked up behind them. "Glass of white wine while you're at it. Hi, Eddie. Good weekend?"

"Till it turned bad," he said. "That's what's happening, right?"

Neither of them contradicted him.

They shook off the three sodden officers of the court and sauntered to the back, where there were actual booths and tables, and not one single patron. Eddie sneezed. Mildew was running amok in the place; or maybe it was that mold that gave you a headache. Something was giving him one.

"Okay, girls. How bad is it?"

"Getting worse," Angie said, causing Ms. Wallis to glance at her anxiously. "But it might be containable—with Talba's contacts."

"Talba's contacts." That was a new one; Eddie was famous for knowing everybody. "You're hurting my feelings."

Ms. Wallis looked mystified. *"Me?"* she mouthed at Angie.

Angie shook her head at her, ever so slightly. "Let's back up, shall we? Start from the beginning?"

"Floor's yours."

And out of his daughter, Angela, the darling little girl who'd cried at her first communion because everything was so beautiful, poured the story of getting thrown in the slammer for possession. He wanted to put his arms around her and hold her—and knew there was about as much chance of that as of petting a tiger. Instead, he caught her eyes. "Angie, I'm so sorry," he said. "I wish I coulda stopped that from happening." He thought he could do it without misting up, but his vision blurred, and his daughter averted her eyes. He went gruff on her. "Ya client screwed ya; ya know that, don't ya?"

"Dad, he didn't. Hell, I wouldn't mind that so much—I'd put it down to bad luck if that was it. Hazard of being a criminal lawyer. The thing is, I screwed him. That's what I feel so bad about."

Eddie felt fury course through his body. He'd raised her better than that. "Ya tellin' me ya had drugs in ya car? What the fuck were ya thinkin'?" He made it a point of forbearing to swear in front of women. "'Scuse my French."

"No, I'm not telling you that. Will you listen? I was set up."

Eddie made a sound like *pssp.* "Yeah, and I got a bridge to sell ya. How 'bout the Superdome? Get ya a good deal."

She ignored him, instead straightening up and leaning forward slightly. "You know Buddy Champagne?"

"Yeah, I know Buddy. Good guy."

"Bad guy."

Eddie considered. That was possible. He knew Champagne mostly from running into him at the Bon Ton, Ruth's Chris, Mandina's, places like that; people he knew knew the judge. That didn't really mean Eddie did, though they'd exchanged plenty of small talk over the years. "Go on," he said.

"Well, awhile back, Buddy bought the old Pelican Marina, out at Venetian Isles. You know it?"

"Run-down old place."

"Yeah. Buddy got it for a song and he decided to turn it into a commercial enterprise, make it pay off for him."

Eddie nodded. "Nothin' wrong with that."

"But the thing is, it's right in town—right in the middle of the neighborhood, and it isn't zoned for commercial use."

"I'm listenin'."

"Think that bothered Buddy? Oh, no. Buddy's a judge, see? He's above the law. Buddy can do what he damn well pleases—in Buddy's opinion. But the neighborhood people didn't see it that way. They tried to stop the development."

That jarred Eddie's memory. "It's comin' back to me now. The *Times-Picayune* ran a little piece about it. Sounded like a technicality or somethin'—like some guy with a grudge against Buddy tryin' to harass him."

"It was a pretty biased story. It isn't just one guy. It's a real grass roots movement. Champagne's doing seafood processing out there. You know how that smells when the wind's right?"

"You gettin' to the point any time soon?"

"I'm the lawyer for the neighborhood group."

Eddie thought about it a minute before the penny dropped. "Let me get this straight. You sayin' a judge planted drugs on ya—you and ya well-known druggie client—to scare you off the case?"

"Actually, I don't think scaring was exactly the point—I think he meant to permanently disable me."

"What makes ya think that, Angie? Ya had a run-in with him in court or somethin'?"

"Several, as a matter of fact. But who hasn't? It's not that, Dad. He's done it before—to Ben Izaguirre, the head of the group I represent. Only Ben saw Buddy's thugs messing with his car, and got there before they could get his bought cops to bust him. Found the stuff and threw it in the lake. Not five minutes later, two cops showed up with some kind of bullshit violation and searched his car."

"Uh-huh. How did he know Champagne was behind it?"

"The guy who planted the drugs works at the marina."

"Don't mean nothin'."

"It might not. But Ben got a couple of warning phone calls first—telling him to back off or else."

Eddie chewed his lip. "Okay, okay, I see what ya gettin' at. Did you get a warning call?"

"Uh-uh. Ben called the judge afterward and got tough with him. Buddy denied it, of course, but I guess he figured out it didn't take a genius to connect a back-off call with a little back-off action. So with me, he played hardball." She stopped and sighed. "And Alabama's paying for it."

Eddie was getting her drift; the more she talked, the more plausible it seemed. Now he thought about it, he'd heard rumblings about Champagne; but then you heard stuff about everybody. He hadn't paid a lot of attention. "Swear to me on ya mother," he said, "that there's no way ya client coulda had the drugs."

"Dad, I swear to you. The drugs weren't even in his stuff. The pot was on the front seat, and he hadn't even been in the car yet. The rock was way in the back of my trunk. Somebody had tucked it away in a real safe place. Very tenderly and lovingly."

Eddie set down his beer with a thunk. "That bastard—'scuse my French—mess with my little girl, I swear to God—"

"Dad, cut it out. I'm not a little girl." She paused and gave him what from her was a beseeching look, though you'd have to be a close relative to pick it up. "But I do need your help."

For the first time in a long while—an unnaturally long while—Ms. Wallis spoke. "Ange. What did you mean when you said it was getting worse? And what in hell was that about my contacts? I don't have any contacts."

"You have one. Evan Farley called from the *Times-Picayune* this afternoon. He's the one who wrote that unfair story about the marina. Champagne's got him in his pocket."

"Called about what?" Eddie asked.

"He knew Al and I got arrested."

"And he's going to run a story about it?"

"Unless we can nip it in the bud."

"Jane Storey!" Ms. Wallis said. Storey was a *Times-Picayune* reporter and a friend of hers.

Angie nodded. "I thought maybe if we could offer her a better story, they might hold off on this one. I mean, I don't know how much clout she's got, but it might be worth a try."

Eddie was seeing his daughter's law school education go down the drain. If the story ran, she might never recover from it—no one would remember she was never convicted of the crime; all they'd remember was that she'd been involved in something shady. He absolutely couldn't let that happen to her.

"I don't care for myself, but Alabama's a public figure. He doesn't deserve this, y'all. I got him into this. The one person he trusted."

"Ya better start carin' for yourself," Eddie muttered. His mind was whirling. "Look, if Buddy planted the drugs, he's dirty."

"Yeah. And you guys are detectives, right?"

"Angie, Angie. Hold it. How we gonna prove somethin' like that?"

"Ben says he's into other stuff."

"What other stuff?"

Angie leaned back, deflated. "I don't know. We need time." She looked at Talba, her eyes pleading—or as close to pleading as they got.

Ms. Wallis was nodding. "Could be done. I've got an idea."

"God help us," Eddie said automatically.

"Look, I'll do one of my undercover acts."

Ms. Wallis had two other talents besides being a pretty decent fledgling P.I.—she was an accomplished poet and a computer virtuoso. Anything that needed doing, she could do, so as long as it involved the infernal machines. She was self-taught, but she could play the computer like a Stradivarius. It made her an invaluable little corporate spy. Somebody needed a nerd, she could get the job; and while she was in the office, nobody had any secrets. Eddie'd never say it to her face, but he was in awe of what she could do. True, he had doubts about her methods, but she swore to him she never did anything illegal.

"This ain't no fancy law office, Ms. Wallis. Ya think ya gonna worm ya way into his chambers, go through his files? Besides, he ain' gon' have anything on paper."

"I'm not going into the courthouse, Eddie. I'm going into his house—as a maid."

There were those who said Eddie was a bit of a racist and even more of a sexist—Audrey and Angela, for two—but this didn't sit right with him. No way was he going to send his associate in as a maid. Uh-uh. He said it aloud: "No way, José."

Even Angie looked at her in horror.

"Yep. I'm gonna do it. And y'all can't stop me. If he's dirty, it'll come out—on the telephone, maybe. Or somebody'll come to the house for payoffs. He'll feel safe at home; that's where he'll be careless. Y'all have probably heard that no one ever notices the help? Miz Clara knows the damnedest things about people. It's like she's invisible. I'm just going to put on my invisible suit and go in there and come out with some dirt."

"Ya not plantin' anything on him."

"Eddie, don't be ridiculous. Give me two weeks; I'll do it. Two weeks' leave if you want to play it that way, because I'm doing it. My mind's made up."

Eddie sighed. Those were the four words she'd never go back on. He could fire her and she'd still do it. *What the hell?* he thought. *The worst she can do is plant bugs and get thrown in jail and get me sued and fined ten thousand dollars.* The thought gave him a stomachache. And yet, when all was said and done, he'd rather go down than see Angie burned at the stake in the *Times-Picayune.* But, come to think of it, that wasn't the only news organization in town. "What about television? How ya gonna stop those guys?"

"I told you," his daughter said. "Farley's in Champagne's pocket. You can bet he's got an exclusive. I mean, anyone could find the arrest records, but they'd have to know they were supposed to look for them. Somebody tipped Farley. It's the only way he could know—and whoever tipped him planted the drugs."

Wheels were turning again. "Okay, I'll work that part of it. If Farley's in Champagne's pocket, it's got to have something to do with a case; I'll find the damn case. Could be pending, or maybe this is payback. Or maybe Farley's a relative. It wouldn't be a bribe—if ya gon' be a reporter, it ain't bucks you're after."

"And if it is a bribe, I might be able to pick it up over at the house," Ms. Wallis said.

"What makes ya think they need a maid?"

"Don't you worry your pretty head," his associate said.

"Here's the question," said his daughter. "Do you know Jane Storey well enough to call her on a Sunday night?"

"Watch me," Ms. Wallis said, and plucked her cell phone from her purse.

CHAPTER
THREE

J ane, I've got a great story for you."

"Well, if it isn't the Baroness de Pontalba." The reporter used her nom de plume. "Hello, Your Grace. What, if I may get to the point, is up? For once I'm not alone on Sunday night."

"Off the record?"

"Sure, off the record. I'm at home, in case you haven't noticed."

"You know Angela Valentino, right?"

"Your boss's kid. Sure. Aka the meanest white bitch in Orleans Parish. That isn't racist, is it?"

"I'm gonna let it slide. Did you know she was arrested yesterday?"

"No. For what?"

"Drugs."

"Now that's a story." For the first time, she heard enthusiasm in the reporter's voice. Angie was a pretty prominent lawyer.

"And not just Angie. She was with Alabama Brazil at the time. They both got popped."

"I'm missing something here. Why are you tipping me? You ought to be on their side."

38

" 'Cause somebody else already has that story—Evan Farley."

"Oh, shit. Funky Farley."

"What? He smells?"

"Damn right. Only not in a literal sense. Something's really wrong about that guy."

"Are you the only one who thinks so?"

"Let's just say he's not real well thought of at the paper."

Talba began to relax a little. "Okay, here's the gist. An extremely prominent citizen set Angie up. Alabama just got caught in the cross-fire. That same prominent citizen then proceeded to tip Farley, and the story's going to run tomorrow. Could you get it stopped?"

"Hell, no. Not unless it's not true. And you just told me it is."

"Maybe we could make a trade. I could offer you a much better story on the prominent citizen."

"Who is?"

"A judge."

Talba sensed tension at the other end.

"Buddy Champagne," the reporter said.

"You were pretty quick with that one."

"Baroness, tell me the truth. Have you really got something on Buddy Champagne?"

"Swear to God," she lied. "Why?"

"He's one of those guys everyone thinks is dirty, but nobody can get anything on."

"How about the marina?"

"Yeah. That's the thing: Someone from the Venetian Isles neighborhood group called a press conference, which some kid got sent to, and Funky Farley asked to follow up on it. Said the kid's story was under-reported, almost got him fired. But then the spin he put on it, sounded like somebody was persecuting poor old Buddy and all his vendors. David doesn't trust him." David Bacardi, she meant, the city editor. Jane had once confided to Talba that she'd had an affair with him. It was long over, but it had come out of a professional closeness that was still bound to be there. She had the feeling Bacardi trusted Jane.

"Look, can you talk to David? Get him to hold the story just one day. Then tomorrow we'll meet and talk. If you think I've got nothing,

Farley's still got an exclusive. I'm pretty sure nobody else knows about this."

"But you're not positive."

"I'm not, but why not ask Farley? If he's got it exclusively, he'll know."

"Let me get back to you."

"Two things—whatever you do, don't tell David who your source is."

"Goes without saying. Number two?"

"Can you bring me Farley's story on the marina?"

"Consider it done." The reporter hung up.

It was half an hour before she called back. "David won't do it. He says no big deal—we run the story and we still get yours when it breaks."

"Jane, I love you, but there's nothing in that for me. Doesn't the word 'exclusive' mean anything to ol' David? Because I swear to God, if you run Farley's, I'll take mine right to your favorite TV reporter and leave you eating her dust."

"Fay Warren. You wouldn't."

"Would."

"That's what I told him you'd say." Jane sighed. "Okay, I'll try again."

This time she called back in ten minutes. "Okay, it's done. He just had to try. You know men. Want to meet for lunch?"

"Sure. How about Elizabeth's? Noon tomorrow."

"TBK, as we say in the news biz." To be continued—Jane had taught her the phrase. Talba hung up, wondering where on earth Venetian Isles was. She would have asked Angie if Eddie hadn't been there, but she wasn't about to let him know she didn't know.

Later that evening, she tried to find it on a map, and couldn't. The Internet wasn't much help, either, but she did glean that it was somewhere in Orleans Parish, and obviously it was on the water. But where?

Talba scoured the paper first thing in the morning, and to her relief, there was no mention of either Angie or Alabama. Their initial hearings were set for that morning, and she waited tensely till Angie called to say that no reporters except Farley had shown up in court. He hadn't tried to talk to her. Following up, Talba gathered.

"The good news is, I got Jimmy Houlihan down there for us, and he got the DA to dismiss the charge against Al."

"Angie, that's fantastic."

"It was a bad arrest; no way they were going to make it stick." She paused and added glumly, " 'Cause it was my car."

Talba barely knew what to say. Angie down was a new Angie. She settled for, "Hang in there, Ange. I'm seeing Jane for lunch. To plot strategy."

Elizabeth's, tucked away in the Bywater, had the feel of an airy, informal Caribbean café. The menu tended toward soul food (though a white family ran it) and it drew a savvy salt-and-pepper crowd—an altogether appropriate venue, and far from Jane's office, which meant they had little chance of being overheard. The reporter was already waiting when Talba arrived.

"Everything cool?" she asked anxiously.

"Farley went to Angie's arraignment."

Jane shrugged. "Par for the course. We'll be okay if we can interest David."

Talba ran the story by her, Jane listening silently till Talba got to the part about the drugs being planted on Ben Izaguirre.

"Farley never had that."

"It was never public."

"Would Izaguirre tell me the story—I mean, not for the record, just to confirm there's something there? That might do it for David."

Talba nodded. "Did it for me. This catfish is unbelievable. I'll get Angie to talk to him."

"Umm." Jane was having a salad. "So, okay, the story's about the drug plants, right? Anything else?'

Talba raised an eyebrow. "One can only hope." She outlined what she proposed to do.

"Girl! You've got guts—wish I'd thought of it." She wrestled lettuce. "It's a great idea, but how in hell do you plan to get the job?"

Talba smiled. "I've got a connection."

"Oh, really."

"Uh-huh." She was lying through her teeth. "Can I have two weeks? That's how long Eddie's giving me."

"I think David'll go for it."

"By the way, why do you think Farley's giving Champagne so much good ink?"

"No idea."

"Well, here's something I'm wondering: Did anybody else cover that press conference?"

Jane thought about it. "I think so—but you know how that is; thirty seconds on television, people forget. Then along came Farley's story and changed the spin. Pretty clever what he did."

And before they parted, she handed a copy of the story over to Talba.

It was a piece about shrimp, mostly—cheap foreign imports versus the more expensive local product ("Louisiana wild-caught shrimp"), a hot topic in certain circles. The state's shrimpers were suffering from the competition, and there were all kinds of pending plans to levy a stiff tariff on the imports. Meanwhile, restaurants were scarfing up the inferior alien product and serving it to unsuspecting patrons. Ben Izaguirre owned a restaurant, but if Farley had questioned him as to which kind of shrimp he served, he hadn't included the answer in his story. Judge Francis ("Buddy") Champagne, who bought his product from local shrimpers, then processed it and sold it to restaurants, was portrayed as a friend to his fellow Louisianans, Ben Izaguirre as their enemy.

Pretty thin, Talba thought, unless Izaguirre also imported shrimp. But if he did, why hadn't Farley had that?

She called Angie and asked her about her client. "Hell, no," she said. "He's dying in the restaurant business, and he's over sixty. He's trying to sell the restaurant right now. Trust me, this guy is no wheeler-dealer. His only interest is in keeping the neighborhood nice for his retirement. Thanks to Farley, half his old friends hate him now."

"Would he confirm the drug plant for Jane? Off the record, of course."

"Sure. I'll call him right now."

"By the way, exactly what are the complaints about that marina?"

"Well, at first, it was just the usual—increased traffic, exhaust from the boats coming in, noise, traffic, oil in the water. But most of all the stink. Venetian Isles is tiny—you ever been there?"

"No, but I know that, as of 2000, it had 772 housing units. Couldn't find anything more recent."

"Sounds like a lot, but wait'll you see the place. Everything's cheek by jowl."

"What'd you mean when you said at first it was the usual—now it's something else?"

"Yeah. Ben Izaguirre says it's against the law to catch shrimp in the winter, but Buddy's still buying it. From poachers, he thinks."

"Well, that part sounds easy. Why not just report him?"

"Talba, you are so naive. Think we haven't?" The lawyer sighed. "Buddy's a powerful man."

"Meaning you got no action."

"Right."

Talba hung up and thoroughly backgrounded Francis Champagne, noting his address, and then worked on another project she had, something she'd need tomorrow. She went home early—she had to be at the judge's first thing in the morning.

The first thing she noticed about Champagne's lovely house was that it was all wrong. It was a genuine Garden District mansion, way too fancy for someone on a judge's salary, whatever that was. It wasn't merely large, it was grand. In fact, it was famous, mostly for the iron cornstalk fence around the extensive grounds. But if the judge had supplemental income, she hadn't found it. However, one thing she did know—his wife had died a few years back. Maybe she was the one with the money. But it was an enormous house for one person, and he hadn't married again, so far as she knew. It needed not a maid, but a staff. Talba cordially hoped she wasn't going to have to clean the whole thing by herself.

She arrived at 6 A.M. and hunkered down in her unobtrusive Isuzu to wait. For an hour, nothing happened. Then a man—presumably Buddy—came out to get the paper. And at seven, a black woman in her fifties walked through the famous gate, strolled up the walk, and let herself in. *Pay dirt*, Talba thought. *The maid.* The only problem was, she hadn't arrived in a car. No way to identify her without approaching her.

Talba figured she either worked half or whole days, so she'd have to come back at eleven, and if the maid didn't leave then, again at three. Given the size of the house, she was betting on three, but she couldn't afford to take a chance.

So she came back at ten, waited an hour—to no avail—and came back again at two-thirty. At 3 P.M. sharp, a youngish black man arrived in a car to pick up the maid. That was better. Talba noted the license plate, then followed the car home—to a shabby house in Central City.

She now had two beautiful leads—one plate number, and one address. She sat down at the keyboard and began to play. The car was registered to a Roman Williams, a mechanic, married to Tawanha Williams, a licensed vocational nurse, and they had three children, one of whom was an outstanding student who'd once won a science fair prize. (Indeed, most of the information about the Williamses had come from the article about the kid.) But they were in their late thirties. Tawahna couldn't be the woman she saw. She was Roman's mother, maybe, or Tawahna's.

Talba brought out the project she'd worked on the day before, a pretext survey. Taking a deep breath, she dialed the Williamses' phone number. A woman answered.

"Mrs. Williams?" she asked.

"We got two of us here. Who you want—Tawanha or Alberta?"

"Let me see—the name I have is . . . uh, Alberta."

"Just a minute," the woman said, and another woman came on the line, one with an older-sounding voice. So far so good.

"Mrs. Williams?" Talba said. "I work for a company that's opening a restaurant in your neighborhood, and we're doing a little demographic survey. We'll pay you ten dollars to answer a few questions. The check is already made out and addressed to you—it'll take no more than ten minutes of your time. That's one dollar a minute. Can you answer a few questions for me?"

"Mmph. More'n I usually make. Go on ahead."

"Okay, thanks very much. First of all, you have been selected at random. May I check your name and address?" That done, she said,

"We're trying to get a sense of the kind of neighborhood customer our client might have."

"Don't see why."

"You know that new Wal-Mart? We did the same thing for them, and they found it very helpful. The idea is, how best to serve the customers."

"Better make it cheap," Williams said.

Talba laughed. "I hear you. Tell me—do you go to church?"

"Yes."

"Where?"

"First Evangelical Baptist." She gave an address.

"When you go to restaurants, what do you generally order?"

"Never go to restaurants."

"Oh, come on—everyone does sometimes."

"Well . . . I like shrimp if it's fried real good. Chicken. Barbecue." She brightened. "Ain't a barbecue restaurant, is it?"

"Could be. The client's trying to decide."

"That go over real good in this neighborhood."

"Do you drink alcohol?"

"Once in a blue moon, maybe. Have me a beer or something."

"I see. Any particular favorite bar?"

"No, *ma'am*. Never go to bars. Just have a beer at home now and then. Maybe at a picnic."

"Okay, do you like to dance?"

"Way too old for that foolishness."

"Have any hobbies?"

"I knit some; for my grandbabies." So far absolutely nothing that could be done in public, where Talba could stage a chance meeting.

"Belong to any social groups?"

"Eastern Star; Ladies Auxiliary kind of thing at the church."

"Well, tell me about the rest of the family."

Williams described her son, daughter-in-law, and their children. No surprises there. They, too, if Williams was to be believed, had no particular interests outside the home.

"Well, how about your job? Do you go to work?"

"I'm a house cleaner. For a family Uptown. Been working there three years."

"You must like your job."

"You know anybody likes their job?"

"I'll take that as a no."

Williams laughed. "You shore catch on quick."

"Well, at least I hope the people you work for treat you well."

"Mmmph. Well, you can hope all the way home, Missy. Ain' gon' make it so."

"Are you well paid?"

"Am I well paid?" Talba could hear her bristling, but she was ready. "Whose business that be?"

"The survey is completely confidential, Mrs. Williams. Our client is trying to determine if the participants have the discretionary income to support an upscale restaurant."

"Beg pardon? Have the *what?*"

"That's just a fancy phrase for excess cash."

That got a big laugh out of Williams. "Now, ain't that a contradiction. Uh-huh. Excess cash. Sho' do got excess cash."

"That means no, right?"

"You one sharp little cookie."

"May I ask what your hourly rate is?"

"You crazy? Callin' up here axin' how much money I make! Whatchoo think ya doin'?"

"Well, actually, that was kind of off the survey. I just asked because my mama cleans houses for a living. She makes fifteen dollars an hour." This was a blatant untruth, but Talba figured it might get results.

"Well, I sho' would like to meet *her* employer. My son ain't well right now, and my daughter-in-law can't even afford child care no more, him not workin'; she cain't work but three days a week. I'm mos' the sole support of the family right now." Talba could hear the anguish in her voice. She was pretty sure Alberta was crying.

And she was also on a roll. "Bad enough I got to clean that great big house without any help. Least one day a week he send me out to that filthy old marina he own—smell like a sewer. Ain't even safe there; kid was killed there a while back. Sometimes I think that man the devil hisself."

Hello, Talba thought. *A kid was killed there. Angie didn't mention that.*

46

"It's none of my business, but why don't you just quit and get a different job?"

"When I'm gon' look?"

Okay, this was it. Talba prayed she wouldn't blow it. "You know what? This could be your lucky day. What about if I said I'd do your job for you for two weeks while you look? I'll pay what your present employer pays, plus a big bonus. Let's say five hundred dollars?"

"Why you doin' this?" Alberta's voice was charged with suspicion. "Who are you?"

"Take it easy, now, Alberta. You just take it real easy. My name's Sandra and I'm somebody who doesn't like Judge Champagne any better than you do."

"Oooooh, I'm in a heap of shit! Whatchoo tryin' to do to me?"

"I'm trying to help you. You said—"

"Call me up, tell me ya somebody ya not. Get me to say things . . ."

"I *know* my mama could get you a better job. People are always asking her to work when she can't. She's got a great reputation, but only so much time."

"I got a *family* to support!" The other woman rang off.

And Talba felt like an idiot. What to do now? She drove home slowly, moodily, trying to think her way out of it. There was a way—and she knew exactly what it was. But it involved manipulating someone a lot more savvy than Alberta Williams—at least where Talba was concerned.

She found Miz Clara with her wig off and her slippers on, rocking and watching the news. "They want to build a new City Hall, baby. Whatchoo think o' that?"

"About time. That horrible building's probably why all the bureaucrats have such bad attitudes."

"Mmm mmm. Tha's a three-dollar word if I ever heard one, but I take ya point." She pronounced it "pernt," the same as Eddie did. He even said "New Erlins" when he wasn't being extra careful; Miz Clara never did that.

"Mama, I got a problem."

Miz Clara was instantly suspicious, whereas it had taken Alberta ten minutes to get to the same place. "Since when ya bring ya problems to ya ol' mama?" But she was pleased to be consulted. Talba could tell by the "ol' mama" part.

"I was trying to get an undercover job and I scared the lady away. See, I need to get into somebody's house for a couple of weeks. This lady works there, but she hates her job, so I offered her money to give it to me while she looks for a new one. I don't know why, but she went all hinky on me."

"What's 'hinky'?"

"That's what the cops say when their snitches get nervous."

"Hinky! Lord, Lord, I'm gon' remember that one. 'Most as good as 'break a leg.'" Talba had taught her to say this before her performances; it never failed to crack her mother up. "What this lady do?"

"What you do. Cleans his house."

Her mother let out a whoop. "Whooooeee! Sandra Wallis, you gon' go cleanin' some cracker's house? Miz Clara's little buppie girl?" Talba had taught her "buppie" also. "Oh, lordy, this I gotta see." She cackled like a witch. "Oh, yeah, I gotta see this with my own old eyes. Now *that* one's worth the price of admission."

"Does that mean you'll help me?"

"Well, I don't know. Depends if any harm's gon' come to that poor woman."

"No, ma'am, it's not. The worst that can happen is she doesn't find a job in two weeks."

"Oh, I can find her a job. Ain' no problem there. Whatchoo gon' do in that house? Anything to make ya mama 'shamed o' ya?"

"Mama! Eddie's sending me. Would Eddie do something unethical?" Miz Clara had a lot more faith in Eddie than in Talba, and her daughter knew in her heart that if either of them knew about some of her methods, she'd get fired by one and disowned by the other, not necessarily in that order.

"Guess not," Miz Clara said. "This a Christian lady we talkin' about?"

Talba nodded. "First Evangelical Baptist."

Miz Clara thought about it. "Antoinette Boiseau go to First Evangelical."

Talba breathed a sigh of relief. The problem could be solved the New Orleans way. It was all about who you knew.

"Lemme jus' give Antoinette a call. What this lady call herself?"

"Alberta Williams."

Her mother heaved her tired body to her feet and padded off in her old blue slippers. She didn't believe in cell phones; still kept an old-fashioned plug-in model in her bedroom. Talba thought she was going to scream with impatience during the thirty minutes it took Miz Clara to get current with Antoinette and then to ask for the reference.

She came back nodding. "It be all right. Antoinette didn't know her, but she know somebody who do—in her ladies' group. Miz Augustine gon' make the call—Versie Augustine. I tell her it's real important, she say she do it right away."

"Thanks, Mama. I've got to go over there right away. You coming?"

"Me? You axin' *me*?" She didn't think she'd ever seen her mother look so surprised.

"I really pissed this lady off. I might need *two* character references."

"Well. Guess I gotta." Miz Clara could hardly contain herself. "Lemme get some shoes on."

Talba parked in front of the Williams house. "Nice neighborhood," Miz Clara said sarcastically. Indeed, it was a few steps down from their snug cottage on Louisa Street.

Talba dialed the Williams number and asked for Alberta.

"Speakin'."

"Mrs. Williams, this is Sandra. The woman who called about the survey? I'm real sorry about that. Did you hear from Versie Augustine?"

"I heard. Says ya on the up and up, no matter if ya lie. Gon' take a lot to convince me, though."

"Well, I got a lot. Look out your window, will you?" Talba waited till she saw a head peek between the curtains. She waved. "I'm out here with my mama. Could we talk to you for five minutes?"

"Mmmph. Guess so."

She didn't let them in, though; kept them on the stoop, while Miz Clara explained that her daughter was a "special investigator" working for the forces of right and decency, and nearly making Talba blanch—it was a crime to impersonate an officer, and this came dangerously close. But in the end, a deal was struck, and Alberta Williams went back in to phone Judge Champagne with some cock-and-bull

49

story about a family emergency requiring her to send a niece to fill in for a few days.

Miz Clara preened all the way home. She was going to be hard to live with for a long time to come.

"Cain't *wait* to see how this one come out," she cackled as she heated up leftover stew. "The Baroness de Pontalba cleanin' white ladies' terlets. Mmm. Mmmm."

"Okay, Mama, happiest day of your life. Let's break out the champagne. But whatever happened to first African-American president?" This was one of the three jobs Miz Clara had always deemed suitable for her offspring. The other two were Speaker of the House and doctor of medicine. Talba's brother Corey had actually achieved the last of the three.

"Might as well see how the other half live," Miz Clara said. "I got one thing to say to ya, ya don't want to get fired first day on the job."

"What's that?"

"Whatever ya do, whatever they tell ya, don't use nothing but Ivory liquid and bleach on the marble. Anything else'll stain, ruin it for good."

"What marble?"

"These folks got any money?"

"Enough for a full-time maid."

"Mmm, my baby gon' be doin' laundry. Bet they make ya iron the sheets."

"Mama, what marble?"

"Rich folks got marble all over. Got bathrooms most paved with marble. You mind Miz Clara now."

Talba promised she would and excused herself. She couldn't wait to call Jane Storey: "I'm in." Jane was howling by the time Talba finished the story of the mama con, especially the "special investigator" part.

"Think I could get thrown in jail for it?"

"Naah. Your word against theirs. Miz C. said 'private.' Williams heard 'special.'"

Talba sighed. "You don't know my mama. She wouldn't lie if it meant I was going to the guillotine."

"Know what it reminds me of? The time when I was traveling in Europe and had to come home for an emergency appendectomy. I'd just been bumming around, filing a few stories here and there—"

"Unemployed, in other words."

"Yeah, and I was so out of it, Mother had to fill out the hospital form. Was she about to put down 'unemployed'? No way—who knew what nefarious hands that record might fall into? And then everyone would know her daughter had actually been out of work for a big three months."

"So what'd she put?"

"'Foreign correspondent.' Thought I'd die."

"Oh, God—seen one mom, you've seen 'em all. Listen, I've got to go—I think I feel a poem coming on."

CHAPTER FOUR

Y ou look all right."

As good as a baroness can in scruffy old jeans, Talba thought. *And I'm early, you happen to notice?* The woman who'd answered the door ought to know exactly how she looked by now. She'd certainly taken a thorough enough gander. Talba half-expected her to inspect her teeth.

This woman couldn't be the judge's lady friend—she was old enough to be his mother, and if she was, Angie must be a secret druggie, because he was bound to be innocent. Nobody who'd been raised by this one could possibly get away with anything. She was tall and erect, with wavy white hair in a short, severe, and way too sensible haircut that still managed to be flattering. And she was wearing a dress. Who wore dresses any more unless they were going to work? And Talba certainly couldn't see this one working. Maybe a volunteer job.

Stranger still, the dress was mauve; vaguely dressy, with a fluttery skirt. She had on earrings and makeup that didn't hide a face full of wrinkles. Her shoes had tiny stacked heels. She was something from another era, and not at all what Talba expected. She'd thought Champagne would be something of a redneck, but if this woman had raised him, he could at least be depended on to have decent manners.

But despite her attempt at elegance, the woman didn't make it. She spoke in a blustery, semicountry fashion that didn't sound like New Orleans at all.

"I'm Adele Reedy," she said, not bothering to offer her hand. "You'd be Alberta's niece."

Talba did offer to shake, and was not rebuffed. She got the impression Reedy was impressed with her politeness. "Sandra Corey. Aunt Alberta said she's sorry she had to be away."

"Hope it's not too serious. Come on in, let's get acquainted. You're going to be working with me, so I may as well tell you what's what."

Yeah, Talba thought. *Tell me everything.*

Reedy led her into a kitchen that was blessedly marble-free, and had a long table in it instead of the usual island. Kind of a beat-up table, the sort that had either been in the family for generations or scavenged from a European monastery. "Sit down. You want coffee?"

"Please, ma'am," Talba said, causing Reedy to raise a stiff gray eyebrow.

"You've got good manners for a maid."

Alberta didn't? Talba wondered. She said, "Guess my mama raised me right," hoping she wasn't laying it on too thick.

"Guess she did." Reedy handed her a cup, and took a seat opposite her new employee. "You got experience?"

"Oh, yes, ma'am. Worked my way through Xavier cleaning houses. I worked for a service."

"Oh, those things." Reedy wrinkled her nose. "We've had some very bad experiences with services. Xavier, did you say? You graduate?"

"Yes ma'am. Degree in social work." (The Xavier part was true, anyhow.) "This is just a favor for Aunt Alberta."

"What about your regular job?"

"It ended about six months ago—agency funds got cut off. I was looking for another, but then this came up and I can use the money."

"I hope you're good at laundry. You iron?" Score one for Miz Clara.

"Happy to. You like your sheets starched?"

To her surprise, Reedy laughed. "Alberta *hates* to iron sheets. We might have to keep you. Listen, laundry's the main thing around here."

Talba groaned inwardly. The house was as big as three houses—how was she going to clean it, much less iron sheets?

"There are five of us living here." Reedy paused. "Well, six if you count Kristin, my son-in-law's girl friend. But you can't because she has her own place—she's just around so much it seems like she lives here. You don't have to do her laundry."

"Your—uh—son-in-law?"

"My daughter passed away a few years back, leaving him with two children. Royce is grown and married, of course, but Lucy's fourteen. We're just one big happy family, all thrown together by a legal dispute." Talba had no idea what she meant by that, but she decided now wasn't the time to ask. She heard clattering on the stairs.

"Ah, there's Lucy now. She goes to McGehee."

A teenage girl entered the room in a school uniform—a girl a little too plump, too awkward to be popular, or even socially acceptable in the fanciest girls' school in town. She had pink skin and pale red hair, nicely cut in a bob—Reedy's doing, Talba was willing to bet. Her sullen look said she'd prefer a Mohawk.

"Lucy, say hello to Sandra."

The girl looked at her without interest and said only, "You making pancakes?"

"Sandra's just getting oriented. By the way," she said to Talba, "can you cook?"

"I think I could manage breakfast. But maybe not pancakes the first day." This was good, she thought. If they ate in the kitchen, she might get to hear them interact as she cooked. She stood. "Shall I scramble some eggs?"

"Ewwww," Lucy said.

Reedy looked at her watch. "Everybody's late today. We usually serve breakfast at seven-fifteen—Lucy's school starts at seven-fifty-five, so it's still a race. But nobody usually turns up except Buddy and Lucy—sometimes Kristin. How about setting the table and getting out stuff for cereal? Missy, you get your own," she said to Lucy. "You're 'bout to be late for school."

Talba heard more stair-clattering, heavier this time, and in a moment a man walked into the room who looked for all the world like a youngish Burl Ives—round belly, round balding head, bland, slightly red face. "You Alberta's niece?" he said. "Welcome to the asylum. We think the world of Alberta, but that don't mean we ain' gon' fire her ass if she don't get back to work soon. Can't cook worth a damn. Burns the bacon every time. Maybe you'll work out better, honey, and we'll just keep ya. You cook?"

"Not this morning, Buddy." Reedy's voice was strained. "We've got to get her oriented."

"Sure, sure. I'll find some roots and berries or somethin'. You show her around."

"Guess it's that time," Reedy said. "You dropping Lucy off?"

"Goddammit, have I got to do everything around here?"

"This is Sandra," Reedy said. "My son, Buddy Champagne."

"Judge Buddy Champagne to you, Adele. You just call me 'your honor,' honey." He winked at Talba.

And I'm "Your Grace" to you, fatso.

Lucy made a face Medusa would have envied. "Daddy, you are so queer!"

"Queer? Who ya callin' queer? Save that for ya brother, princess. Ya daddy's anything but."

"Royce is not queer!"

Oh, boy, Talba thought.

"Let's go, Sandra. Let me show you where everything is."

"Yes, Miss—uh—do you prefer Mrs. Reedy or Miss Adele?"

"Lord, honey, we don't stand on ceremony around here. Call me anything—"

"Except late for supper," Lucy finished with a sneer in her voice.

"Young lady, you are way too big for your britches. Now eat your breakfast and get on out of here."

Talba saw that both Lucy and her father had managed to find cereal and serve themselves. Good—they weren't completely helpless.

Reedy showed her the kitchen products, told her what to use on what (she'd never seen a stainless steel cleaner before), and had just ushered her into a stately but somewhat dusty hall when a gorgeous young woman came running down the stairs in a black suit she'd probably bought in New York. Her golden hair glistened and her skin looked as if it had been scrubbed with stainless steel cleaner. She was the only one other than Reedy who deigned to shake hands with a mere maid.

Once she stopped moving, Talba could see that she was really quite petite—but she had a presence, no question. "Hi. I'm Kristin LaGarde."

"Sandra Corey."

"Good to meet you. Gotta grab coffee and run." She clacked into
the kitchen and Talba heard her say, "Morning, Princess. Sleep well?"

For the first time, Lucy showed signs of life. "Hey, great suit."

"We can't exactly start at the top," Reedy said to Talba, "because
that's where Royce and Suzanne live." She pronounced it *Suzonne*.
"They're never up before nine or ten. So let's start on the second floor."

As they climbed the stairs, she added, "Royce keeps irregular
hours—he's learning the seafood business, working for a friend of the
family. And Suzanne's a consultant." She seemed a bit uncomfortable,
as if feeling a need to explain their sloth.

"Oh," Talba said noncommittally, a word she used a lot when she
wanted more information.

She got it. "You ever heard of feng shui?"

"No, ma'am, don't believe I have," though Talba was more than
familiar with the concept.

"Some Chinese thing—it's about arranging furniture, far as I can
see; big on mirrors. Suppose to make the chi flow right so you'll have
good luck and get rich."

"Ma'am? Not sure I understand."

"Listen to me, I'm talking like she does. Chi is energy. Anyway,
that's what Suzanne does. Goes into people's houses and pushes things
around; I call her a fluffer."

Talba said nothing.

"Fluffs things up."

Talba made her eyes go big. "Really? She get a lot of work?"

"Mmmph. Not so you'd notice."

Talba thought this was a classic case of the shoemaker's children.
If ever a house could use some good chi, this one could. It looked as if
it hadn't been rehabbed in thirty years or more, and a good thing,
Talba thought—maybe the bathrooms wouldn't be paved with marble. It was well lived in, but not, if its condition was any indication,
particularly well loved. It had the slightly dingy, musty look and feel
of neglect. Alberta was probably so overworked she couldn't get
around to everything, but that wasn't the whole story. The furniture

needed reupholstering, the walls needed painting, the curtains needed replacing. It was a bit like a time warp—as if its mistress had suddenly died, and no one had loved it since. Talba suspected that was more or less the case, and wondered if Kristin was going to be moving in soon. If so, the Champagnes had better get their marble order in.

The second floor twisted and turned, so that two distinct sections—maybe wings—were set far enough apart that Lucy and Adele (as Talba was beginning to think of her), who occupied one, probably couldn't hear Kristin's cries of passion from the other, where the judge had his chambers, so to speak. She was relieved to see that Adele and Lucy shared a bathroom on the hall, though the judge had his own. There was probably one more upstairs and a powder room on the first floor—only four if she was lucky.

Lucy's room was painted lavender, a color Talba wouldn't have picked for someone with her coloring. It was the usual jumble of heart-throb posters, stuffed animals, wadded-up clothes, and machines—TV, CD player, and computer. No telephone, though—she probably had her own cell phone.

Adele's room, by far the neatest in the house, was surprisingly un-frumpy. Its floral curtains and duvet cover seemed new. A few good antiques—dressing table, bed, writing table—had been chosen with care—and the walls were a light yellow. Talba liked it; she couldn't see how this woman could stand to share a bathroom with a teenager.

The judge's bed was a store-bought sleigh style—clearly a repro-duction—and he had some old but shabby pieces that Talba found com-fortable and masculine. The walls were dark green and the bedding was a green, brown, and burgundy paisley—probably Adele's choice. Very suitable; utterly lacking in imagination.

What deeply interested her was this: Buddy's home office opened off his bedroom, so that in the second room she could probably hear anyone who entered the first room in time to get her nose out of whatever it was in.

Starting at the front door, the first floor consisted of a wide hall, powder room, living room, dining room, sun room, library, kitchen, and a small sitting room the family evidently used for watching television, which Adele called the den.

"We hardly ever use the living room," Adele said. "It probably won't need much."

Except a paint job and new furniture, Talba thought. It was painted a kind of dirty mauve, as depressing as it was downright unsightly, and it was hung with dusty photos, mostly, and a few dark-hued oil paintings, mostly still lifes and nature scenes. The furniture was old—not antique, just old—and upholstered in patterns that looked as if they'd been designed about fifty years ago.

The dining room was deep forest green, with windows on the garden. To Talba's mind it was the best room in the house, except for the library, which she loved. It was painted a deep wine color, and in here, old furniture looked good. It was worn tan leather, and there was even a library table, piled with books, and a fireplace. On the mantel stood matching statues of black figures in turbans, the sort known as "black-amoors." Adele had the grace to flush slightly when she saw Talba looking at them. "Sorry about those," she said. "This is Buddy's favorite hangout—the original smoke-filled room, where he brings his cronies to drink and puff on vile cigars. Someone gave him those old things and nobody's ever been able to talk him out of them."

"Too bad—I know somebody who'd like them, and he's a black man. Collects what he calls 'insult art.' Aunt Jemima clocks, those little jockey statues, mammy salt shakers, the whole thing. Let me know if the judge ever wants to sell them."

Adele looked as if she didn't know whether to wince or smile. Instead, she just stared. "Uh—I prefer the sun room myself," she said, finally. But even that seemed hopelessly out of date, its wicker furniture covered in a floral print on a black background that had gone out of style sometime before the Kennedy era. But it did afford a view of Adele's pride and joy. "Gorgeous garden," Talba said.

"Thank the good Lord for it," Adele said. "It's the only thing between me and a padded cell."

That sounded so promising Talba held out a bit of bait. "Things get pretty crazy around here?"

Adele rolled her eyes, though rather unsuccessfully—it took a teenage girl to pull that one off. "Families," was all she said.

Aside from the library, the den was the most user-friendly of all the rooms, having been recently painted a soft cream. The furniture looked relatively new, and a great deal less expensive than the maw-maw stuff on the rest of the first floor. It even had a built-in television console.

"We built this out of the old pantry," Adele explained. "Had to have some place to relax."

They ended up in the kitchen, where Reedy had a desk for paying bills, which seemed to be about it for her personal space outside the bedroom. Talba found the tour alone had nearly exhausted her.

"Monday's the day we change the sheets," Adele said. "So that's done. Alberta usually does the rest of the laundry on Tuesday, and irons the sheets she did the day before. That way she can do the rest of the ironing throughout the week, when she has some spare time."

Good Lord, Talba thought, wondering when she was going to find any.

"I think she does the bathrooms on Tuesday, too, so they're probably pretty dirty. And of course she makes the beds and straightens things every day. Then she's available to make lunch for whoever wants it, and I don't know what the rest of her system is."

"Kitchen every day, of course," Talba ventured.

"Certainly. Do you do windows?"

"Yes, ma'am. Long as the Pope's still Catholic."

"Good. Because Alberta doesn't. You could make that a project while you're here."

"Happy to. Place'll be glowing time I get through."

"You're on your own, then."

"I'd better get my laundry going." Adele had by now shown her where the laundry room and the various hampers were, except, of course, those belonging to the still sleeping beauties.

She had gotten the first load of laundry in, and was just putting the finishing touches on Adele and Lucy's blessedly marble-less but completely trashed bathroom when a male voice roared, "Hey! Can I get some breakfast around here?"

She returned to the hall, still wiping her hands, almost colliding with a man probably in his early thirties—around Kristin's age— wearing ripped khaki shorts and nothing else. His hair was greasy and hadn't been combed. She could smell alcohol from three paces, that stale day-old reek that comes from a hard night of heavy drinking.

"Well, hello!" he said, giving her what he obviously believed was a charming smile. He was tall and skinny—way too skinny for her taste—and his dirty hair was brown, with natural blond highlights. His face was somewhat obscured by a fashionable goatee, but mostly, it was handsome—straight nose, unremarkable brown eyes, okay lips, high brow, and decent chin—not exactly strong, but decent. He had premature wrinkles around his eyes, probably from too much partying, and one of those bracelet-of-thorns tattoos on his right bicep. Talba never could get the hang of those things. If you were going to get a tattoo, why not get a jaguar, say, or a parrot? What was up with thorns?

She stepped backward, to make a statement. "Mr. Royce, I presume."

"You presume, do you? You a Harvard Ph.D. or somethin'?"

"Something," she said. "That's for sure. Something named Sandra Corey." Once again she offered to shake, not sure whether this was wise with a nearly naked white guy still drunk from the night before, and sure enough, it wasn't: The jerk kissed her hand.

"What would you like for breakfast, sir?"

"Oh, drop the 'sir' bit. And that 'Mr.' crap too. Call me Royce. We're equal-opportunity assholes around here."

"Yes sir, Mr. Royce." She gave him a sideways glance to see how he was taking it, then added, just in case, "Sorry—just kidding."

"Oh, man, we got a comedian here." He shouted up the stairs, "Hey, Suzanne. Come on down. Ya gotta meet Edwina Murphy here. Hey, that's good—maybe I'll call you Eddie."

Okay, a license to smart off. "You do that Mr. Royce, suh. And put in a word with Comedy Tonight, okay? I don't cook so good; I'm scared I'll get fired when you taste my eggs. I got a poor ol' mama and a crippled little brother."

He did an approving double-take and called again, "Suzanne! You're missin' the show."

A woman appeared on the third floor landing, which was as big as a sitting room, and furnished like one, with a sofa flanked by tables and lamps, a console table on the wall across from it. She was also tall and skinny, also brown-haired, with one of those Hollywood-looking mussed coiffures that wasn't a whole lot longer than her husband's, which was way too long for a judge's son, in Talba's limited experience. The woman's beak was long, narrow, and a bit turned under—very French—and it gave her face the kind of character she didn't see in Royce's. Her lips were full and her cheeks rosy from sleep. She looked elegant even in the sweatpants she was currently tying. She wore them with a tiny white T-shirt that showed a hint of midriff. "What's going on down there?"

"Alberta's niece is a regular clown."

Talba was afraid she'd gone too far. "Years of working with kids—lose your sense of humor, say good-bye to your sanity," she said in the general direction of upstairs. "Sandra Corey, at your service."

"Edwina Murphy to me," Royce said. "Hey, Eddie, want to whip us up some eggs and grits, maybe a little boudin?"

"Okay on the eggs and grits—I don't know if I can do boudin on short notice. How about I ask my mama how tonight, make you some tomorrow?"

"It's a deal."

"Royce Champagne," Suzanne said, "you are not coming to the table without taking a shower. Hi, Sandra, nice to meet you."

Talba was glad Suzanne hadn't called her Eddie. She wasn't crazy about appropriating her boss's name.

She went down to the kitchen and found grits, eggs, and bacon, which ought to substitute nicely for boudin, and some bread for toast. She made more coffee and offered some to Adele, who was working at her kitchen office.

Absently, the older woman accepted a cup and then turned back to her checkbook, which she appeared to be balancing. "Those two!" she said, shaking her head and looking at her watch.

Suzanne came down first, now wearing a hint of makeup. She poured herself a cup of coffee as Talba started the eggs. " 'Lo, Mama Dell. I heard that. We only sleep late to avoid the Whore of Babylon."

Whoo, Talba thought.

"She already gone, by the way?"

"I presume," Adele said, "you aren't talking about your sister-in-law."

"My, uh—oh, Luce. Somehow I don't think of her that way. More like a niece."

"In that case, Kristin, who I find a very lovely young woman, has gone to work. You've heard of work, right?"

"Hey, Royce," Suzanne yelled, "coast is clear!" She turned back to Adele. "If you don't think what I do is work, maybe you should come with me sometime. See what a difference feng shui can make in a house."

"My family's lived in this house for twenty-two years. We like it like it is, thanks."

Royce joined them, actually smelling fresh and soapy, his wet hair slicked down, a loose shirt covering his torso, the same old ripped shorts tickling his knees, beat-up running shoes on his feet. He gave Adele a kiss. "Mornin', Granny Goose."

She gave him a swat, the first sign of affection Talba'd seen in any of these people. "Mommo to you, young man. Tell your wife to button her lip about Kristin—she's probably gon' be your stepmother."

Talba, who was now serving the eggs, looked up to see Royce roll his eyes. "Now isn't that just charmin'."

Adele, sitting in one of those desk chairs that spins on command, executed a one-eighty, so that she faced the starving masses. "You two need an attitude adjustment. You are here as guests of your father and me. If you do not learn to accommodate your father's wife, I can't be responsible for what he might do. She'll move in, and neither one of us will tolerate unnecessary strife in Lucy's life. Lucy loves the girl and she needs a female role model the worst kind of way."

Talba cut her eyes at Suzanne, who hadn't missed the fact that she was the target of Adele's barb. Her fresh rosiness had become a red-hot flush.

"Aren't we jumping the gun, Mommo?" Royce said. "They're not even engaged."

"How stupid can you be, Royce? Hear this: They soon will be. And you are gon' have to adjust to it." She rose and left the room.

"Oh, hell," Royce said. "Forget breakfast. I'm going to work."

Suzanne shrugged. "This is delicious. Alberta cooks her eggs too hard."

CHAPTER FIVE

Fortunately, no one but Adele wanted lunch that day, and taking pity on the new kid, she made herself a tuna fish sandwich. The afternoon was running, running, running—five loads of laundry, eight sheets and sixteen pillowcases to iron, beds to make, bathrooms to clean. Talba had to stay well past four—and then well past five—to feel she'd done a good enough job to warrant a second day. She had only a moment to snoop, and that was in Buddy's night table, where she found a vial of Viagra, a box of condoms, an excellent collection of sex toys, and a gun nestled amid the happy clutter of true love. Buddy came home shortly before she left and went upstairs with a curt nod. She was just walking out the door when she heard him roar, "Can't anyone take a crap around here?"

Good timing, she thought, and closed the door behind her.

At home, Miz Clara was dozing in her rocking chair, wearing her old blue slippers and no wig. "You look like death warmed over."

"Mama, I'm in no mood. I've got to go lie down."

"Ain'tcha got a date with my baby?" Sometimes that was Talba, sometimes Sophia, but this time she meant Darryl.

"Can't do it," she said. She'd phoned to cancel on the way home. She kicked off her shoes and threw herself on her bed, wondering if her body was ever going to be the same. Two hours later, she woke from a deep sleep, teased into consciousness by a black cat purring in her ear, a white one nibbling her toes. "Don't bite, Blanche," she snapped, and forced herself to go forage for food.

Her mother had made chili. Miz Clara had already eaten, but she sat down across the old black-painted table from her daughter, having first poured her a glass of Chardonnay—an unaccustomed attention. "Ya gotta either drink or read the Bible if ya gon' clean houses," she said, "and I know ya mama raised a heathen."

"Have some wine with me," Talba said. "I've got to talk to you."

"Why, I b'lieve I will," said Miz Clara, who never drank unless invited, and then only one glass. She retrieved the wine, which she'd already put away, and poured a glass for herself. "My baby have a hard day?"

"Mama, I'll be honest. I don't know how you do it."

"I got my systems." Miz Clara looked like the Cheshire cat.

"What would you think about sharing? Along with some recipes."

"Recipes! They want ya to cook?"

"You don't have to?"

"These people are animals."

Talba considered it. "Well, one of them is," she said, thinking of Buddy. "Jury's still out on the rest. How do you do it, Mama?"

She meant the question literally, and Miz Clara took it that way. "First of all, ya gotta start at the top. If ya do the floor and then the chandeliers, what's gon' happen?"

Talba didn't know, but apparently she wasn't required to. Miz Clara answered herself. "Ya gon' get a second coat of dust on that floor. Have to clean it twice. See what I mean?"

Talba'd never considered the effects of gravity on dust—this was actually very educational. "Ya gotta look for cobwebs while ya up there—most housecleaners don't even notice 'em. But they up there; they up there catchin' dust, holdin' dust, makin' everybody sneeze. Get them cobwebs and the room's gon' be a lot cleaner already. They gon' like that.

"Another thing. Clean the windows before you do any other heavy stuff. Why? Because the whole house looks cleaner when the windows are clean. Right away, they gon' be impressed."

"Oh, good. Alberta doesn't do windows."

Miz Clara nodded, satisfied. "Ya gotcha work cut out for ya. And here's a little insider tip—ya want to impress men, clean they windows. Ya want to impress women, make those mirrors shine. Spend extra time on the glass stuff—quickest way to impressin' a new client.

"Now here's somethin' real important. Never touch they guns."

"Funny you should mention that—I found a gun today. In the drawer with the sex toys."

Again, Miz Clara nodded. "Sometimes they be in there. Drugs, too. Lot of folks keeps they drugs in there. Here's somethin' I notice. Folks rich enough to have an everyday maid—specially ya judges, ya city officials, folks like that—they got drugs all over.

"They don't have the least little fear about the po-lice or the law. What they paranoid about's people turnin' on 'em."

Which I fully intend to do, Talba thought, and was momentarily disappointed that she hadn't found drugs. But the moment passed—a private stash wasn't a news story and the cops were probably already bought, anyhow. She needed something a lot better than a little pot.

"Ya don't never find no loose change in those kinda people's houses," Miz Clara continued. "Guns, though. I find 'em everywhere—under the mattresses, under the chair pillows. Once I come across one in a kitchen drawer, all tangled up with a corkscrew. Like to scared me to death. Dangerous? Whooee! But don't touch, whatever ya do. Folks is funny about they guns."

Unfortunately, you could have an arsenal in your closet and it still wouldn't be illegal. But Talba was glad for the advice. A gun was the last thing she wanted to touch.

"And they gets dusty, too," Miz Clara said. "People forget they have 'em. Best ya can do, just tickle 'em a little with a feather duster kinda thing—only they ain't made out o' feathers no more. Another thing—don't go in no cabinets—tha's where people keep they good stuff. They weddin' china, Aunt Bertha's antique tureen, stuff like that. They keep it put away 'cause it might get broken if they didn't. And you don't want to be the one to break it. Don't touch nothin' in a cabinet."

That applied, Talba thought, to the maid without benefit of P.I. license. In her job, it was cabinets or quit.

"Anything else?" she asked.

"Under the bed. Whole lots o' dust collects under the bed. Gotta get under there and chase it. Be surprised what else ya find there. Ya got rubber gloves?"

"Why?"

"You find out." Miz Clara laughed like she'd had a lot more to drink than one puny Chardonnay. "Oh, yeah. You find out."

Talba didn't want to find out. "I'm going to bed—I've gotta cook 'em some boudin in the morning, but I'm too tired to ask you how to do it. Can you remind me in the morning?"

"Boudin? That ain' nothin'. Ya just put it in the pan, tha's all."

"That's it? Do you turn on the gas or anything?"

"Lord, child, I gotta draw ya a picture? Add a little water, cook it low—takes 'bout twenty minutes. Oh, and throw the casin' out."

"Before or after I cook it?"

"After. Heat'll break it."

That was what she was after—Talba'd never understood how boudin began as a sausage and ended up on your plate all soft and mushy.

She slept a solid ten hours and needed every minute of it. She'd promised Eddie she wasn't going to plant anything on Buddy, but she only half meant it. She wasn't going to plant drugs, of course. But to her mind, there was no substitute for the occasional tiny receiver/transmitter, available at certain Internet spy shops she knew about. Of course, she could get thrown in jail if she were caught, and Eddie could get sued and fined, but where Angie was concerned, he might be lenient about that part. However, she wasn't about to get caught. She slipped a couple of bugs into her jeans pocket and set out for the salt mines.

Buddy himself met her at the door, still tying his tie and smelling of shaving soap.

"Young lady, you just don't know how close ya got to bein' fired ya first day on the job. Hadn't been for Adele, your ass'd be outta here."

Talba's heart thumped. Maybe he'd Googled her or something—she was famous as the Baroness de Pontalba, even had a Web site with her picture all over it and newspaper stories prominently mentioning her day job.

"As it is, my ass is burned—not to mention certain delicate other parts."

What the hell was he talking about?

"Think about it," he said, and stood aside to let her in. "When you cleaned my toilet, did you forget anything?"

"Oh, shit!" She knew immediately what he meant—she'd sprayed on the bowl cleaner and let it soak, but she hadn't come back to swish it around and flush it away. Buddy must have flushed the toilet himself— at a highly inopportune time.

"Now there's no need for profanity." Buddy went on into the kitchen. "Just be more careful next time."

She followed him in, pleading. "Oh my God, Judge, it'll never happen again."

He'd now poured his coffee, and turned to face her, holding the cup. "It does, you and Alberta are both history. Ya hear me?"

"Yes sir. I promise."

She turned to dig the boudin out of the refrigerator, but Lucy bounced in before she could hide her face, which was in danger of displaying unseemly mirth. "Sandra? Sandra, you're my hero—swear to God, you shoulda seen Daddy dancing around."

"That's enough out of you, young lady." Her father's voice banished all thoughts of girlish giggles—on Talba's part, anyhow.

"Oh, Daddy, don't be such a dork."

Enter Adele. "Sandra. I have to speak to you about something."

"Done," the judge said.

"Miss Adele, I swear to God it'll never happen again."

"Better not."

Kristin was next, followed closely by Royce and Suzanne, who for some reason had decided to rise at a decent hour. Kristin looked ready to take on the board of Bank One—all ninety-nine pounds of her—but the other two looked like they'd had about two hours' sleep.

"Hey, Kristin. Hey, Royce," Lucy said, ignoring Suzanne as if she were a piece of furniture. "We're not having boudin, are we? I hate boudin."

"Young lady, goddammit! I've about had enough out of you," her father said.

Kristin shot him a "go easy" look and Suzanne said, "Do you really think we care what you hate?"

Kristin stood. "You leave her alone." She moved a step closer to the girl.

"You shut up," Suzanne said. "You aren't a member of this family. Who needs your mealy little Pollyanna mouth? I'll be putting up with the no-neck monster when you're just one of Daddy Buddy's fond little memories. He's got lots of those, haven't you, Daddy Buddy?"

Daddy Buddy! Talba was thinking. And *Tennessee Williams*. She recognized "no-neck monster" as Maggie the cat's favorite endearment for kids. She'd landed straight in the second act of *Cat on a Hot Tin Roof*, complete with Burl Ives, and Suzanne seemed to know it. Why else would she have quoted from the play?

"You don't get to call me that!" Lucy shouted. "Only Royce." Well, that explained that, but, except for the fatal cancer, these people were six characters who need search for their play no longer.

This is surreal, Talba thought, and caught Kristin giving her a sympathetic glance, though she was the one who'd been insulted. The petite blonde looked at her watch. "Oops. Time to go." Talba guessed she was used to it. "Run you to school, Luce?"

Buddy said, "Wait a minute, sugar tit."

"Daaaaady!" Lucy wailed, dying of embarrassment.

The judge got up and kissed his sweetie. "I'm comin' home for lunch," he murmured. "Join me?"

Please God, not a nooner, Talba thought. *Some things simply cannot be endured.*

"Love to, darlin', but I've got a meeting with Gary Blancaneaux. The state senator."

"Watch ol' Gary—they don't call him Groper for nothin'." He patted her bottom as she click-clacked smartly out the door, an adoring Lucy more or less clinging to her coattails.

As soon as they heard the front door snick, Talba served the eggs and boudin. And Buddy became a firebomb. "Suzanne Champagne, you will not speak to my friends like that in my house! And Royce, you will control your wife, you lily-assed pansy, or I swear to God I'll toss you both out to beg on the street."

He threw down his napkin, strode out, and headed upstairs. Royce, red-faced, followed as soon as his father was far enough ahead that he didn't have to talk to him.

And then Adele followed, saying, "I just don't seem to have much appetite."

Which left Suzanne. "Well, I do," she said, and Talba gave her an extra helping.

"Bet you're wondering," Suzanne said, "how I can eat with all this going on around me?"

"No, ma'am." *I'm trying to stop shaking in my shoes.*

"Meditation. You've got to be serene to live in this house. That, and practice. Daddy Buddy's little chickies come and go. He blows up, Royce backs down. Lucy pouts and mouths off." She shrugged. "You get used to it."

Talba profoundly hoped she got the goods on the judge before she had the opportunity to get used to it.

She had three goals before lunch, to which she wasn't looking forward—getting every window in Judge Champagne's suite sparkling clean, planting a bug in his office phone, and pillaging at least half his files. If she got that done, she could work on Adele's mirrors.

As it happened, she did get the bug planted and the office windows done, but there was no time to rummage files if she was going to get the beds made by noon. Since most courts recessed at noon, she figured Buddy'd be home by twelve-fifteen, at which time, she'd have a toothsome lunch waiting. Anything to buy time.

Entering the third floor sanctum, she saw that both of the younger Champagnes had long since departed, leaving a room that stank of alcohol and dirty clothes. More laundry to do. After straightening the bed, she tossed the noisome garments in the hamper and worked her way down, entering the kitchen exactly on time. Adele was working in the garden, having exchanged her church-lady dress for a pair of baggy khakis. Talba tapped the window and waved at her.

The older woman smiled, looked at her watch, and came in. "Gardening keeps me calm," she said. "I'll just go up and change for lunch. Can you manage by yourself? There's plenty in the refrigerator. But no sandwiches—Buddy likes a hot lunch."

"Kitchen or dining room?" Talba asked.

Adele looked at her as if she'd asked what a cat or a dog was. "Why, dining room for lunch and dinner. Just the two of us today, I b'lieve."

Talba thought, *what a little tête-à-tête that ought to be*, but then, *maybe not*. These people seemed so used to drama, they hardly seemed to notice it. She found some leftover chicken and vegetables for a stir-fry, to be preceded by a lovely salad, complete with hearts of palm, a can of which Talba found in the pantry.

Things went swimmingly until she set the second course in front of her employer and target. "What the hell is this?" Pronouncing it *hail*.

She was disconcerted. To her mind, it was the best lunch you could have. "Uh, chicken stir-fry?"

"Female food. Adele, she's givin' me goddam female food!" He looked up at Talba, furious, definitely not kidding around. "I look like a woman to you?"

"Umm . . . stir-fry isn't unisex? I know I've seen men . . ." But *had* she seen a man eat it?

"Oh, for heaven's sake, Francis," Adele said, "you could stand to lose a couple of pounds."

Frantically, Talba searched her memory for a substitute. "Omelet and home fries? Hamburger?" Nope, no sandwiches. "I know"—she'd seen a microwave—"stuffed potato."

To her surprise, he boomed out a laugh. "Honey, you're all right. Quick little thinker. Omelet and home fries'd be great. Take this slop away, will ya?"

Talba left to cook the third meal of the day. The omelet came out so perfectly that all might have gone well after all if Royce hadn't walked in the door the instant she served it. By now, Adele had finished her veggies and excused herself.

"Royce? That you?" his father called. "What you doin' home in the middle of the day. Get ya ass in here and have lunch with me."

His son came in looking disheveled and smelling, once more, of strong drink.

"You been drinkin'?" Buddy asked.

"Daddy, I've got something bad to tell you. I got fired."

Buddy's face flashed pink. He threw his napkin down on the table. "Fired? What the hell ya mean fired? Tell me you ain't sayin' Jesse Partee fired ya. How in the name of fuck does a man's son get fired by his best friend?" By the time he finished his speech, his pink face had turned deep red. Talba might have feared a heart attack if she'd had the slightest sympathy for the man.

Royce shrugged, hunching his shoulders and looking deeply embarrassed. "I didn't understand the rules, that's all. I thought I was just there on a fill-in basis. All I ever did was watch other people, what they were doing. I didn't know I had to keep nine-to-five hours."

"It's a job, son. J-o-b as in w-o-r-k. That means nine-to-five to me, or something close to it—whatever hours Jesse works. What'd *you* think it meant?"

"Well, I was religious about it for the first month or so. Then, after that, there just wasn't that much to do—I mean it ain't shrimp season! So I started going in a little later—I mean, not real late—I just wasn't all that careful, but I swear to God, I always stayed eight hours. Every day of my life."

"How late?"

Royce shrugged again, looking ever more uncomfortable. " 'Bout nine-thirty usually."

Maybe sometimes, Talba thought. *But definitely not yesterday.*

"You know what I think? I think he was trying to get rid of me. I *begged* him for something to do! Swear to God, Daddy. He kept sayin' I had to learn the business before he could give me any real responsibility. 'Real responsibility.' Like that was different from any responsibility at all. I mean, I could have broken heads or shoveled ice, come to that. You know I'm willin', Daddy. He just wouldn't give me a damn thing to do."

"You tellin' me the truth, son?"

"Have I ever lied to you?" Royce's voice had risen to match his father's.

Talba stole a glance at Adele, whose face told her that if he was lying, it wouldn't be the first time.

"Are you lying now?"

"No!" Royce was outright yelling.

" 'Cause I'm gon' kill ya if ya are." Buddy's voice was much lower now, cold and dangerous.

"Daddy, I swear to God."

"Jesse Partee, you are on my enemies list!" the judge roared. "I will ruin the man. I will destroy his business and I will destroy *him*. I can promise ya that, son. No two-bit shrimp seller's gon' treat my son like shit. Meanwhile, I'm gon' do what I shoulda done in the first place. Ya gon' work for me. Out at Venetian Isles. Ya definitely gon' shovel some ice. I'm gon' let Brad teach ya the business."

Royce let his shoulders relax. Casually, he drew out a chair and sat on it, drawing it up close to the table across from his father. "Daddy, I just don't know if I'm cut out for this business."

"Well, what the hell *are* ya cut out for? Tell me that, will ya? Every job ya ever had, ya lost. And ya always got some excuse. The boss didn't like ya, ya didn't understand the rules. The boss had it in for me, and he was takin' it out on you. Just what the hell ya think ya gon' do? Live off ya wife's fluffer earnin's?"

"Feng shui."

"*Fuck* shui! What am I gon' do with ya, son?"

"I was thinkin' I might go to law school."

"Law school! With a straight C minus average from one of the worst universities in the country? What law school's gon' have ya?"

"What law school's gonna turn down Buddy Champagne's son?"

Unexpectedly, the judge laughed. Laughed so hard you'd have thought his son was Billy Crystal. "Only every law school in the country. I'm tired of cleanin' up ya messes, boy. This time ya gon' stand up and be a man—if I have to tan ya hide to make ya do it."

Royce turned as red as his father, got up, and walked out of the room. Talba thought possibly a pattern was forming.

She cleared the table and busied herself in the living room, having decided to eat an elephant one bite at a time, as Eddie would say. She started at the ceiling, with the cobwebs, chandeliers, and ceiling fans, teasing the dust off with a feather duster, and there was plenty of it. Evidently, Alberta didn't use Miz Clara's system.

Next, she applied herself to the pictures, mirrors, wall sconces, and finally the furniture, to which she also applied the special polish prescribed by Adele, eschewing supermarket products, which, she was assured, left an ugly buildup and ruined the wood.

She was vacuuming the upholstery when Buddy came down from his office to go back to work. "Hey, Sandra, what'd ya do to my office?"

"Not nearly as much as I wanted, but I was afraid to move your papers around. I know a lot of people don't like their desks touched."

"Whatever ya did, keep doin' it. Place looks like ya shined it up with car wax."

"Really? I did a good job?" *Thank you, Mama,* she was thinking. She made a vow to get to Adele's mirrors before the day was over.

"I may have to fire ya aunt. But ya right—don't touch any of my papers."

Wouldn't dream of it, Talba thought. *Certainly not me.*

She couldn't wait to see what was on her tape. She figured he'd come home for a reason—most probably to make private phone calls.

CHAPTER SIX

O nce again, she cancelled out on Darryl. She wasn't quite as tired as the day before, but if she'd had to go out, she'd still have fallen asleep over dinner, and besides, she had a lot of catching up to do.

First, she listened to the tape, and there was one good thing on it— a conversation between Buddy and Evan Farley:

> **Farley:** *Hey, Buddy, thought you'd like an update. Sorry we couldn't run a story about that bust the other day. The city editor didn't think it was really a story. At this point, anyhow.*

> **Champagne:** *Evan, I really need you here. These scum are 'bout to run me out of business—along with about half the remaining shrimpers in Louisiana. You know how bad it is for the shrimpers, boy?*

> **Farley:** *Well, that's the story they want to focus on. I appreciated your tip, but the powers that be here just don't think what the lawyer does in her spare time has anything to do with it.*

Champagne: *This is about integrity, Evan. This is an ex-ample of the kinda people out to get me. Druggies and lowlifes. That bitch ought not to even be practicin' law in this state. Probably loaded half the time and incompetent as hell.*

Farley: *Well, I'm working on it. Just wanted to let you know I appreciate what you're trying to do for me here.*

Champagne: *I'm expecting great things outta you, boy.*

Now this was fantastic intelligence. It didn't prove Buddy had Funky in his pocket—that "what you're trying to do for me" could be construed as helping with a news story—but it was provocative. It confirmed a connection between Farley and Champagne, and it implied the connection might be based on tit for tat. The only problem was finding the tat. Maybe Eddie was having luck on the Farley beat.

Next, she had to background everybody but Buddy, whom she'd already run through her personal wringer.

To her dismay, Adele and Royce had pretty much managed to stay out of the papers, though she was able to find out a reasonable amount of Adele's story. Suzanne had been no newsmaker, either, under her married name, but there was a wedding announcement for her and Royce. She'd been Suzanne Gautier, and there wasn't much on the former Miss Gautier, either—just one story about feng shui becoming popular in New Orleans. She'd had a few things to say about the proper flow of chi, but that didn't do much for Talba. Lucy had never hit the paper once.

The one she was interested in was Kristin LaGarde, who was quite a little mover and shaker, and who was also living proof of the commonly held belief that love is blind. What a young, gorgeous, smart, reasonably wealthy woman saw in a crude old snake like Buddy Champagne, Talba had no idea. Father figure, probably, although Kristin had a very much alive and not only kicking but ass-kicking father. The lovely Kristin was the daughter of Warren LaGarde, a wealthy developer who built hotels, and she'd gone into the family business, working her way up to vice president in charge of development. She was only thirty-two, but she'd been married and divorced—to and from a lawyer named Daniel Truelove. Evidently, there wasn't all that much in a name.

Still, Truelove was a great moniker—Talba could only imagine the inner struggle the woman must have gone through trying to decide whether to remain Kristin Truelove—who could resist that?—or going back to being Vice President Kristin LaGarde of LaGarde, Inc.

Pragmatism seemed to have carried the day.

Just for the fun of it, Talba did a little work on Daddy Warren, though most of the city already knew his story. His father had started with the flagship Hotel LaGarde, and when he died, sonny had expanded the business. He now owned four hotels, and he was always building more. Not a day went by that his name wasn't in the paper— getting yet another height variance, speaking out on the need to support tourism (more or less the city's only industry), collecting civic awards, announcing new chefs at his hotels' various restaurants.

Talba just loved that height variance thing—all the hotels did it, and it went like this: They applied for a permit to build a hotel to be ten stories, maybe; and then, halfway through the building of it, they said they'd go bankrupt if they couldn't go to fifteen. And, not wanting to lose the business, the powers that be usually went for it. Why on Earth the city kept falling for such a simple con was one of life's great mysteries.

Warren was divorced, too, and Kristin's mother now ran a little antiques store in Covington, which had more than once made it into some kind of local story.

Adele was from Texas, which explained, to Talba's mind, why her manner and accent were somewhat more bluff than that of the average Uptown lady. Her husband, Hollis, who'd founded a company that sold supplies for oil rigs, had died a few years back. That, Talba thought, might explain the fancy house.

She added the background files to the one she'd made on Buddy, which was unremarkable (law school, law practice, judgeship) except for the fact that his wife hadn't died a natural death. Celeste Champagne had been killed in a hit-and-run accident, which might or might not be suspicious.

Talba couldn't yet piece together how Buddy and Adele happened to live together, but her bet was that it had something to do with Celeste's and Hollis's wills—especially since Celeste had died suddenly. Or maybe it was simply an accommodation for Lucy's sake.

She would have done a little work on Farley, to help Eddie out, but that was as far as she could go for one night, and anyway, Miz Clara was calling her to supper. Once more, Miz Clara'd taken pity on her and made her a hot meal—red beans and rice, with some leftover greens on the side. Since Miz Clara hadn't been able to stew them forever, she'd decided to sauté them in bacon grease after steaming. But this was no time to register a heart-healthy protest.

"Thanks, Mama," Talba said as she sat down. "Listen, what can I make for lunch tomorrow? Judge Champagne wouldn't eat my famous chicken stir-fry."

Miz Clara all but curled her lip. "Mmph. Cain't blame him. Why don't ya take the leftover beans for tomorrow? Meanwhile, I be thinkin' o' some things that make up easy."

"Really? You got enough?"

"What I'm gon' do with those beans? Can't feed 'em to the rats—give 'em gas." She bent over to pet the black cat. "Idn't that right, Koko? Ya want some chicken, baby? I berled some up for you and you and that white gal."

Once again, Talba was in bed by eight, rattling pots and pans eleven hours later.

Once again, Kristin took Lucy to school after a couple of sassy exchanges, and the morning's fight took place between Adele and Buddy, who said he couldn't see a reason in hell why the kid was so bratty, but maybe if somebody just paid her a little attention once in a while . . . Adele said okay, she'd take the kid shopping, maybe some new clothes would help, and Talba rejoiced.

With luck, she'd be alone in the house that afternoon.

She tidied the kitchen, getting ready to make the second-floor bedrooms look like they'd just come back from the laundry, while Adele worked the phones in her kitchen office—ordering liquor from Martin Wine Cellar and checking up on an order from a caterer. No surprises there, she thought, with the Champagnes practically on the Mardi Gras parade route. A party was no doubt in the offing.

When Adele had finished, she confirmed it. "Whew! Bacchus party Sunday. I've got a million errands—you be okay while I'm gone?"

"Sure. Anything I can do?"

Adele sighed. "We've got food for a hundred coming in two days, but in the meantime, I guess the rest of us have to eat. Could you look around, see what we need, and run out to Langenstein's for me? I hate to make you do that, but they just *will* not deliver any more."

"Sure; be glad to. Anything else?"

"Work on Buddy's bedroom, will you? He loved the job you did in his office. Anything to keep him happy."

"Glad to, Miss Adele." *Just get the hell out and let me rifle some files.* She had a new cell phone with a camera in it; if she found anything good, she could photograph it.

Adele left, but Suzanne was still around, Royce having left early for his brand new job at his daddy's marina. Talba made her grocery list and went upstairs to clean Adele's mirrors, a casualty from the day before. No sooner had she gotten into a rhythm than the doorbell rang. She found the intercom and spoke to it: "Who is it?"

"Delivery from Langenstein's."

"I'll be right down."

Puzzled, she descended and opened the door, already talking. "I don't get it, I didn't order. Anyway, I thought Langenstein's didn't deliver."

The delivery guy smiled. He was a white guy, a little shabby, but maybe a bit old for this kind of work—and he carried two things only, both of them hams. Beautiful hams. "This time they do—picked these babies up myself. Champagne residence, right?"

"Right, but—"

"You new or something? Where's Alberta?"

"Family emergency."

"Oh. Well, these are from Mr. Nicasio. He said to be sure I got them over here before the party."

"Okay, thanks." Talba tried to tip the guy, but he assured her it wasn't necessary. She found the gift card, and photographed it: "A little something from the God of High Living. Happy Mardi Gras—Harry." Bacchus, he must mean. The hams were for the parade party. And Harry Nicasio was the same bail bondsman who'd posted Angie's bond. Was there some kind of connection? Talba's skin crawled.

She looked at her watch, sighed, and decided she just had time to shop before lunch—she had Miz Clara's beans, but the lettuce was too tattered to serve. She stowed away the hams, went out to procure the items on her list, then put on the beans to heat, started rice, and built a salad, which she dressed with her mama's famous lemon vinaigrette (only Miz Clara didn't call it "vinaigrette"). She set the table for three, thinking Suzanne might smell the beans and get tempted, and no telling who else would show up.

Adele and Royce, as it turned out. Adele ate only the salad, the other two only the rice and beans. Fair enough, Talba thought—I'm getting better. To her amazement, the three ate in relative peace, except for a few cross words between Suzanne and hubby-dear.

"For Christ's sake, Royce, do you have to chew with your mouth open?"

"Do you have to sleep all morning while other people work?"

That kind of thing.

Royce caught her eye as she cleared, "Hey, Eddie, I got a pure-D mess down at that marina—you got a few minutes to help me out?"

Adele fixed him with a steely eye: "Are you crazy, boy? We've got a party here Sunday night. She can't take time off now."

Wrong, Talba thought. She was itching to get a look at that marina. She broke out in smiles and nods and made her voice high and feminine—by nature, she wasn't much of a pleaser, but she'd seen other people do it. "Oh, yes, ma'am, I could do that. I didn't know you had a party here, or I wouldn't have been working so hard on the upstairs. I could work Saturday if you like, get the dining room and sun room ready. The living room's already coming along."

"You could work Saturday?" Adele sounded as if she'd won a door prize.

"Yes. Ma'am, I could. I've got some bills and . . . you know how it is. I'd be glad to."

"Done deal." Adele leaned back in her chair, looking as satisfied as if salad was enough lunch. "Royce, she's yours."

"Come on then, Eddie," he said. "See if you can make me laugh—I could use it."

"Hang on a minute. I've got to go apply my blackface."

He did laugh. "You are way too sharp to be a maid."

This was getting dangerous. On the other hand, she and Royce were developing rapport, and she needed allies. She decided to keep up the routine.

"Very good, sir. I'll fetch my stupid-hat, sir. By the way, what about if I follow you in my car? So you don't have to bring me back."

"Great idea. But from the looks of the place, don't plan on coming back any time today."

"Royce." Adele spoke firmly. "You can have her for two hours. Two hours only."

Talba followed Royce out Highway 90, aka the colorfully named Chef Menteur Highway. It was commonly thought to have been named after an actual chef, but Talba, struck that the literal translation was "chief liar," had looked it up. One explanation was that the Choctaws had once had a mendacious leader who'd been exiled there, another that they'd disliked an early governor, whom they'd nicknamed "lying chief." A third held that it was named after Chef Menteur Pass, the tidal estuary connecting Lake Borgne with the Mississippi Sound, which had treacherous—or "lying"—currents.

Talba was going with the governor.

The Chef Highway cut through New Orleans East, which she'd visited a few times—a very few—usually on shopping expeditions and once on a case, but it wasn't an area she knew, any more than she'd know the West Bank if Darryl hadn't lived there. It was odd, she thought, how many New Orleanians, black and white alike, seldom ventured beyond their own neighborhoods. She'd once met a waitress in the French Quarter who'd lived in the suburb of Kenner her whole life, yet never been to the Quarter before she took the job.

But there was a Home Depot in New Orleans East, and a Wal-Mart, so Talba'd been there. She knew there was a Vietnamese neighborhood somewhere in the East, but she'd certainly never seen that.

Today, she did, though. Royce continued on the Chef until businesses began to appear with signage in Asian characters, and still he kept driving. Finally, they passed something she'd seen on the map—a large wooded area called the Bayou Sauvage National Wildlife Refuge—and a little ways past that was a sign that said VENETIAN ISLES. It was a subdivision bounded on its other end—north or east, Talba wasn't sure—by a body of water clearly marked CHEF MENTEUR PASS.

There were several marinas on the right side of the highway, where there was open water—Lake Borgne, if she remembered correctly. Venetian Isles lay on the left. It seemed to be on a peninsula between Lake Borgne and Lake Pontchartrain, which were connected by the pass. The map had indicated that if you crossed the bridge over the pass, you got to a little community on a smaller body of water called Lake St. Catherine. On the other side of this lake, another pass, The Rigolets, flowed from Lake Pontchartrain into Lake Borgne, and also, by taking a small jog, into Lake St. Catherine. If you kept going, you got to Slidell and eventually to the Gulf Coast. All new territory to Talba—she wondered if Eddie and Audrey came this way when they went to the coast for their famous weekends.

Exploring that area was for another day, however. Today, Royce turned up a street in the Venetian Isles neighborhood and came out on a canal where the marina was nestled. It seemed to consist of a small office, a big refrigerator, a few berths for boats, some conveyor setups, and a longish dock that ran the length of the property. There were a lot of baskets lying around that looked like ordinary bushel baskets, except that they were made out of wire. There were also some plastic ones, more or less strewn about, along with enormous plastic bins. The place wasn't much to look at, and there was absolutely nothing going on.

But another truck was parked there, and a man came out of the little office as Talba got out of her car. "Good," Royce said. "Brad's here."

"Hey, buddy," he called, and gave a large wave.

Brad waved back and as they drew nearer, Talba saw that he was a slim, well-built young man about Royce's age, with a shaved head. There was something about his face that Talba didn't quite like, but couldn't put her finger on. A slightly calculating look, maybe. He wore an old Saints T-shirt, a pair of cutoffs, an earring, and some kind of abstract tattoo on his right arm.

"Sandra, Brad Leitner. Hey, buddy, this is Sandra, but you can call her Eddie. She's on cleanup duty."

"Why Eddie?"

"She's a laugh riot—regular little Eddie Murphy."

"Hey, Eddie. Say something funny. We could use a laugh."

"Man walks into a bar—"

Leitner was already shaking his head.

"Okay. There's a priest, a rabbi, and a minister—"

Leitner looked beseechingly at Royce. "This is seriously not working for me."

"You want *good* jokes," Talba said, "my hourly rate's fifty bucks."

"Think I'll pass. Place smells like a garbage dump. You're just in time." He went back into the office.

He was right. The place was filthy, and stank. Stank badly. The dock was littered with—among other things—decaying shrimp heads and even whole shrimp. Very dead ones. She could see why the neighbors were upset.

"Ever been here?" Royce said. "Whole place is on canals. Almost every house has a water view. A lot have docks."

The neighborhood must be a find for house hunters. It seemed very modest—the figures she'd found put the average mortgage somewhere in the $800 range, though surely that had changed—and yet it still seemed to offer that nearly untouchable amenity: affordable water views. The American dream for a song. Yet she could see the neighborhood was changing. Many of the houses looked as if they'd been built between the '50s and '70s, but they were dwarfed by new ones that she bet hadn't been included in those five-year-old figures. It looked as if some of the older dwellings had been torn down to build the monsters, a sure sign of gentrification.

So, of course the neighbors were mad. Not only had they bought a little chunk of paradise, it was a crowded paradise. The last thing they wanted was commercial activity in their haven.

"What goes on here, exactly?" Talba asked. "I mean, I don't see any action. Shouldn't there be boats here, unloading shrimp or something?"

"This is the slow season. But I'll show you how we do it. See, the boats dock right here, and we unload with a thing like a large vacuum cleaner that goes down into the hold—you know what the hold is?"

"Not exactly."

"It's like a big bin, or bins, where the boats keep the shrimp, packed with layers of ice. The shrimp goes into our bins, here"—he indicated deep plastic vats on the dock—"and then we put it on the conveyor, where it's separated from the water and ice, so we don't have to pay for that too—see, it's done by weight. Then it goes into those wire baskets, which hold a hundred pounds each. Used to go into the plastic ones—those are called champagnes, nothing to do with our family.

They hold seventy pounds, and they were used when shrimp was sold by the barrel. But now it's by the pound. We weigh it and put it back in our own bins, once again packed with layers of ice. They can hold seven hundred pounds. Then the bins go in the refrigerator, and from there the shrimp's sold. All there is to it."

Talba couldn't really see what there was to learning the business, but she supposed it had to do with how large the shrimp were, and what the going rate was. She nodded as if she got it.

"Stack the bins and the baskets, and hose everything down, will you? That's a fire hose, by the way—use both hands. Don't worry about the trash—just throw it in the water."

"In the water?" Talba couldn't believe what she was hearing. That meant more or less in people's front yards. "No, we better haul it. Got some plastic bags?"

"Don't worry about it. Catfish'll eat the shrimp heads. It's all organic; natural recycling."

"What about the other stuff?" Styrofoam cups, papers, assorted other detritus.

Brad shrugged. "Who's gonna haul it? You or me?"

Talba sighed. "Ideal situation, you."

"Well, listen up, Eddie. You want to be environmentally correct, you do it; just don't expect any help from me."

Of course he didn't have plastic bags, but he did steer her to a market across the highway. On her way to get bags, she took the opportunity to explore the neighborhood, which wasn't easy, considering that nearly every street ended in a cul-de-sac. The place had been carefully constructed so that almost every house was on the water. How it got its name was clear—the canals. The streets had names like Genoa, San Marco, and Murano. It was a kind of Disney Venice, without reproduction Italian palaces. Instead, the new homes—though semipalatial—came in any style you could name.

Some were Southern, with columns, some were Caribbean, some looked like Spanish or Moroccan villas. A couple sported Grecian statues, an unfortunate few were a postmodern mess, and one or two even looked vaguely Italian. Most of the newest ones seemed to be at the end opposite the pass, and Talba began to see that if you lived at this end, the development looked very new and shiny indeed.

Oddly—at least to her—the streets were clogged with cars. Maybe people used the money they saved on housing to buy cars to get them back to civilization. And at least three of the vehicles were Orleans Parish district cars. It must be a popular haven for cops. *Fits*, she thought. *Cops never live in high-crime neighborhoods.*

When she'd had a decent spin, she drove back to the marina and started filling a bag with crustacean corpses and coffee cups. While she was doing it, she listened. And watched.

Royce sat in his little office drinking coffee and flapping his jaw at his buddy, but doing very little else so far as she could see, until a man drove up and went in—a dark white man, maybe a Cajun. They talked awhile, but Talba couldn't hear much until Royce gave him a tour. She was still bagging garbage, and black women bagging garbage, it turned out, were as invisible as rumor had it. "Nice little operation ya got," the man said. "I want ya to know how much me and my buddies appreciate what ya doin' for us. Seem like nobody wants to buy the real stuff no more."

That word "stuff" caught her attention, but it turned out the man was talking about shrimp. "Hell, we believe in y'all," Royce said. "Louisiana wild-caught shrimp's the best in the world."

"That what they callin' it now?"

"Branding, Tom. It's called branding. Only way to compete."

"Well, I leave that to you marketing geniuses. All I know, Mr. Brad and Judge Buddy take damn good care of us. What few of us we got left."

"Hey, Tom, we don't want to see shrimping die out in this state any more than you do. How much product you figure you can supply us with?"

"Oh, couple thousand pounds every three days or so. We stay out about that long. Maybe more, we get lucky." Royce nodded and shook. "Done deal. We can use 'em." He waved good-bye to Tom and got on his cell phone, looking out over the water, acting as if he were on vacation.

"Hey, Randy, this is Royce Champagne—you know, from Jesse Partee's? Well, I'm not working for Jesse any more. Yeah. Yeah. I'm over at my daddy's place."

Talba was on the hosing part now, and it was harder to hear, but a phrase came through now and then. "We can afford it 'cause we're doing a volume business. Lots of Jesse's customers are coming over to us—that's the reason I left."

And then, "Oh, come on, Randy, you don't want to do that. Nice place like yours, you don't want to serve that inferior chink stuff." He listened a few minutes. "Well, I'm telling you you can't afford *not* to." Pause. "No, that's not a threat. I'm talking quality here."

It went on like that for a while, but it didn't sound to Talba as if he'd made a deal.

Royce hung up, swore, and tried again, pacing up and down the dock, staring at pelicans and gulls, acting like he thought he was important. And striking out, Talba was pretty sure.

His voice was getting louder and louder; nastier and nastier. Some salesman. And then suddenly, it sounded like he was talking to a woman. "Hey, there, darlin', what are you doin' here? You're way too cute to be hangin' around a place like this."

Oh, right, whoever she was, she was definitely going to go for that. Talba glanced his way, just to get an idea of what Royce's idea of cute was, but she didn't see anybody. He was down on his knees.

"Come on now. Come on, don't run away. Hey, Eddie, head him off!"

Him? Talba thought, and something jumped off the dock and disappeared in the bushes.

"Damn! He'll starve to death. You see him? Looked like he hadn't eaten in a week."

"Did I see what?"

"Little calico kitten. Cutest thing you ever saw—tiny black nose in a snow white face. Wonder where his mother is?"

This was a side of Royce she hadn't suspected.

"I'm gonna leave some shrimp out for him. Anybody's got enough, it's us."

She left to find a place to dump the trash, then spent two more hours downstairs at the Champagne house, trying to make it presentable for a party. She wasn't doing too badly as a maid, she thought on the way home, but detecting was another matter—she was no closer than ever to finding any evidence connecting Buddy to Angie's drugs.

That night Miz Clara taught her how to make shrimp étoufée. Talba figured that was appropriate.

And something good happened the next day. Judge Champagne didn't go to work—simply played truant, to all appearances. Stayed in his office and talked on the phone. She couldn't wait to get home and listen to her tapes. Adele was out doing errands again, Kristin and Royce were working, and Suzanne had a yoga class followed by a massage.

It was a good day to impress Buddy with her étoufée, and she didn't even have to make it—she'd brought in the sample batch she'd made with Miz Clara, after first saving some for their dinner Friday. But she did make bread pudding for dessert, one of her own specialties.

Before lunch, though, she had to get Adele's and Lucy's rooms in shape. She'd been slowly working on Adele's, but she'd barely been in Lucy's except to make the bed. She might as well try to sort out some of the clothes strewn all over the floor. Most of them went into the hamper in the bathroom, but there were a couple of jackets that needed hanging up.

On a shelf in the closet, she noticed a box marked with a skull and crossbones and a simple, enticing legend: LUCY'S. KEEP OUT. Maybe there was a diary in it. For all she knew, Lucy'd overheard a conversation she shouldn't have, and written about it.

She took down the box.

Indeed, there was a journal in it, the first entry marked, "Love Spell." Followed by, "Spell to Bind Suzanne." And other spells. She closed the book, and found another in the box, this one printed. It was titled, *A Teen's Guide to Witchcraft*. There was also a miniature cauldron, a stemmed glass, an ordinary stick, candles, incense, shells, and feathers. The guide outlined the tools a teenage witch would need, enabling Talba to identify the stick as a wand and the glass as a chalice stand-in. Talba knew enough about neopaganism to realize the apparatus was harmless. Lucy certainly wasn't a practicing Satanist, but this wasn't the sort of thing that usually went over in Catholic families. She'd known the kid was a rebel.

And when she thought about it, if there was a diary, it would probably be in Lucy's computer. This was Talba's specialty—she had a great program that could get a simple password in about fifteen seconds, but she'd have to do without it today. No problem, though—she also had a knack for passwords, and Lucy's was bound to have something to do with the stuff she'd just found. She tried out a few—"girlwitch," "witchgirl," "abracadabra"—with no success, and finally got out the witch book again, looking for likely buzzwords and finally happening upon "magick," which worked. As simple as that. The kid believed in magic. She went to Lucy's "favorites" file and clicked on "blog."

There it was: she had a weblog. No juicy stuff there, but to Talba's surprise, Lucy wrote poetry. Pretty good stuff, too. And she, Talba, was one of the best-known poets in the city. Now here was a hook.

She logged off and went to fix lunch.

She set the table for four, just in case, but Suzanne and Buddy were the only ones who showed up. Suzanne sat across the table from him, in a tight tank top, though it was February. "Lookin' good, honey," Buddy said. "But aren't ya cold in that?"

"Oh, no, I'm warm-blooded."

The judge laughed. "Now, that I can believe."

Uh-oh, Talba thought, and sure enough, when she brought in the dessert, an uneasy silence had descended. "I don't think I'll have any," Suzanne said. "I seem to have lost my appetite." She looked pointedly at her father-in-law. Then she stood, tossed her napkin on the table, and left the room.

"You gon' pull a Royce on me?" Buddy called after her. "Come on back, I was just kiddin' around."

She didn't come back.

"On the rag," Buddy said, and winked at Talba.

Uh-huh, she thought. *Buddy, you are a bad, bad man.* He wasn't close enough to have groped Suzanne (unless he'd tried to play footsie), but he'd sure as hell said something that freaked her out.

"Now, this is what I call lunch. And very nicely served, if I may say so."

"Thank you, sir," Talba said demurely. "Will you be in this afternoon? I thought I'd give your bedroom a good going-over."

"Do your worst," he said. "I got some bidness to take care of."

She excused herself and went into the bathroom to call Eddie, to see if he could tail Buddy. But Eileen Fisher, the office manager, said he was out on a job. Well, no matter. If everyone stayed away, she had a lot of time to go through files.

She repaired to Buddy's office to dig up dirt, first checking his medicine cabinet, where she found Oxycontin. The date on the vial was recent. Something might be made of that, but she was bound to find something better. After a cursory search, however, she hadn't. There was a checkbook, though, and she photographed all the names of the payees, just in case some of them were cops, deputies, or possible drug planters. It would take a while, but she could background them all.

Lucy and Adele came home as she was finishing up. Quickly, she straightened the office and went out in the hall, where she loitered long enough to hear Lucy shouting, "I hate that! I'd never wear that in a million years."

"Lucy, you know Mardi Gras's your dad's favorite time of year. The least you can do is show him the respect of wearing something to his party that covers your belly button."

"You just don't *get* it, Mommo!"

"And you may *not* ask Danielle."

"Why? Because she's black? I'm outta here." And the girl burst out of her room at a run, sideswiping Talba with a fair-sized object she was carrying. "Omigod, I am so sorry."

"I'm okay. What's that you hit me with?"

The girl held up the object proudly. "Camcorder. I got it for my birthday."

Actually, Talba already knew that—it was in the blog. She also knew it was Lucy's most prized possession.

Lucy looked sheepish. "Listen, I'm sorry you had to hear that."

"What? I didn't hear anything." Talba winked and continued down the stairs.

"Turn around," Lucy said, and when Talba did, she saw that she was being taped. "Say something brilliant."

Here goes nothing, Talba thought, and declaimed, " 'Call the roller of big cigars, the muscular one, and bid him whip in kitchen cups concupiscent curds.' "

The budding filmmaker stared admiringly. "Awesome."

"Translation: Want some ice cream?"

"That was Wallace Stevens."

"Never heard of him," Talba deadpanned.

"Give me a break. How do *you* know Wallace Stevens?"

"They let black girls go to school. Last I heard, anyhow."

Lucy turned off the camera and followed her downstairs. "Nobody else in the asylum knows any poetry."

Talba was drunk with power. Enough time invading people's privacy, and you could conquer the world. "Asylum?" she asked.

"You mean you haven't noticed? Even Daddy calls it that. You don't think it's weird that we all have to live together like this?"

"I thought maybe you liked it that way."

"Mommo does, I think—so she can keep an eye on me. But Daddy says he's looking after my interests. 'Cause I'm a minor."

"Too deep for me, kid."

"Well, my grandfather died when I was little, but he wanted Mama to inherit the house—see, it was always in his family, and he and Mommo didn't really own it together. So his will said she could live in it till Mama got it—'right of habitation,' it's called. But then Mama got killed." Talba searched the girl's face for sadness, and saw it settle there. "And her will left it to Daddy, and we moved in so he could 'look after my interests.' 'Cause Royce and I are supposed to get it eventually, and I'm a minor. I think there's some kind of fight about it, though—or would be, except that everybody wants Mommo to take care of me. Except maybe me."

"Lucy, you know your grandmother loves you."

The girl sighed. "She's old-fashioned, that's all."

Not liking the shadow of sadness that still sat on Lucy's face, Talba said, "Come on—there really is ice cream."

"Maybe a Coke float. With Diet Coke, of course." The kid giggled.

Talba led her into the kitchen and opened the refrigerator, but Lucy pushed her aside. "You don't have to make it. My best friend's African-American. I hate it when, uh . . ."

"Uh-huh, I get it. That would be Danielle, I presume?"

"Yeah, these assholes won't even let her come to the Bacchus party."

"Language, young lady."

"You too, Brutus?" the girl said.

"Oh, boy, a closet intellectual. You hide it pretty well, baby."

"It's a lonely job," Lucy said, taking a bite of vanilla ice cream.

Talba finished the sentence. "Yeah, yeah. But somebody's gotta do it." An ancient line to her, but Lucy seemed to want to hear it, and Talba figured it wouldn't hurt her to oblige. She was right—evidently the kid hadn't yet heard it enough to make her wince. Instead she smiled, clearly delighted to find an adult who'd kid around with her.

But then her eyes filled up and she turned back to her food preparation.

"What?" Talba asked. "What is it?"

"Oh, nothing. I just wish . . ."

"What?"

"I wish they'd let me have a pet or something."

"Hmmm." Talba's mind raced to figure out what she was getting at, and failed. "I give up. Can you spell 'non sequitur'?"

"Awesome," the kid said again. "You are way smart."

"Not smart enough to get that pet thing."

"Oh." Lucy looked forlorn. "I thought of it because I said 'lonely,' I guess. I don't have a boyfriend—I mean, look at me—I'm not the boyfriend type. And my best friend's black and half the time that gets weird. And, like, I live in an asylum. I need, like . . ."

"Something to love?"

Lucy looked embarrassed.

"Well, why can't you have a pet?"

"Suzanne's allergic. Or says she is. She's a bitch." She put a hand to her forehead. "Ooh. I ate that too fast."

"I heard that, young lady," Adele said, stepping into the room.

"What? That I ate my ice cream too fast?"

"What you called your sister-in-law. Go to your room."

"Whatever." Lucy sauntered out, not the least nonplussed.

"What am I going to do with that child?" Adele said to Talba. "She's such a brat, Buddy's at his wit's end. I try, but with this party and all, things are just getting away from me. The damn caterer misunderstood the order and now she's got to double it and doesn't have time."

"Guess she better make time," Talba said.

"That's what I told her. And she's only sending me one server. She's piss-poor. Are you good at serving?"

Talba shrugged. "I can get by."

Adele exhaled. "Well. Are you free Sunday night, by any chance? I hate to ask you, but I'm really—"

Talba interrupted, to save her the trouble. "Sure, I could do it. I'd love to. I could really use the extra cash."

The older woman closed her eyes in relief. "I'll dance at your wedding. Wear a white shirt and black skirt."

"Blue skirt okay?" Talba had a dozen of them. White shirts and blue skirts were her invariable work attire—practical, always suitable, nearly invisible.

"Blue's fine."

Talba had a great idea. "You sure you're going to have enough help? I know a real good waiter—probably I could talk him into coming." Darryl was no waiter, but he'd just love this—and a high school English teacher ought to be smart enough to figure out how to pass hors d'oeuvres.

"You've got to be kidding. You could really get me somebody?"

"I can try."

"I swear I don't know what we ever did without you. I've got to go see about the flowers. See you tomorrow then? About two o'clock to set up."

"Yes'm, I'll be here."

Talba went home, lined up Darryl to serve, and wrote two poems. She had a reading tomorrow, after her setup date, and she needed something new. Whatever else happened, she was still the Baroness de Pontalba. The day's tapes could wait. She couldn't drink while working, and she could while listening.

When she was finally able to get into bed with a glass of wine and her tape player, she got so excited she nearly phoned Eddie and Jane Storey. But she had a meeting with Eddie and Angie the next night, after her reading. The content of the tape would keep till then, and it was so good it deserved personal delivery.

CHAPTER SEVEN

She slept till nearly noon and woke up feeling as if she'd been issued a fresh skeletal system. It was a gorgeous February day—more spring than winter—so she wore a tank top under her chambray work shirt, thinking to strip down if necessary.

At two sharp, she arrived at the Champagne house—to a scene of chaos. Furniture was in disarray, tempers were frayed, and no men were in sight.

All the women except Lucy were, though. "Thank God you're here," Suzanne said instead of hello. "Daddy Buddy and Royce went off to an Iris Party with Brad and left us to do everything—although Daddy Buddy said something about some guys coming to help. Naturally, they aren't here. Don't you think the food table ought to be in the dining room, and the bar out in the hall?" She was wearing denim capris and a tank top that showed a sun tattoo on her upper back.

Kristin, in jeans that looked ironed, joined them. "Buddy wants the bar in the dining room."

"Then everything will just get jammed up. Come on, Sandra, what do you think?"

"If I start thinkin', I might have to charge overtime."

Kristin laughed, Suzanne didn't. "Come on, Suze, you know how Buddy is about this party. . . ."

She was about to say more, but Suzanne cut her off. "How many times have I asked you not to call me 'Suze'?"

Kristin glared at her. "Suzanne, what do you really care? This party's Buddy's pride and joy. You know Mardi Gras's more important to him than Christmas and Thanksgiving put together. Why are you being such a crybaby?"

"Crybaby! How dare you? Since when are you an expert on traffic flow? What do you think feng shui's all about, anyway? You've got me—why not take advantage of me?" She was shrieking.

Adele entered the dining room and put a hand on the younger woman's shoulder. "Suzanne. We'll do it Buddy's way."

"Fine! Just fine. Do it Daddy Buddy's goddam way. Whatever Buddy wants, Buddy gets." She glanced sideways at Talba, suddenly remembering the new maid had witnessed the disturbing scene at lunch. "He wishes!" she finished.

"Well, he's getting his bar where he wants it," Adele said crisply. "Get that, will you, Sandra?"

Someone was at the door—two burly brothers, dressed in baggy jeans and T-shirts. "Can I help you?" Talba asked.

"We're here to do the heavy lifting," one of them said, a youngish guy with a shaved head like her brother Corey. He was cute and he knew it.

Talba played dumb. "I didn't know we were expecting . . . uh . . ."

"This the Champagne residence, right? Mr. Nicasio sent us."

"Of, of course. The guys to do the heavy lifting."

"Now ya catchin' on."

She was catching on, all right, and beginning to worry about her offer to help serve. "Mr. Nicasio coming to the party?" she asked casually as she let them in. That was all she needed; she wondered about Jimmy Houlihan, too.

The two men exchanged a look. "Don't think he invited," the cute one said. "But he like to help out whenever he can."

In a way it was too bad. Sure, he might have recognized her, but she'd have loved the chance to photograph a bail bondsman at a judge's party.

"Miss Adele! The guys are here to help."

Adele bustled into the hall. "Oh, good. Can you two go in there and work with Kristin? She's the blonde one." To Talba she said, "How'd you do with my extra server?"

"I don't know if it's going to work out. He'd love the job, but this is the weekend he has his daughter."

"How old is she?"

"About ten."

"Perfect. She like parades?"

"What kid doesn't?"

"Good, get him to bring her—Lucy can babysit. She won't like it, but she can do it. How are you at arranging flowers?"

"I could give it a shot. But wouldn't that be more Suzanne's thing? Seems like she's the aesthetic type."

Adele looked bemused. " 'Aesthetic.' Well, aren't you a case. Never use a ten-cent word if you got a three-dollar one. Good idea, though— might make her feel important. Suzanne! Hey, girl, I need you." She winked at Talba.

Talba spent the rest of the day ironing tablecloths, which Adele had just discovered she'd forgotten to send to the cleaners, and came out of the laundry room to find Suzanne in tears, crying out her woes to Royce, who had by now gotten home from a day of drinking beer and catching throws. Kristin seemed to have left, and Adele was nowhere to be seen.

"Kristin thinks she owns the goddam house, and Mama Dell takes her side. Can't you do something?"

"Well, Suzanne, for God's sake, what do you care? This party's all about Daddy, not you. Can't you just do your meditation and your feng shui and call it a day?"

"This *is* my feng shui. This is what feng shui's all about. If they do it her way, it's going to screw up the traffic flow. Everybody'll congregate in the front of the house."

"So? Once the parade starts, they'll be that much nearer. Give it a rest, will you?"

"Kristin thinks she owns the goddam place."

"Are you jealous of her or something? Who cares? Daddy has a different girlfriend every six months."

"You know what, Royce Champagne? You are a wimp! An unmitigated coward and a craven little kid."

"Suzanne, I am so sick of your whining I could scream."

Me too, Talba thought. *I'm out of here and you can all rot in hell.*

She took her weary bones home and transformed herself. Half the fun of being a baroness was dressing the part, and she had a new outfit from the Ashro catalogue, "the animal magnetism duster set." The dress was layered, the outside layer being a jungle print with leopards and zebras frolicking in a turquoise jungle and the bottom layer a chiffon leopard print, which brushed and swirled around her ankles a good foot below the jungle layer, which matched the duster. Both pieces were banded in gold and trimmed with bronze beads. Not everyone could get away with it, but a baroness could, with about five pounds of turquoise jewelry.

Miz Clara, as always on reading nights, deputized herself into the fashion police: "Wait'll Eddie see that. He gon' fire ya fine behind."

Talba was used to this—once, her mother had pronounced her "a rummage sale on the hoof." The threat of firing was mild.

Talba was more or less the house band at a restaurant called Reggie and Chaz, famous for its poetry readings and its cheap and cheerful décor, which was notable mainly for the dozens of Guatemalan belts that hung from the ceiling like so many multicolored streamers. It was one of the few literary hot spots that drew a salt-and-pepper crowd of poets. At most other venues, just about anyone might show up in the audience, but the poets themselves tended to be all one color or the other.

Talba liked the multicultural aspect and indeed admired a number of white poets, though she couldn't understand why they tended to read in a monotone instead of memorizing their poems and performing them. She blamed T. S. Eliot, who, in her opinion, had a lot to answer for. If people could be bothered coming out at night to hear poetry, the least she could do was give them a show.

She never got to read first at Reggie and Chaz. So many people came just to see her that they liked to save her for last, but tonight she had begged to go third and had finally negotiated fifth.

The poet immediately before her was white and political, her favorite kind of act to follow, since her own material was so different. She had two new poems, the first of which was called "The Night They Busted Big Chief Alabama Bandana," which, due to its topical nature, was guaranteed to kill. (And couldn't possibly reveal Angie's arrest to anyone who'd care, considering that the audience was sure to consist mostly of Bywater and Marigny hipsters, sprinkled with artistically inclined brothers and sisters.)

But first she read another inspired by recent experiences. She called it "The Intersection."

The Intersection
Mr. William Butler Yeats wrote that
"Love has pitched his mansion in the place of excrement"
Tha's what ya call a poem within a poem
And I always loved that line.

But I'm gon' go ol' Bill one better.

'Cause somethin' I seen
Was even more obscene
Than nature.

I was over at my buddy Bubba White's
And Bubba gets a nosebleed,
So I go lookin' for a tissue,
Happen to open the wrong drawer

And this is what I see:
I find his favorite trove of sex toys.

Now I'm real happy for ol' Bubba,
Who's kinda gettin' on these days,
Got a nice young girl friend
I was kinda wonderin' how he was gon' keep.

And in that drawer I see a cache of
Them Viagra pills
And I feel even happier

P.I. on a Hot Tin Roof

For him, 'cause I hear the young
Kids, not more than twenty-one—
Talk about how it keep 'em goin'
Maybe thirty-six hours straight,
And I think even thirty-six minutes
Probably make ol' Bubba
Want to jump the moon.

And then I see a great big box
Of condoms, and I know ol' Bubba
Even in his joy,
Be playin' it safe.
Now ain't that nice, I think.

And then I see the gun.

Just nestled in there snug and cozy.
And I ponder what ol' Bubba
Might be afraid of,
'Cause all the condoms
In the entire state
Ain' gon' protect us
From that kinda mess.

I'm pretty sure that
Firearm be loaded
And ready to go, too,
Just like Bubba on a good night

In the event he know what that is.

Put me in mind of two streets
Intersect here in our city—
Desire and Law—
And that's for real.

Think to myself—
Hope that never happens.
Hope ol' Bubba keep them two
Separate for sure.

Hope that nice young girl friend
Never make him mad
At the wrong time.
Hope nobody else in the house
Come in his room one night
Lookin' for a tissue,
End up
Full of bullets.

'Cause all the nice young girls
In all the world
And all the Viagra
In the whole parish of Orleans
Ain' gon' cure what Bubba's got.

Or what we all got.

It was a dark poem, and though the other didn't have a happy ending, it did leave 'em laughing—at least in a rueful kind of way, which
was the way she liked it. She signed off in her usual way, "The Baroness
myself thanks you," and stepped gracefully off the stage. The others in
her party—Eddie and Angie—had sat in the back, and the three of
them slipped out into the bar.

Eddie wasn't much for poetry, but he loved the sound of Ms. Wallis's
smooth-as-butterscotch voice, which was probably the only thing
that kept him from firing her sometimes. Like tonight—for wearing a
dress that looked about right for Mardi Gras.

The other thing, he had to admit she had a pretty good sense of humor. But he couldn't for the life of him understand why an educated woman wrote in what he called Ebonics.

"I don't get it either," she'd told him. "It's just the way I hear the poems." Like she was Joan of Arc.

Angie said, "Nice dress, Your Grace."

"Mama said your daddy'd fire me for it."

"I might," Eddie said. "I might. Weren't you a little on the realistic side tonight?"

Ms. Wallis shrugged. "I read Angie the poems in advance. She said full speed ahead."

Eddie cocked an eyebrow at Angie, then turned back to his young assistant. "That true about the gun?"

"Uh-huh. And you can guess who Bubba is—but unfortunately, there's nothing illegal about it. I found Oxycontin, though."

"Who cares? It's a prescription drug."

"Yeah, but you could argue he was taking it when he made important decisions."

"That's not gon' get us anywhere," Eddie grumbled. "Whatcha drinking?"

"White wine," Ms. Wallis said.

"Bourbon for me," said Angie, and Eddie said, "Make it two."

"You two are not going to believe what I've got."

"Am I off the hook?" Angie asked.

"Well, that's the bad news. I haven't got that piece yet. But Buddy's definitely dirty. He's dirty and lazy and so incompetent we could get him thrown off the bench tomorrow."

"Lazy?" Eddie raised his voice. "Lazy? Since when's it a crime to be lazy, specially in Louisiana." As he saw his associate's face relax into an I'm-going-to-enjoy-this expression, he realized the trap he'd fallen into. It was never a good idea to give Ms. Wallis an opening like that.

"What if you're a judge and you're so lazy you phone in court?" she asked smugly.

He tried to process what she was saying. "Go on," he said.

"He didn't go to work yesterday. Just sat back in his office and called his clerk and said he was going to hold court from home that day. The lawyers made their arguments over the phone, and he ruled over the phone. And that's the truth, the whole truth, and nothing but the truth."

"Wait a minute. Hold it. How could you hear all that?"

"I was making up his bed. His office is just off the bedroom."

The back of his neck was pouring sweat. Ms. Wallis was honest to a fault—on most things. But he didn't completely believe her when she said she never resorted to illegal listening devices. She knew way too much and she was way too sure about what she knew. But if she was lying, she wasn't about to admit it if he asked her. "How'd you hear what was happening on the other end?"

"He left the speaker phone on, can you believe it? Miz Clara was right when she told me nobody notices a maid. Anyhow, I was pretty quiet—I'm not even sure he knew I was in there." She sipped her wine and gave him a don't-mess-with-me look. "Easy enough to prove, anyhow. Plenty of witnesses—the clerk, the reporter, both lawyers . . ."

"All right, all right." He was thinking it over, wondering if it was possible. And in his heart, he knew it was—that he'd probably even witnessed something similar a few times. The truth was, there were plenty of stories about judges not showing up for court. He could think of one or two who were notorious for it; their clerks really ran their courts.

He knew perfectly well you couldn't really hold court on the phone. Yet here was what he'd seen: lawyers waiting to argue, witnesses waiting to testify—Eddie among them—and then the clerk would come out and say the judge was on the phone, and the two lawyers would disappear into chambers. Presumably they'd argue their motions or have their status conferences with a judge sitting by his pool—maybe even on the beach in Florida—while they sweated in the courthouse. It had always pissed Eddie off. Personally, he loved the idea of someone getting caught at it—but it didn't solve the problem at hand.

"So you can make Jane Storey's day," he said. "It ain't right, but it doesn't make him dirty."

"What about if I told you Harry Nicasio sent over two hams for his Mardi Gras party, and some guys to help him set up?"

"Harry the bail bondsman?"

"That Harry."

Eddie pondered. "Guess I'd say it doesn't look too good. But I got a problem with it—who'd sell himself for a coupla hams?"

"What do you bet it's the tip of the iceberg?"

"And how do we get to the base of said 'berg?"

"Well, I was thinking of handing that part over to Jane Storey. He's got to be doing favors for Nicasio—she can probably run it down pretty easily. Oh, and I overheard another conversation—with Evan Farley, about the story Farley couldn't write about Angie. No specifics, but something smells there. Did you get anything, Eddie?"

Eddie shifted. "Yeah, I got something. Custody case. Farley's trying to get his kid back from his ex-wife. And guess who the judge is?"

"Come on," Angie said. "That's a really blatant conflict of interest."

"Uh-huh. Oughta be enough to get Farley off the story, anyhow. But we need proof Buddy set you up if we're gon' get the charges dropped." He turned to Ms. Wallis. "Which is the object of this little exercise."

She got her canary-feathers look again. He hated that look. "Well, I've got a lot of names from his checkbook. We can check them out, see if any are involved with Angie's case—like maybe we'll find Buddy made payments to the cops who busted her. Want me to do it, or do you want to?"

It was the last thing Eddie wanted to do, but he took pity on her. In their few phone conversations that week, she'd sounded so tired he didn't see how he could pile any more work on her. And anyhow, this was Angie—if anyone was going to screw up, it ought to be Eddie. "Hand it over," he said. "I'll get Eileen to help me with the damn machine." His kindest name for the computer.

But it wouldn't take a lot—he could just phone the police personnel department and determine whether any of the names belonged to cops.

Ms. Wallis pulled a list out of her bag. "Thanks." She smiled, but he saw that she looked exhausted.

"You got eye bags as big as mine. They been workin' ya hard?"

She shrugged. "Miz Clara does it every day and she's more than twice my age. I'm just not used to it."

"Ya think we got enough or ya want to keep goin'?"

She looked horrified. "Are you kidding? All we've really got's possibilities—I mean, so far as Angie's concerned. Sure, we've got enough to keep Jane eating out of our hands for the next decade, but I can't stop now, Eddie. Uh-uh. Negative."

"Talba," Angie said softly, "you really don't have to . . ."

"Shut up," Eddie said. "Yes, she does."

101

CHAPTER EIGHT

For the third time since she'd known Darryl Boucree, Talba didn't
feel like driving across the bridge to spend the night with him. She
was so tired she was afraid of falling asleep at the wheel, but she hadn't
seen him in a week, and he'd been wonderfully generous about agreeing
to help out at the Bacchus party. Not that he didn't want to—it was his
kind of thing: an adventure in unknown territory. And he really did
think Raisa would enjoy the parade. So, even though Raisa was there,
she made the trip.

Raisa was a love child who lived with her mother, and Kimmie was
what Darryl called "difficult" when he was in a good mood. He said
"crazy" a lot, too, and he wasn't speaking lightly. He really thought she
was. He hardly knew Kimmie, except as his child's mother. They'd
barely dated at all before Kim became pregnant, a sobering development that made them realize they didn't even like each other. So they'd
gone their separate ways—his family had sent him to Yale, mostly, he
claimed, because they were so freaked—and she'd married someone
else. But she'd gotten divorced, and reappeared one day with the kid,
needing money. For a long time, Darryl had worked three jobs to help

support Raisa—as teacher, musician, and bartender. But when Kim finished beauty school and got back on her feet, he'd been able to quit bartending. By then, though, he was hooked on Raisa, and the feeling was mutual. Kimmie, on the other hand, no longer had any use for him, so he more or less kowtowed to her, to keep the kid in his life.

In Talba's humble opinion, Raisa was every bit as difficult as her mother, just in a different kind of way. She was prone to tantrums, for one thing, single-mindedly dedicated to getting whatever she wanted. Some might have said she was spoiled, but Talba thought the opposite. Whatever it was she needed, she wasn't getting—enough of her father, for one thing. But Kim was a rigid, withholding, judgmental woman, and selfish. She alternately clung possessively to her daughter and dumped her on Darryl when it was convenient. Talba suspected a lot of promises were broken in that household, which now included a stepfather to whom Raisa apparently hadn't taken any better than she'd taken to Talba.

She didn't take at all well to sharing her daddy.

Thankfully, the kid was in bed by the time Talba arrived. Darryl kissed her and offered wine, which she gratefully accepted. "Hate to say it, handsome," she said, "but I'm going to be a pretty dull date tonight. I feel like I've been run over by a truck. I've got a new respect for what my mama does."

"Maybe a foot massage."

"Umm. Maybe." And so she sat on one of his rust-colored sofas and let him rub away the tension and weariness of the last few days while she filled him in. Technically, every case was confidential, but where Darryl was concerned, Talba took the notion of secrecy as more of a guideline than a rule. What was the point of having a job if you couldn't share it with your boyfriend? But not even Darryl knew about her penchant for illegal listening devices (the prohibition against which she also viewed as a mere suggestion).

"Sounds," he said, "as if you've got enough to keep Jane Storey busy for a month."

"Oh, man, is she going to owe me. That's got to be a good thing."

"Bringing down a crooked judge could be even better."

"I just have to get Angie off, that's all. And then I can go back to my cushy job as a computer wiz and brilliant poet."

"How'd the reading go, by the way?"

"I killed. *I* am a baroness."

"Uh-huh." He'd only heard the line about a thousand times.

"A nearly dead baroness."

"Would Your Grace agree to be tucked in?"

"My Grace would more or less demand it."

They were awakened at 8 A.M. by an easily identified flying object—a hungry ten-year-old landing between them. "You keep sleeping," Darryl said. "I'll feed her."

But Raisa's oatmeal was too lumpy, and when Darryl made her some eggs instead, they were too runny, as she so elegantly put it. It was going to be one of those days.

Talba heard it all from the bedroom. Unable to sleep for the ruckus, she dragged her bones out of bed. She was sure Raisa heard her feet hit the floor, because the next thing out of the kid's mouth was this: "Daddy, why does that lady always have to be here?"

Talba stumbled sleepily into the kitchen. "I don't have to be here, sweetheart. I'm here because I love you." She had her fingers crossed. The kid wasn't all that lovable.

"Well, I don't love you," Raisa volunteered.

"You will, though. Everyone does. *I* am a baroness."

"*You* are a baboon."

So Talba had little choice but to do an ape impersonation, which would have made her niece Sophia Pontalba fall down laughing, but Raisa, as always, was unmoved.

"Oh, hell, I need coffee," Talba said. Darryl handed her a cup.

"I'm gonna tell my mama you used a bad word," Raisa said. Darryl glowered at her. The last thing they needed to do was give Kimmie ammunition—lately, she'd been telling Raisa she didn't approve of Darryl, and because of their situation, he didn't have formal custody rights. Exactly what she found of which to disapprove, Talba couldn't imagine. Darryl was an English teacher at a public school, which made him practically a saint in Talba's opinion, and he was a well-known musician as well, which made him a catch. But then, Kimmie was a whack job.

"Guess what we're going to do today?" Darryl said. "We're going to a party."

"Don't want to go to no party."

"Any party," Talba said automatically, and Darryl said, "You're turning into your mama."

"You ain't got no mama," Raisa said, to which Darryl retorted, "You don't have any mama."

"That's what I said."

"Well, she has. You even met her once, at a crawfish boil at Mr. Valentino's house."

"Don't know no Mr. Valentino."

"Well, you met Miz Clara at his house, and she's one of the great cooks of the parish. Some day, maybe, if you're good, we'll take you to see her and you can try her fried chicken."

"Hate fried chicken."

"You like mansions?" her father said. "You want to see a mansion?"

"What's that?"

"A really, really big house. And beautiful. This one's beautiful, right, Talba?"

"It ought to be. I just spent a week shining it up."

"Is it your house?" Raisa asked, interested for the first time.

"No, I just work there. And tonight your daddy and I are going to help some folks give a party. And you know what we're going to do?"

The girl was silent.

"We're gonna have fun!"

Raisa made her patented you're-an-idiot face and left the room.

"That's it," Talba said as they pulled up to the Champagne house.

"Now that," Darryl said, "truly qualifies as a mansion. What do you think, kiddo?"

"That's a house?"

"A big one."

Raisa, for once, was speechless.

"You cleaned *that*?" Darryl asked.

"Tell my mama, will you? Listen, Raisa, your daddy's got something to tell you."

This was the tricky part. "Raisa," Darryl began, "can you keep a secret?"

105

"How much ya gon' pay me?"

Darryl was ready for that. "Well, I *am* going to pay you."

"You are?"

Raisa had expected him to say, "I'll tan your little bottom if you don't," the way he usually did, to which she invariably replied, "Oh, *Daddy*!"

"We're detectives tonight, you understand? We're undercover. We're getting paid, so you're going to get paid, too. One dollar if you do things right."

"What I gotta do?" She was understandably suspicious; Darryl didn't believe in bribes.

"All you have to do is call Talba 'Sandra.' That's her secret name. Can you do that?"

"Think I'm a baby? Sandra. S-a-n-d-r-a."

Darryl nodded. "Very good, double-o-seven. And one other thing. You can't tell anyone we're detectives. They think we're here to help out with dinner."

"Two dollars."

"Three."

"Oh, *Daddy*!"

"No, I mean it."

"For real?"

"Shake on it?" He held out his hand. Raisa didn't move.

"Three dollars. Going once, going twice . . ." Raisa shook. But Talba wouldn't rest easy till they'd left the house. The kid was so perverse she might go out of her way to blow their cover.

"Ready? Let's go."

No one was downstairs except Adele, who seemed impressed by Darryl's good looks and better grammar, and who positively raved over Raisa. "Why, you look just like a little angel! You want to meet my granddaughter?"

"No, ma'am."

Talba was amazed by the "ma'am" part, pretty used to the other. "Well, it's nothing personal," she said. "Raisa's having a 'no' kind of day."

Adele laughed. "So's Lucy. They're made for each other." She turned her head toward the stairs and hollered, "Lucy! Luuuucyyy! Come on down, the little girl's here."

Lucy, dressed in a short skirt and a pink T-shirt that looked awful on her, walked slowly and grandly down the staircase, if a disgruntled fourteen-year-old could be said to be grand. Raisa stared up at her, hatred in her eyes.

One look at Darryl, though, and Lucy perked up; he had that effect on females. Shaking hands with him, she blushed. And when she finally condescended to look at Raisa, it was with a look of such haughty disdain she nearly gave off sparks. But then she *really* looked at her, and did a double-take, moving back a step to get a better view.

"Omigod! You are adorable."

Talba tended to forget it, given the kid's disposition, but Raisa was one of the prettiest children on the planet. She had smooth, light-mocha skin and crinkly, fine, golden hair—not really blonde, just gold—that (now that she was older) curled in shiny ringlets unless she brushed it, and if she did (which was seldom), turned into a golden cloud. Talba had thought it would turn dark as she got older, but it hadn't, just developed those curls. Neither Talba nor Darryl had been able to get her to brush it tonight. But the curls were something out of a storybook.

"You're exotic," Lucy said. "Do you know what that means?"

Raisa said nothing, her brows meeting in the middle and almost, but not quite, covering the frown that brought them together.

"It means you're really unusual. I've got to get my camera." The girl turned tail and raced up the stairs.

"Lucy! Luuuucyyy!" Adele called after her, to no avail. Shrugging, she said, "Raisa, would you like a piece of king cake?"

At least that was a sure thing. "Yes, ma'am," Raisa said, turning her attention to the gorgeous spread laid out on the dining room table.

But Adele wasn't a grandmother for nothing. "Maybe a ham sandwich first." Raisa's face fell, but she could see she was going to have to eat ham to get cake. Darryl grinned at Talba. Things could be worse.

The kid was spreading mustard when Lucy returned with her camcorder. "Hey, Raisa, look at me. How's the ham?"

Raisa frowned. "Haven't tried it yet."

"Well, eat some. Let me get you eating some." And Raisa started performing.

She circled her mouth with the sandwich, popped it in, and said, "Mmmmm," which made everyone laugh.

"Great," Lucy said. "Fantastic."

"Now say, 'Thank you, Miss Adele,'" Darryl admonished.

Raisa turned to her hostess, "The baroness myself thanks you, Miss Adele." And she curtsied, in perfect imitation of Talba taking a bow.

Even Adele cracked up. "Where on earth did she learn to do that?"

Talba cringed. What if the child blurted out the truth?

But she said, "Saw it on television."

"Fantastic," Lucy said. "Want to see yourself?" She played the tape back, and Raisa laughed delightedly.

"Did someone mention ham?" Adele asked, and Talba realized for the first time that Raisa had a sense of humor: She'd simply never bothered to display it before. But the thought of herself in a movie had made her drunk with power.

"Hey, Lucy, want to see me eat king cake?" she said.

Talba stared at Darryl, who shrugged. "There's nothing like an audience. You and I both should know." He had spoken low, but Adele heard it. She looked from one to the other. "Do you two moonlight as actors or something? You're attractive enough."

Talba felt blood rush to her face, but Darryl laughed. "I'm a musician," he said smoothly, "and Sandra sings with the band sometime."

Suzanne came running down the stairs. "Are the caterers here yet? Ohhhh." The last part was about Darryl. Talba was so used to him she tended to forget how good-looking he was. He was coffee-colored, tall, reedy, a little bit devilish (as befitted his night job), and a little bit professorial (ideal for his day gig). With fabulous teeth, close-cropped hair, and an appealing, wiry energy, he made a really great first impression, and an even better second one.

"Darryl Boucree," he said. "Sandra's friend."

"Oh. Well, I just need to check on the vegetarian stuff."

"Come on," Adele said. "I'll get you two set up. You're so attractive—do you mind passing hors d'oeuvres?"

"Darryl's the showman," Talba said hastily. "I'm clumsy as an ox. Why don't I just stay in the kitchen?" She'd called Jimmy Houlihan, but if Patsy came with him, all bets might be off.

"Nonsense. I don't trust these people." Meaning the caterers. "Sandra, I really don't know what we'd do without you."

Darryl barely had time to roll his eyes before the doorbell rang: the first guest.

It was five minutes before the next one, but after that, they came thick and fast. In no time, the place was so full that Talba figured she could always duck behind somebody if she spotted the Houlihans.

But in about an hour, they were the least of her problems. Lucy had disappeared with Raisa, happy to have a new black friend, since Danielle had been disinvited. Darryl was having a ball pretending to be a waiter—and carrying it off beautifully. Talba passed hors d'oeuvres and smiled and even made the occasional joke, not particularly worried about being recognized unless she did see the Houlihans. It wasn't really a poetry crowd.

She picked out Brad Leitner, talking to Adele and a guy in cutoffs, various celebrities lite, like local pols (all white, which excluded the mayor), and a few blue-collar types she thought might be cops.

Automatically, her head turned at the sight of fellow African-Americans, checking out members of her tribe, and indeed there were quite a few more than she'd seen at the Houlihans' party. Political buddies, she figured. But she almost dropped a tray of Louisiana wild-caught shrimp when she found herself face-to-face with her own brother.

He nabbed a plump crustacean and let his face crack in a wide grin. "Moonlighting?"

"Omigod, Corey, think of a cover story, quick. How about this—I used to work for you, okay? Best housekeeper you ever had. If anyone sees us talking. Is Michelle here?"

"Housekeeper?" he guffawed. "Are you kidding?"

"Jesus, here comes Kristin. My name's Sandra, okay? Darryl's who he is, except not a schoolteacher."

"Who's Kristin?"

"Quick. Go warn Michelle."

But it was too late. Kristin was upon them. Ignoring Talba, she stuck her hand in Corey's direction. "Hi, I'm Kristin. Hope you're having a good time."

"Corey, uh, Wallis." He looked at Talba uncomfortably. They hadn't consulted about last names.

Talba nodded at him briefly, to signal it was okay, and got out of

Dodge, weaving through the crowd in search of her sister-in-law. She spotted Michelle across the room, taking a cheese puff from Darryl. The bad news was, Suzanne was talking to her. This thing was going south fast.

Worse, she wondered how the hell her own flesh and blood knew the Champagnes.

She was trying to get to Darryl for a quick conference when a bell rang, loudly and insistently. Silence fell.

"Now that I have your attention," Buddy intoned, causing a few sycophants to titter, and Talba to wish for a law against saying dumb stuff. If one more person mentioned the "see-food diet" to her, she was going to have to smack him. That "attention" thing was just about as bad.

"I just wanted to welcome y'all all here and let you know that Zulu came early this year. Look what I got!" He held up a coconut decorated with gilt and glitter and feathers and one other thing.

Zulu, the most venerable and far the most colorful black krewe, traditionally parades on Mardi Gras morning, hence the "early" part. The coconut was a reference to the most prized throws of the season, the krewe's decorated coconuts. And the other thing on the coconut was a name, spelled out in glittery letters: KRISTIN.

"Looks like this is for my good friend, Kristin LaGarde. Honey, would you come here and get your present?"

Kristin, dressed like Lucy in a short skirt, had topped the skirt with a rose-colored sweater that picked up the color in her cheeks. She looked like a movie star at play. "Buddy, you shouldn't have," she cooed, slinking forward to receive her prize.

"Hey, let's make sure everybody's here—Lucy, where are ya? Royce and Suzanne?

"And there's Adele over there. Come here, y'all, and check this out. Lucy, ya got ya camera on?" He turned back to Kristin. "It's a magic coconut, honey; it opens up like a box."

Kristin looked up at him quizzically and then pulled at both ends of the coconut. Nothing happened.

"You've got to twist it."

She gave it a dainty twist, then a harder one, and the two halves came apart. One half had been fitted out with a little center-slit black velvet cushion, the sort used to display rings. And it did display a ring, set with an emerald-cut diamond the size of a knuckle.

"How ya like that?" Buddy asked.

The crowd had begin to ooh and ah and buzz.

Kristin seemed to have lost the power of speech.

"Kristin LaGarde," Buddy said, "will you be my wife?"

And the corporate vice president squealed like a sorority girl. Then, throwing herself around his neck, she spoke huskily, choked with tears. "I can't believe it! You mean it, Buddy?"

"Never meant anything more, sweetheart. It's a cold world out there. I finally found out what makes a house a home and I gotta make sure she's gon' stick around. By the way, you accept, or what?"

Kristin had stepped away from him, eyes wet. "I thought I was going to have to ask you."

"Okay, folks! We got a meetin' of the minds, and we're headin' for a weddin'!" He planted a big one on his intended. "Want to try the ring on?"

She nodded, and someone stepped forward to offer a tissue for her tears. Delicately, she held out her hand, amid the requisite cheers and applause, as Buddy slipped the ring on.

Once again, she hugged the groom-to-be, who kissed her again and broke off to say, "Does this mean we can go on ahead and do it now? How 'bout if you quit your grinnin' and drop your linen—right about now?" A shocked silence fell, broken by nervous titters.

Kristin blushed. "It's going to be uphill work civilizing you." At that, the cheering began again, and a man stepped out of the crowd, one about Buddy's age, but much better looking. He was tall and prematurely white-haired, with a longish face; very distinguished looking. He wore a striped shirt and khakis.

"Let me be the first to congratulate my little girl!"

Kristin fell upon him and clung. "Daddy, I'm so happy!"

Warren LaGarde, Talba realized. After him came a woman who looked to be even younger than Kristin, and resembled her. After she'd hugged the bride-to-be, she leaned possessively against LaGarde, who put an arm around her. Talba saw that she wore a ring much like Kristin's and a gold band as well. Apparently, the May-September thing ran in the family.

"Lucy, where are ya?" Buddy said. "Let's get everybody up here. Hey, Adele, Royce, Suzanne, let's pose for our first official family video."

Lucy was in her element. She'd captured the whole coconut thing on tape, and she was still at it, Raisa at her heels, her tiny face lit with excitement. Both girls looked happier than Talba had ever seen either one of them.

But as the family came forward for an engagement toast, Talba noticed that the LaGardes' smiles seemed tense and forced. Royce raised a go-cup no doubt filled with beer, but his hand was shaking. Suzanne looked as if she might bite, but managed to compose herself in front of the camera. Only Adele and Lucy seemed genuinely happy.

Something's wrong with this picture, Talba thought. *Big surprise.*

She was a little nonplussed herself. She liked Kristin. The last thing she'd wish on her was Buddy Champagne and his coming downfall. The upside, though, was that the bride-elect had time to find out before the wedding who her fiancé really was.

If Jane Storey moved fast enough.

Lucy was playing the part of reporter. "Kristin, are you surprised?"

"Surprised? Hey, I thought I was going to have to tackle him."

"Daddy, did you really think a great person like Kristin was actually going to say yes?"

"Young lady, go to your room. Next question."

"Tell us the story of how you met."

"She found me drunk in a gutter and saved me from three approaching muggers."

"No, really."

"We met in court," Kristin said. "Where else?"

"And was it love at first sight?"

"For me it was," Buddy said. "The minute she set foot in my courtroom, I thought, 'Buddy Champagne, you're going to stop your tepee-creepin' and marry that li'l ol' gal.'"

"Oh, Buddy, come on. You gave me such a hard time!"

"Well, that was just to get your attention. Hey, ya know what I hear? Sirens. And y'all know what that means." It meant the parade was approaching. "Y'all go on and enjoy the parade now. And thank you all for being here on such a memorable occasion."

112

Memorable was right, Talba thought. She was pretty sure nobody there was ever likely to forget it. She checked out the family again. LaGarde was at the bar, reaching for something amber that wasn't beer. I'd drink heavily, too, she thought. Suzanne was leaning on Royce, who was whispering to her. She was as pale as shrimp meat.

Warren LaGarde drained his glass and walked out the door, his young wife scurrying to catch up. Whether they were going out to see the parade or making a hasty exit, Talba didn't know. But she was betting on the latter.

CHAPTER NINE

Lundi Gras dawned cloudy and threatening, and by the time Talba got to the Champagnes', the rain was so heavy she got soaked running in from her car. "Look at you!" Adele said. "I'll get you one of Suzanne's sweat suits." And she headed upstairs. The house was a shambles from the night before and Lucy and Buddy were in the kitchen with Kristin, who was wearing sweats herself, evidently intending not to go to work that morning.

"Thought I'd stay home and help clean up," she explained. "We'll just have cereal this morning so you don't have to cook. Oh, and Adele says, after seven days straight, she's giving you the afternoon off."

"Well, I appreciate it. I've been working so hard I feel like I've been in a wreck."

"I'll bet you do." Buddy was wearing jeans himself. He must be calling in court that day. "You're a drowned rat," he said. "You can't work like that."

She was surprised he'd noticed. "Miss Adele's getting me some clothes. That was beautiful last night, Your Honor. Congratulations."

"Can you believe this ol' gal's really gon' marry me?"

Lucy sidled up to Kristin and put an arm around her. "She wouldn't leave me alone with Suzanne, would you, Kristin?"

Kristin nuzzled her head as if she were a pet.

"Hey, Sandra, Darryl's really handsome," Lucy said. "Was he married to a white woman? I mean, before?"

"Lucy!" Kristin was horrified.

Lucy flared. "It's a reasonable question."

"It's okay, Luce. You mean the blonde hair? No, Raisa's just a freak. Pretty freak, though."

Buddy said, "Prettiest little freak I ever saw in my life."

"She's really a great little kid," Lucy said. "I taught her how to work the camcorder and she went crazy with it. Smart as anything."

"You bring out the best in her," Talba said, and meant it. She'd never seen Raisa take to anyone the way she had to Lucy.

Adele came back with the sweats. "I've got to get Lucy to school. Did Kristin tell you? Half day's enough for today—and Mardi Gras off, of course." Talba hadn't even considered coming in the next day. Mardi Gras in New Orleans was like Christmas anywhere else—business as usual was cancelled. "Clear off the tables, will you? And get a load in the dishwasher."

Talba went to the downstairs powder room to change, and came out like a powerhouse. Today she had a concrete manageable chore, and help. At noon, she'd be free. Nothing was going to stop her.

She and Kristin worked together like a machine, not talking, just clearing and cleaning. When Adele returned, she joined them with a merciless efficiency. Buddy disappeared to his office.

There was no sign of Suzanne and Royce till ten-thirty. By then, most of the heavy work was done, which was "a blessin'," as Miz Clara would say—Suzanne tried to pitch in, but she didn't have a clue how to make things happen, and she sniped at Kristin every chance she got. Royce grumbled for a while, then repaired to the den with a cup of coffee. Business as usual.

By noon, it was all done but rearranging the furniture. "Don't you worry about a thing," Adele said. "I'll get Buddy and Royce to do it after 'while. Let me pay you, and then you just run on home and have a happy Mardi Gras with that man of yours—and that cute little girl."

Decent woman, Talba thought, and regretted, not for the first time, what she was about to do to the household.

She intended to put the unexpected afternoon off to good use. But first, she went home and made herself some tomato soup and an egg salad sandwich, reading the paper as she ate. The bad news was the weather: The storms were going to get worse that afternoon, and Mardi Gras was a crapshoot.

She listened to the morning tapes before going into the office, and what she heard was beautiful. Absolutely gorgeous. Buddy had made one important call—to Funky Farley, asking why he still hadn't seen anything in the paper about Angie's arrest.

And he'd received a call from a man who identified himself as Mac Boudreaux: *"Hey, your honor. Just wanted to make sure everything worked out. I got a little worried 'cause I didn't see nothin' in the paper about it."*

"Everything's fine, Mac. I'm gon' take care of ya. Don't you worry about a thing."

"Well, I wasn't worried for myself, but my buddy Frank's got some medical bills—"

"You boys did just fine, Mac. I'm gon' get ya checks off today."

"Uh—if you don't mind—would cash be possible? I mean, nobody wants no records."

Buddy's voice was impatient. *"You come by the house Wednesday. I'll take care o' you boys."*

"Everything gon' work out at the marina?" Boudreaux sounded tentative. *"I know a lot of guys who'd sure enjoy doin' business with ya."*

"Ya brother-in-law brought me a load of shrimp just last Friday. You tell him things are fine—we got 'em on the run—not a peep out of ol' Ben since last week."

"Shame about the Chief, though."

"Ah, he's just another nigger likes his drugs. Bound to go down some time for somethin'."

Bingo, Talba thought.

Boudreaux was a pretty common name, so she didn't go through the usual backgrounding process. If this was the guy who planted the drugs, he was probably a cop. She called the police department and asked for Mac Boudreaux. She was immediately put through.

Smiling, she hung up.

This was it. With luck she'd be at the house when the transaction occurred.

She absolutely couldn't wait to tell Eddie.

Eddie was half thinking of going home—nobody was in any kind of mood for business on Lundi Gras—but now he had to do Ms. Wallis's work as well as his own. He was in his office wrestling the damn machine when she careened in, bouncing off the walls.

"Eddie, we got him. I heard him on the speakerphone—promising to pay the guys who did it."

He looked at her over the top of his glasses. "They said they did it? On the phone?"

"Well, not in those words." She reported what the guy had said, and her subsequent confirmation that he was a cop. "With any luck, I can photograph Buddy paying them off. With my trusty spy phone."

"Ya ridin' for a fall, Ms. Wallis. They catch ya, no tellin' what they might do."

"Hey! Who's the baroness? Catching me's not in the cards."

She was way too cocky for her own good. If it wasn't Angie's reputation at stake, he'd order her not to do it. But he wasn't about to—because she was right. They probably had enough already to bring Buddy down—and get the charges dropped against Angie. Maybe not by going through the usual channels, but Eddie had friends in the police department; he wondered about Boudreaux's reputation. He could find out by asking around, but he said to Ms. Wallis, "Ya find anything on Boudreaux? He ever been in trouble?"

"Yep." She was grinning. "Suspended two years ago. For failing to book valuable evidence—sometimes drugs, once a wallet with a lot of money in it; also 'borrowing' from the property room. He busted an armed robber, the guy had Rolex watches, Boudreaux turned up wearing one."

Eddie thought about it. It was almost too seamless. He really didn't see how she could have been so lucky with the speakerphone. "Ms. Wallis, ya know about the fruit of the poisoned tree?"

"Sure. Tainted evidence." She shrugged. "But this isn't evidence. It's journalism."

117

"It's still poisoned."

"What are you getting at, Eddie?"

"Ya know about going to jail if ya been doin' anything ya shouldn't, right?"

"EdDEE! You mean illegal listening devices? You know I wouldn't do a thing like that. Besides, I wouldn't even know how."

In a pig's eye, she wouldn't. She was an electronics expert. Well, it was her ass if she'd done it; the worst that could happen to Eddie was a lawsuit that would ruin him. But then again, if she did get photos of a judge with a dirty cop, who was going to sue? The P.I. board could still fine him, but what was a few grand to get Angie out of this mess?

Inwardly, he squirmed a little, but there wasn't a damn thing he could do about Ms. Wallis's methods except fire her. He'd eaten the fruit of the poisoned tree himself a time or two, when he was a Jefferson Parish deputy.

He narrowed his eyes at her, anyhow. "Just be sure ya never learn."

"Let's get Angie over here. And Jane Storey."

And so they powwowed, the four of them, and that tightass Jane Storey nearly wet her pants. "We are going to cook him, baroness. This is enough for a whole series."

"Maybe a Pulitzer in it for ya," Eddie said.

"Lot of legwork to do, though. Talba, you really think you can get Buddy paying them off?"

She shrugged. "Depends if I'm there when Mac shows up. If I am, I'll get it."

Eddie had no doubt she would. She had that little phone camera, and a beeper camera as well. She'd get something. But she couldn't record audio. He reminded her of that.

"EdDEE!" she said again. "Think I'm crazy?"

"I'll take that, as Buddy would say, under judicial review. Look, tell ya what. I'll surveil the house; I can get them going in if they show up—with my new little toy." Ms. Wallis had made him buy a state-of-the-art digital camcorder, one you could almost hide in the palm of your hand.

"Great idea!" Jane Storey cried. "Why don't you let me go with you? I can see it for myself."

What the hell had he gotten himself into? "No, ma'am! Absolutely not. I could be in that car eight hours or more. I am not takin' you with me. I gotta have peace and quiet."

"Okay, I'll go in my own car."

Damn! He thought, and wished he'd kept his infernal trap shut. He glared at her. "No. You stay away or we don't give you a damn thing."

But he was bluffing and she knew it.

"Eddie, it's not like this is your idea. I was going to be there, anyway—I just didn't mention it."

He offered up his palms to the heavens. "Well, what the hell; we don't need two of us. You go with a photographer. I'll stay in the office and do Ms. Wallis's work."

Storey was as capable of getting it as he was. He turned to Angie. "Say, ya got Alabama off, right? He gonna be out and about tomorrow?"

"*I* didn't do anything—Jimmy Houlihan did. The charge was dismissed, thank God. So Al'll be out bright and early, with bells on—or, at least, with his new suit on. Talba, you and Darryl ought to bring Raisa."

"What time?"

"You know the Indians. It's irregular at best. But he'll probably be all over everywhere, he's so proud of that suit—and so damn glad to be free."

"Don't see how we can miss him, then. We're definitely going to be in the 'hood." She turned to Eddie. "Hey, Boss Man, can I ask you something? Raisa's got a sudden fascination with videotape. I was wondering—you ever use your old camcorder?"

He shrugged. "Haven't since I got the new one. It's so big I don't know how I ever stood it. Whatcha thinkin'? Ya want to let Raisa try her hand tomorrow? Maybe catch some Indian dances?"

"Do you mind?"

"Knock yaself out," he said. And then, "Ya done good, Ms. Wallis."

He never said anything like that. But she had done good. Even if she'd been very bad in the process. If she ever talked to anyone about it—and she never planned to—she knew their argument would be that listening devices had to be illegal for privacy's sake. Otherwise, they'd say, think how many black people could be entrapped. And her answer would be, "Tough, if they're doing something illegal."

But in her heart, she still wouldn't want the cops doing it. She could live with the doublethink, even if she couldn't explain it.

She accepted the praise, put the whole sticky business out of her mind, and drove across the bridge to Algiers Point, her thoughts turning to the coming holiday.

In New Orleans, there are probably as many forms of Mardi Gras as there are neighborhoods, ethnic groups, and bands of eccentrics with agendas. This year, Darryl had Raisa, who usually spent the holiday with her mother in St. Bernard Parish. He and Talba planned to show the kid a traditional African-American Mardi Gras, beginning with the Zulu parade and moving on to the neighborhood called Tremé, which still boasted some of the old ways, like the Indians, and was trying to revive others, like the Baby Dolls and the skeletons.

Living out of town as she did, Raisa had never seen Zulu and didn't even know about the Indians, the most spectacular sight of all Mardi Gras.

But Fat Tuesday dawned gray and threatening.

Still, if you looked hard and had an optimistic nature, you could see patches of blue here and there. Talba had hopes, but they were nearly dashed when Raisa threw her cereal bowl on the floor and said it was the worst Mardi Gras ever because it was going to rain and she and her dad couldn't even have the day to themselves. That wouldn't have been so bad if Darryl hadn't said, "That's it, young lady. Go to your room and stay there till you're ready to apologize."

Raisa fled the room, crying and yelling over her shoulder, "I'm not coming out all day. I wish I'd stayed home with my mother!"

Darryl leaned on the kitchen counter and spoke to the wall. "She's going to tell Kimmie we wouldn't even take her out."

"She'll come out."

"You don't know her."

"You forget. I do. All too well."

Darryl put his arms around her. "Talba, I'm sorry. I honestly don't know why she has to be such a brat."

Talba had been wondering about it herself—for all the time they'd been dating. But knowing Lucy was making her mellower toward the kid—her life couldn't be easy, and kids were supposed to have it easy. "Know what, Darryl?" she said. "I think it's partly my fault. I never know what to do when she acts like this, so I just leave her alone. When what she probably needs is attention."

"Well, she sure doesn't want it from you."

"She could learn to love me. I'm very lovable."

He laughed. "That's what she's got against you."

"No, really. It's not just jealousy. I'm going to go talk to her."

"She'll take your head off."

"No, she won't," Talba said confidently, and strode off to Raisa's room. She was back in ten minutes, Raisa in tow. The kid was still in her nightgown, looking like the cherub she wasn't.

She stood sweetly before her father. "Daddy, I'm sorry. I want to go see Zulu and the Indians."

Her dad folded her into his arms, telling her it was all right. And over her head, he mouthed to Talba, "What did you do in there?"

"Bribed her," Talba mouthed back.

"Talba brought me a present."

"Well, it isn't exactly a present."

Raisa actually smiled. "Well, it is for one day. For just one day, I get to have it."

And Talba went to the car to get the camcorder she'd cadged from Eddie. "Guess who's about to go into show biz?"

Darryl broke out in a delighted grin. "Raisa, you can really work that thing?"

"Yep. Lucy taught me. I'm a videographer now. Can I have some breakfast?"

"First you better clean up that mess you made." He had saved it for her.

In half an hour, they were on the ferry, having decided driving on Mardi Gras was foolish at best. Darryl was coaching Raisa on her coconut supplications. "Now, you've got to get up right next to the float. Tell you what—you're too big for it, but I'll put you on my shoulder."

For a moment, she was wide-eyed. "Really, Daddy? You never do that."

"Yeah, but this is important. Know what else? You can lie today, too. I mean, exaggerate—'cause the best story gets the coconut."

"But don't they just throw the coconuts like beads?"

"Not any more—because people kept getting hurt. So mostly they just hand them out these days. Think there's even a law about it."

But Raisa was hardly listening. She was already fabricating her coconut tale, intoxicated with the notion of sanctioned prevarication. "Okay, Daddy, how's this: Please, Mr. Zulu-man, my mama said if I didn't come home with a coconut, I don't get any dinner."

"Good. And then if he gives you a silver one, say she said no dessert if it isn't gold."

"And then the minute he hands me the gold one, I'll pass the silver one to you. And keep 'em both."

Talba laughed. Darryl frowned. "Let's not push our luck. You want to hear about the Indians?"

"Yeah. Are they real Indians?"

"They're black, just like us. They just dress like Indians. Call themselves gangs."

"But why, Daddy?"

"Well, in the old days, I guess they identified with Indians. Because Native Americans weren't treated very well, either."

"I mean why do they call themselves gangs like the Crips and the Bloods? I thought gangs were bad guys."

"These gangs just pretend-fight. They send out a Spy Boy to let them know when another gang's coming, and the Flag Boy has a great big flag that he can use to signal the chief it's there. And then, when they meet up, each chief tries to make the other one bow to him, and they do war dances and sing to each other."

"But why, Daddy?"

"Ah, the eternal why. 'Cause it's Mardi Gras, and it's fun. Then, these other gangs dress up like skeletons. And some of the women are Baby Dolls."

"I don't want to be a Baby Doll. I want to be an Indian."

"I think they're mostly men. But, listen, want to meet one? Talba has a friend who knows Big Chief Alabama Bandana. She might introduce you."

"That his real name?"

"Hey, the boat's docking."

Zulu was just turning onto Basin Street when they got there. On sighting the first float, Raisa was as shocked as any Yankee. "Those are the stupidest costumes I ever saw!"

The famous Zulu warriors wore their trademark blackface, with cartoon white lips and fright wigs. They sported grass skirts and carried spears. "Daddy, this is embarrassing!"

"Baby, are you a sociologist or a videographer?"

That got her into gear. Immediately, she started taping. But when the time came, she didn't get to do her spiel: A lady Zulu beckoned her over, said, "You're the cutest little girl I ever saw," and without further ado, presented her with a gold coconut, "to match your hair."

Undone, Raisa blurted, "Hey, could I have a silver one, too?"—and two other riders fell all over themselves bestowing silver ones on her, whereupon she cracked them all up by shouting, "Oh, man! This is the best Mardi Gras ever!"

Talba could have kissed those Zulus. "One for each of us," she said. Raisa retorted, "What'll you pay me for one?"

Talba had thought the Indians might be an anticlimax after that, but their finery was so far beyond spectacular even Raisa was awed. As soon as the first Spy Boy came into view, she blurted, "Look, Daddy, he looks like a purple cloud!"

"It's the Poison Oleanders," Talba explained, and she had to admit that Raisa had nailed it—the Indians' forest of waving plumage did indeed resemble a gorgeous cloud of feathers. "If the Oleanders are here, Angie'll be around. My friend."

And when the chief marched grandly into view, Angie was in the second line, dressed in her accustomed black, accessorized with a Goth wig and a lot of temporary tattoos.

For a while Raisa occupied herself taping a little girl about her own age decked out head-to-toe in pink feathers facing off Alabama himself, whom she actually called "Sir" when Angie finally introduced them.

And then she turned to Talba: "You didn't say your friend was white."

Angie shrugged. "Can't help it. Born that way."

"It's okay," Raisa said. "I got a white friend too."

Talba wondered if she meant Lucy, and hoped not. They weren't going to be friends after Jane Storey got through with Lucy's daddy. And again, she thought about the others in Buddy's life. Kristin would be devastated, but better off in the long run. Royce and Suzanne were so self-involved she couldn't bring herself to care much, and Adele had seen a lot worse. Lucy was the one who bothered her. Lucy and one other person, whom she called that night.

"Alberta, it's Talba Wallis. Look, it's happening. We got what we need. Are you okay with it?"

"Okay with it? I'm happy with it. Got me another job with a real nice family. Lady's an artist; orders me sushi for lunch—whatcha think o' that? You ever had raw fish? Yes, *ma'am*—let hell come down on those people. I'm just glad I don't never have to go back in their mean, back-stabbin', unhappy house again. Miss my Lucy, though. How my baby is?"

"Mean as ever, as Miz Clara would say. Wish it was me that never had to go back."

But she did have to go. For one thing, to retrieve the bugs she'd planted; for another, to keep suspicion to a minimum.

Ash Wednesday went fine, or the first half of it did. She busied herself upstairs, catching up on ironing mostly, so she'd have an excuse to hang around downstairs after lunch. In the course of it, she got the bugs.

At twelve-thirty Buddy came home, and just after lunch two men showed up and talked to him at the door.

But Talba couldn't get anywhere close.

That was a bummer, but an even worse one occurred after school, when she regaled Lucy with Raisa's Mardi Gras exploits.

"Three coconuts!" Lucy squeaked. "I've never even *seen* Zulu. Take me with you next year—promise?"

"Sure. If it's okay with Judge Buddy." She hated saying that. If ever anything wasn't going to be okay, that was it.

She couldn't wait to get the reports from Eddie and Jane Storey. In the car on the way home, she accessed her messages: The good news was, they'd gotten the transaction on film. The two men had come in a police car, and they'd gotten the plate number: It was registered to Mac Boudreaux. They'd filmed the conversation at the door, and they'd seen Buddy hand each of the men something, but what it was, no one could say. This was the bad news.

They had enough to file a report with Public Integrity, the department's version of Internal Affairs, but not enough to clear Angie outright.

Talba got Jane Storey on the horn: "Hey, brace yourself, Baroness. There are going to be at least three stories. The first one's running tomorrow. We did it! We really did it."

"Yeah, but what about Angie?"

In her mind's eye, she could see the reporter shrug. "Nobody's going to believe a word out of Buddy's mouth when I get through with him."

Next, she called Angie. Who had one word for the situation: "Shit!"

"You'll be okay, Ange. Jane won't let it go. Don't worry."

But she couldn't shake her disappointment.

The first story, which Talba read the next day in her own kitchen, was about the illegal marina, the boy who'd died working there, the opposition from the neighborhood group, and the fact that Evan Farley had been dismissed from his job after it was discovered he'd covered stories about the judge in his own custody case.

It pointedly named Angela Valentino as the lawyer for the neighborhood group (neatly setting the stage for later revelations) and ended with a teaser mentioning chumminess with a bail bond firm "and other improprieties."

Jane Storey called before Talba left home. "Keep an ear out today. I've got the other stuff, or I will by the time it runs. I'm calling today for Buddy's side. Maybe you'll hear something good on the speakerphone."

"I don't think so," Talba said. "I'm working downstairs today." It was too bad the bugs were gone, but if ever Buddy were going to look for them, this would be the day.

She arrived to find the family in the kitchen, all except Kristin, poring over the paper. Buddy's face was nearly purple. "Goddam, what a bunch of lies!" was the first thing she heard from Royce.

Adele looked at Talba anxiously. "I already made coffee. I don't think anyone'll be able to eat today." She pointed with her chin. "And Royce is having his with brandy."

"What's wrong, Miss Adele?"

"Oh, that *Times-Picayune* rag's printing some lies about Buddy." Then she muttered, "Guess they're lies."

"I can't go to school," Lucy wailed. "Everybody'll feel sorry for me." Talba saw that her face was chalky and mottled.

"Oh, baby, I'm sorry," she said, and cuddled the girl.

"Mommo, can't I stay home?"

"Your room could use a real good cleaning," Talba said. "Maybe you could help me with it."

Adele took pity. "Okay. You can stay home."

"I need some nails to chew," Suzanne said, opening cabinets as if she expected to find them there.

"Fix you some eggs?" Talba asked, and to her surprise, everyone wanted them. And grits and biscuits, too. She took an odd, penitential pleasure in feeding them.

For a while, as they ate, an eerie silence descended, which was finally broken by Adele. "Any of it true, Buddy?"

Buddy didn't even stop chewing. "Adele, you know better than that. Can't believe you've got the nerve to even ask."

"But the bail bond guys . . . ," Lucy said, and her father stopped her with a slap.

"Whose side you on, huh?" he shouted. "Ain' nothin' wrong with that. Everybody does that."

Lucy retreated, chased by Adele, and Talba wished she could follow.

"What I don't get," Royce said, "is why they're doin' this to us. Somebody's been talkin' out of school, Daddy, and you know it." Talba's heart pounded.

Buddy stuffed a biscuit in his mouth and talked with his mouth full. "Got me a feelin'. Just got me a feelin'—somethin' to do with that lawyer bitch."

Talba's face heated, and she looked fruitlessly for an escape route. If they connected her with Angie, with the mood Buddy was in, who knew what he'd do to her?

"You watch," Buddy continued. "Gon' turn out she's behind this. And it ain' gon' do her a bit of good. We got that bitch cold. She's goin' down behind this."

"Ben Izaguirre," Suzanne put in. *Angie's client.* "Daddy Buddy, I knew you shoulda let me put up whirligigs in his direction. This would have never happened if we had some decent feng shui going."

"Royce, can ya shut this chatterin' monkey the hell up?" Buddy said, and stood, crumpling his napkin in lieu of Suzanne. "I'm goin' back to bed." He looked around for a bottle of bourbon to take with him. He might have gotten drunk, Talba thought later, but he certainly didn't sleep. The phone rang all day.

Talba spent most of the day in Lucy's room, sorting through stuff that needed tossing, but she heard enough to be able to report to Jane Storey that the reporter had given Buddy the worst day of his life.

On her way out, Royce intercepted her. "You about caught up here? I need you at the marina tomorrow. First thing after breakfast."

CHAPTER
TEN

If ever the term "TGIF" had resonance, it did for Talba the last day she worked for the Champagnes. "If I get through today," she told Miz Clara at breakfast, "I may go to church Sunday, and get down on my knees and give thanks."

"Hallelujah," her mother said in her saltiest tone. "Hard work's gone and done what a good Christian upbringin' couldn't."

But of course it wasn't only the work. It was the sensation of being in Pompeii while the lava was flowing. She was almost looking forward to a day of mucking around with piles of shrimp hulls.

Jane's subject that morning was Buddy's relationship with Harry Nicasio. Her story talked about gifts and services in return for what it called "favorable bonds" for Nicasio's clients—high ones, she meant. The teaser said tomorrow's piece would be about Buddy's habit of phoning in court.

The scene Talba walked in on was like an instant replay of the day before except for two things: Royce had had the crudeness to come to breakfast in his undershorts, and Buddy was missing.

Once more, Kristin wasn't there.

Once more, everyone was sitting around reading the paper and muttering about mendacity.

Lucy, still in her pajamas, was still playing the role of the kid who ratted out the emperor. "But is it allowed for them to come and give us hams and stuff? I mean, they do. Is there really something wrong with that?"

And she was still getting slapped down, this time only figuratively. Adele snapped, "You don't know what you're talking about, young lady."

"But, Mommo, I'm *asking*!"

Talba felt for the kid.

Suzanne finished her section of the paper and looked up sleepily. "Where's Daddy Buddy this morning? Should one of us go wake him up?"

Royce said, "I'll go. Sandra, can you make me some eggs over easy?"

"I need pancakes," Lucy said miserably. Obviously, school wasn't in the cards today, either.

Talba hustled for the next half hour, turning out a different breakfast for everyone except Adele, who consumed only coffee and stared distractedly out the window. She was starting to clean up when Royce returned in grubby jeans.

"Buddy still asleep?" Adele asked.

"His bed hasn't been slept in. Must be at Kristin's."

One less bed to make, Talba thought, and put on Royce's eggs. She glanced anxiously at Adele, not wanting to make her life any more difficult. "Royce wants me at the marina this morning, Miss Adele. Would you rather make it afternoon?"

Adele was holding a tissue to her face. She sniffed before answering. "Oh, go ahead now," she managed to croak. "I think we need some time alone."

Royce certainly seemed to, even on the drive over. He was bleakly silent, a cloud of despair seeming to emanate from him, making Talba deeply uncomfortable and unexpectedly sad. She knew there had never been any choice. It was either the Champagnes or the Valentinos, and the Valentinos were her tribe now. But she had never been so close to the damage one of her cases had caused to the family of the wrongdoer.

Intellectually, she knew it was Buddy's fault, not hers; that he was the one who should have thought about his family. But it was one thing to know it and another to assimilate it. This must be like survivor's guilt, she thought, and broke the silence only once, to ask, "Got bags?"

"Shit!" Royce answered. He stopped at a convenience store for garbage bags, handing her a five-dollar bill without a word. Neither spoke when she returned to the truck. As soon as they arrived, Brad Leitner came out and stood on the dock, hands on hips.

"Hey, Royce? I just did twenty thousand dollars' worth of business."

"Sure, you did," Royce said sarcastically.

"Listen, buddy, I'm real sorry about all this mess with your daddy."

Royce tried to smile and failed. "Ah, it'll turn out all right. Daddy's not doin' anything wrong." But he couldn't control the hurt in his face. Talba just had time to register the other man's distress before she averted her eyes, feeling like an intruder. Out of the corner of her eye, she saw that Brad was hugging Royce as if someone had died.

Sighing, she went up on the dock and started to fill her bags, her sympathy for the Champagnes quickly forgotten. *What kind of people would let this kind of mess accumulate?* she thought. *Place should be closed down.*

Except for Brad, the marina was deserted. He'd undoubtedly been busting Royce's balls with that windfall story. But they'd definitely been working the marina since she'd been here, so maybe they were buying from poachers. A worse-run place she'd never seen, and she wondered why. Laziness, she thought. Royce was a man who felt entitled, who got by on his charm, such as it was. And so was his daddy.

Royce had walked out on the dock, again with this cell phone, and she tried to listen. It didn't sound like business he was talking—at least not the usual good ol' boy, jokey business she'd have expected. He was whispering. Probably something about Buddy; or maybe it was Buddy he was talking to. She needed an excuse to get closer.

Looking around, she saw a net on a pole standing against the rail near Royce. All she needed was a reason to use it. Accidentally on purpose, she dropped some debris in the water, and went to get the net to retrieve it. But Royce was watching her. "Gotta go," he said into the phone, and returned the instrument to his pocket. Lazily, he leaned against the rail, watched her get the net. "Whatcha need that thing for?"

"Dropped something in the water."

"Let me get it. I've got longer arms."

He leaned over the side with the net, Talba trailing beside him, and suddenly he cried, "Daddy!" He dropped the net in the water and took off at a dead run toward the other end of the dock. "Brad!" he yelled. "Daddy's out there—in the Grady White."

Talba looked over the side. There was a little powerboat tied to the dock, and in the boat was Buddy Champagne, toppled to the right on a cockpit seat, his feet on the deck, the rest of him lying on his side, as if he'd been sitting up and had fallen over. His right arm was flung out behind his head, fingers hanging over the side of the stern. He was white as a fish belly. Still as a rock.

And as dead as the boat he sat in. She saw it instantly. No live person was that pale, that still.

Talba was frozen. She thought of taking out her phone, calling 911, calling Eddie—but she could think only of Lucy.

Brad and Royce raced toward the boat with Buddy in it. Helplessly, she watched, too much in shock to dial, as Brad said, "Let me do it." He jumped into the boat, nearly capsizing it. The motion caused Buddy's head to roll ever so slightly, just enough for Talba to see the wound—a rather neat hole—on the right temple. Surprised there was so little blood, she tried to remember if it had rained the night before. It hadn't.

"Shit!" Brad hollered, and Royce uttered a scream with no syllables.

Talba took a deep breath. "Don't move him!" she yelled. But Brad had scrambled back onto the dock. Again he held Royce, neither of them speaking. Fingers shaking, Talba dialed 911 and gave the address of the marina.

Then she called Major Case Homicide and asked for a cop she knew well, Detective Skip Langdon, formerly of the Third District, but returned to headquarters after one of the department's many reorganizations.

"Baroness," she said. "What's up?"

"Skip, get out to Venetian Isles—the old Pelican Marina. Buddy Champagne's dead in a boat. Looks like a suicide."

"Jesus. Call 911."

"I already have."

"I'm on my way. What the hell are you doing there?"

"Working a case. Long story, but you've got to get me out of here."

"That *Times-Picayune* thing?"

"I'll tell you when you get here. But here's the short version—I've been working undercover as a maid for the Champagnes. It's going to get ugly when they find out. Oh, and one other thing—they think my name's Sandra. Could you possibly refrain from calling me 'Baroness'?"

"As you wish, Your Grace."

Talba hung up, and called Eddie, who, in turn, promised to call Angie. Finally, because she owed it to her, she called Jane Storey.

Then she ran down the dock to the two men, but Royce was already driving off in his truck. "What's he doing?" she asked, outraged.

"All he could say was, 'Oh, shit! What's Lucy going to do?' He went to break it to her before the police came and kept him for hours. You got a cell phone?"

"I've already called the cops."

He raised an eyebrow. "Well. Quick thinking. How the hell could a thing like this happen? He must have had a heart attack. Or fallen, maybe."

"Uh-uh. He's got a hole in his head."

"Shit!" Brad said. "Shot? Is that what you're saying?'

"Well. You saw it. What did *you* think?"

Brad lowered shoulders tensed against the truth. "All right. Guess Royce and me thought the same thing. His daddy couldn't take the heat. Offed himself."

Talba's knees felt weak. The last thing she'd meant to do was cause this man's death.

She knew what to expect in the next few hours. The coroner would come to pronounce the judge well and truly dead; the crime lab would take photographs and gather evidence; the cops would ask endless questions, and then they would take her to the station and make her sign a statement. She wouldn't get away for hours.

And she'd smell like dead shrimp all day.

Her cell phone rang: Angie. "Don't say a word till I get there."

"Whatever you do, don't come down here." Pointedly, she avoided using the lawyer's name, but she walked away from Brad just the same. "You don't want to be connected to this. Are you crazy? Everything's

132

going to come out. You want to be on television at the scene? Don't do it, all right? I'll be fine."

Silence hung like a weight on the line. Finally, Angie said, "Okay, I see what you mean. I'll get Jimmy Houlihan."

"I do *not* need a lawyer, okay? I didn't do it."

But try to tell a lawyer you don't need a lawyer. It took her another five minutes of arguing, and by that time, Langdon had arrived, along with Lieutenant Adam Abasolo, whom she also knew. To her amazement, they obliged by pretending they'd never seen her before in their lives. After a decent interval, Langdon took her aside to get her story—and the backstory to her story.

During the interview, she asked a question Talba was to remember later: *Had she seen a gun in the boat?* Talba visualized the scene. She had seen both of Buddy's hands, and they were empty. It was a small fiberglass boat, white, so a gun would have stood out.

"No," she said.

"Are you sure?"

"Positive. But one of his hands—"

"I noticed. Like maybe he dropped it. Try to be patient, okay? I'll be awhile."

Meanwhile, Jane Storey arrived, in a feeding frenzy. Talba had also warned Jane that for purposes of this encounter, they were strangers. But she'd forgotten about the police radio. Soon the television stations, smelling blood like buzzards, began to converge.

It wasn't the first time Talba'd made news, either in her detective persona or that of well-known poet about town. Someone from Channel Seven shouted, "Hey, there's the Baroness de Pontalba. Baroness, whatcha doin' here?"

And she ran to the tiny office for cover, almost wishing she had Jimmy Houlihan to deliver the "no comments."

Finally, after a couple of hours, during which she gave Eddie and Angie periodic phone updates, Langdon took her away, complaining the whole trip about the way she smelled.

CHAPTER ELEVEN

No matter how loathsome the man, it's a terrible thing to think you might have caused someone to commit suicide—and suicide was what it looked like to her.

Langdon had gone relatively easy on her—though she'd have thrown the book if she'd known about the illegal tapes—but Talba wasn't about to give out information on an open case—at least not yet. Talba hadn't seen a gun, but still, she didn't dare hope it was anything other than suicide. She was on the hook and there was nothing she could do but twist.

She wondered how Jane Storey felt, but there'd been no reaching her later that day. She knew perfectly well what Angie's reaction was—and it wasn't sorrow. It was anger. She'd be mad that she hadn't gotten the public revenge she wanted and that she was still accused of possession. Talba'd be able to get her off with the speakerphone story as long as Boudreaux caved, but Angie had wanted Buddy to take the rap for setting her up.

Alberta Williams was distraught. She phoned Talba in tears. "I didn't wish him no harm, Miss Wallis," she wailed. "I wish to God we never done this thing." And Talba didn't have to get a phone call to know how Lucy and Royce felt.

Adele she didn't have to speculate about. The first television broadcasts had identified Talba as being on the scene, mentioning both her jobs. Adele left a message on her cell phone: "Hello, Baroness. I hope you're happy. We knew there was a rat somewhere, but we never suspected you. We trusted you. How does it feel to deprive a little girl of her daddy? To betray a whole family's trust?"

A quote from somewhere popped into Talba's mind: "Loyalty to an employer is the most vulgar of loyalties." *At least*, Talba thought, *I'm not guilty of vulgarity*.

Darryl was next on the phone: "Oh, God, Talba, you're all over the news. I'm just so sorry it turned out this way. You okay?"

"I've had better days."

"Look. You did what you had to. This was Buddy's doing, pure and simple. He did the crimes, and he got caught. If he chose to take this way out, it was his decision. As long as you didn't pull the trigger, you didn't do it. Do you get that?"

Talba sighed. "Miz Clara always says, as long as you do your best, an angel couldn't do better. Well, actually, she just said it for the first time today. I'm trying to take it to heart."

That in itself spoke to the gravity of the situation: When Miz Clara got warm and cuddly, you knew things were bad. Talba took refuge in her work—beginning a poem about trust and how it could be abused.

And two days later, she got a call from Jane Storey. "Talba. Got stuff from my buddy Grissom—this crime scene guy I drink with."

"Grissom? Isn't that the name of the guy on *CSI*?"

"That's this guy's alter ego. He'd kill me if I told you who he is. Fact, he'd kill me if he knew I was telling you anything. Swear on Miz Clara you'll keep it to yourself."

Talba's heart speeded up. "Girl Scout honor."

"Ready for this? Buddy may have been murdered."

"What?" She was almost happy. If the man hadn't killed himself, she hadn't pushed him over the edge.

"It's true," the reporter said. "I've got the whole technical skinny. You want the long version, or the short?"

Talba asked for the long.

"Well, for openers, Grissom says there wasn't much blood."

Talba thought back to the scene, how she'd wondered if rain had washed the blood away. "It could have been washed away, though. By a wave or something."

"It's possible, but Grissom doesn't think so. Buddy's clothes weren't wet and it wasn't a hot morning—they wouldn't have had time to dry."

"And that means?"

"Well, if he was alive when he was shot, there should have been a lot of fine spray, what Grissom calls high velocity blood spatter."

"You're saying someone shot a dead man? Like, he had a heart attack or something—*then* they shot him?"

"Hear me out. And then there was the absence of a weapon. They thought he might have dropped it, but they dived for it, and they couldn't find it. Also, Buddy did have a gun, but it was still in the drawer of his bedside table."

"With the sex toys."

"Oh, yeah?" Jane was vaguely interested. "No secrets from the maid, huh?"

"What else?"

"Lots. It wasn't a contact wound. See, if you put a gun to your head and fire, the skin rips in what they call a stellate, or star pattern. This hole was clean."

"Don't remind me," Talba said.

"The bullet was still in his head, by the way. Anyhow, on a contact wound, there'd also be tattooing from gunpowder and stuff Grissom calls 'other artifacts of oxidation.' There wasn't a lot of that, like he was shot from a few inches away. Right away, Grissom gets suspicious. So he tests Buddy's hands."

"That's standard," Talba said wearily. "Paraffin tests."

"Uh-uh to both. First of all, paraffin's so five minutes ago—they've got much better stuff for GSR now—'gunshot residue' to you. Lead, barium, and antimony. Second, did you know it can cost a thousand dollars to run those kinds of tests? NOPD rarely does them. But Buddy's kind of high profile, and anyhow, Grissom can't be stopped. There's whole bunches of tests you can do, like with nitrites, alternate light sources, lots of stuff—sounds like they've got their choice, on the rare occasions they pop for them. Anyhow, Grissom does one, gets nothing. But he's not satisfied, so he sprays the hands with something called Ferrotrace, which'll turn them purple if the victim's handled a blue steel weapon. Now, granted, not all weapons are blue steel, but this one comes up negative, too. So Grissom can't really find anything to substantiate suicide."

"But why would you shoot a dead man?"

"Here's a better question—how'd the guy get dead? Grissom saw something else on Buddy's head—I mean, besides the bullet hole. A line on the tissue that the gunshot wound didn't obscure, like there was a subdural hemorrhage. Where something hit him, maybe."

"You're losing me."

"Autopsy's not in yet, but Grissom thinks he was bludgeoned to death—or somehow hit his head—and someone shot him later."

"I repeat—why shoot a dead man?"

"Okay. That's the million-dollar question. Maybe it was the coup de grâce—whoever killed him didn't know he was dead. Pushed him off the dock, maybe, then shot him to make sure."

"Uh-uh. The way Buddy was sort of half-sitting, half-lying wasn't haphazard. If he didn't shoot himself in the boat, somebody very carefully placed him in it."

"Okay, then. First they hit him—or he falls—then they shoot him and put him in the boat."

"But why?" Talba repeated.

"Why don't you ask your buddy Langdon?"

Langdon wasn't going to give her a damn thing unless she got something back.

"Who" was a better question than "why." And Talba still wasn't off the hook. If her investigation had brought one of Buddy's many enemies out of the woodwork, she was still responsible. But at least she felt a little better about writing Lucy the sympathy note she'd been contemplating, but hadn't had the nerve to compose. She made it a poem:

Day Cat
Death is a feral cat that comes in the night.
And a friend is a daytime beast
That prowls your dusty corners
And destroys you
Unwittingly.

An enemy is an accident,
Or circumstance itself.
And appearances cannot be trusted.

But magick is real,
And transformative.

A daytime cat is only an animal
Blind to the future
And it grieves to lose its own friend
As a child does, to lose her father.

But magick transforms.
Blessed be, my daytime cat.

The last line was a reference to something she'd seen in Lucy's witch book. She wasn't entirely sure what it meant, but she took it at face value. If Adele saw the note, she'd flush it down the toilet, and Royce would probably come after her with a machete, but Lucy had a subtle mind. There was an outside chance she'd see it as the expression of grief for her own actions that Talba meant her to. And it was the only way she knew to apologize. As she expected, she never heard back from the girl, and life settled back into a routine for a couple of weeks.

Then one fine Monday afternoon, just as Talba was getting ready to close down her computer and clean off her desk, Kristin LaGarde waltzed into her office. Eileen Fisher nipped at her heels, trying to intercept her.

"Kristin!" Talba was alarmed. "What can I do for you?"

"I just want to talk."

Best, Talba thought, to confront her worst fear directly. "You wouldn't be armed, would you?"

Kristin looked flustered. "What? Oh. No. Look, I'll give my purse to the receptionist. She can go through it."

"I'd appreciate it."

But Eileen said, "I'm not going in that thing," and Talba had to do it herself. Her fears allayed, she sent Eileen away.

"I'm sorry for what happened," she said.

"You should be. Do you have any idea what havoc you caused?"

"Look, I have to live with it too. If you want an apology, you've got it. I wish I'd never heard of this case."

"I want to know why you did what you did."

"It was a case, Kristin. I was asked to do it. By someone close to me, as a matter of fact. I'm really sorry about Buddy—and I'm sorry for you and Lucy and all the rest of you—but someone who matters to me was being threatened. More than that—they were being badly hurt. By Buddy."

Kristin's face changed, contorted itself into something between fear and curiosity.

But she charged ahead anyway. "I think you did it for money."

Talba shook her head. "If it's any comfort to you, I didn't get paid for the job. I lost money on it, as a matter of fact. I could say it was a favor to a friend, but it was more than that. That's really all I can tell you."

"I want to trust you. I really do. Or I wouldn't be here."

"I can't make you trust me, and you have every reason not to. All I can do is tell you that I'm sincerely sorry for your loss—and for all the suffering I've caused you and your family." It occurred to her that Kristin was taking a long time getting to the point. "What is it you wanted to talk to me about?"

Kristin's eyes flooded. "I want to know what happened. Who killed Buddy."

Talba remembered just in time that she'd sworn on Miz Clara not to mention what Jane Storey had told her. "Buddy killed himself," she said.

Kristin shook her head. "Uh-uh. I talked to the cops today. It's still an open case. One thing, they never found a weapon and anyway—are you ready for this?—he was shot after he was dead. They think he was—" She stopped, trying to get control, lowered her head a little, and spoke on the uptake. "They think he was bludgeoned first."

"That makes no sense, Kristin." Talba was doing her best to feign amazement. "Why would somebody do that?"

"That's what I want you to find out."

"Bludgeoned," she said. "In the boat or somewhere else? I mean, did someone move his body there? And *then* shoot him?"

"They don't know," Kristin said impatiently. "And frankly, I don't think they're going to until they find out who killed him. And they're not about to do that. You know these cops . . ."

"Hold on, hold on—Skip Langdon's on this. She's the best there is."

"I want to hire you to work on it too."

"You want to hire me? Me, of all people?" Talba had so many questions she didn't know where to start.

"Well. One thing we know—you're a pretty good detective." Her lips pulled back in something resembling a smile.

"But—" Talba stopped cold. "I can think of a million 'buts.' Don't you feel I betrayed you? You and all the Champagnes?"

"The Champagnes do feel that way—and I don't blame them. But you may have saved me from making a horrible mistake. If Buddy was guilty, that is."

"Okay, I saved you. So why not leave the whole thing alone—why do you want to go further with it?"

"I know you're not going to understand this, but Buddy had a good side to him. I know; I saw it. I loved him for the warm, caring man he was. Do you believe a person can be warm and caring, and still be a criminal?"

It was on Talba's lips to say, *Sure. Look at Tony Soprano*, but she thought better of it. Instead, she simply said, "Everyone has two sides."

"Well, somebody killed Buddy. Is there any doubt in your mind about that?"

"No, I think you're right."

"I want to know who. I want them brought to justice—for killing the man I loved. Or the part of the man that I loved. I might not have loved the Buddy I was about to get to know, and I guess I thank you for that, but the part I did love is dead, too. Does that make sense?"

"I'm thinking about it."

"He deserves justice. Everyone does."

"And you think you're the one to get it for him. What about the cops?"

"Sandra, try and get this—he was the man I was going to marry. It's the one thing I can do for him."

"Okay." It occurred to her she might have the same reaction in Kristin's shoes, but she still couldn't see why the woman had come to her. "The Yellow Pages are full of detectives."

"Look, I know you're good at your job, and I like you. I've always liked you—you're a lot more intelligent than most people I meet in the course of a day, and who knows what kind of person's walking around with a P.I. license? I don't know any of them, and I don't want to have to audition a bunch of bozos. Besides—"

She paused. Whether she was gathering her thoughts or creating drama, Talba couldn't decide. She rode out the silence.

Finally, Kristin said, "I just have a feeling you've got a personal stake in this."

Bingo, Talba thought. Whoever had killed Buddy had probably come out of the woodwork as a result of her investigation. She most certainly did have a personal stake in it. "You mean you think I might have some guilt about what happened."

Kristin said nothing, but her expression changed subtly—to eagerly inquisitive. Talba had to give her points for shrewdness. "Okay. You guessed right. But I'm not sure I don't have a conflict. And there's another problem. I'd want to interview the Champagnes about what happened that night. But I'm the last person they'd talk to."

"Conflict? I'd say it's more likely you have a duty."

It was a point that hit home. The fact was, Talba still felt responsible. Knew it was irrational. Couldn't shake it. "What about the Champagnes?" she sighed.

This time Kristin's smile was real—and a bit smug. "I ran this by them before I came here. They're dying to talk to you. They think you ought to have to do this. As a kind of penance."

"Ah. And that's what you think too. Make the punishment fit the crime."

"Besides, they want to tell you what they think of you."

"I just can't wait for that. But why would they trust me? I betrayed them."

"They wouldn't trust you, but so what? I'm the client, remember? Anyway, if I don't like what you're doing, I can fire you—I can expect regular reports, can't I?"

"Of course. We can set a limit on the number of hours I work before I report and you can see if I'm worth what you're paying me."

"And how much would that be?"

When Talba explained the agency's rates, Kristin nodded. "Why don't you do ten or twelve hours and see if you get anything?"

Talba shrugged. She was still nonplussed by the whole thing. "If you like. But I can't promise anything. All I can do is go over the ground the police will have already covered."

"Call me crazy," Kristin said, "but I have a feeling you're smarter than the average cop."

"Are you kidding? Skip Langdon was a department star when I was still at Xavier."

"Sandra, you know perfectly well the police often solve cases they can't prove in court. You don't have to prove anything. I just want to know."

"Why?"

"Wouldn't you feel the same?"

"I guess so." She was sure she would—in fact, she felt that way now and she'd hardly known Buddy; moreover, she'd disliked him.

Kristin stuck out her hand. "Deal?"

Talba considered one more time, decided to go for it. "Deal," she said, taking the woman's hand. She was dying to poke around in these particular ashes.

"Thanks, Sandra."

"Call me Talba. One thing, though. The way we work, the client's identity is usually confidential; but in a case like this, it'll be a lot easier to get people to talk to me if I can say who I'm working for. Okay with you?"

Kristin considered. "I don't see how that could hurt."

Talba nodded, satisfied. "First order of business, then—how's Lucy?"

"Not great. Adele's got her in therapy. She appreciated your note, by the way."

Talba wondered if Kristin had seen it—and had understood how she felt. "Give me her cell number."

"No. She's just a kid."

"I thought you said you trusted me."

"What do you want it for?"

"You know how I said I had a duty? My first duty's to Lucy. I need to see if I can do anything for her."

"Oh, all right."

A s usual, Ms. Wallis had her hair on fire. "Eddie, we've got a new client. You will never guess—"

He didn't let her finish. "Ms. Wallis, just sit down and take a few deep breaths."

She sat but she didn't pause to breathe. "Kristin LaGarde wants us to find out who killed Buddy."

He took off his glasses and stared, thinking that if his ears didn't work, at least his eyes might.

She said, "Your bags are violet today. Tell me that's a good sign."

"Kristin LaGarde. What's the matter, she doesn't think Langdon can handle it?"

Ms. Wallis shrugged. "Survivor's guilt? I don't know. People are crazy—they just need to think they've done everything they should, I guess. I told her we'd do it. What do you think?"

Turning it over in his head, he could see only one possible conflict. "You didn't kill him, did you?"

"No. Did you or Angie?"

"No motive," he said dryly, "thanks to you and Ms. Storey. What color's her money?"

"I thought you'd say that."

"So. Ya background the client?" He knew she had, of course—E. V. Anthony and Associates had a hard and fast rule that this was the first thing Talba did after a prospective client left the office. You never knew if they were crazy or a criminal or a chronic liar or could pay the bill.

"Sure—for Angie's case."

"Well? Anything interesting?"

"Her dad's Warren LaGarde, the hotel man."

"Hoo boy—she was some catch for Buddy."

"Yeah." She seemed distracted.

"What's bothering ya? It's somethin'. I can tell."

"I think there's a loose end."

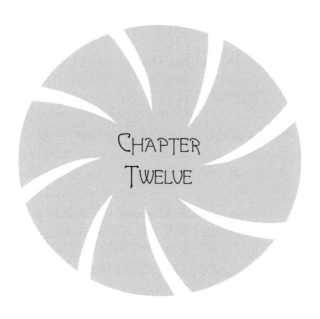

CHAPTER
TWELVE

There was a loose end, all right. That thing Kristin had said at the Bacchus party, about meeting Buddy in court. That could mean one of only two things—either she'd been a juror or a witness in a case before him, or she'd been involved in a case herself. To find out if it was the former, Talba would have to ask outright. But if it was the latter, it ought to be easy enough to figure out—because chances were it involved her father's company.

Talba went back to her computer, but there was nothing about a lawsuit in any of the local papers that she could find. Great. That meant braving the bureaucracy at the courthouse, every P.I.'s least favorite chore. She went out to buy pralines, and then drove to the courthouse. The city's cops weren't nearly as corrupt as people thought—there'd been a cleanup in recent years. But a myth she'd found to be true was that New Orleans had the least helpful bureaucrats of any city in Louisiana, and possibly in the world. The point of the candy was to sweeten their dispositions. Eddie had taught her the trick, and, just as he said, their response soon became Pavlovian. When they saw her come in, their often-surly faces lit up. It wasn't a tip and it wasn't a bribe. It was just a nice way to say thanks for a job well done.

Or so she and Eddie rationalized it.

She found two suits filed against LaGarde, Inc.—both involving hotels LaGarde wanted to build that preservationists had sued to stop. Both had been settled in LaGarde's favor. And both had been heard before Judge Buddy Champagne. Technically, she supposed, there was no conflict if Buddy and Kristin had begun their relationship after the cases were settled, but who cared now? Talba added the case names to the client's file and called Lucy.

"Hi, it's Sandra."

Lucy sounded drugged. "Oh. Hi."

"I want to see you. Can I come over?"

"I don't care."

"That means 'yes,' right?"

No answer.

"I'm on my way."

Adele would be the first hurdle, of course. She answered the door herself, wearing one of her too-fancy dresses, this one black. "How dare you show your face around here?"

"Kristin said you'd see me."

"You're a plague on this family."

"Well. You're right—I know I have been. Kristin said you'd want to tell me so yourself."

"That poor child has had nightmares every night."

Talba apologized for what she'd done, and finished with, "Look, I hate what happened—especially to Lucy. The only thing I can do now is try to find out who did it. I owe that to your family."

To her surprise, Adele fought tears, something she didn't think happened often. "I'm going to tell you something. Buddy was a plague on us, too. We might have not known it—or maybe we just didn't want to admit it—but he was, and he was going to bring us down eventually, whether you or someone else was the instrument of it. Think I didn't know he was skipping court? Didn't know who those people were from Nicasio's office? Come in, and let me talk to you."

Kristin had been right. Adele had been more or less lying in wait for her. She took Talba into the sun room, explaining that it was "just about the only room I can stand anymore."

The house seemed bereft in a physical as well as spiritual way. Crumpled napkins lay forgotten on the dining room table, and in the kitchen languished half-read newspapers. Dust you could write in covered the surfaces. Small, stray bits of paper and detritus like bottle caps and pencils—even a Ritz cracker—had been dropped on the floor and abandoned by a family too demoralized to bother bending over to retrieve them. Instead of furniture polish and the lingering scent of the morning's bacon and eggs, sour mildewy smells pervaded the entire first floor—the odors of neglect. Apparently, the Champagnes hadn't replaced Alberta.

"Sit down. I'm seeing you for Lucy's sake. You almost killed her."

Talba obeyed. "You mean because of what happened to her father?"

"Because of what happened to her. Do you understand what a hard thing that was for a child? To learn what her father was—and have the whole world know?"

"And then to lose him."

"Her world is in ashes, and you lit the fire that made it happen. You betrayed us, Sandra."

"Yes, ma'am. I've been worried about her."

"Like I said, she's been having nightmares every night since Buddy died. And you made it happen." She twisted jerkily, seeming to come to some kind of decision. "You know what? This idea of Kristin's is crazy. I'm sorry I ever agreed to it." But Talba didn't think so. Adele was a shrewd woman. She wouldn't have agreed without reasons of her own. Talba wondered what on earth they were.

"Well, yes and no," she said. "About it being crazy. She guessed right about how badly I'd feel. She knew I'd work harder than any other P.I. in town to find out what really happened."

"You're being well paid for it."

"Well, I *wasn't* paid for exposing Buddy. I did it because it needed to be done."

She was testing the waters. To her surprise, Adele didn't jump on her. "Buddy was a wicked man. Living with him was hard on all of us. But that doesn't excuse you."

Talba had the sense she was just saying what she thought she ought to say. "Well, enough about me," she said. "May I see Lucy?"

Adele shrugged. "Up to her."

"Can you ask her?"

"I'll ask her. But I want to be with y'all when you talk to her."

"Fine with me."

Adele disappeared and came back with the girl, who looked as if she hadn't washed her hair since her father's death. She had lost weight; actually looked better in one sense. But Talba felt terribly for her; she'd suffered a monumental loss, and it wasn't only her father's death. It was dealing with who he was, and with school, after everyone found out. She wondered if the girl was still at McGehee.

She had to go through the same thing with Lucy as she did with Adele—a million apologies and a thousand recriminations. And in this case, tears.

"Hi."

Lucy said nothing.

"You hate me, right? I don't know what to say, baby. Except that I'm sorry."

"It's not good enough." And so it went.

But, as with Adele, she didn't get the feeling Lucy really blamed her. She took a chance. "There was a piece of you that knew all along, wasn't there? About your father?"

Water pooled in the girl's eyes. "No! I thought my father was a god." It came out as a sob.

Talba had enough sense not to mention the way the girl had treated him—more or less as if he were a loathsome insect. That was just hormones, she supposed.

"Baby, I—"

But Lucy interrupted. "Do you know what it means to worship someone, really *worship* him—and discover he's a crook? I mean, your parents are the ones who teach you how you're supposed to act—what are you supposed to think when—" It seemed for awhile she couldn't go on, but she finally said, "When you find out it's all a farce? All *lies*!" She lowered her voice. "Everything falls apart, that's what happens. The world turns upside down."

Talba started to apologize again, but thought better of it. What had

147

happened to Lucy—the loss of innocence—had to happen to everybody. It was the first sad thing in the average kid's life, but every kid had to work through it. Talba hated being the instrument of it, but she couldn't take the rap for Buddy. "Can I ask you something, Luce?" she asked. "Just to clear the air between us? Would you agree that when all this started, I wasn't even around? That your dad's own actions set it in motion?"

"Somebody killed him! Am I supposed to like that?"

"Neither of us likes it. But I like you. And I wouldn't have had this happen for anything. You know that, don't you, baby?"

That started another flood. But before the tears spilled over, the girl said softly, "Yes." Adele tried to hold her as she cried, but Lucy resisted, and when the tears stopped, Talba spoke to both of them, very softly, "Can we talk about who might have wanted to kill him?"

"It was that lawyer bitch," Adele said.

"You know it wasn't, Adele. She didn't hate Buddy. She was doing her job, too. Listen, I've been to that marina. The neighbors have a point. The place stinks like a sewer."

Lucy nodded. "I've been trying to look at things from her side. Daddy hated her, but that doesn't mean she hated him." *Not until he planted the drugs*, Talba thought. *That kind of changed things.* But they didn't need to know about that.

"But there were people who did," she said.

Lucy nodded. "You know a boy died out at the marina, don't you?"

"It was an accident, I heard."

"Yeah, but his family hates us. Just *hates* us. Like Daddy hated the lawyer."

Talba took out a notebook and wrote in it. She wasn't likely to forget, but this whole interview was a performance in a sense—on both sides, she suspected.

"What's their name?" She already knew, of course.

"Dorand. Faye and Billy Dorand. The boy was called Jimmy." Lucy turned her face toward the just-budding garden. "I knew him."

"You knew him well?"

"No. But I liked him. I was sorry for what happened." And that explained a lot, Talba thought, about why she was there. Lucy, at any rate, understood her position. "I wanted Daddy to do something for them. But he wouldn't."

"Did they file suit against him?"

Lucy looked confused. Adele nodded. "They did."

"You think they might have killed Buddy?"

"Yes!" Lucy said. Adele remained silent.

"Anyone else?"

"I guess," Lucy said, "it could have been someone involved in a case. Someone that he . . ." She couldn't bring herself to go any further.

There might be hundreds, Talba thought.

"All right. Can both of you stand to talk about that night?"

"You mean the night he was killed?" Adele said, ever the bluff Texan. "That's what you're here for, isn't it?"

Talba nodded, keeping her eyes on her notebook. "Did he have dinner at home that night?"

"Yes," Adele said.

"And then what happened?"

Lucy said, "I went upstairs to do homework. And then I went to bed."

Adele said, "I went into the den to watch TV—by myself. Royce and Suzanne were out or something. Buddy went up to his office—he's got his own TV up there. Maybe he had calls to make; I don't know."

"Did either of you see him again that night?"

Grandmother and granddaughter looked at each other. Finally, Lucy shrugged. "I didn't," she said.

Adele shook her head.

"Hear anything?"

Again, they exchanged glances; then both shook their heads. They might be checking each other out, Talba thought, or they might be lying. Either idea was interesting.

"Okay, that's all for now. Mostly I came by to see you, Lucy. Listen, whatever happens, I want you to know I'm not your enemy. Or yours, Miss Adele. I was Buddy's, yes, but I'm not yours. We're in it together now." She looked at Lucy when she spoke; that was the person she wanted to get through to. "Okay?"

Adele nodded. "Fair enough. I might not like it, but I've agreed to it."

Lucy looked relieved. "Sandra," she began.

"Call me Talba."

"Oh. I forgot. You're a poet. Wasn't there a real Baroness de Pontalba? Why do you call yourself that?"

The original was a New Orleans historical figure, an intrepid nineteenth-century woman who'd developed and built the Pontalba Apartments at Jackson Square despite being, on one occasion, pumped full of lead by her own father-in-law. She'd survived with two fingers missing and two bullets in her chest. But all that had nothing to do with why Talba had become a baroness. "I stole her name," Talba said, "because somebody stole mine a long time ago. When I was born, my mother asked the doctor what she should name me, and you know what he said? 'Urethra.' It's on my birth certificate."

Even Adele registered horror. Lucy's was mixed with bewilderment. "Why would anyone *do* that?"

"He thought it was a joke. And when I grew up, I just declared myself a baroness—because I wanted to be one. And she was the only one I'd ever heard of."

"Oh. My. God." Lucy said. "That's . . . inhuman."

Talba smiled. She'd long since come to terms with it, partly by writing a poem about it. "Water under the bridge," she said.

Lucy seemed hugely embarrassed, as if she herself was the perp. She seemed to be searching for a bone to throw. "Hey! I just had a thought—can you come talk to my class?" She paused. "I mean if I had a class. I guess I'm changing schools."

"Lucy may be going away to school," Adele interjected. "We have to decide if that's the best thing."

Lucy put on her sullen look. "It's not my idea. How's Raisa?"

"She's fine. She talks about you all the time." Not strictly true, but close enough. "And I borrowed her a camcorder for Mardi Gras. She got some great stuff."

"Ooh, could I see it? I mean, could I see her? I'm a little short on friends right now."

"How about Danielle?"

"Her family won't let her come over any more."

An interesting irony, Talba thought. And a pity the girl had to resort to a ten-year-old for a friend. "Sure, you can see her," she said. "I'll set it up."

Talba left and went home to her mama. It would be a good night to chill and read a book—she had a heavy day tomorrow, beginning with a drive to the marina. She wanted to know more about the kid who'd been killed there.

S he checked into the office first and arrived at Venetian Isles about ten. Both Royce and Brad were in the office. Royce didn't speak to her; left when he saw her. So much for Kristin's diplomacy.

Brad shrugged. "He's not talking to anybody much these days. He's sad about his father and he feels bad about"—he paused—"some other things."

"What other things?"

"Goddammit, I'm trying to be patient here. Listen up: Royce is one of the good guys. He didn't like a lot of the stuff his father did, but he was trapped, you understand? He couldn't do a damn thing about it, and he's like, all messed up inside. About his daddy dying and—shit!— just the way things work around here." Talba didn't know if he meant the marina or Louisiana, or maybe the world. "His daddy's dead and he's stuck with the mess he left and he's trying to figure his life out. Give him a break, okay? Back off."

Good idea, Talba thought. "Sorry," she said. "I guess we got off on the wrong foot. Do you know what I'm here for?"

Brad had been sitting at a small table that served as a desk. He stood now, apparently unable to tolerate being shorter than she was. "Yeah. Stupidest thing I ever heard of. If you don't mind my saying so."

"Royce think so too?"

"Royce is more or less still in shock. I don't know what he's think-ing anymore."

"His daddy treated him pretty badly."

"He was still his daddy."

"Brad, you saw Buddy a lot, right? Who wanted to kill him?"

Brad walked out onto the pier, looked off into space, making her follow. A power play. "You, maybe."

"Uh-uh. I already had what I wanted. Tell me Buddy didn't have enemies. He was a judge, and he was dirty. A lot of people must have thought they'd gotten a raw deal."

Brad picked up something, maybe a stick, and threw it into the water. "Ben Izaguirre hated him—the guy was trying to close down the marina. But you already know that."

"How about the Dorand family?"

Brad turned to face her. "Now you're onto something. They sure made enough threats."

"Oh, really? What kind of threats?"

Brad laughed. "Not death threats. Just that they'd see the Champagnes in hell if they didn't pay up. All they wanted was a settlement. Didn't give a damn about their kid." He turned away. "Trash," he muttered.

A man in an aluminum flatboat chugged toward the pier. He cut his engine and hailed Brad. Up close, Talba could see that he was dressed like a shrimper, in a flannel shirt thrown over an old T-shirt and a pair of jeans. "I'm here for my money."

"Excuse me," Brad said to Talba, which she took for a dismissal. She turned away but didn't leave.

"You remember me? We had a deal. I give you shrimp, you give me money. Simple, yeah? Where's my money?"

Brad glanced at Talba, who noticed that Royce was running back down the pier, apparently sensing a need for damage control. "Bob, it's not a good time. We've had a death in the family."

"Well, I'm 'bout to have one in mine—from starvation, I don't get my money."

Brad glanced nervously at Talba. "Eddie, give us some privacy, will you?"

"Sure." Talba walked back toward her old Isuzu.

She waited in the car, bored out of her mind, and finally reached forward to turn on the radio. Just as she was fiddling with the dial, she was sure she heard something, and it definitely wasn't music. It was like a . . . there it was again: A definite "meow." And rather authoritative.

She opened the car, got out, and nearly stepped on a kitten that looked like it would fit in her pocket. "Well, hello, baby."

The kitten arched its back and crab-walked. She knelt. "You must be Royce's little friend. You don't look so bad." It was small, but its coat was healthy, and its ribs didn't show. It spoke to her again. She spoke back. "Come on, sweet pea. You look like you need a square meal."

But it had a lot better sense than to come on. Uh-uh. This thing with the big feet was going to get it vaccinated and make it suffer the indignity of a cat box. Talba figured its long-gone mama had explained that it must never, ever fall into that trap.

"Suit yourself," Talba said, and looked up to see the stranger turn his boat around and head out of the canal into the pass. When he was gone, she went back to tackle Royce and Brad again.

Royce gave her a hostile glance, again walked away. She yelled after him, "Hey, Royce, I found your kitten." No answer. Brad sighed. "Guess I've been elected troubleshooter. Surprised he didn't answer, though. He loves that little thing, but Suzanne won't let him bring it home. He's been feeding it shrimp."

"Why not?"

"Right. One thing we got, it's shrimp."

"No, what's the problem with Suzanne?"

"She's afraid of cats." He looked disgusted. "You beat that? A grown woman."

It was funny about fuzzy animals. Talba figured he was sufficiently softened up by the kitten to be civil. "Tell me more about the Dorands."

He snorted. "Trash. Mean bastards. What more do you need to know?"

"Okay, let's leave that for a while. Tell me about yourself."

"Why the hell should I?" His face was red, and his scalp was reddening as well. Civil indeed.

"You're close to the Champagnes, aren't you?"

"What the fuck is it to you?"

"You know what I'm doing. I'm trying to help them."

"Best thing you could do is get the hell away from them."

"You want to at least tell me where the Dorands live?"

"Round here."

"Can you be more specific than that?"

"No. I sure couldn't."

She couldn't figure out why he'd turned so hostile. She tried another tack. "Okay, next subject. Were you here the night Buddy was killed?"

"Are you crazy? Of course not."

"Well, who was? Is there a night watchman?"

153

"Yeah, there's a night watchman." He spoke in the mocking, know-it-all tone of a twelve-year-old. "The cops already talked to him."

"What's his name?"

"None of your goddam business."

Royce finally came out of the office, and joined them. "Name's Wesley Burrell. He doesn't know a goddam thing."

Talba took out a notebook. "Mind telling me where he lives?"

"*Goddam* Kristin LaGarde," he said, and went back in the office.

Talba took advantage of the moment with Brad, figuring, when in doubt, try the direct approach. "What's wrong, Brad?" she said. "Why do I get the feeling I'm missing something?"

When he turned toward her, his face was livid. "You goddam little bitch! What the hell are you trying to do here?"

She must have hit a nerve. "Must be something on your mind. Otherwise you wouldn't be so mad. What was Buddy doing here that night?"

Making a sound like a growl, Brad turned around and walked down the pier, much as Royce had earlier. After a moment, he broke into a jog, the better to work off his anger, Talba thought. "What's the matter with him?" she asked when Royce returned.

Royce stared down the pier after his friend. "He doesn't like you much. You blame him?"

"Not really." She smiled. "Got that address for me?"

"Wes lives in Arabi. Ya gon' leave us alone now?"

"Thought you wanted me to find your daddy's killer."

Royce winced, and went back in the office. She followed him. "Listen, one more thing."

He didn't answer.

"The kitten's down by my car and she looks hungry."

His face relaxed slightly. "Oh, Gumbo. Take some shrimp to him, why don't you? Hell, take him home—he's just going to die out here, anyhow. Everybody else does."

Despite its mama's admonitions, the kitten was so hungry it ate out of her hand. Talba grabbed it by the scruff. Royce was probably right—and Raisa was going to love this animal.

And she was going to love Talba for bringing it to her.

Gumbo—if that was its name—seemed to think the worst had happened, but fortunately Talba had a few more shrimp, which she laid on the seat beside her before releasing the cat. Apparently, as far as it was concerned, rules were meant to be broken. It was far too hungry to stand on ceremony.

Talba turned her attention back to the interview. The two men were almost laughable. They seemed to be trying to play good cop–bad cop, except that neither of them was convincing as the good one. It was more like each had come to the other's rescue when he had to.

She wondered why the hell they hadn't just clammed up—and then realized, with some frustration, that they more or less had. They hadn't said what Buddy was doing at the marina, they hadn't given her the Dorands' address, and they hadn't even told her where Wesley Burrell lived.

CHAPTER THIRTEEN

Ben Izaguirre might as well be next, she thought, *and then the Dorands.* Izaguirre's restaurant was more or less in the neighborhood, in the Lake Catherine area, going toward the Rigolets, and she figured he'd probably be there in the middle of the morning.

The restaurant was a musty-smelling old white-shingled dockside joint that looked like it didn't do much business anymore, if it ever had—the kind of family-owned eatery that was getting harder and harder to find in New Orleans these days, but probably served great seafood. A sign out front announced, FRIDAYS BOILED SEAFOOD—BIKERS WELCOME.

Talba wasn't too sure what to do about the kitten; but it was a cool day, so suffocation ought not to be a problem, and it was busy sleeping off its meal. She figured it could fend for itself for a while.

Inside the restaurant, two or three formica-topped tables looked as if they'd just been deserted by the breakfast crowd, and hadn't yet been cleared. Each of the others was equipped with salt, pepper, Tabasco, ketchup, horseradish, small bowls of lemon wedges, and tiny paper cups for cocktail sauce.

A white woman was already setting up for lunch, busily ignoring the mess. She was overweight and motherly, the kind of waitress who calls you "dawlin'" and makes you feel like she's serving her own cooking. Talba was willing to bet she'd lived in Lake Catherine all her life.

"Mr. Izaguirre here?" Talba asked.

The waitress put her hands on her hips. "Sorry, dawlin', we not hirin'."

"Tell him I'm a friend of Angie Valentino's. I work with her father."

"Oh. Sorry." The woman was clearly dismayed, knowing she'd screwed up. "I'll get him."

In a moment, a squat mushroom of a man waddled out behind her, beaming, hand already sticking out like a fin. "You must be that detective gal."

Talba let him pump her hand. "Oh! You heard about me. I'm Talba Wallis."

"Ben Izaguirre."

Like Brad Leitner, he was bald, but in his case, it was natural. He still had a fringe of white to prove it. "Ya want some shrimp? Guarandamtee ya it's Louisiana wild-caught. Got some nice ersters, too." Oysters, he meant. Eddie's pronunciation.

Talba smiled. She liked him; he reminded her of Eddie. "Maybe some coffee," she said.

"Denise, coffee for the lady," he told the waitress. "Iced tea for me. Sit down, sit down—anywhere ya like."

Talba obeyed, and he lowered his bulk into a chair at a right angle from her. "Sure ya wouldn't like somethin' to eat? Least I can do's feed ya. Miz Valentino says ya did a real fine job over at Buddy's, rest his evil ol' soul. What can I do for ya?" He didn't stop to let her answer. "It's a terrible, terrible thing they did to Miz Valentino and that Indian fella. Real shame about that. And all she cared about was her client— didn't think about herself at all. Fine, fine woman, Angela Valentino. Don't come any better than her." His face hardened. "Listen, whoever knocked off ol' Buddy did us all a favor. Thought about it myself once or twice."

"Somehow, I don't see you as a murderer," Talba said truthfully.

"Oh, I got a temper on me. Ask Denise—or my wife. Anybody'll tell ya that. More than once I thought about takin' the law into my own hands. But no need, no need; thanks to Miz Valentino. And you, of course. I have to thank ya for what you did."

"It kind of backfired on me, though. I didn't mean to get the judge killed."

He patted her hand. "Course ya didn't. Man like Buddy, though, he had enemies."

"Sure you didn't kill him?" Talba smiled when she said it.

"Killin' him wasn't exactly my fantasy. I had one, though—don't think I didn't. Thought about torchin' that hellhole more than once. Too close to home, though; mighta spread."

"The marina, you mean?" she asked, wondering whether he was serious.

"Garbage dump's more like it. Buddy's shrimp mighta been 'wild-caught,' but I don't want to think about sanitary conditions over there. Not to mention safety considerations. Whole neighborhood was up in arms about that poor little Dorand boy."

"I hear he lived around here," Talba said. "You know his family?"

"I do now." He looked uncomfortable. "Simple folk. Salt of the earth—didn't know what hit 'em. Ya never did say what I can do for ya."

"Still got a few loose ends on the case. Angie isn't off the hook quite yet. She said you almost got the same treatment."

"Hell, yeah, I did. Goddam those bastards—think they own the earth."

"What bastards? I mean—Buddy and who else?"

"People in power that take advantage of the little folk. That's all I meant. Why?"

"I heard you saw who planted the drugs on you."

He shook his head. "Well, I did and I didn't. Saw a couple guys get out of my car and run away. Only saw 'em from the back. But one of 'em was bald as an egg. Pretty sure it was Brad Leitner. I thought they were stealing something, but nothing was missing. Right away I knew what happened."

"How?" Talba asked.

"Pretty obvious. There was a bag of pot on the front seat." He picked up a cellophane pack of saltines and began to worry it open.

"In plain sight," Talba said.

"Right. So anybody walking by could see it. See what I'm getting at? It wouldn't take an illegal search to find it. So puttin' two and two together, it had to be a plant. Because Buddy'd threatened me. Or rather, he'd gotten Brad Leitner to do it." There was something odd about his face when he mentioned Leitner, as if a whiff of Buddy's marina had wafted by.

"What did Brad threaten you with?"

"Just that I'd be sorry—that kind of crap." Izaguirre was now pouring ketchup into one of the little sauce cups. "So I just took the package and threw it in the water. By the time I got back to the car, a couple guys were looking in the window—sheriff's car was parked right down the street."

"That was pretty quick thinking."

Izaguirre looked up from his sauce-making. "Ya know something, Miss Wallis? I wasn't thinking at all. I got the hell scared out of me, that was all. Besides, I know Leitner. My kid went to school with him—always was a sneaky little bastard."

Talba smiled. "What'd he do to your kid?"

"Turned half the school against him—told lies about him."

Since he hadn't mentioned what kind of lies, Talba didn't feel comfortable asking. Instead, she waited while Izaguirre added horseradish and Tabasco to his concoction.

Finally, he said, "They were both on the track team. Said Mikey tried to grab him in the shower." He stirred the sauce with a cracker.

Talba smiled. "Oh. What'd Mikey do to make him mad?"

"Little pissant was jealous. Mikey was the captain of the team." He stirred the sauce again.

"Was Leitner ever in any kind of trouble?"

"I don't know if he was ever arrested, but I can tell you this—he's an ex–Orleans Parish sheriff's deputy—with emphasis on the 'ex.' What's that tell ya?"

"You mean, with that sheriff's car parked near yours? Tells me he knows where to find the dirty deputies."

Izaguirre nodded, sniffing at the cracker and making a face. He picked up the Tabasco and sprinkled it liberally before he spoke. "That's what I think. The sheriff's department runs the jails, and Buddy was a judge. You know what the paper said. He set high bonds for Nicasio's clients. Lot of room there for cooperation with the deputies. And Leitner's tight with the Champagnes, always has been."

"Wonder if he quit the sheriff's department to run that marina?"

"Now that I don't know. All I know is, he turned up there a few months ago."

Talba had a thought. "Royce go to your kid's school, too?"

"Oh, yeah. De La Salle. Another little punk." His nose wrinkled again. Another rank whiff. He chewed a sauce-sopped saltine. "Ya ever try this? Poor man's ersters. Been doin' it since I was a kid."

Talba couldn't help but smile. "Sure." Every kid in Louisiana did it, but very few grown-ups did.

She wondered if Angie knew about Izaguirre's long-running relationship with the Champagnes—if it could be called a relationship. Maybe there was something personal in his opposition to the marina. But she still couldn't find a motive for murder in it.

"But the drug thing," she said. "Do you have any reason to think Leitner was involved with drugs?"

"Hell, anybody can get drugs. Anyhow, there were always shady characters hanging around that marina. Tried like hell to find out if anything funny was going on over there. Never could, but there was enough wrong without that. How would you like that place in your neighborhood?"

"I'd really hate that," Talba said truthfully, which for some reason Izaguirre found hilarious.

When he'd quit laughing and wiping his eyes, he said, "There ya are, then."

"Well, I thank you for your time. I'd like to go see the Dorands, but I'm not sure where they live. Can you help me out with that?"

Izaguirre looked at his watch. "Sure. They live just up the road. You'll probably find 'em home. Billy doesn't work—he's got some kind of disability or other—and Fay runs some kind of half-assed beauty shop out of the house. Say, ya want to take some shrimp home with ya?"

"Thanks, but I'm going to be out for a while. Last thing I need's my car smelling like your neighborhood."

That got another belly laugh, the term being particularly applicable in Izaguirre's case.

160

"By the way, it's not shrimp season, is it? But I can see they've been working that place. Was Buddy buying from poachers?"

"Damn right he was." He shrugged. "Whatcha gonna do?"

When she had the address, Talba left, hoping Fay wouldn't be washing someone's hair when she got to the Dorands. The cat, still napping, stirred when she got in the car—in fact, had a near freak-out and ended up hiding under the seat. Good place for it, Talba decided.

The house was on the little two-lane highway, Old Spanish Trail, that led to the Rigolets Bridge. It looked like a converted fishing shack, rising on short stilts, about two and a half feet high, and the house proper was dwarfed by an old-fashioned screened-in porch—or would have been, if not for the vast satellite dish perched somewhere at the back of the little building. The house had white siding and a great deal of peeling green woodwork, but no amount of dressing up could erase the gloomy effect of all that dark screen. Timidly, she tried the screen door, unsure whether it constituted the beginning of the residents' private space, and it opened on a man, evidently Billy, sitting in an old wooden porch chair, staring into space and looking sad. Every inch the broken man. What had happened to him—the death of a child—was the worst thing that could happen to anybody, people said. She didn't doubt it.

"Mr. Dorand? Sorry, I didn't know if I should knock or not."

"We leave it open. Wife operates a bi'ness outta here. Whatcha need?"

"I'm a friend of Ben Izaguirre's. Wonder if you could talk to me a few minutes."

He grunted. "Whatcha need?" he repeated. He didn't sound like he cared much.

"I'm doing some work for Angela Valentino. Looking into what happened to your boy."

His eyes reddened and watered. His expression didn't change.

"Is Mrs. Dorand home?"

He grunted again, and heaved himself up, no easy feat. He was a large man—a lot bigger than Izaguirre—diabetic, perhaps. Pale, too. Maybe heart trouble.

"It's all right, I'll knock."

"I'll get her." He evidently didn't want her going into their house. A racist, maybe. In fact, she'd bet on it.

Fay Dorand was a shortish, plumpish woman with an air of vitality about her. She had short, thick, auburn hair, more crinkly than curly, that sat on her head like a small bush. If she was a hairdresser, she should probably stick to other people's heads. But she wore a pink smock, indicating that Izaguirre had been right.

"It's all right," she said to her husband, as she slipped out onto the porch. "I just put her under the dryer." She spoke to Talba. "Billy told me you want to talk about Jimmy."

Talba pulled out her license and a badge that could be had for eighty dollars if you were a P.I.—Eddie scorned the whole idea, but Talba found hers useful in cases like this. "I'm a private investigator, and a friend of Angela Valentino. Just talked to Ben Izaguirre—he said you might be able to clear up a few things for me."

The Dorands didn't ask her to sit down, though Billy lowered himself again into a chair. "I know this is difficult," Talba said. "I was wondering if you can give me some information about the accident."

Billy's red-rimmed eyes bored into her so savagely she nearly had to look away.

"They electrocuted him," Billy said. "Just like a criminal."

There was so much anger in the man she wanted to take a step back. Willing herself to stand her ground, she spoke carefully. "Mmm. Mmm. Sounds like you're saying you don't think it was an accident."

Billy grunted again. "Bastards don't care about nothin' but money. Idiots wired the place wrong. Somethin' wasn't grounded, and Jimmy stepped in water while he was runnin' the conveyor belt." He sniffed. "Wasn't but seventeen."

"I hear you filed suit against the marina."

"Our luck," Fay said, "it woulda been heard in Buddy's court."

Did she really think that could happen? Talba wondered, and thought it possible. These weren't the kind of people who understood the finer points of law. "You think?" she said.

"Hell, Buddy got what he deserved. I'm just sorry he won't be around to pay us what he owes us."

"How about the electrician? Did you sue him, too?"

"Hell," Billy said. "There wasn't no electrician. That homo Brad Leitner did all the wirin' over there. Buddy was too goddam cheap to even hire a professional. And him with that mansion Uptown." The word "mansion" came out as a sneer. "Ya ever seen that place? Makes Anne Rice's house look like a cabin in the woods."

So Brad himself was responsible for the boy's death. That, Talba thought, was what he was hiding. But maybe it wasn't the whole story. Eddie had coached her carefully in lying and playing dumb and she was getting a lot better at both, but this time she wouldn't even have to fake dumb. She had no idea if that homo remark was a routine insult or actually meant something. "Leitner's gay?" she ventured. "I didn't know that."

"Shit, you met the guy? Got a cute little earring in his ear and a shaved head. What more ya gotta know about him? Probably shaves his legs too. Him and that Champagne boy's what we used to call asshole buddies. Go over and watch 'em in action."

Now that Talba thought about it, it was possible. They hugged a lot, but then, they'd suffered mutual tragedy. They behaved more or less like parts of a machine, too—or parts of a couple. And then there was that locker room story of Izaguirre's—maybe Brad had been the grabber instead of Mike. But where all that got her she didn't know.

"Tell me something," she said. "In your opinion, who is really responsible for Jimmy's death? Buddy or Brad?"

The Dorands looked at each other, maybe weighing the effect their answer could have on their lawsuit. Finally, Billy said, "Buddy, no question. Had to know better. Leitner's only crime's bein' a moron. That and a fudgepacker."

Talba kept her face steady; wincing wouldn't win her any points. "Mrs. Dorand? You agree?"

Faye nodded, slowly. "Buddy. Family still owes us. This thing's not goin' away."

Well, I am, Talba thought. *And the sooner the better.*

But she still had a question or two. "Y'all home the night Buddy was shot?"

Again, they looked at each other. Finally, Fay shrugged. "We don't go out a lot. Must have been."

"You didn't hear the shot, did you?"

"I'm not sure we didn't," Billy said. "Heard somethin' funny."

"What?"

"Some kind of noise."

"How can you remember that if you're not sure you were home?"

Billy flared. "You callin' me a liar, girl?"

"No, sir." She turned her palms up to signal she wasn't armed. "Just asking."

"Well, get on down the road now. I've 'bout had enough of the likes of you."

She got on down the road. Happily; no matter that the kitten was nowhere in sight.

Still hiding, she figured. And hoped it wouldn't decide to go exploring while she was driving.

She wondered what Jimmy had been like. Lucy'd said she liked him. In that case, he must have resembled his parents only in having two arms and two legs. "Simple," Ben Izaguirre had called them. A serious understatement.

Clearly they were racist, homophobic, and prejudiced against anyone better off than they were. They'd seen Buddy's house and that had probably whetted their greed. She wasn't sure she could believe a word either of them said.

CHAPTER FOURTEEN

"Eddie, you got connections in the Orleans Parish Sheriff's office?"

Eddie couldn't believe Ms. Wallis sometimes. "I been in business thirty years, or what?"

"I take it that's something like 'Who de man?'"

Eddie sighed, feeling weary. "You got it, Ms. Wallis. Criminal or civil?" Because of a separation of jurisdictions after the Civil War, Orleans Parish had the only criminal sheriff in the country, whose main duty was to run the jail.

"Criminal."

"Whatcha need?"

"Royce's best friend used to be a deputy. Might have gotten fired."

Eddie raised an eyebrow. "Ya gotta piss somebody off to be fired from that job. It ain't civil service. You can be fired at will."

"Ah. Even more interesting. Can you find out what happened?"

"What's the matter, it's not online?"

"Well, the guy's not in rapsheets.com, but even a baroness can't get personnel records."

"Hang on there—forgot to wear my shock-absorbing tie today."

"You should let Audrey pick out your ties."

That annoyed Eddie. Audrey didn't like the damn tie, either. What was up with women? Were they telepathic or something? "I'll make some calls," he said.

"Good. I've got to get going. I've got a kitten in the car."

"Ya got a what?"

"Rescue kitten. For Raisa."

"Darryl know about that?"

"He'll love it—it's a really sweet little thing."

"Oh, boy," was all he said, thinking about the time Audrey'd brought home a rescue kitten for Angie and her brother, Tony. He hadn't loved it.

Instead of making calls, he decided to go over to the sheriff's office, shoot the shit a little to keep his hand in. He asked at the receptionist's desk for Chief St. Pierre, then waited till his old buddy St. Bernard came to get him—they didn't let you roam the halls here. The guy's name was Bernard St. Pierre, but anybody who'd ever met him understood the doggy thing—he was a big, shambling, broad-backed, slow-moving guy, loyal to a fault, who didn't seem all that smart at first glance. Eddie'd had more than one glance.

"Eddie, my man, how ya been keepin'?" The Saint wore a slow canine grin that hid the fact that he'd probably taken in all the data Eddie offered by his mere presence. "Let me guess," he said, "ya gave up desserts for Lent."

Eddie had. "What makes ya think that, Saint?"

"Put on a few, haven't ya? And ya not gon' give up beer."

"Pound or two," Eddie shrugged. Ten, in fact. And he had given up desserts. The Saint was starting to bug him already. "Came by to ask about a former employee."

"Ya know I can't talk about that." The Saint favored him with a wink that was more like a tent door flapping. "Come on into my office."

Eddie followed. "Guy named Brad Leitner. Ever know him?"

"Oh. *Him.* Got rid o' *his* sorry ass."

"Uh-huh. I knew there was somethin'."

"Queer as a quacker." The Saint had his own language.

"Ya mean he's an odd duck? Or ya mean he's gay?"

"Oh, he's an odd duck, all right. Kept to himself when he was here. Never one of the boys. I think some judge got him the job. And also queer as a quacker."

"What judge?"

"We don't say that name here anymore. FBI might be listening."

"Ah. The one that was just in the news? Pals with Harry Nicasio?"

"The one Harry offed."

"*Harry* offed!" Eddie hadn't thought of that one. "Why would Harry off him?"

The Saint shrugged. "Knew too much. Kill the witness, ya kill the messenger. Nobody to testify, Harry stays out of a cage."

"I don't want to get too personal here, but seems to me some of your guys might make pretty good witnesses. Whatcha gonna do, keep 'em under guard?"

"Hell, they're armed."

"Ya really think Harry offed him?"

"Just a theory. But, my opinion? They don't call Harry the Old Nick for nothin'."

"I didn't know they did."

"Eddie, Eddie—ya been out of circulation too long. Sit down. Take a load off."

The Saint sat in his own chair and picked up a mug of coffee. He didn't offer Eddie any.

Eddie sat, too. "So about my queer duck. Ya sayin' he *is* gay?"

"Gay as a blade. That don't go down too well around here."

"What, did he grab the other guys or something? How would anybody know?"

"Hell, he didn't hide it. Talked about it all the time. Real popular dude." The Saint rolled his eyes.

"Last I heard it wasn't a firin' offense, though."

"Naah. He roughed up one too many prisoners." Here, the Saint paused, pregnantly. "But, hell. You been around, Eddie. You know how it is. Assholes get out o' line, somebody's gotta control 'em."

The Saint was subtle, but Eddie thought he was getting his drift. "Meaning he didn't do anything that wasn't standard procedure."

"Usually, one deputy don't report another." The Saint's eyes were hooded, his voice low. "Like I said, real popular guy."

167

"Come on. The guy had juice. Didn't Buddy Champagne pull any strings?"

"Nope. Just let it happen."

Eddie wondered what that meant. He said, "Think there was any kind of falling-out with the judge?"

The Saint just shrugged. "Buddy was a big boy. He knew how things work here."

"So what you're sayin' is, Leitner was more or less drummed out."

"We gotta have some standards here."

"No quackers."

"No quackers who *brag* about bein' quackers. Ya see what I'm sayin'?"

Eddie saw. There'd been a time when he'd been perfectly in sync with what happened to Leitner. He was surprised to find himself annoyed with the Saint's smugness. "I musta moved on," he said. "Hell, I'm a paragon of tolerance these days. Got me a black female associate. Young, too."

"God help ya."

"Yeah, well, that's not the bad part. This one's a college graduate and smarter'n your whole staff put together, which wouldn't take all that much. And got a mouth on her."

The Saint laughed. "Know what I'd do with that one? I'd fire her ass."

Eddie stood up. "Can't. Audrey and Angie'd fire me. Besides, she does all the work anymore."

He thanked the good Lord Ms. Wallis would never find out he'd bragged about her to the sheriff's main man—and then he thanked the sheriff's main man. He left to report his findings, secretly chortling that he'd learned a new phrase to annoy Ms. Wallis with.

For once, she was in her office, doing the employment and prenuptial backgrounds (which she called "sweetie snoops") that he loathed with every fiber of his sixty-six-year-old Luddite being. Give him a good insurance fraud any time. What he loved was to be out there with his camcorder, snaring some bozo who was supposed to be half-crippled building himself a new addition he intended to pay for with his insurance windfall. Guy like that deserved what he got. Eddie found it highly gratifying.

"What'd ya do with the kitten?"

"Took it home. Koko and Blanche weren't pleased." Her own two cats had been inherited from another job. Animals were sticking like lint to her lately.

"Had a talk with the Saint," he said, helping himself to a seat.

"Who? Oh. St. Bernard. At OPP." Orleans Parish Prison. "What'd he say?"

"Says Buddy got Leitner the job."

"Big surprise."

That annoyed Eddie, but it gave him the opportunity to use a word he thought she'd really hate, coming from his mouth. "You dissin' me?" he said.

Instead of being annoyed, she laughed. "Eddie, how does a guy like you learn a word like that?"

"Hey, I'm as hip as the next guy. Ya want to hear the rest of it or not?"

"Spill, as they say in your generation."

He decided to let that one go. "The Saint says he's as queer as a quacker."

He waited for her to go on for twenty minutes about homophobic bubbas. Instead, she only nodded. "I get it. Walks like a duck, talks like a duck."

He'd overlooked that possible meaning, but he didn't let on. "Specially talks like a duck," he said. "He's queer and he's here, and he doesn't care who knows—a real no-no down at OPP. Saint says they drummed him out on some kind of trumped up charge."

She pondered that one. "What kind of trumped-up charge?"

"Some kind of bullshit unnecessary roughness thing."

"Ah, so he's a sadist."

Eddie was disgusted. "Ms. Wallis, ya usually smarter than this. The Saint said he didn't do anything anybody else doesn't do." He wasn't sure whether that was proper grammar or not, but he was pretty sure she'd tell him if it wasn't. "They just didn't want a queer in the ranks, get it?"

"You never heard where there's smoke there's fire?"

"Look, say what you want about the Saint, but he's a fair guy. He says it, he means it."

"From what I hear about that jail, they've got a lot of sadists down there. If Leitner got fired, he was probably worse than most."

"I didn't get to the good part yet. He thinks Harry Nicasio whacked Buddy."

"Eddie, I know you didn't tell him what we're working on. Are you saying he just volunteered that?"

"Well, yeah. Yeah, he did. But I'm not a hundred percent sure he was serious. Said it was a witness protection thing, with a kind of a twist—protection *from* the witness."

"Possible." But she seemed dubious. "Lots of other witnesses out there."

"That's what I told him. You know what, though? I got an idea— what about Leitner as the perp? The Saint says Buddy didn't lift a finger to help him when it went down. Maybe he didn't trust him. Maybe he thinks Leitner was behind the newspaper story, and he asks for a meeting at the marina. They get in an argument, and Leitner kills him."

"Heat of passion kind of thing?" She seemed doubtful.

Eddie shrugged. "Guess it'd have to be. Anyhoo, just a thought. How come you didn't react to Leitner being gay?"

"Someone else told me that—said he and Royce Champagne are an item."

"Thought Royce was married." Too late, he realized his mistake.

"EdDEE! How naïve can you be?"

Nothing to do but ignore her. "Know who I think you should be talking to?"

"The night watchman, right?"

Eddie stood up and glowered at her. "Yeah. If you think you can find him." It pissed him off when she acted like she was one step ahead of him.

Talba had backgrounded Wesley Burrell in Arabi, but the most interesting thing she found about him was that he didn't live in Arabi. He used to, that wasn't hard to figure out, but he was living in Westwego now. Perhaps Burrell had had to put former addresses on his employment form and Royce had read it wrong. Surely he hadn't tried to misdirect her deliberately—what would be the point? Childishness, she decided. And it could as easily be directed at Kristin and her great idea as at Talba and her investigation.

Burrell was a retired postal worker, which might not augur a towering intellect, but you never knew—by all accounts, the Saint was a pretty smart dude for the sheriff's office. The good part was, if the guy worked as a night watchman, he ought to be home sleeping. She liked talking to sleepy people—they let things slip.

What she found was a dapper, well-built sixtyish guy in shorts, setting out spring begonias, now that it was getting warmer. Westwego was a working-class white town and this guy, despite his absence of beer gut, was probably a bubba who'd pretty naturally be suspicious of a black chick in the neighborhood. She pulled out her badge and license as she approached.

"Mr. Burrell?"

He stood up from his planting, his bony knees caked with dirt. "You FBI?"

She grinned. "Not nearly so bad as that. I'm a humble P.I.—you expecting the FBI?"

"I was involved in a murder—thought they might come around."

"Well, they haven't yet. I'm Talba Wallis." They shook hands.

"You want to come in and have some iced tea?" This guy was no bubba.

"Sure," she said, and followed him into a tiny white bungalow so neat she thought at first he was one of Brad's gay friends. It wasn't capital-f Fabulous, but it might be the Westwego equivalent. However, Burrell evidently wasn't gay. A very neat, short-haired woman who looked a good ten years older than Burrell was working at a laptop on a table that clearly doubled as a desk in a dining room that clearly doubled as a library and office. It was completely lined with books.

"This," he said with a flourish, "is my wife, Mary Ann. Mary Ann, this is Miss Wallis. She's a private eye, come to call on us for some reason. You haven't been up to anything you shouldn't, have you?"

She made to stand, but Talba said, "Don't get up."

Mary Ann ignored her and stood up. "Sorry the place is such a mess. We're putting in a little garden—just moved here last fall." Talba saw that the laptop (which was wireless) was connected to a gardening site. Seed catalogues covered the table.

"We're newlyweds," Wesley Burrell said proudly. "I work contracting jobs from time to time. Came to remodel Mary Ann's kitchen, and it was love at first sight."

Talba said, "I thought you were a postal clerk."

Both Burrells laughed. "I was, I was. Been most everything. Bartender, waiter, night watchman, you name it. Let me get you that iced tea."

He bustled off, giving Mary Ann a chance to lead Talba into a living room that seemed to have been furnished by Pottery Barn. Obviously, Mary Ann was a great catalogue shopper. "Had to buy all new stuff," she said. "My husband got the furniture."

You little devil you, Talba thought. *Carrying on with the contractor.* If anybody didn't look the type, she was it. "All but the books," she said.

Mary Ann laughed. "I'm afraid I've got this little habit. I'm a retired librarian. But those are mostly Wesley's. We bonded over *The Lovely Bones*—neither of us could stand it."

"Why not?" Talba asked. "I kind of liked it."

Mary Ann shivered. "All that heaven stuff. Gave us the willies. My ex-husband," she added, "isn't much of a reader. It's true what they say—you can't break up a happy marriage." She held her hands apart like parentheses, containing her words. "And the kids were grown, so why not? Matter of fact, the grandkids are almost grown. We were both marking time. Lenny married his secretary the minute the divorce was final."

"A win-win situation," Talba said, and Wesley came back with the iced tea.

"Let's sit down, shall we?" he said, handing Talba a tall cool glass. "If I can coin a cliché, to what do we owe the honor?"

"It can wait a minute," Talba said. "You piqued my curiosity. Did you say you were involved in a murder?"

He nodded. "Client of mine was killed. It's probably what you're here about, right? I mean, Mary Ann and I lead kind of a blameless life—but not every day does a client get killed on my watch. And everyone else has been here to talk about it—I figured the FBI was next. Instead, I bet it's you." He gave her a shrewd look. "Besides, you discovered the body—we saw you on television."

Mary Ann did a double take. "You're that poet! I looked you up on the Internet, but I didn't recognize you."

Talba figured they'd appreciate her Baroness routine. "The Baroness de Pontalba, at your service," she said. "But you can call me Your Grace."

Wesley raised a bemused eyebrow, but decided to go with it. "Okay, Your Grace," he said, "you want to hear my story, right? Who are you working for?"

"That part's usually confidential, but in this case, it's not. I'm working for the judge's fiancée."

"Never met her," Wesley said. "I just came at night and did my rounds. Place stinks like hell, doesn't it?"

"Was there ever any activity there—at night?"

"Just me. Otherwise, quiet as a tomb. Why?"

"I think Buddy was buying shrimp from poachers," Talba said.

"Ah. It's not shrimp season, is it? I should have thought about that. Well, if he was doing it, he was doing it in the daytime—which you'd have to at Venetian Isles. Quiet place like that, night work'd be even more noticeable. Damn!" He seemed to be kicking himself. "Well, I was about to quit, anyhow. The judge's death kind of turned the trick. But anyhow, I was embarrassed—people aren't supposed to die when you're looking out for their property." The average person might have looked suitably grim at this point, but Wesley didn't. He seemed to be enjoying the diversion.

Mary Ann patted his knee. "I need you home at night. It wasn't a job that really used your talents."

He wiggled his eyebrows. "Hubba-hubba," he said.

"You two need some privacy?" Talba asked.

Mary Ann blushed. "Sorry."

"Listen, it's the damnedest thing," Wesley said. "Somewhere around midnight, the judge called and told me I could go home. Left a voice mail while I was on my rounds."

"Did he say why?"

"Said he was headed out there for a meeting."

"Voice mail," Talba said. "You sure it was him?"

For the first time, Wesley looked chagrined. "Ever since then, I've asked myself that a hundred times, but at the time, I had no reason to

173

doubt it." He gave Mary Ann a glance. "And as you can see, I've got a lot to come home to. Here's the bad thing—I erased the voice mail."

"Oh. Did he tell you to?"

This time he looked downright ashamed. "No. Just habit. Hell, it was his marina. I figured if he wanted me to leave, I'd be glad to. Wouldn't have to smell that place all night."

It was a pretty pat story. Talba asked if he knew the judge before he took the job.

"Nope," he said. "He ran an ad on the Internet. Didn't know him or Royce or Brad. Didn't have a clue the place was controversial. Course, I heard about that kid being killed. But, hell, accidents happen. Between you and me, though, they do run a pretty loose ship."

"Yeah, so I've heard. Tell me, did you get the sense they were doing anything illegal? Besides that poaching thing, I mean."

"What kind of illegal?" Talba could have sworn he looked a little wary.

"Like drugs, maybe."

He shrugged. "All I ever saw was a closed-down stinky old place."

"The neighbors said shady characters hung around there."

Wesley laughed. "Probably meant me."

"Oh, yeah? You're a suspicious character?"

"Mary Ann does call me Slim Shady."

It took Talba a minute to get the reference. "You two," she asked incredulously, "are into rap?"

"Not by choice," Mary Ann said. "My grandson's an Eminem fan, more's the pity."

"I hear you," Talba said.

She asked Wesley if he'd left right away (he had) and if he had any idea who Buddy might be meeting (not really), and what he thought of Royce and Brad (they seemed like pretty good guys), and then she drank her iced tea and stood to leave, wondering why Buddy had wanted to leave his property unguarded, even for a short while.

She thought of one last thing. "Was there anything odd about Buddy's voice? Anything to indicate it wasn't him?"

"Well, he had that redneck thing going. 'Hey-Wes-ol'-buddy-why-don't-you-head-on-home?' kind of thing. I don't know anybody else who talks like that. Do you?"

It occurred to her the whole interview had gone way too smoothly, been far too civil. She tried out one last thing. "In your heart of hearts," she said, "do you think it was him?"

"Well, I'll say this—it didn't cross my mind that it wasn't. Hell, it was midnight. Figured he got to drinking, wanted to bring some woman out there."

"To *that* place?"

"It was private, anyhow. He brought women there all the time."

"Even though he was engaged."

Wesley laughed. "I've been working there almost a year—don't think he's known your client that long."

"Did he bring them out there to . . . uh . . ."

"Naah. Not even Buddy was that crude. Place is nasty. He just showed 'em around. If they were impressed, God help 'em."

"Well, look. Can you think of anything—any incident, anything at all—that gives you an idea who'd want to kill him?"

"Lots of 'em. You name somebody, they've got a motive."

Talba pursued that for a while, eliciting only a list of the same old names, and advice to go through Buddy's court cases. Wesley's theory was, someone out there had a grudge.

CHAPTER FIFTEEN

The trouble with the same old names was that none of them belonged to anyone Buddy would leave the comfort of his home to meet in a dark, deserted place. Ben Izaguirre? Hardly. The Dorands? When pigs flew. Someone he'd ruled against in court? Sometime around the year 3000.

But if Burrell was to be believed—and Talba decided for the moment to believe him—Buddy had gone there to meet someone. That tryst thing—maybe that was something. Maybe it was a former lover who'd heard about his engagement. Someone with something on Buddy, maybe.

A woman, come to think of it, would be a great suspect. Buddy wouldn't have been afraid of her.

That made Talba think of Suzanne. She didn't seem to like anybody very much. That ought to make for very loose lips. But she had to be approached correctly, and Talba knew exactly the way to her heart. She called her on the cell phone.

"Suzanne? Talba Wallis."

"Oh. The snitch. Thanks for everything."

This was one difficult case.

Something occurred to her for the first time—maybe the real reason Kristin had hired her was that she thought it was one of Buddy's nearest and dearest who'd killed him. After all, they could hardly refuse to let her do it, or they'd tip their hand. And contrary to the story she'd been given, they were resisting like Talba worked for the IRS.

She went into her apology routine again—she had it down pretty well by now—and concluded by saying that wasn't what she was calling about, anyhow. (Well, it almost wasn't.) "I do need to talk to you about the murder, just to cover my bases—you know what I mean—but the thing is, you got me curious, so I bought this book on feng shui—"

"Oh! Don't you love it?" All seemed to be forgiven.

"Adore it. Crazy for it. I want to do my office right away, but I'm confused about something. My door's kind of at a funny angle—I'm not sure how to place the bhagwa. I mean, if I get it wrong, I reverse my marriage and money corners, right?"

"Oh, sure. And there are different schools of thought on it, anyhow. You really have to be careful."

"I mean, like, when you're standing in the doorway, you have to turn to—"

"Look, does your desk face the doorway?"

"Well, sort of, but—"

"You want me to come take a look? I have some time tomorrow if you like." Eager as anything. A fish on a line.

Oh, yeah. Come to me, baby, Talba thought. "Oh, gosh," she said. "You aren't too expensive, are you?"

"If your office is small enough, I could do it for about a hundred dollars."

"I don't know, I—"

"Look, I'll do a free consultation. Then you just refer me to somebody and we're square."

"Really? Okay, that'd be great. Tell you what, let me at least take you to lunch—are you free?"

"Let me see." Suzanne paused, evidently consulting her date book. "I could rearrange something."

"Done deal," Talba said. "Come about noon." She knew earlier wasn't going to fly.

Suzanne might not like people much, but she was in love with her job.

Time to knock off and go home, after a quick stop for kitten food, cat box, and litter, none of which escaped Miz Clara's notice. "Why we need more cat stuff?"

"We don't," Talba replied, "but Darryl's going to. I got Raisa a kitten."

"Ya what? Ya went out and bought a kitten?"

"Rescued it. Want to see?"

"Whatcha mean, do I wanna see? Ya brought another animal in this house? No wonder the Queen and the Duchess actin' so strange." Miz Clara pretended to hate Koko and Blanche, but they were getting fat from the treats she slipped them. "They hidin' under things, makin' noises like they a couple of toms."

"Well, Gumbo's in their territory. They'll live; it's just for one night. I'll take her over tomorrow. You want to see or not?"

"Last thing I wanna see's another damn cat in this house." But she trudged after Talba to her daughter's room and followed her in. "Where's it at?"

"Hiding, probably." They lured it out from under the bed with an open can of cat food. The kitten looked like a tiny, skinny, cat-shaped canvas upon which an artist had painted an intricate design in white, black, and gold. It had a white background and an all-white belly, with meticulously applied spots and patches on its back, one black leg, one gold leg, three spots on a white leg, and a face out of a Kabuki play—matching black spots like kohl around its eyes, and four black spots on its nose, spaced like a lopsided cross.

"Lord, that ain't no kitten! It's a Rembrandt."

Talba considered. "Picasso, I think. Pretty, isn't it?"

"That's the most beautiful animal I ever saw in my life—'cept for bein' so scrawny. And it ain't no bigger than a minute. Gumbo? That thing's named Gumbo?"

"Nickname, I think. Nobody knows its real name."

"Well, it oughta be Cleopatra or somethin'—that's one pretty kitten. Raisa's gon' love that—mmm mmm. Don't know 'bout Darryl, but—"

She was interrupted by the sound of galloping, then a great hissing and spitting that caused the kitten to go Halloween on them.

"Omigod, Mama," Talba yelled. "Get Blanche and Koko out of here!"

"Scat," Miz Clara yelled. "Y'all wanta traumatize that baby? All Darryl needs is another psychiatrist bill—that daughter of his is gon' cost him plenty down the line. Come on, y'all—scat!" She raised her arms like a grizzly bear, causing poor Koko and Blanche to turn tail and run, in the certain knowledge that their best friend had just flipped out.

Suzanne arrived at noon the next day with four potted plants and assorted mirrors. "Hmm, this doesn't look so bad. But this is an office, so you're going to need plants in your career, helpful people, and money corners. And I brought some mirrors just in case—but your desk does face the door, that part's okay. Tell you the truth, I expected a lot worse."

Talba didn't inquire as to the reasons for all these things, but she got told anyhow, and in little more than half an hour, her office was ready for anything. Suzanne wanted to do the reception area, too, but Talba called a halt after a while—the last thing she needed was Eddie's post facto input.

There was a newish Thai place in the neighborhood, and, remembering how much Susanne liked her food, Talba eventually enticed her pad thai–ward. "I don't usually drink at lunch," she said, "but I'm feeling kind of reckless today."

"Kind of light and airy? A lot of people report that after getting feng shui'ed. Let's celebrate. Go ahead—have a glass of wine. Or maybe some beer."

"I will if you will." Anything for the cause. But Suzanne refused, so Talba got to keep her head clear.

Talba asked her how Adele and Lucy and all the gang were doing and Suzanne said they were muddling through, except for being in shock and everything. "And you?" Talba asked.

"Well, Royce is taking it pretty hard; I'm just trying to help him get through."

"He must be a difficult man to be married to."

Suzanne seemed surprised. "Why do you say that?"

"May I speak out of school? Sometimes you just don't seem happy, that's all."

"Well, uh—I'm having kind of a hard time getting my business started."

Talba said, "It seems like he drinks a lot."

"Oh, he does," Suzanne admitted. "I'm terribly worried about him, if you want to know the truth."

"I was wondering about Brad. He can't be a good influence."

"Oh, Brad," was all Suzanne said.

"I get a weird vibe about him. Do you happen to know if he's gay?"

Suzanne looked at her quizzically. "You must be very perceptive. He's so macho and everything, hardly anyone ever guesses. But of course Royce has known him since fifth grade—pretty hard to be in the closet with your best friend."

"I see what you mean. But I'm wondering—did Buddy know?"

"Oh, sure. He just accepted it, like we all do."

"Suzanne, I hope you don't take this the wrong way, but Buddy seemed awfully prejudiced. I mean, something like that . . ."

"Oh, it never bothered him at all. Old redneck that he was, that didn't stop him from being crazy about Brad—damnedest thing. Sometimes I used to think he loved him more than Royce. You ever read that book, *Rich Dad, Poor Dad?*"

Talba shook her head. "Is it a novel?"

"No, it's about a kid whose best friend's father kind of took him under his wing and taught him things. Daddy Buddy was like that with Brad, only he didn't teach him things about money, like the kid in the book. Brad was like a second son, that's all. The favorite son. Sometimes I think that's the root of Royce's problems."

"Problems."

"Oh, you know—his insecurity. You've noticed it, right?"

"This stuff is hot!" Talba interjected. "I think I'll have a beer after all. Sure you won't have one?"

"No, I—can you keep a secret?"

"I'm a P.I., remember? Secrets-R-Us." She hoped Suzanne wouldn't remember that she'd just spilled more secrets than the Champagnes knew they had. "What's on your mind?"

"Well—there's a reason I'm not drinking. Think about it."

Talba remembered how Suzanne was hungry all the time, and

seemed to sleep a lot. And all of a sudden something fell into place. "You're pregnant, aren't you?"

Suzanne giggled. "Maybe just a little bit."

"Hey, congratulations."

"Keep it quiet, though—I don't think this is exactly the time to tell Royce."

"Oh. Maybe not."

This was a weird development, but Talba couldn't see a reason in hell why it should stop her. "Well, that's a relief," she said. "I thought maybe Royce and Brad were—you know . . . lovers or something."

Suzanne laughed. "Royce? Omigod, that's a major hoot! Royce! Royce is usually way too drunk to be interested."

"But—uh . . ." Talba was confused about the pregnancy, but it seemed indelicate to mention it.

"Well, usually he is," Suzanne said. "We did it on Lucy's birthday a couple of months ago." She patted her stomach. "No drinking at the party." She looked slightly bleak. "I still haven't decided whether to have an abortion or not—I've still got a few weeks to make up my mind."

"Oh. Why would you have an abortion?" It was way too personal a question, but Suzanne didn't seem to notice.

Suzanne put down her fork, making Talba think she was getting somewhere. It took a lot to kill this one's appetite. "The drinking, like I mentioned. Also, I was doing quite a bit of it myself till I found out I was pregnant—I worry about the baby, you know? Also—" She stopped and stared at the food as if trying to figure out what it was. "There's another reason I know Royce isn't gay. Or anyway, isn't involved with Brad."

"Yes?"

"He—uh—gets tired of people fast. Believe me, if they'd been lovers, Brad would be history."

"You mean he fools around."

"Yeah. He fools around. Would you want to bring a kid into that?"

Talba suddenly felt sorry for her.

Eddie, tell me something—you're a guy." Ms. Wallis had just regaled him with her latest adventures. "How likely is it that a macho straight guy would be best friends with a gay guy?"

Sometimes she could be so naïve, she floored him. He shrugged, getting ready to educate her. "Could happen, Ms. Wallis. Anything could happen. Been in this business long as I have, ya seen everything." He paused. "Specially if the straight guy didn't feel threatened."

"That's what I mean. Royce seems like the type who would feel threatened."

"Maybe Brad's got a boyfriend—ever think of that?"

"Let me get my notes." She stood up and left the room. But she was back in half a minute, staring at a printout. "He lives alone. At least, there's no one else at his address."

That was worth another shrug. "What, ya staked out his place? He pays the rent, the other guy might not be in that database ya patronize."

"Boy toy–type thing?" She chewed on her lip. "Could be."

Royce's sex life interested Eddie not nearly so much as a salient point she seemed to have missed—and he did love to catch her missing something. "Know what's bothering me—how come nobody heard the shot?"

She thought about it. "Well, maybe somebody did. But I think I see what you're getting at—it would be odd, if they hadn't. Better canvass the neighbors, huh?"

"I would."

She nodded and stood again. "Got you. Will do."

One thing about her, she was up for anything.

Talba figured she could ask Adele whether Brad had a boyfriend, but that could wait. She hated to admit it, but Eddie was right about the shot. She hadn't even asked Ben Izaguirre about it.

She phoned him first. Nope, he hadn't heard anything. But he'd been at the restaurant. His wife, who was home, hadn't heard a shot.

So that meant another trip back to Venetian Isles. She tried Izaguirre's next-door neighbors on the marina side first. They'd been out that night, but maybe their babysitter had heard something. Mrs. Stern, a white woman in shorts and a halter top despite the cool weather, invited her in and called the girl. Nope, she hadn't, either. Stern suggested trying the Dobrescus next, across the street—Mrs. Dobrescu had an elderly mother who didn't miss a lot. "Can she hear?" Talba asked.

"If she was a cat, she could hear a mouse squeak at fifty paces."

But old Mrs. Matocha hadn't heard a peep—but then she'd been watching *The Wild Bunch* on television, which had involved a whole lot of shots.

And so it went, up and down the street, and the next one, and even the next one. No shots heard, just one teenaged girl who said she thought she might have heard one, though at the time she'd thought a raccoon had simply overturned a garbage can. There'd been some kind of strange noise, anyhow.

The best thing she got was a man who'd taken his dog out shortly after midnight, and he was adamant that he'd heard nothing and would have if there'd been anything to hear. But Talba didn't think the coroner could fix the time of death within the half-hour period he'd have been out. She'd have to ask.

If the judge had been shot at the marina, someone had to have heard it. So you had to wonder if he'd really been shot there.

Yet he'd called Wesley Burrell and announced he'd be there soon. What to make of that? It was a distinctly unsatisfying exercise.

But one good thing—about halfway through it, Jane Storey called and asked her if they could meet for a drink. She had big news.

And Talba could really use a drink.

They met at the Loa Bar at the International House, a pretty fancy watering hole for Talba's taste, but Jane had a date there later. She seemed to have a pretty active social life these days.

Indeed, the reporter seemed to have taken more care with her appearance than usual. Her highlighted hair was piled on her head and she had on a crisp white blouse with silky black pants.

"Hey, you look great. What's going on behind my back?"

"You're the detective."

"At first glance, I'd say true love."

"Try a second glance."

Talba thought a minute. "Okay, you're not wearing a slinky dress, and you're having a drink, not dinner. So, first date, maybe. And you had a date the other night that obviously wasn't a first date. So more than one guy. Lots of dates. Elementary, my dear—Match.com."

"Actually, no. But you're close."

"Okay, okay. I got the idea right but not the right service. What kind of guy would you want to meet? Someone smart, that goes without saying. And creative. So, a specialized service."

Jane was laughing. "One for writers. Writeyourheartout.com."

"Damn, I'm good."

"Uh-uh. It is elementary. If you're not Internet dating, you're not cool."

"And I'll bet it's really easy to get dates—because every writer on it's doing a story about it. You work for the *T-P*, your date probably works for *Gambit*—or one of the TV stations. Better be careful—you might be about to find out what it's like to be a source."

The reporter blushed. "Omigod, I never thought about that!"

"You *are* doing a story."

"I'm a reporter, right? Of course I am. It's a great assignment— what the old guys call a four-bagger."

"A baseball term, I presume—so what's a home run?"

"You get fed, get drunk, get laid, and then boot the story."

"Boot the story? You mean you're not going to write it?"

Jane sighed. "Well, I was until you mentioned that counter-espionage thing." She sipped her cosmopolitan. "Gives one pause. Maybe I ought to quit while I'm ahead."

"Oh, go through with this one anyhow. Might turn out to be true love."

"Yeah, and it might turn out to be George Clooney." She tried look-ing world-weary, but it didn't fly on her girl-next-door face. "What are you drinking?"

Talba looked around at the sleek surroundings. "Campari and soda."

"What? Not Chardonnay?"

"Doesn't go with the décor."

"Cool place, huh?"

"Damn near cold. But I like it, I like it. What's this really big news you've got?" The bartender brought her drink.

Jane said, "Did you know about the lawsuit over one of Warren La-Garde's hotels?"

"Before Buddy, you mean. Old news, girlfriend. Two suits, by the way."

Jane leaned back and widened her eyes, showing a lot of sparkly eye shadow. "Okay, I take it back. You are good."

Talba shrugged. "With Buddy's record, it figures, right? I knew it had to be there and I found it."

"But this is big. How can you be so cavalier? It argues for some kind of merger. Or at the very least, a strategic alliance—between a huge corporation and a judge. Meaning Kristin and Buddy's ill-fated nuptials."

"You journalists talk like you write." Talba tasted her drink. "I forget how good these things are. But about Kristin and Buddy—I just don't see it that way. I was there when Buddy proposed, remember? And so was Daddy Warren. Believe me, he looked anything but pleased. Couldn't wait to get himself first a stiff drink and then out of there, all in the space of five minutes."

"Well, how would you expect him to feel? Buddy was *his* age. At least."

"Well, you should see Warren's wife. Still in training bras. But you can't have it both ways—either it was some kind of arrangement or it wasn't. Anyhow, the cases have already been settled. What's to be gained now?"

"The romance obviously didn't start now. Maybe it's some kind of payoff."

"What, the king offers the princess to his most faithful vassal? You're getting medieval with me."

"Okay, okay. But these people aren't like you and me. You've heard the LaGardes are connected, haven't you?"

"Mob? The LaGardes? No, I haven't heard that." Some things, alas, just couldn't be looked up on the Internet.

Jane nodded smugly. "Oh, yeah. And guess how they're connected? Through Kristin."

"You're losing me."

"Okay, listen. You know she was married before, right?"

"Right. To a Daniel Truelove."

"The son of Patrick Truelove and Victoria Mancuso Truelove, who happens to be the granddaughter of Joseph Mancuso. Surely you've heard of the Mancusos?"

185

Talba was flustered. "Oh, come on," she said. "Old Joseph's long dead."

"Nonetheless, he had three sons, who own half the bars in the French Quarter, and most of the video poker machines in the state. Victoria's on the board of every one of the operative corporations."

Talba was about to say something, but Jane held up a finger. "Wait. And, upon graduation from Loyola Law School, young Dan joined his dad's law firm, which represents the Mancusos."

"Oh." Talba tried to digest the news, annoyed that she hadn't thought to background Truelove. "So what do you think it means? He and Kristin are divorced."

"I'm working on it," Jane said. "Now get out of here. My date's due in ten minutes."

Talba grinned. "Happy hunting," she said, and left for her own date.

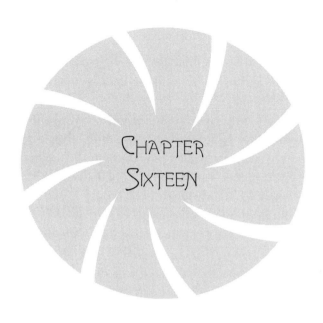

CHAPTER
SIXTEEN

The thing about the kitten was that Talba was going to rescue it whether Raisa existed or not. The kitten needed rescuing, and it was a cute little thing, and who'd notice one more at home? No problem with Miz Clara—she was already in love; Blanche and Koko were bound to be next, if worse came to worst. But she was 90 percent sure this thing with Raisa would work out, and if it did, the kid would be indebted to her forever.

Plus, she had an ace in the hole—she was seeing Darryl that night, and Raisa wouldn't be there. So, in the event Darryl had some major objection, it would be as if it had never happened.

And so, with all the confidence in the world, she wrestled the cat into a cardboard box, gathered up the feline supplies, and set off for the West Bank. Everything went swimmingly until Raisa answered the door.

Seemed her mother had had some kind of emergency. *Damn. Wish I'd known so I could have canceled*, was Talba's first thought, but the kid was unexpectedly friendly. "Hey, you gotta see the Mardi Gras stuff. Come on, let's look at it." And then: "Whatcha got in the box?"

"I brought you a present," she said, looking guiltily at Darryl. "A kitten," she mouthed at him, and he began shaking his head, turning, she could have sworn, slightly pale.

But by now it was way too late. Gumbo had begun to protest the box, both vocally and physically—the animal was scratching at the top and sides of the box, finally managing to get a paw through the top.

Raisa stood back in awe, unable to believe her good fortune. "Is it . . . what I think it is?" She looked anxiously at her father.

"I think it might be," he said, trying to recover.

"Careful," Talba said. "I rescued it. It's about half wild." She opened the box and without further ceremony, Raisa reached in and grabbed. Talba had a bad moment, terrified the animal would take the skin off the kid's arm. Instead, it relaxed into her hand, purring loudly.

"Oh, Daddy, look! A kitten! It's really a kitten! I thought you said I couldn't have one."

Darryl was gaining poise by the moment. "Do you think you're old enough to take care of it?"

"Yes!" And then, "I don't know—how old do you have to be?"

Gumbo struggled to get loose. Raisa let the kitten go, and immediately it began an extended inspection tour of the Boucree residence. It looked adorable, poking its spotted nose into all the corners, making sure all the smells were kosher—no lions or goats in the vicinity. "We'll see," Darryl said. "We'll see." And then he sneezed.

"Uh-oh," Talba said, but Raisa didn't notice. Her attention was so thoroughly fixed on the kitten that Talba and Darryl were able to whisper unnoticed.

"I didn't know she was going to be here—I was just going to try it out on you."

"It might be okay—I'm only allergic to some cats."

"Omigod, I'm sorry!"

"Maybe it could live outside."

But Raisa heard that one, and had her own opinion: "No!"

Darryl busied himself making dinner, apparently not ready to deal with it. Meanwhile, Raisa asked for its provenance (though not exactly in those words) and Talba told the story of finding it starving at the marina and luring it home with shrimp. And its name—Gumbo.

Raisa asked, "Do I have to call it that?"

"No, you can name it anything you want."

"Gumbo!" she said. "I love that name." She was in heaven. Darryl was sniffling. She fixed up the cat box, and fed the little beast, and then took Talba and Gumbo into her room to see her Mardi Gras Indian tape. It was the first time Talba had ever been invited in.

By the time Darryl called them to dinner, they were a happy family unit for the first time ever—except that Darryl's eyes were getting redder and redder.

Raisa was alarmed. "Daddy, what's wrong? Are you crying?"

"Honey, I've got a little bad news."

"Is that why you're crying?"

"Sort of. Gumbo is making me cry. I'm allergic to him."

"Her," Talba said automatically. "All calicos are female." She hadn't bothered to mention this to Royce.

"Oh, Daddy, she's a girl cat!" Raisa's face was a montage of pleading and disappointment.

Darryl patted her. "Honey, we'll try to work with it. Could we put her in your room for now?"

Raisa did that, and Darryl got up to get an allergy pill, but even as they ate, Raisa chattering, uncharacteristically happy throughout the meal, his face continued to swell.

Having finally exhausted the subject of the wondrous thing that had come into her life, Raisa moved on. "Hey, Talba, have you seen the tape Lucy took at the Bacchus party?"

Darryl and Talba looked at each other, silently deciding to ignore the elephant in the room. "Haven't had a chance yet," Talba said.

"Is it okay for me to have a white friend, Daddy? I really like Lucy. Could I see her again?"

"Sure you can have a white friend, if Lucy's willing. But that's kind of up to Lucy right now."

"Good. I already know she likes me. She called me her precious little angel. Can't we call her, Daddy? Talba, you could call her."

Again, the exchange of glances. Finally, Talba said, "Honey, Lucy's kind of going through a hard time right now. Something bad happened to her daddy."

"Her daddy? What happened to her daddy?" Raisa looked anxiously at Darryl, as if she'd never considered that anything bad could

189

ever happen to a daddy, even though something bad was happening to hers right now.

Suddenly Darryl made a decision. Before Talba could speak, he said, "Sweetie pie, let's not talk about it right now." And Talba doubted the girls would ever get together again. Darryl would probably do anything to protect his daughter from learning about the death of a daddy.

"But, Daddy, I want to know."

On the other hand, he'd also do anything to keep her from going into a full-on pout. "When you're old enough, baby doll. How was school today?"

Lame, Talba thought. No kid was going to fall for that.

But Raisa bit—for once, something unusual had happened. "Kyra's taking ballet lessons. Do you know what ballet is?"

"I think I've heard of it—something to do with dancing?"

"Yeah, it is. They wear these really cute skirts and stuff—she showed me pictures of her recedure."

Both adults took a moment to ponder. "Recital?" Talba ventured.

"Yeah! Recital. Hey, Daddy, can I take ballet lessons? I really want to. Can I do it, Daddy?"

Oh, God, just say yes, Talba thought. *This kid's never in her life wanted to do anything but watch television and torture adults—and not in that order.*

"You really want to, huh?"

"Yeah! I really want to!"

"Well, what are you going to do for me if I say yes?"

"I don't have to do anything for you." The pout was starting.

"Yes you do. You have to eat your soup."

"Hate soup!"

"No soup, no ballet."

And Raisa knew she had won. Talba felt she had, too—she barely recognized this child. Was it possible that so simple a thing as a day with a camcorder had begun to pry open her world? But things happened that way. She could recall learning to read as if it were yesterday—how for the first time she understood that she could make sense out of all those squiggles by herself, without adult assistance.

And the time a poet had come to talk to her sixth-grade class, and it was a black female poet. She had had no interest in poetry up till that

190

moment. But here was a woman who was her color and she could make words sing as if they were birds. And more, she'd taken an interest in Talba—in some stupid classroom poem she'd written. That woman had changed Talba's life forever. Come to think of it, her first-grade teacher had also taken a shine to her, given her special attention. Maybe Lucy could play that role in Raisa's life—or maybe she already had. Maybe the kid was destined to be a great cinematographer just because an older girl—a teenager, however geeky—had called her a precious angel and showed her how to work a camera.

Or maybe miracles didn't happen.

They were clearing up the dishes when her cell phone rang. Normally, she would have ignored it, but things were hot enough at the moment that she checked her caller ID. None other than Warren LaGarde was on the line.

She clicked him into her life.

"Miss Wallis? We haven't met, but I'm Kristin LaGarde's father. I wonder if you'd have lunch with me tomorrow. I have some things to talk to you about."

Talba asked no questions. This was definitely a man she wanted to meet. "Sure. I'd be happy to."

"Good. The Rembrandt Hotel at noon. Have the desk call me." He rang off without waiting for an answer.

As she hung up, she saw that she'd just missed a call from someone else. *Speak of the devil,* she thought. There was a voice mail from Lucy: "Talba, I wrote a poem I want to show you. Could you come over tomorrow?"

Every kid, she thought, wanted an older friend: Raisa wanted Lucy, Lucy wanted Talba. Well, that was fine with Talba—in fact, it was the least she could do. She wondered if she'd be working off her guilt about the Champagnes for the rest of her life.

Later, when Raisa was in bed, she told Darryl about the two calls. "Pursue that Lucy thing," he said. "I smell a great little babysitter here."

"Think you can keep Raisa from finding out about Buddy forever?"

"Damn, that was close! Wonder why she didn't pursue it? You know how she can be."

"She's changed, Darryl. Has Kimmie been giving her Nice Pills or what?"

"Don't get too excited. When I put her to bed, she asked if we could ever have a night without you."

"That's my girl. But you know what? She might really be turning a corner."

"Oh, sure. And it just snowed in the Amazon. What's new in the case?"

"Well, I finally know what happened that night—or what I think did. Buddy apparently called the night watchman and said he could go home because Buddy had to meet someone at the marina."

"So all you have to do is find out who it was."

"Can't be bothered. I'm too busy having lunch with hotel tycoons. Did you know the LaGardes have mob ties, by the way?"

"With what mob? There isn't one in New Orleans."

"Right. The Baptists run the video poker racket." And she switched back to the subject on both their minds. "Look, I'm really sorry about the cat. I had no idea Raisa was going to be here."

"It's okay. The worst that can happen is she'll get her heart broken."

Walking into the Rembrandt Hotel, Talba was struck by how similar it was to the International House, where she'd been the night before. But whereas the latter was light and airy, done up in whites, this one went for a denlike effect, lapis with the occasional touch of black. Quite sophisticated, but it had about as much New Orleans charm as a toaster oven. Why not go to New York if you wanted that style? Practically feeling her way to the reception desk—on account of the dimness— she took in the sort of customer who frequented the place, and was surprised to see a lot of jeans, shorts, and T-shirts, as opposed to business suits. But the men who sported them had shaved heads and soul patches, very hip. Quite a few were Asian, with baseball caps. So it must be the kind of place that catered to the Hollywood and jet-set elite. She placed her order for the owner and snuck a look in a dark, sleek bar that probably filled up with little black dresses on the stroke of six.

LaGarde tapped her on the shoulder. "Miss Wallis, I presume."

Talba turned around. "Ah. I see Kristin described me." He was even handsomer than she remembered; very distinguished, in fact, with an aristocratic manner that was the exact antithesis of Buddy's redneck act. Taking him in, she had a revelation: *Jane's theory is completely backwards. Kristin might be in the family business, but she's rebelling like a teenager.*

LaGarde gave her a full-wattage smile. "She said you were a baroness."

"By night only. By day a humble P.I."

"Well, let's go eat Chef Andre's not-so-humble food."

He took her into the restaurant, where rich draperies and borders carried out the lapis theme, this time with touches of gold instead of black. Gorgeous abstract paintings hung on the walls, which were blessedly white, along with the tablecloths.

"I'd recommend the mushrooms with goat cheese as a starter, followed by the salmon."

But Talba spied a fancy stir-fry on the menu and ordered that instead, preceded by a salad. "The baroness eats her veggies," she explained.

LaGarde, seeming slightly put out, went with his own suggestions, and offered wine, which she declined, feeling that if ever sobriety was needed, it was now. She noticed that her host passed as well. This was definitely a business lunch.

It began with LaGarde quizzing her so hard on her life history that she finally said, "I should have backgrounded myself and brought a dossier."

He laughed. "Sorry. I'm just naturally curious, I guess. Interested in how people got where they are."

"My mama wonders about that, too. She thought she was grooming me to be the first African-American female president. Failing that, either Speaker of the House or a doctor. My brother did manage that one. Corey Wallis—maybe you met him at the Bacchus party."

"I did meet a black doctor. One with a beautiful wife—one of the Tircuits, I believe."

Talba made an inadvertent face. "That'd be Michelle. My sister-in-law." The Tircuits were a big name in New Orleans.

"You don't like her?"

"No, I do. But she's one of those women who gets her nails done a lot. I'm more the ambitious type—though not according to the aforementioned mama. She doesn't care much for the humble part of the

193

profile." Talba was getting tired of talking about herself. She said, "Kristin seems the ambitious type herself."

"That she is," LaGarde said. He quirked an eyebrow. "Could be an understatement."

They were starting on their main course. Talba deemed it time to get down to business. "May I ask you something rude?"

He laughed again, and wiped his mouth, replacing his napkin meticulously. Mr. Charm. "How rude?" he asked.

"I was wondering what you thought of your prospective son-in-law."

"You mean did I dislike him enough to kill him?" He was still being Mr. Charm, but the question was serious.

She feigned shock. "Mr. LaGarde! I'm not *that* rude."

"Why don't you call me Warren? Shall I call you Talba?"

"I prefer Your Grace." She meant to be playful and hoped it came out that way.

But he said, "Don't we take ourselves seriously," which threw her off her stride.

"Sorry." She was flustered. "Call me Talba. The baroness thing's just, uh . . ."

"It's fine. Your Grace is good." He smiled again, almost flirting. She was getting the impression he liked to keep people off balance.

"Well?" she said. "You're avoiding the question."

"Listen, nobody wants their daughter to marry an old crook. But it's the sort of thing Kristin would do."

There were two good hooks there. Talba could barely decide which one to go with. Finally, she decided to take them in order. "Ah. So you knew he was an old crook."

"There was gossip."

"Had Kristin heard it? She doesn't seem the naïve type to me. But on the other hand, she genuinely seemed to love him."

The waiter had cleared the plates and asked if they wanted coffee. La-Garde used the moment to put his napkin on the table. Decisively; making a statement. "Your Grace, nothing about my daughter is genuine."

"I beg your pardon?" This was definitely not what she was expecting.

"I think you're in a bit over your head."

Talba kept silent.

"It pains me to say this. I do hope you realize I wouldn't do it if there were any other way." He stopped, and again she held her tongue. "My daughter's manipulating you, Talba."

So much for honorifics. "Manipulating me." She thought about it. "She's paying me to do a job. What more do you think she wants?"

"I wish I knew, Talba. I really wish I knew."

She sat still, trying to wrap her mind around this one, but all she could think was how much she hated people who used your name in every sentence. "Why," she ventured, "do you think she's manipulating me, then?"

"Because that's what she does. She's never had a straightforward thought in her life." He was quiet himself for a moment, letting her absorb it. "I'm sorry to say it, but my daughter's psychotic."

"Psychotic. What kind of psychotic? Schizophrenic? Bipolar?"

"Sociopathic might cover it better. Even as a child, she was different. Never told the truth when a lie would do."

Talba wasn't impressed. "Kids lie."

"Using drugs in high school. Selling them in college. Stealing. More lying. My God, you should have seen what she put that poor husband of hers through."

Talba waited, but no more was forthcoming. "Well? What?"

"The gamut." He stopped to sip coffee. "Other men. Spending all his money. Mind games."

"Let's go right to mind games."

"She'd pretend to be obsessively jealous—cut up all his clothes; call him at the office and accuse him of having affairs."

Talba wondered how he could possibly know. "When Kristin was the one who was having them," she said.

"In fact, she'd accuse him of anything she could think of, including dishonesty in business."

She wondered if she dared mention the supposed mob connection, but decided to pass. As for the other things, she couldn't identify anything any judgmental, old-school, extremely controlling parent might not say about his child. It might all be true, but none of it sounded psychotic. "Why," she asked, "are you in business with her, then? She's an officer of your company."

He laughed, but this wasn't the polite laugh of before; it was more like an astonished guffaw. "I'm not in business with her. You can be vice president of a company and do practically nothing. However, Kristin stays perfectly busy. She's in charge of acquisitions, which means she looks at property we might want to buy. Spends the day making Realtors' lives miserable, then makes reports. And sure enough, sometimes we take her suggestions—certainly when it comes to décor, a field in which she excels. I never said she was stupid or talentless; merely crazy. But she has no real responsibility. Certainly no access to our accounts."

"Or she'd steal from her own father."

"You never know what she'd do. She's unpredictable. And dangerous."

"Okay then. I'm going to ask you the million-dollar question. You don't even know me—why are you telling me all this?"

"Listen to me, little girl. I'd be best pals with the maitre d' here even if I didn't own this hotel. Do you have any idea how many of these little talks I've had to have with people she's gotten involved with?"

In that case, Talba wondered, *why didn't Kristin move out of town?* She had a better question. "Was Buddy one of them?"

"Buddy?" He snorted. "My first take was, he deserved her. But there was a child involved." He thought about it. "Eventually I might have had to do it. Even with Buddy."

Talba remembered how patient and loving Kristin had been with Lucy. She was one of the few adults the girl seemed to approve of.

"You still haven't answered my question—why are you telling me all this?"

"I don't want to see you get hurt, that's all."

That struck a chord. He had said his daughter was dangerous. "It sounds oddly as if you're talking about physical peril."

"Peril. Good word." He fiddled with the tiny doily under his cup, buying time. "Anything's possible, Your Grace. Anything at all."

The light was beginning to dawn. "You think *she* killed Buddy."

"I don't know. I just don't know. And I don't want to know. I'm prepared to pay you to stop your investigation."

"Bribe me, you mean."

"Not at all. I'm trying to protect you."

"Look, if she's dangerous, why not just go to the police?"

For the first time he actually looked sad. As if having such a daughter weighed on him. "She's my daughter, Talba. I'm trying to protect her, too."

There were lots of things Talba could have said to that, but she decided not to go there.

He was dead serious now, no longer Mr. Charm. In fact, he was doing a fair impersonation of a distraught father. "Look, Your Grace. Nothing good can come of this. Only harm."

Talba was torn between insult and pity—there was at least an outside chance he was sincere. She was trying to think of something semipolite to say, when LaGarde started in again. "You and I both know Buddy was a small-time crook. Accepting hams to set bail, for Christ's sake! How the hell are you going to sink any lower than that? He was a lecherous old skirt-chaser who couldn't leave the young stuff alone. You read the paper. Hell, you were there in the house—you're the one who fed that reporter the information, weren't you? You know what, I've always wondered what your motivation for that was, but I'll forget about that for now. Champagne deserved to die and if anyone knows it, you know it. Can't you just goddam well leave it alone?" He hadn't raised his voice. It was his own restaurant, after all. But he'd spoken in a low growl that was even more frightening.

Talba struggled to keep her cool, but in the end she was just too damn mad. She fished for her purse and pulled out a credit card. "Let me take you to lunch. I'll put it on Kristin's bill."

"Hell, you're as goddam crooked as Buddy was."

She was signaling frantically for the waiter when suddenly someone did raise his voice. "Where the hell is that goddam bastard?"

She swiveled her head to see the maitre d'—a little dapper guy—struggling with a man twice his size, a man who didn't look at all as if he belonged. He was deeply tanned and dressed in scruffy jeans and a baseball cap. "I want to talk to goddam Warren LaGarde," he yelled.

LaGarde got up and strode over to him, walking tall, every inch the intimidating aristocrat. "Let him go, Russell," he told the maitre d', who didn't actually have him at all. He spoke to the intruder. "What can I do for you, sir?"

The restaurant had gone silent. Talba could hear every word without even straining. "Mr. Royce said to come talk to you. You know who I'm talkin' about?"

197

"Let's go to my office, shall we? I'd be delighted to talk with you." The guy was smooth, Talba had to give him that. The big guy was now more or less shuffling.

She would have paid the bill and left, but the waiter declined to bring her one. She settled simply for leaving.

By the time she got out to the lobby, LaGarde and the man were getting into the elevator.

She stepped into the sun, shaking. It had been one of the most unnerving lunches of her life. The thing was, the man with the cap seemed familiar. She stood there a few moments, free-associating, trying to put his face in context—and finally, she had it.

He was Bob, the shrimper who'd appeared at the marina in a flatboat the day she found the kitten, demanding money from Royce Champagne.

CHAPTER
SEVENTEEN

S he was dying to go back to the office to get Eddie's take on the seeming madness of Warren LaGarde—not to mention the meaning of Bob's visit—but duty called in the form of her guilty conscience. School was nearly out, and she didn't have time before her scheduled visit to Lucy.

She was a bit early, but fortunately her favorite bookstore, Garden District Books, was right across the street, so she took a few minutes to browse, thinking to pick up a book for the kid. She settled on one she figured no teenager could resist—especially a kid who'd just been orphaned.

Lucy herself answered the door, still in her school uniform, an unprecedented occurrence in her experience. "Hi. Adele's not home?"

"We got a new housekeeper. I think Mommo's upstairs showing her how to clean mirrors."

Talba hadn't shared her mother's mirror-cleaning theories with the Champagnes, but apparently they'd been noticed. She handed over her package. "Brought you a book."

Lucy took her to the sun room, offering iced tea without looking at the book. Talba accepted the drink and noticed that the house was looking a lot better. She was glad of that—the chaos had gotten her down the last time, and if it depressed her, she could imagine what it was doing to the family. She'd almost been tempted to offer to clean it one last time. But not quite.

It took a long time for Lucy to return, but when she did, she'd changed into torn jeans and a skimpy T-shirt in a startling chartreuse. She served the tea on a silver tray that also held a manila folder, and picked up her package. Staring at the book, she looked puzzled. *"Life of Pi?* It isn't about math, is it?"

Talba smiled. "Nope. It's not like any book you've ever read. You like animals, right?"

"Sure. You already know I'd kill for a pet. Not even a dog. Just one little kitty-cat."

"Well, check the cover art." It showed sixteen-year-old Pi in the lifeboat he shared with his friend and enemy, Richard Parker.

"Is that a *tiger?*"

"Uh-huh. Be careful what you wish for. See that kid? He spends nearly a year in that boat with his little kitty-cat there."

She turned up her nose. "Oh. A fantasy. I hate fantasy."

"No, it's not. It's so realistic it'll curl your hair. It's all about animals—and survival. You like metaphor, right? It's like one big prose poem about your life."

"My life, or anyone's life?"

Talba felt smug. "Read it and see if you identify with it."

The kid put down the book. "Whatever."

"So. How're you doing?"

Lucy didn't answer immediately. She stirred her tea a lot longer than she needed to. "Well. At first I was afraid no one at school would speak to me because they thought my dad was crooked. Now they're avoiding me because they don't know what to say. And they feel sorry for me." She spoke matter-of-factly, in that straightforward way children have of avoiding pain. Talba almost wished adults could do it. Lucy smiled. "I kind of think I'd rather be in a boat with a tiger."

"Baby, I'm sorry." Talba pointed to the book. "Just get in that boat with that tiger. You've heard of escapism? That's why God made books."

"The goddess."

"Oh, right. You're a pagan."

The girl's eyes widened. "How did you know that? I mean, I know you're one—you put witch stuff in your poem. That's one of the reasons I wanted to see you—because we have that in common."

Talba laughed. "I hate to disappoint you, but my mama says I'm a Baptist and I let her get away with it sometimes. But I know about pagans and I know you're one because nobody has secrets from the housekeeper." Instantly, she regretted the last part.

"Well, not from you, anyhow." Lucy's tone had turned sullen.

"If that's a secret, it stays right here." She tapped her chest.

"You sure? I mean, I'm not going to read a headline that says, DEAD JUDGE'S DAUGHTER CAUGHT IN SATANIC RITES?"

"Give me a little credit, okay? I didn't see anything Satanic in your room. Just nice girly witch stuff."

"Girly! Jesus!"

It seemed to Talba nothing she could say was right. "Look, I know how powerful magic is. I come from the ethnic group that brought you voodoo, remember?"

"Voudoun."

Talba decided to ignore that one. "But Wicca's warm and fuzzy, besides being powerful, right? Who's the goddess if not your mama?"

"You've got an answer for everything, don't you?"

"Uh-uh. I'm just smarter than most adults."

Finally, the kid cracked a smile. "Wouldn't take much."

"I was kidding, okay? No flies on your grandma."

"Naah. She's just kind of a bitch."

Even in her current kid-friendly mode, Talba knew she couldn't let that one go by. "She's a pretty nice lady, actually. And you know it."

"She's a racist!"

It was on Talba's lips to say, "And your dad wasn't?" but she let it go. Instead, she said, "She's just kind of old-fashioned. And aside from the goddess, she's the closest thing you've got to a mama."

"Lucky me."

Talba shrugged. "Hey, you could be on the open sea with a tiger."

"Sign me up."

It was moments like this that made Talba think Darryl was a hero. She'd be in a straitjacket if she had to teach high school. "So," she said. "The poem."

201

"Oh, forget about it. You'll probably just think it's stupid."

The kid was still in a lousy mood, but at least now they were on Talba's territory. She straightened her spine and began to lecture. "Let me tell you something you may not know. Writing is all about people thinking you're stupid—or being afraid they will. Nobody ever wrote a word and showed it to anyone else without breaking into a sweat. So don't think you've cornered the market on that one, kiddo."

"Don't call me kiddo." But she reached for the folder.

"Is 'kid' okay?"

"Kid's fine. Tougher."

"Read, kid."

"Huh? You want me to *read* it to you?"

"You've heard the term 'poetry reading'?"

"But that's, like, a performance. This is just you and me."

Talba was stern. "Read."

But to her surprise, her little ploy to boost the kid's ego backfired. Lucy's shoulders started to shake. She closed her eyes, presumably to hide tears. She shook her head violently.

Not knowing what else to do—the girl definitely wasn't a hugger—Talba put her hand on Lucy's shoulder, giving some contact, but not infantilizing (she hoped). "Steady, kid. Steady. Okay, you've got stage fright." It wasn't that, but she was trying to distract the girl from her grief. "Happens to the best of us. You go in the bathroom and throw up while I read your poem." *And cry your little eyes out, baby. In private, so it won't hurt your dignity.*

The poem was called "The Crow":

The Crow

A crow flew into my house
And spread its terrible wings
And shook its hideous tail
And spoke in its terrible voice
And insulted me.

That other bird said "Nevermore,"
But this one said "Neveragain."

Neveragain will you know a mother's gentle hand
Or a father's soothing words
Neveragain will the sun be gold and warm
Or the weather be inviting
Neveragain will you be a child.
Or be whole.
Or be the person you were.
Your wing is broken
And you cannot fly.
Neveragain will you spread your wings like mine

But henceforth you will be me.

And the crow grew as large as the room itself
And folded me in its wing
And I lay there in the dark
And I leaned into its harsh feathers
And all was dark
And all was black—

And the crow was wrong.

When I lie in its fearsome embrace,
Against its pulsing ribs,
A captive in a feathered womb,
Encased in darkness,
In impenetrable stillness,

I am me.

Talba was frankly appalled. Better, she thought, that Lucy had written it than dreamed it, but she had rarely read so terrifying a document of hopelessness. Her only positive thought was that thank God the girl was in therapy. She hardly knew what to say when Lucy came back, her eyes slightly pink, her ice cubes melting in her glass.

But Lucy wasn't about to let her off the hook. "Well?" she said. "Did you read it?"

"Sure I read it. Nice homage to Poe. Good use of imagery. Only thing is, I had to call up a shrink to keep from slitting my wrists."

Lucy smiled. Happily, almost. "Really? It got you?"

"Yeah. It picked me up in its beak and chewed me up."

"Hey, that's *good.* Can I put it in?"

"It's yours, kid. What does your therapist say about *this* baby?"

"Think I'd show it to that asshole? He's not exactly literate, you know. Just some hack they've hired to hold my hand."

"Well. Good thing you've got somebody to do that. Hey, Raisa misses you. Could you stand to babysit some time?"

"Babysit?" She seemed to be thinking it over. "Yeah, sure, I could babysit. But I'm writing a film and I thought maybe she could star in it."

"Really? I'll bet she'd be thrilled." This could only be good. As long as Lucy was writing, she couldn't be contemplating self-immolation.

"So, the poem, you know, it's about depression."

"I gathered," Talba said, trying to keep the irony out of her voice.

"You know, I just have to live with it for awhile. I have to give in to it and let it, like, embrace me, and then I might come out the other side."

" 'Hello darkness, my old friend,' " Talba said.

"Ooh, that's good. Can I have that too?"

"It's not mine. It's a line from an old song."

"Too bad. It would have really made me sound smart."

She was okay—or at least she was going to be. "Keep writing, kid," Talba said. "It's doing you a world of good."

She looked up as footsteps approached. Adele entered, in black pants and T-shirt. At least she didn't look like she was going to church. "Well, if it isn't our favorite P.I."

"Hello, Adele. How are you?"

"Getting along." Adele stood, pointedly declining to sit, and Talba wondered if this was some kind of hint.

"Hey, listen," Lucy said. "I've got this really cute tape of Raisa at the Bacchus party. Grandma, why don't you keep Talba company while I get it?"

"You've got homework, young lady. Be quick about it." Definitely a hint.

Lucy left, and still Adele didn't sit. "She's still having nightmares."

Talba squirmed. "I'm so sorry."

There being nothing else to say on that subject, Adele gave in to politeness and attempted to bridge the awkwardness that had settled upon them. "Well. How's the investigation going?"

"It's going great," Talba lied. "But I've got a question for you. Did you know Brad Leitner's gay?"

"You could hardly miss it. He and his partner were here the night of the Bacchus party. They're around all the time."

Her memory clicked back to Leitner at the party, talking to Adele and someone she didn't know. "The guy in cutoffs?"

Adele shrugged.

"What's the partner like?"

"Nice enough, I guess." She definitely wasn't in a talkative mood.

"May I ask his name?"

"Whatever for? Brad had nothing to do with this."

How do you know? Talba wondered, but she kept her peace, which was easy enough—Lucy had just returned with a copy of the tape.

Talba stood, and Adele relaxed almost visibly. But Talba wasn't finished. "Hey, kid—"

"Could we drop the kid routine? It's working my nerves."

"Hey, precious—"

Lucy made retching sounds.

"I was wondering   would you like to go to a poetry reading sometime?"

"Whatever."

That was too much for Adele. "Lucy, for heaven's sake!"

"Why, sure, Your Grace, I'd just love that." Talba couldn't tell whether she was being sarcastic or just pimping her grandmother.

"I thought maybe you'd like to read."

"Me? Uh-uh. No, I couldn't."

"Sure you could. Your poem's as good as anybody's and a lot better than most. Thanks for showing it to me."

"Really? You really think so?"

"I really do," Talba said. "Maybe I could find a reading just for kids."

"They have those?" Lucy's interest perked up. "Do boys go?"

"I don't know. Why?"

" 'Cause I'd be too self-conscious."

"You could handle it."

As she left, she heard Adele saying, "What's this about a poem, young lady?"

So," Ms. Wallis concluded, "should I tell the client about her father?"

Eddie considered. "Don't see what good it could do."

"You don't think I'm ethically obligated?"

"Hell, no, 'scuse my French. You were obligated to do just what ya did—refuse the money and blow him off. Ya not obligated to start a family feud—maybe get him murdered."

"If *she's* the dangerous one."

Eddie nodded. "Ya gotta wonder. Ya just gotta wonder."

"What I wonder is what that shrimper was doing there."

"Somethin's up, Ms. Wallis. There's a wrinkle here."

"Yeah. Here's another. Jane Storey says the LaGardes are connected."

"Not that I ever heard." And Eddie prided himself on hearing most things. Ms. Wallis trotted out Storey's story, which seemed worth checking out, and Eddie had another idea. "You could talk to Truelove. See if he confirms what LaGarde said. Maybe she did off ol' Buddy. But it don't seem likely to me. Ya don't commit murder and then hire a P.I. to prove ya did it."

"Good point, Eddie."

"But, just to be sure, why don't ya check out the mother as well—the former Mrs. Warren LaGarde? If anybody's likely to know which one of 'em's got a screw loose, it'd be her."

"Eddie, you're a genius."

"Naaah. I'm just smarter than you."

"Yep. You are. Swear to God you are."

Even when she gave him a compliment, she sounded arrogant. "I'm sure ya mean well," he said, to take her down a peg or two.

Talba got online and on the phone. She needed to find a kids' poetry reading for Lucy. But there didn't seem to be one. Lucy was just going to have to make her debut with the big guns, but that should be all right. The more she thought about it, the more she liked that crow thing. It wasn't all that subtle, but neither were most of the poems you heard in coffeehouses. Hers weren't, for that matter. She prided herself on telling a story in each one—verbal athletics made her tired.

Next, she tried to figure a way to background Bob the shrimper without a last name. She could ask Royce, but that might be tipping her hand. She decided to let it go and concentrate on Daniel Truelove and Kristin's mother, Greta. Her fine-honed investigative instincts detected a Swedish strain somewhere on the maternal side of the family. But she found nothing more about either than she already knew—yes, Truelove's mom was a Mancuso, and yes, Greta LaGarde still owned an antiques store in Covington.

She gave Truelove's firm a call to ascertain that he was in, with the thought of popping over immediately—why not? He was in the neighborhood.

But first Darryl called. "We can't keep the cat. I had a full-blown asthma attack after you left this morning."

"I didn't know you had asthma."

"Neither did I—I haven't had an attack since I was twelve."

"Oh, Darryl, I'm so sorry. Have you told Raisa?"

"I didn't have to—it was her idea. She doesn't want anything to happen to me, like Lucy's dad."

"Oh, God!"

"You're not kidding."

"I'll come get the kitten after work—and vacuum your house for you."

"Just get the damn critter. I'll vacuum myself."

" 'Critter'?" Talba said, but he'd already hung up.

She still had time for Plan A—dropping by Truelove's law firm, to which she gained access by the simple expedient of dropping the La-Garde name, and where she was invited to cool her heels for twenty minutes before the lawyer came out of his lair.

207

Truelove was tall and thin. He had black hair, as a Mancuso might be expected to, but his features were much finer than she'd imagined, and his eyes were green. Even Talba could see the man was gorgeous, and she didn't go in much for white guys. His accent was Deep South, his manners elegant, and yet he had a natural, down-home quality that must render the lady jurists and jurors helpless.

He seemed to be trying to puzzle out what she was doing there, which was fine with her—it was a pretty awkward subject. "You're a P.I. and you work for the LaGardes," he said, giving her an opening.

"Well, not exactly. I've been hired by your ex-wife on a matter that doesn't involve you at all—"

"I should certainly hope not."

"—and her father suggested I talk to you."

"Oh. Warren. Up to his old tricks." He sighed, maybe with relief.

"I beg your pardon?"

Truelove sighed again. "He doesn't seem to have accepted the fact that Kristin's a grown woman. Tries to control every aspect of her life."

"Hard on a marriage," Talba said.

"Hard on a bachelor," he said. "I don't think Kristin and I ever had any idea how we happened to end up married. At least I didn't. Warren engineered it—at any rate, it seems that way in retrospect." His mouth twisted in a bitter little smile. "And we've both been paying for it ever since. Make no mistake, Miss Wallis—he's a very dangerous man. Frankly, I wouldn't believe a word he says. Kristin was very young when we got married—did you know that?"

"She's still young."

"That man more or less turned her out—and I was too stupid to see what was happening."

Talba was fascinated, but more or less in the dark. "What—um—exactly *was* happening?"

"It was simple. Or it seems simple now. Our family owned some land that he wanted. He made a big point of throwing Kristin and me together. You've seen her—she's beautiful. She's incredibly beautiful."

Talba could have done without the adverb, but she nodded anyhow.

"Well . . . men are stupid. Meaning me. He sicced her on me and I was helpless. She was young and sweet and innocent and incredibly beautiful and smart and she was all over me."

Talba remembered what she'd said so scornfully to Jane—*You're getting medieval with me.* Truelove was, too. If she understood correctly, he was telling almost the same story Jane had made up about Buddy and LaGarde, with a twist—a feudal king trading his daughter not to his most faithful vassal, but to a prince, in exchange for part of his family's kingdom.

"LaGarde got the land, I gather," she said.

"Of course he got the land—we were more or less partners at that point. Our two families were, I mean. Swear to God, he'd have done anything to get it. If my father weren't alive, he'd probably have seduced my mother. Maybe he did—I wouldn't put it past him. Mom pushed the thing as hard as Warren did—but maybe for her own reasons."

What the man's supposed mob connection had to do with this, Talba couldn't see—Truelove sounded like a very disillusioned man. "And my family didn't give it up cheap—but that's another story." Maybe that was the mob part of the deal. "Leave it at this—they needed the money, and they got certain other concessions from La-Garde. Look, I don't do business with my family—you may have heard things about them. Kristin and I were both pawns." He looked away. "God, I wish I had it to do all over again!"

Suddenly he seemed to come out of a trance. "I'm sorry." She noticed that he was blushing slightly. "My friends tell me I should be in therapy—I can't seem to stop telling the story. What was it you said you were here about?"

"Your ex-wife hired me to investigate her fiancé's death."

"Buddy Champagne. I thought it was a suicide."

"The police think not. I came to you because Warren LaGarde sent me."

"But—what would I know about Buddy Champagne?" His puzzlement seemed real.

She decided on a smallish lie. "Mr. LaGarde sent me because he said I was in over my head—that his daughter was psychotic and you could verify it. Now you're telling me in so many words that he's the one who's dangerous. Frankly, I'm wondering what else you can tell me about him. Like why you think that."

He steepled his hands. "Warren LaGarde is a major piece of work.

All I can tell you is that he was willing to throw his daughter at me because he wanted something—so maybe he wanted something from a prominent judge as well. But that doesn't help you, does it? That wouldn't be a reason to kill said judge."

She backtracked—there was more than one way to get at this. "Well, tell me. *Am* I in over my head? LaGarde said Kristin put you through the wringer—that she's a chronic liar and therefore must be manipulating me."

He raised an eyebrow. "Does that strike you as a little self-serving?"

"A little."

"Look, maybe she did put me through a wringer, but I was probably just as toxic for her as she was for me. She was just a kid when we met—didn't know what she wanted, or who she was, or who I was. I put her through school, and then she dumped me. End of story."

"I don't mean to pry—"

He smiled. "Oh, yes, you do. That's your job."

Taking that as a license to pry, she said, "LaGarde said she had an affair along the way."

"*An* affair! She was a slut. But then so was I. We were just—fucked up, that's all."

Talba was so used to Eddie she half-expected Truelove to excuse his French. It was restful to meet a white man who could swear guiltlessly.

"But make no mistake about it, that is one hardheaded woman. And bright—whoo! She might have been young and dumb when we met—meaning no street smarts—but she's smart as hell. I couldn't believe it when she dumped me—I mean, no matter what, you can't just dump family . . . I thought."

Talba interrupted him, having sudden second thoughts. "Meaning you still consider her family? Still see her and talk to her?"

"Are you kidding?" he said. "That one I got over without a therapist. I never want to see the woman again. She may not be the devil, even if her father thinks so, but she's so selfish and manipulative"—his mind wandered off—"then again, guess who made her that way? I always wondered about Warren."

"About Warren?" Talba wondered if he was going where she thought he was going. "Meaning you think he has a sexual hold on her?"

He seemed relieved that she'd been the one to say it. "I just don't know. But I sure don't rule it out. It would explain why he tries to control her every move, wouldn't it?"

"Yes, but so would insanity. Which is what he's claiming for her. What do you think—crazy or not?"

"I think he's the quintessential overprotective parent and she's way too close to him. When she left, I told her—fool that I am—that her family would never get another penny from mine." He stopped to get Talba's reaction. "Yeah, yeah, I know how dumb that sounds—I'm over that kind of stuff. But listen, know what she said? She said, 'Fine. We don't need it.' Now tell me she isn't too tied up with Daddy."

"Well, in that case, let's take another tack. You really don't seem to think much of Warren. What if she finally did break away? What if he didn't actually want her to marry Buddy—would he kill to keep it from happening?"

So far, he'd impressed Talba as thoughtful and balanced. But on this one he didn't hesitate. He began to nod before she got the words out. "Definitely. She'll always be Daddy's Little Girl—so far as he's concerned. And he's a *ruthless* bastard."

This, Talba thought, *from a mob prince.*

He smiled. "Gonna get me an ugly woman next time." Like beauty made you mean.

But this was no time for a feminist lecture. "Make sure she's poor, too," Talba said. "Then you've got your bases covered."

211

CHAPTER EIGHTEEN

Eddie, you up for a drink?" Ms. Wallis had a bottle of wine with her, waving it around with a couple of glasses like some movie seducer.

He slid his spectacles down in a vain attempt to hide his eye bags, but it didn't work. "You're aubergine today," she pronounced.

"Hell, I don't even know that word."

" 'Scuse your French."

"I'm gonna need a drink, right? Is that what this is about?"

"Well, I do, anyhow. Had a pretty interesting afternoon."

"Ya got any bourbon?"

"No, but you do. In the back room." And she went to get it.

When she returned, she poured generously and told him yet another outrageous story. Hell, if he did half the things she said she did, he'd be out of business—and he figured there was plenty she didn't tell him. But she could make the infernal machine sing and that was what made life in the office worth living. That and her butterscotch voice. Damn beautiful voice the woman had.

It was the things she used it for that gave him pause. She'd just point blank asked Truelove if his ex-wife was crazy. Now if it was Eddie, he'd have had a drink with him, worked the subject around—the guy wouldn't even have known he was being interviewed. But somehow, she'd gotten away with it. "Interesting family," he said.

"Yeah, but the jury's still out on them. And furthermore I don't see where any of this is getting us. What I want to know is, what was that scene with LaGarde and Bob the shrimper all about?"

"There's somethin' funny about it. They've gotta pay the fisherman when he unloads the boat. I don't see how Buddy could have owed him money."

"Well, I could ask him, but I don't know how to find him."

"Thought that was ya specialty, Ms. Wallis."

"I'm kind of stuck. There's a Louisiana Shrimp Association, but from what I gather it's not exactly a trade union. And anyhow, the guy's name is Bob—pretty hard to figure out which Bob, even if he's a member and they've got a roster and they'd be willing to show it to me. I was thinking about a shortcut."

Eddie didn't like the sound of this. "Like what?"

"Well, I've got to ask somebody. I just can't think up a good lie. Thought you might be able to help."

"'Cause I'm so good at lying."

She shrugged. "Well, that's your story."

It was, actually. He didn't really have an answer for that. He thought about it. "Who'd know who the guy is?"

"Royce or Leitner, but they're still a little disturbed about my maid act. They're not going to cooperate."

"Okay, let's think. It goes like this, am I right? Buddy was the shrimpers' friend, but the shrimpers don't like LaGarde—or at least Bob doesn't. Wonder if Kristin hates her father as much as he hates her."

"Omigod. Eddie, that's it. You are a genius."

"Yeah, you mentioned that. What's your big idea?"

"You don't want to know."

It occurred to him that she was thoroughly and completely correct. "Ya right about that, Ms. Wallis. It's the last thing I want to know—ya goin' home or what?"

"Yeah. Or what. Good Night, Moon."

He kind of liked that. It reminded him of when he used to read to Angie.

"Hey," he said. "How'd the kid like the cat?"

"Let's put it this way. I'm still her least favorite person."

And she left to go get the damned cat, feeling somewhat mortified about the whole incident. As she was driving across the bridge, her cell phone rang. She checked her caller ID and saw that it was a call she had to take. "Hey, Luce, how're you doing?"

"Terrible." The girl was crying. "I hate my life. I wish I'd never been born."

Hoo boy, Talba thought.

"Something bad's wrong with Royce. Suzanne and Mommo took him to the hospital."

"You're alone there?"

"Yeah. He called Suzanne to come get him at the marina, and she yelled at him on the phone. God, why do people who hate each other get married?"

"He got hurt at the marina?"

"I guess so. And then Suzanne yelled at him!"

"What about?"

"I don't know. They're married, that's all—they're always fighting about something. She says Royce drinks too much and he says she's a lazy bitch. Mommo says they're both ungrateful and they ought to be glad to have a roof over their heads. I'm never getting married. I'm going to be a lesbian."

Glad for the distraction, Talba said, "You don't think women fight with each other?"

That stopped her, but only for a minute. "I'm going to be a hermit. Have you talked to Kristin? I hate Kristin."

"I thought she was the only adult you could stand—besides me, of course. And now you hate her?"

"She's deserted me. She never cared about me at all."

"Honey, she's had a lot on her mind."

"She's a phony bitch."

You should hear what her own father has to say about her, Talba thought, and said, "She has her own grief. You should give her a break."

"Oh, God, I just want to die."

"Well, don't die, Luce—I'd miss you. I'm on my way over, but I've got to go somewhere else first. I have to pick something up. Can you just sit tight for awhile?"

"I guess so."

"Good. Look, about Royce—did Suzanne bring him home?"

"No. Mommo went with her to the marina, and she called from there and said they were going to the hospital."

"And you don't know what's wrong?"

"God, I don't know anything! I'm all alone here." She began to cry again.

"I'll be there as soon as I can."

Talba rang off, having decided what she was going to do with the cat. She'd actually gotten the idea the minute Darryl's allergy became apparent—after all, Suzanne wasn't really allergic. She probably just needed the opportunity to work through her fears.

She found Darryl's house as sterile as a hospital. He'd already vacuumed and confined the innocent offender to the bathroom, and he was breathing as normally as she was. Talba bundled the kitty supplies into the car, boxed Gumbo up, and vacuumed the bathroom—it was the least she could do. And then, after a little rehashing, she left, forbearing to tell Darryl her plan—he'd probably just point out the foolishness of trying to take an animal where it wasn't welcome.

She wasn't up for that.

This poor cat needed a friend and so did Lucy. Even if they were only together for a few days, it had to help—if it didn't work out, the animal could come live with her and her mama and its wicked stepsisters, Koko and Blanche. If it did work, the kitten would be another bond between Lucy and Raisa. They'd have to see each other if they had a pet in common.

Nearing the Champagne palace, she got Lucy on the phone again. "You okay?"

"I'm better. Mommo called and said Royce is just banged up a little, and they'll bring him home as soon as they run some tests—but she said they'll be awhile."

"Good. Just what I want to hear. Have you read *Life of Pi* yet?"

The first response was a scream so piercing Talba had to put down the phone and rub her ear. It was followed up by a wall of words, some of them the same. "Oh. My. God. That is the best book I've ever read.

Oh. My. God!! I stayed up all night. I cried and cried when the ship went down. That poor zebra. Thank you sooo much."

"Was I right? Did you identify with it?"

"Yeah . . ." She hesitated. "Except for one thing—at least Pi had a friend. I *really* cried when he left."

"Hold on five minutes, okay? Then meet me at the back door."

"Why the back door?"

"Because I don't want anybody to know I'm there. And neither do you."

She had the supplies on the back porch by the time the girl got there. For once, the animal was blessedly quiet. Seeing the box, Lucy said, "What's that?"

"Richard Parker." The tiger in the book. "You take the litter and food, okay?"

"Richard Parker? There's a *cat* in there?"

"Litter box, cat food, cat," Talba said. "Brilliant, Holmes." And Gumbo said something, too—something more protesting than piteous, like *Let me out of here, you two-footed scum.*

At the angry little sound, Lucy's face took on an expression similar to the one Raisa had worn to watch the Bacchus Parade. And just as quickly, the childlike wonder was gone. Lucy was suddenly a character in a spy movie. Soundlessly, she picked up the equipment, kicked off her shoes, and padded upstairs, Talba behind her, cooing softly to the kitten.

They reached Lucy's room (which looked like Pi's ship after it went down), closed the door, and Talba said, "Christmas just came early. Go ahead—see what Santa Claus brought."

The kid approached the box as if it contained the crown jewels. Sensing freedom, the kitten began to vocalize. One white paw came up through the opening between the box flaps. "Oh. My. God." Lucy folded the flaps back and beheld her new pal. "Oh. My. God." She picked up the animal, which began to purr, and tears began to run down her face.

Talba was alarmed. "Don't tell me you're allergic."

"Allergic?" But she quickly lost interest in anything human. "Oh, you precious baby. You're so *little*." She held the kitten up and looked at it. "Oh. My. God. This is the prettiest kitten I've ever seen in my life. Is he really named Richard Parker?"

"No, that's just her description. She's actually a female. She was an orphan who hung around the marina—Royce called her Gumbo."

"She can be Rikki."

"Rikki it is."

"Did Royce know you were going to bring her?"

"No, but he told me something he didn't think was important. Guess what? Suzanne's not allergic to cats—she's afraid of them! And he didn't make it a secret or anything—if you get discovered, you can quote me." She chuckled. "*Then* you'll see some fighting. But why don't you shut Rikki in your room when you're away? That way she'll have time to adjust. And by the time they find her, she'll already be ensconced. Know something? Royce loved this little thing—he wanted to bring her home, but he couldn't because of Suzanne. I have a feeling he might be an ally."

"I can't believe you brought her to me." The change in the girl was nothing short of astonishing. Whereas before she'd looked as if she'd lost her last friend, now she was animated and . . . hopeful. Like any child who had a reason to live. Talba would have said "happy" if she hadn't known better.

"Well, it wasn't actually my first thought, but if any two creatures ever needed each other, it's you two." She told the tale of Raisa and Darryl and the asthma attack, while Rikki went on patrol, poking her mottled nose into every cranny and corner, exactly as she'd done at Darryl's house.

"Raisa can come see her whenever she wants."

If they let you keep her, Talba thought. "Listen, what's the new maid like? Maybe I could talk to her for you—see if she'll keep quiet."

"Oh, Mommo already fired her. Said she was worse than Alberta. So we don't have anybody right now."

"Uh-oh. Who cleans your room?"

Lucy laughed. "Are you kidding? Nobody in this house lifts a finger."

"Well, why don't you start keeping your room neat? Then nobody'll have to come in."

"Oh, Rikki's a bribe, is that it?" She was laughing.

"Kid, you can live in a hellhole for all I care." She looked around her. "In fact, you do. Just a thought, that's all."

Lucy surveyed her surroundings. "It *is* pretty bad. Maybe I could do a little something. That way when I change the litter, they won't know."

"Smuggling it in might be another matter, but I'll leave that to you. But, listen, if worse comes to worst give Rikki back to me—don't take her to the shelter, whatever you do."

"I'm keeping her." Somehow or other, she made her jaw look like Harrison Ford's. Talba wasn't about to argue with her.

"Good. By the way, I couldn't find a kids' poetry reading. So do you want to read Saturday night?"

"Saturday? That's day after tomorrow."

"Come on, kid—let's jump-start that career. There's a place called Reggie and Chaz that has readings all the time. I'll take you."

"It's not my career—I'm going to be a cinematographer."

"Well, this'll give you something to fall back on."

Not recognizing this as a stab at humor, Lucy didn't crack a smile. Instead, she made a big show of nonchalance. "Whatever." And then, "What should I wear?"

"Something that covers your midriff."

Lucy grumbled something about Talba sounding like Mommo and saw her out the back door.

Mission accomplished—Pi now had a pal on the lifeboat. Talba just hoped the kid didn't write some cute kitty poem for her debut.

After asking once more about Royce (there was no more news) she went home to call the client, her reasoning being this—if in fact the La-Garde bad blood was mutual, Kristin would happily put her in touch with someone who hated her father. She curled up with Koko and Blanche—who were singing loudly for their supper—and dialed, ignoring the two furry heads that kept trying to bonk her into action.

Kristin was all sweetness, her voice lilting over the line as if Talba were her oldest friend. "Hey, Talba. I was going to call you tomorrow, to see how you're getting along."

"You know who'd really appreciate a call? Lucy. The kid's going through a rough time."

"Oh, I know, I've just been so swamped. I'll call her after school tomorrow."

"I'm sure she'd appreciate it. Also, she might need your help. I just took her a kitten, and Suzanne claims to be allergic to cats—they're probably going to try to make her give it up."

"Oh, Suzanne. She's such a manipulator." That word again. "Sure. I'll put in a word with Adele. She loves me. So how about the investigation? Are you getting anywhere?"

"A few things are falling into place. But I'm puzzled about something. Does your dad have anything to do with the marina?"

Silence for a minute. Finally, "No. I'm sure of it. He hated Buddy."

"Oh, really."

"The day after we announced our engagement, he called me into his office and fired me. I said okay, I was going to marry the man I love."

"He fired you." That didn't jibe with what Talba had been told.

Kristin laughed, and her laugh was like mercury flowing. "Oh, he hired me back before the day was out. He needs me and he knows he needs me. But he did say he wasn't coming to the wedding."

Talba was getting a lot of information she hadn't bargained for. She said, "Can I ask you a delicate question?"

"Sure. You already know everything else about us."

"Do you suspect your father of killing Buddy? Is that what this is all about?"

"Oh, no. Omigod, absolutely not. When I say 'hate,' I mean he didn't think Buddy was the right man for me. Old enough to be my father, he said—can you believe that? Considering Tootsie-pop."

Talba assumed she meant her stepmother. "So you don't suspect your father?"

"Talba, he's my *daddy*."

"Okay, I just had to ask. Look, I have an off-the-wall question for you. I found out a guy who did business at the marina is mad at your father, and I'm wondering why."

"Well, that could be anybody. Lots of people don't like Daddy—he's kind of a difficult man."

"The guy's named Bob, and he's a shrimper. Do you have any idea who that is?"

But Kristin's mind had gone off on a tangent. "Wait a minute. I heard something about this. How do you know about it?"

"I hear things."

"Oh, no, you didn't hear it. It happened at lunch, I heard. You were

219

there. My father took you to lunch and gave you The Speech, right? I hope you had the sense to tell him to go to hell. He does that every time I get 'out of control,' as he likes to say. He doesn't like me trying to find out who killed Buddy."

"Why?"

"Says to let sleeping dogs lie. Why does that generation love clichés so much?"

"Well, I figured it was just some kind of family stuff. Don't worry about it. I didn't take it seriously." She tried again with her question. "But, listen, what was going on with this Bob guy?"

"I don't know. Is it important?"

"Let me put it this way. I'm thinking Buddy's death had something to do with the marina—and I saw this guy there. Can you find out his name?"

"Probably. Let me call you tomorrow. By the way, haven't you put in about twelve hours by now?"

"At least. Should I stop?"

Kristin didn't answer right away. Finally, she said, "Let's keep on it."

Talba hung up, feeling like the phone call alone was a day's work. She went to feed her own whiny cats.

And by morning, she had the shrimper's name—Kristin had left it on her voice mail at work. The guy was Bob Cheramie, and he lived near Lake St. Catherine, just up the road from Venetian Isles, the area where the Dorands lived. What, she wondered, was a shrimper's schedule like? (Assuming he came home at night, that is—she knew they often stayed out a few days at a time.) Well, she had to assume it. The old Benjamin Franklin, she surmised—early and early. And she'd missed the first early. Just in case, she made a pretext call to the Cheramie home, and ascertained that Mr. Cheramie, to quote his voice mail, was out. So it would have to be sometime between the first and the second earlys: just before dinnertime, perhaps.

This would be a perfect day, she decided, for a drive to Covington—to see if Kristin had two parents who hated her. Like Venetian Isles, Covington was a place Talba had never been to—though she'd heard plenty about it. It was in upscale St. Tammany Parish, across the lake, and there just wasn't much reason to go there if you were a young

African-American starving poet and computer jockey. Add "P.I." to the mix, and there might be, but so far it hadn't come up.

What she *had* done before was cross the causeway over Lake Pontchartrain, and she dreaded doing it again. Unlike the more familiar—and attractive—suspension bridge, with its sweeping views, this one was built on concrete pilings, and crossing it felt like driving an endless white road across an infinite stretch of nondescript water. In truth, it was only twenty-four miles long, but it felt like a hundred. It had to be the most boring bridge in the world. The "north shore," as St. Tammany Parish was known in New Orleans, was a popular white-flight area, and there were times when Talba simply couldn't understand white people. The idea might be to get away from crime and grime, but to her, no amount of safety and fresh air was worth twice-daily ordeals on that soul-destroying span.

On the other side, she encountered tree-lined highways and—yes!—relentless cleanliness. The malls seemed brand new, the grass freshly mowed, the cars scrubbed shiny. It was about seven miles from the end of the bridge to Covington, and the town itself was preceded by the usual stretch of Anywhere, U.S.A.—fast-food emporia, gas stations, supermarkets, Kinko's, Wal-Mart, and Office Depot.

She followed the signs for the Covington Central Business District, and immediately after crossing the Bogue Falaya River, found herself on a street boasting offshoots of the more local businesses you could find in New Orleans itself—but upscale ones only. Here was another Villa Vici (furniture), Mignon Faget (jewelry), and Ballin's (clothing), plus a couple of familiar restaurants, one of which was a branch of the world-revered Acme Oyster House. At least those with no need to commute didn't have to hit the causeway for food and spiffy supplies.

But the business district wasn't at all what she pictured. She'd been expecting a picturesque main drag lined with storefronts housing darling boutiques and adorable gift shops, of the sort you'd find in a tourist town. But Covington wasn't a tourist town. Its business seemed to be conducted largely out of several streets' worth of converted houses, mostly bungalows that seemed to her to date from the 1920s or so. Spanish moss hung from the trees, a phenomenon you didn't see on the other side of the lake. It was quite charming in a completely unself-conscious way.

Inside the bungalows, according to the signs, were lawyers' offices, health-food stores (three that she counted), coffeehouses, a cigar store, and a pub or two. She found Greta LaGarde's antiques shop in a cottage nestled between a store that sold musical instruments and one that housed a day-care center.

The store was a far cry from the dusty flea-market sort, and another whoop and holler from the elegance of Royal Street. It was actually more like a gift shop. There was a lot of good stuff for wedding gifts with price tags taped to them set out on beautifully restored tables. Huge bowls held decorative painted balls that had no reason for being except to fill empty bowls. Silver and brass candelabra, some with crystals hanging on them, held fancy beeswax candles that also could be had for a price. Festooned sconces and gold mirrors hung on the walls. It was almost painfully Tasteful. Talba itched to hang some Mardi Gras beads and strew some ethnic fabrics around to funk it up a little.

And its proprietor, if it was she, was a step up from the store itself. She looked as if she could preside with perfect poise over the snootiest emporium of elegance. In fact, she more or less personified elegance, and she was a step up from the current Mrs. LaGarde as well—in appearance, at any rate. She wore her age the way Diane Keaton did—as if she came from a distant planet where a beautiful older woman was as much prized as a beautiful older table.

Her thick silver hair cascaded in a lush bob, and her lavender sweater and midcalf black skirt perfectly complemented it. Small gold and diamond earrings that veered over the line from merely Tasteful to baroquely elegant glittered at her ears, though they showed only when she flicked her hair a certain way. She was every inch a Greta, and almost a baroness, though in a European kind of way.

"Mrs. LaGarde?" Talba asked, almost timidly.

"Yes? I'm Greta LaGarde." She looked at her visitor with curiosity but no disrespect, as if hardly anyone approaching her description ever entered the premises, yet was welcome anyhow, on the off chance she happened to have a pocketful of bucks.

Talba introduced herself. "I'm Talba Wallis, and I'm doing some work for your daughter. I'm a P.I., actually—she hired me to try to find out what happened to her fiancé."

"Really." It wasn't a question.

"I was wondering if you knew Buddy Champagne." Talba watched her face carefully, and was not disappointed. A telling little eleven formed between her brows—the gorgeous Greta evidently eschewed Botox along with vulgar hair color. There was anger there—though at whom it was directed Talba could only guess. "What *happened* to him?"

"He died, he didn't disappear—or am I missing something?"

"What happened the night he died, I mean."

"You mean who killed him? Don't we have police for that? Leave it to Kristin to think she can do a better job than they can."

"I've noticed she has her own opinions."

"Well, that's an understatement, one opinion being that her mother didn't need to meet her fiancé." LaGarde turned her back, straightening a candle that looked perfectly upright to Talba. "I'm afraid I never knew the man. I wasn't even at her engagement party."

"Oh. Well, I happened to be there, and I don't believe she knew it was meant to be an engagement party—Buddy kind of sneaked up on her."

"You were there?" She turned around and stabbed Talba with a thrust of blue eyes. "You must be . . . I thought you looked familiar."

"Guilty as charged. Yes, I'm the woman you may have seen on the news."

"I'm afraid I don't understand. Why would Kristin hire you, of all people?"

Talba tried out a weak little laugh, a nervous one. She should have seen this coming. "Good question. I'm a little confused about it myself. But I guarantee you she did—if you like, you can call her and confirm it." Talba held her breath—this was the one thing she didn't want Greta LaGarde to do.

"No, I believe you. It's the sort of thing Kristin would do. She always likes to make herself look good—it's her stock in trade."

Talba wasn't following. "I beg your pardon?"

"Look, if you're successful—and you've already shown yourself to be competent—then she gets the credit for solving Buddy's murder."

"Why would she want to do that? Couldn't it be simpler? Couldn't it just be that she wants to know the truth?'

LaGarde laughed. "Kristin? Nothing's ever simple with my daughter, Miss Wallis. You must know that by now."

The time had come, Talba thought, to let down her hair. "To tell you the truth, your ex-husband went so far as to warn me against her. I was wondering—it *is* kind of an odd situation—can you shed any light on it?"

"I'm sure Warren has his own agenda. He always does. What was it you wanted to see me about?" She was getting haughtier by the minute. And on her, haughty looked intimidating.

"Sometimes the tiniest piece of information can lead to something. I was just curious to know what you thought about the man your daughter was going to marry."

"I only know what she told me—after the fact. The fact of his death, I mean, not their engagement. I first heard they were engaged when Warren called me in a fury—after the damn engagement party."

"That must have hurt."

She didn't seem to know how to answer that one—didn't seem to have considered hurt. Finally, she said, "Yes. It did."

"I gather you aren't close."

At that, her eyes watered. "I'd like to be. The good Lord only knows I've always wanted that. My daughter pushes me away at every opportunity."

Bitterness here, Talba thought, and wondered if she could capitalize on it. "She seems to be close to her father."

Greta snorted, and it isn't pretty when a personage like Greta snorts. "If you can be close to a glacier."

"I gather he didn't approve of the match. I'm wondering . . ." Talba geared up for a lie. "Well, here's the real reason I wanted to talk to you. It's a little delicate, but I get the impression Kristin's worried that he may have killed Buddy to stop the marriage. Is that possible?"

Greta was back in possession of herself. "That Kristin would knowingly set her father up for exposure? Or that Warren would kill someone? No to the first. She'd take the information and find a way to use it to get what she wants from him."

"Which is?"

"I've never understood a single thing about my daughter—or my ex-husband for that matter."

"I see—and the second question?"

"Would Warren kill someone if it suited him? Certainly. That night he called, he ranted about what trash Buddy was. He said he couldn't see why the girl's mother—that was what he called me—'the girl's mother'—couldn't do anything to stop it. I said it was none of my business, and he said, 'Goddammit, I hope I'm not going to have to kill him.'"

Talba felt a need to double-check what she was hearing. "He threatened to kill Buddy?"

She sniffed. "If that's a threat, I guess he did. I know one thing. He's certainly capable of killing someone if that person's in his way. I'm not sure he hasn't."

Where to go with that one, Talba wondered. Was this too much information? "Uh . . . I'm at a bit of a loss. Are you saying you suspect him of killing someone else?"

Greta laughed, her laugh as bitter as her words. "Certainly not. You wanted to know who he is, and no one knows better than me. A man who'd leave his wife of twenty-five years and the mother of his child for some tacky little floozy—after everything those two put me through— would probably kill someone too. Wouldn't you say?"

Talba laughed too, but with a certain amount of humor. Greta had unwittingly said something funny, to Talba, anyway. "It would depend on what he'd put me through."

"Kristin. That was enough. I never wanted to have children, but Warren wanted a son."

This was a woman who was at least a couple of stitches short of a sweater. Maybe a whole row of stitches. "Toxic parents" was a term Talba had heard, but never really understood. She was getting the hang of it now. The question was, which parent was the more toxic?

For all she knew, Greta might have killed Buddy for no better reason than to derail Kristin's happiness. She was also beginning to see what Kristin saw in Buddy—with parents like these, he was a prince.

"By the way," she said, "what was it Kristin told you about Buddy after the fact?"

"She told me I'd have hated him. But she was wrong. Anybody who can handle that one is welcome to her."

CHAPTER NINETEEN

After that dose of cyanide, Talba felt disoriented. She stopped for gas in Mandeville and, seeing that she was on a lovely road lined with peaceful-looking pines, decided to continue for a bit, to have a drive in the country to see if she could shake Greta's ghost.

She passed a plethora of upscale subdivisions, some of them gated, but she never got the feeling of being crowded, or even particularly in the suburbs. It still felt like the country, and even more so once she came to the Tchefuncte River in Madisonville, whose banks were planted with wide swaths of grass. She stopped the car and sat on a concrete bench under an oak on the far bank, thinking to digest the experience while looking at water.

Kristin was coming into much clearer focus. Talba thought of the way Adele loved her, Lucy loved her—the way she worked so hard for their esteem, the way she was always volunteering to do things. She must be one of those pleasers who tap-danced for every audience she could muster because no matter how fast she'd moved her little legs as a kid, her parents saw only missteps. It would explain her extramarital affairs, too—probably no amount of approval was ever enough.

Poisonous as the interview had been, Talba was glad she'd had it. It was a somewhat unconventional way of backgrounding the client, but a lot more informative than surfing the Net (though she'd never admit it to Eddie).

But her bread and butter came from surfing and she went back to the office to put in a day of it—on other cases—to pass the time until she judged a shrimper might be home. Six-ish, maybe. She left the office at five, once more taking I-10 to Chef Menteur and cruising the Chef until she came to the picturesque community of Lake Catherine.

On the right side of the Chef, the Lake St. Catherine side, each street was a tree-lined lane that curved just enough that you couldn't see the end. She explored a little first, and decided she'd come too far when she came to a sign that said, UPTOWN LAKE CATHERINE. POPULATION A LITTLE MORE OR LESS THAN DOWNTOWN. She reversed direction and turned down Bob's street, which may have been downtown or uptown—it was difficult to tell in a settlement consisting of only a few small lanes, some jumbled up with old fishing shacks on canals, some boasting newly built Caribbean-style houses. At the end of Bob's street, she found a cul-de-sac with four houses in a row, Bob's being the first. Strangely, it had windows, but no door. Two cars were parked in the driveway, a good sign.

She parked and walked toward the front until she could see through a window. She was looking at a sort of watery garage, filled (in the garage part as opposed to the water part) with equipment and ropes, and populated by a number of cats and kittens climbing on a rope pile. If felines around here bred like this, no wonder Rikki had needed a home. Though only a dinghy occupied the berth, a chaland was moored a few feet further out. With a surprised (and somewhat delighted) chortle, she saw that the roof of the boat garage was actually the floor of the family's abode, though the structure was designed in such a way that you couldn't tell from the street. Talba had never seen anything like it. She made her way to the side of the house, where she found a few steps leading up to a door, upon which she knocked as boldly as if she hadn't just fetched up in a foreign country.

The door was opened by a teenage boy wearing a T-shirt and half-wearing the ubiquitous low-slung baggy jeans of his generation, the fashion statement that had once inspired a state lawmaker to introduce a legislative remedy that quickly became known as "the butt-crack law". Ridiculed by the media as a "cheeky but assinine" idea bound to make the state the "butt" of jokes throughout the nation, it never passed, though there were times when every adult in the state (however supportive of civil liberties) thought of it with longing. Talba did at the moment—the kid was fat and probably thought he dressed to make himself look thinner. It wasn't working.

He had a curious choir-boy haircut like the Beatles had worn some forty years earlier. It went poorly with the hip-hop pants, but beautifully framed a round cherubic suntanned face that probably concealed the mind of a master criminal. No one who looked that angelic could possibly have an honest bone in his body.

His face made Talba smile. "Hi. Your dad home?"

The kid looked suspicious. "You selling something?"

Talba reached in her backpack for the leather case containing her license and badge, which she flipped open, figuring the kid would appreciate the badge, even if Eddie didn't. "I'm a private investigator."

He wasn't impressed. "No, you're not. P.I.s can't have badges."

"You're misinformed, sir." Talba gave him a smile that she hoped was slightly mischievous, yet a little schoolteacherish as well. "We don't need no stinkin' badges, but we can *have* them if we want."

That did it. "Really? You can? How do you get to be a P.I.?" A kid was a kid.

"You take a course and pay some money—that's all there is to it. Of course, it helps to be brilliant and resourceful, but it's not a requirement."

He ignored the last part—kids never seemed to get her jokes. "Wow. They didn't cover that on career day at school."

"At my school either. Can I talk to your dad?"

"Depends."

Uh-huh. As evil as she'd figured. But she humored him. "Depends on what?"

"Lemme see your piece."

She was taken aback. "You mean my gun? I don't carry a gun. My weapon of choice is a T-ball bat—want to see that?"

"Don't mess with me, man."

A man's voice came from a few feet away. "Who's at the door, Donnie?"

The kid turned around and the man came into view. Bob Cheramie. "Mr. Cheramie," she said. "I wonder if I could—"

But he could see her now. "Hey! You're the chick I saw yesterday. With Warren LaGarde."

Behind Donnie, he opened the door a little wider. She could see that the room was a kitchen. The more you knew about the house, the stranger it got. Cheramie was holding a Budweiser.

"What the hell are you doin' here? Donnie, go on now." The kid cast an evil look at Talba and disappeared. "Any friend of that asshole's no friend of mine."

Talba laughed. "I'm no friend of LaGarde's. I'm investigating him." She showed her license.

He studied it carefully; not many people did that. "Well. You better come in then. Want a beer?"

"No thanks. Driving."

"Sit down. Sit down." He himself sat down at a yellow fifties-style table. Or perhaps it was the real thing—the house could easily have been fifty years old; maybe it and all its furnishings had been in the Cheramie family that long.

Talba made herself at home.

"Whassup?" Cheramie said unceremoniously.

"Someone's hired me to look into some things regarding Mr. LaGarde—and I might have a piece of information for you. How much do you know about LaGarde?"

"I know he's a cheatin' rat bastard. Ya got somethin' else?"

"I think so. Did you know his son-in-law's a Mancuso?"

It seemed to take him awhile to process it. "Mancuso. I shoulda known. It's in the goddam blood." Clearly, he was no geneticist, but Talba let it go. He sighed. "And Buddy Champagne was no saint, either. Goddam 'em both."

"Okay, let's trade," Talba said. "I want to know what kind of trouble he was giving you—might be something I can use."

"Against him, I hope."

Talba let an eyebrow go up a little. "Well, you never know."

"All right—don't see the harm in it. I had a deal to sell my shrimp to Judge Champagne. Simple enough, right?"

Talba nodded. No news there.

"So Buddy dies, I don't get paid. I go talk to Royce, and he says he's sorry, but some big deal Buddy had didn't come through. They dumped my shrimp right there in the canal, you believe that?"

"Easily. The way that place smelled."

"Man, I was mad. I haul off and hit Royce, I was so goddam mad— you ain' gon' report me, are you?"

Talba shook her head, thinking that at least the puzzle of Royce's injury was cleared up. "I'm not an officer of the court," she said. "Like a lawyer." (Though she really had no idea whether a lawyer would have to report a crime she'd only heard about.)

"Well, I hit him a few more times, tryin' to knock some information out of him. Ya understand? And sure enough, I pry some loose. He says Buddy's got a contract with LaGarde to buy shrimp for his restaurants, but LaGarde reneged on it. Flat out wouldn't buy the shrimp. So I say, well, goddammit, sue him! Get the money any way ya have to—why have I got to suffer for this? Wasn't only me, either. Come to find out, it was happening to the other boys as well."

He paused to guzzle beer. "Buddy Champagne, the shrimpers' friend. Oh, yeah. Ya see that boat out there? Thanks to Judge Buddy, it's being repossessed. You don't know what kinda problems we got, all those chinks dumpin' cheap shrimp on the market. Fact: They got ninety percent of the U.S. market. I ain't exaggeratin'—ninety percent! Aquaculture, baby, aquaculture—it's wipin' us out. Ten, fifteen years ago, shrimp was a luxury in this country. Fact: Wholesale prices for shrimp have dropped forty percent since the year 2000. Meanwhile, my operatin' costs are gettin' higher and higher—price of fuel, insurance— hah! Insurance, hell. Just about nobody can afford that no more. I'm behind on my credit cards, I'm behind on my electric bill, I owe every-body under the sun. Hell, I'd have already lost my house, my folks hadn't paid it off, rest their souls." He put the can down and got up in her face, his eyes like coals. "So I knock some more information outta the sumbitch—and he says he don't have nothin' on paper. Ya under-stand? Ya see where I'm goin' with this?"

Talba didn't. "I'm not sure," she said.

"It was somethin' illegal, see? LaGarde promised Buddy all his seafood business—and it's got to be considerable—and Buddy stakes the whole goddam business on this one order, but it don't come through.

LaGarde's buyin' that cheap foreign shrimp just like all the other scum-bags in this town. Nobody' cares that shrimpin's dyin' out in Louisiana—for the simple reason that the big guys don't give a shit about the little guys. Ya know what the goddam *New York Times* said? Now, don't get me wrong, I ain't one of those guys think any paper not published in Louisiana's automatically a commie rag. I got a lotta respect for the *New York Times*. But they had the gall to attack the shrimp tariffs in an editorial. Said it was unfair to goddam Vietnam and China! Said it was political, and what was even worse, complained that some of the money would go to the people who're hurtin'. That's *Americans* they're talkin' about. That's *me*. Assholes don't understand a goddam thing about people with families to feed."

Talba was actually fairly interested, not to mention sympathetic. But she felt a need to get the conversation back on course. "Where does the illegal part come in?" she asked.

"Buddy's a judge, see? Think about it."

Once he put it that way, Talba didn't have to think about it at all. It was incredibly obvious—so exactly like Buddy down to his toenails, she didn't see why she hadn't already seen it. She told him what she'd known since her records search. "LaGarde had a case before Buddy, and Buddy ruled in his favor."

"Two cases. It's a matter of record, ya know that? I went down and looked 'em up myself. Goddam matter of record. That's what I went to see goddam LaGarde about. I was so goddam hot under the collar I coulda killed him, too."

Talba smiled. "So how come he's still alive?"

Cheramie took another dose of medicine, wiped his mouth, sighed, and pointed with his chin to the back of the house. "Only thing stoppin' me's I got a kid to raise. His mama left us three years ago. I coulda got arrested for beatin' Royce up if anybody'd seen us, but nobody did, and I went right out after and got me an alibi. But a whole hotel full of people woulda known if I up and killed LaGarde." Hearing what he'd just said, he gave Talba a sly look. "Look, you know I don't mean that. I'm not a violent man. Figure of speech."

"I understand." *And really, really don't want to get on your bad side.*

"So anyway, I couldn't even beat him up, much less kill him And that I'd'a gladly done if it wouldn'ta been my ass."

"But you did talk to him—I saw the two of you get in the elevator. What'd he say?"

"Said Royce made the whole thing up. Said he never had no deal with Buddy." He guzzled again, and shook his head. "How ya like that, ya know? 'S why this country's in the shape it's in. Ain't even honor among thieves anymore."

Talba smiled, seeing the irony. "That's the lowest." She could feel his pain, all right. But the timing bothered her. "Tell me something— when was Buddy supposed to pay you?"

He repeated his routine—guzzle, wipe, lower can. "On delivery. And I made quite a few deliveries. Buddy's been owin' me for weeks, tell ya the truth."

"And you never confronted him before?"

"Ah, he always had some story."

"It isn't shrimp season, is it? So you had nowhere else to sell the shrimp."

"Now don't you get all righteous with me, Miss Private Investigator. Here I am, about to lose my boat, can't even stay out a coupla days 'cause I got a kid to take care of—what I'm gonna do? I gotta catch shrimp to make a livin'—I don't *know* nothin' else."

"I'm just surprised you put up with it, that's all."

"You know how Buddy was. He could charm the pants off a *picture* of a nun. Or maybe ya never met him."

"Oh, I met him. I met him all right." She winked. "But he wasn't my type, in case you're wondering. Did you know he was engaged to LaGarde's daughter?"

"He was *what?*"

Talba repeated what she'd just said. "But don't get too excited. I don't think the father and daughter get along."

"That is one fucked-up family."

"Two," Talba said. "So. You have any idea who killed Buddy?"

"I know it was a righteous dude, whoever he was. Huh! Shrimpers' friend. Tell me about it." He finished his beer, whereupon Talba thanked him for his help and left, wondering how Royce was.

She called Lucy to check and also to confirm their reading date. "Hey, Luce, it's me. How's Royce?"

"Omigod, he's got a broken rib. He looks like someone beat him up."

"Is that what happened?"

"He says he fell over something. But his face is all bruised up, and so's his whole chest and everything."

"Well, I'm sorry to hear it. How's the little princess?"

"She is sooo wonderful! And no one knows yet."

"Try and keep it that way. Pick you up tomorrow at seven—we'll have dinner first. Did you clear it with your grandmother?"

"Uh—I was wondering if *you* could."

Talba called Adele and argued her into it. Reading between the lines, her main reluctance, it seemed, was permitting her precious niece to spend an evening with a black person, but she couldn't say that, so it was fairly easy to break her—especially when Talba said Raisa would be along, too.

That one required a call to the club's owners. They said, sure it was a bar, but it was also a restaurant, and kids came all the time. So that part was okay. Next, the kid's dad.

That wasn't hard, either. Raisa was thrilled that the kitten had gone to live with Lucy, and Darryl, in turn, was so grateful that he readily agreed to the outing, although he grumbled a few things about Raisa needing her sleep.

The only glitch was thinking up a reason why Raisa couldn't see Gumbo—nobody wanted to mention that this was a case of adults conspiring against other adults. She and Darryl finally settled on a story about Lucy's brother being hurt and needing peace and quiet. But they forgot Raisa didn't yet know that Buddy was dead. "Oh," Raisa said. "And how's her daddy?"

Talba thought Darryl was going to stroke out. His distress was so evident, Raisa picked it up. "He died, didn't he? That's the bad thing that happened."

"Oh, honey!" Darryl gathered her close to him. "I'm sorry you have to know something like that."

"I'm just sorry for Lucy." She wriggled away and went to her room to think about it.

She didn't ask what had happened. But she did want to know what would happen to Kristin. "She's a strong woman," Darryl said. "It's hard, but she'll be all right." That part, at least, Talba felt okay about—no part of it could be considered a lie.

They took Raisa to the aquarium that day, which delighted her, and also gave Talba an idea for a poem, which she scribbled on the way home. She didn't plan to read—she was something of a celebrity at Reggie and Chaz and didn't want to upstage her protégé—but since she planned to introduce Lucy, she wore one of her performance outfits. It was a long lime-green skirt, matching scarf wound around her hair, and matching empire-style tunic with a black and white design on it, in quadrants—lime right boob, the left covered in black squiggles on lime, then a long lime drape on the left hip, and on the other, big white swirls on lime. The flowing sleeves were lime with deep cuffs of the black-squiggle pattern. Even Raisa was impressed. "You look . . . ," she struggled, ". . . really strange."

"I'll take that as a compliment."

"I didn't mean it that way."

Adele nearly flipped. "Where the hell are y'all going? To some concert or something? You didn't lie to me, did you?"

Talba laughed. "Nope. I didn't. *I* am a baroness."

Seeing Adele's blank stare, she said, "It's my shtick. Want to see my Web site? It explains it all."

She regretted it instantly. They'd have to go to Lucy's computer, and the kitten was in her room. "Oh! I forgot. We took it down to work on it. But here's the short version—I have this affectation, and it's . . ." She posed, indicating her outfit. ". . . this." Then she had an inspiration. "It's a black thing."

"Oh. Will there be any other, uh, I mean . . ."

"Is it an all-black restaurant? No, indeed. This is one of the few integrated poetry readings in town, thanks in large part to *moi*. You do thank My Grace, don't you?"

Lucy stared in amazement. Talba realized that she was behaving in character, already the baroness, already on stage.

Adele looked ready to change her mind.

Quickly, Talba said, "Sorry. I forgot I didn't have an audience."

Adele's face was grim, but she said, "Well, have a good time. Lucy, remember your manners."

Lucy giggled. "Oh, Mommo. Nobody says that any more."

"Just be a good girl." As she kissed her granddaughter, Talba saw Adele's eyes fill. Probably because of the giggle. Lucy wasn't doing much giggling these days.

They were nearly out the door when Lucy said, "Hey, I forgot something," and raced back upstairs.

"She seems better," Talba remarked, setting the stage for Rikki's eventual discovery, hoping to weight the judgment in the kitten's direction.

"She does." Adele seemed puzzled. "I guess kids are more resilient than we think."

"The poetry helps her, Miss Adele. It really does."

Adele smiled. "I'm grateful to you. I didn't even know she was writing."

"She said Royce got hurt. How's he doing?"

She shrugged. "It's nothing a bottle of whiskey won't cure. That's his theory, anyhow."

Lucy clattered back down, clutching her camcorder. "Almost forgot the most important thing. Raisa can tape me for you, Mommo. We can watch it tomorrow."

Adele kissed her again, and Talba sensed the tenderness between them. How much Adele had cared for Buddy, Talba didn't know, but she knew she was hurting on Lucy's account.

"Break a leg," Adele said, and before Lucy had time to protest, Talba explained what it meant.

"Tell Royce I'll break a rib," Lucy retorted, and the minute they were out the door, she said, "You didn't tell me to dress up."

She'd opted for jeans turned up almost to the knee and a tight-fitting T-shirt with a design of Hindu deities, which Talba pronounced perfect. "Half the poets who read," she said, "will probably be dressed like you."

After she and Raisa had hugged and Raisa had said, "I'm sorry about your daddy," and Lucy had said, "Thanks," Darryl asked them what they wanted for dinner.

"Big Mac!" Raisa hollered, to which Darryl replied, "Bleeagh!"

"Oh, Daddy."

"This is a big night, kid—we're having an adult dinner. We can eat at Reggie and Chaz if you like. They have pizza."

That went over with both the girls, so Reggie and Chaz was elected. Talba could see immediately that neither of the girls had ever seen anything like it. Reggie—half of the gay African-American couple who ran it—met them with a bow. "Ah! The Baroness. It's an honor, Your Grace. And Darryl Boucree. Long time." He kissed Talba and slapped palms with Darryl, after which he greeted each girl with outstretched hand. "And two princesses. Princess Raisa, I believe? And you'd be Princess Lucy."

They were wide-eyed (even Lucy) not only at Reggie's excess, but also at the place, with its Guatemalan belts hanging like snakes from the ceiling and its distinctly salt-and-pepper flavor. Both had seen a sprinkling of other races at restaurants, but neither had evidently been in a place where it was more or less fifty-fifty. And then there were the clothes. People who frequented Reggie and Chaz tended to come from the Faubourg Marigny and the Bywater, neighborhoods known as havens for artists.

A lot of the men sported what Talba called "musicians' clothes"— loose, short-sleeved, square-tailed shirts worn outside the pants, and porkpie hats; the women wore gauze and Indian or African prints and vintage outfits and zany hats, more conservative versions of Talba's baroness look. Plenty of tattoos and piercings on both sexes. A good fifty percent, as Talba had predicted, were dressed like Lucy, in jeans. True, lots of midriffs showed, but Lucy didn't seem to feel too deprived that she'd been talked out of it.

She seemed to be in heaven. "This place rocks."

"Told you."

"Does everyone have a performance name?"

"Nope. Just royalty."

"Henceforth from this moment, I shall be known as Princess Lucy."

"That's a long time. You sure?"

"Yeah!" Raisa said, though it was none of her business.

"Okay, that's how I'm introducing you. But hear this—you don't outrank The Baroness. Nobody does."

Lucy smiled. "Not till I get some better clothes, anyhow."

And then she and Raisa got into a big discussion about taping. Raisa had brought Eddie's camcorder (which Talba hadn't yet returned), and wasn't sure how she could get everything on both cameras. Finally, Lucy agreed to let Darryl operate hers so Raisa could make her own tape, which she'd get to keep "and cherish," as Lucy put it, striking a princess pose. The kid was showing real performance instincts.

But for a while, Talba was worried. They finished their pizzas and the evening moved into the drinking part of the evening (Shirley Temples for the girls, Chardonnay for Talba, beer for Darryl), which made the girls restless and argumentative, since they had neither the mellowing advantage of alcohol, nor other kids to distract them. Talba had warned them that the reading would start half an hour late, but what good was a warning when you were young and impatient? Lucy's stage fright was so nearly palpable that Talba left for a while to bribe the night's emcee, Lemon Blancaneaux, to let the kid read second. She figured first would send her over the edge with fright and third or lower would require hospitalization.

The bribe consisted of only a couple of drinks, but it did mean Lemon's self-important company for half an hour. Lucy was going to owe her.

Lemon began the evening with his customary greeting, so well known to the habitués that they shouted it with him. "How y'all tonight?"

And then everybody shouted and high-fived, leaving Lemon to inquire loudly if they were making fun of him, which caused even more hilarity and a mock attempt on Lemon's part to leave the stage, which meant he had to be shouted back, however insincerely. Lemon had a reputation for loving the sound of his own voice.

So they endured a good ten minutes of inane patter before he even condescended to announce the first poet, also a young white girl—though considerably older than Lucy. She had written a love poem, which contained words that neither Raisa nor Lucy (with any luck at all) had ever heard. Throughout the recitation, Darryl squirmed like a kid who had to pee. Not wanting Lucy to have to follow that, Talba had a whispered conversation with Lemon—switching the Princess to third place—and causing him to do what he always did when he was a little confused, or at a loss for words or just lonesome for his own voice. Once again, he shouted out, "How y'all tonight?" and over the ensuing uproar, Talba could hear Raisa whispering to Darryl, "Daddy, what's 'come juice'?", which Lucy caught on tape. Talba could only pray the tape never fell into the hands of the dread Kimmie.

The next poet was a house favorite (though not the house star, who was the Baroness de Pontalba). Serenity Prayer Jones was renowned for his alcohol consumption, known as "Prayer" to his many friends and

237

drinking buddies, and well known for his doggerel about the joys of being an unrepentant reprobate. Tonight's poem, entitled, "Lounge Lizard," was about himself and was mercifully short.

Lounge Lizard

I slither to the corners of the bar,
Drinkin' everything that ain't nailed down.
They say I don't work,
But shirk's its own form of work.
Know what it takes to charm
A hundred people a night,
And get me sailin' like a kite?
I ain' no use, I ain' no help.
Got no beauty, got no brains,
All I got's a few refrains—

"How y'all tonight?"

Folks like me 'cause I ain't
The mayor
And I ain't Rumsfeld
And I ain't the emcee—

"How y'all tonight?"

And I ain't the poor
And I ain't the rich.
I'm just a broken down
Son of a bitch.

When Lucy mouthed that line along with him, sure of what was coming next, Talba knew everything would be fine. And then when everyone shouted the last line together—"How y'all tonight?"—the kid whispered, "I can do a lot better than that," which Raisa caught on tape.

Lemon came back on, with a hearty, "How y'all tonight?" and introduced Talba for about a year and a half, after which Her Grace took the stage, to foot-stomping and shouts of "Baroness! Baroness!"

She quieted them down with what they recognized as her usual exit line, "The Baroness myself thanks you."

"But I'm not going to read tonight," she continued. "Instead I've discovered a great young talent—a very young talent, folks—only fourteen years old. A young talent who's making her debut tonight. She's going to read two poems for you, so join me in welcoming another member of my royal family, Princess Lucy of the House of Champagne!"

Because of the "family" remark, everyone, of course, was expecting another black poet, and so all was silence till Lucy shouted, "How y'all tonight?" And the audience was hers.

Sensing it, she took over the stage like a pro. "Debut," she said.

Debut
No long and glittering gown for me,
Nor social pedigree,
No silver spoon,
No mother.
And no hope.
A lovely life for a cockroach.

I lived so quietly before!
As simple social insect
And household pest,
Foraging for crumbs
In a kitchen of dissension.

And then my father died.

And so begins the moment
Of my reinvention.
My body is a carapace that cracks
And spews upon the pantry floor,
And my soul scuttles into darkness,
And an animal eats it.

I am dead.

But I am sticking to its ribs!
I am clotting,
I am holding.
I can feel that I am staying,
Cleaving, clinging,
My carapace in tatters,
My entrails scattered.
But I am sticking,
I am holding!
I am making my debut
As part of something other,
Something different,
Something innocent
And insignificant,
Yet bigger and more solid—

My own tears the glue

The crowd, which had gasped when she got to the part about her father, and had held its collective breath ever since, was utterly silent until Lucy bowed and said, "The Princess myself thanks you," and then wild applause erupted. The audience was cheering for her, pulling for her—maybe not so much for her career as a great young talent, but for a kid in a bad place, struggling to stick, to cling. She had done what Talba had seen few poets do—she had touched them.

Lucy's face turned as red as her hair, but she was undaunted, fine to keep going. When she read her "Crow" poem, it was safe to say there wasn't a dry eye, certainly not Raisa's—or Darryl's. Again, the Princess thanked her subjects. Again, applause, at first somber, cautious, and then building, becoming ever more confident. Standing behind her, Talba held her hands palms up, and raised them slowly, but there was no need—half the audience was already on its feet.

Lucy was crying, really bawling, but she managed to get it together to thank her subjects once again, and Talba stepped forward to ask the audience, "Didn't I tell you?" which started the whole thing all over again. And then the foot-stomping began anew, with loud shouts of "Baroness, Baroness! Come on, Your Grace, poem, poem!"

Talba refused and left the stage, but they wouldn't stop till she came back, Raisa capturing the whole thing. She read "Calamari," the poem she had written that afternoon. It was inspired by something she'd seen at the aquarium about the largest animal in the world, a monster bigger than a whale, with an eye as large as your head—the giant squid. The poem had images about tentacles and darkness and deepness, and barbs about scientists not being able to go deep enough in their own planet to study it, though they could send a spacecraft to Mars, and then it riffed on Martians and foreignness for awhile, rather cleverly, she thought. It was a lighthearted poem, a funny poem, and the perfect foil for Lucy's gloom and doom and crazy hope.

"They love you!" Raisa said later, amazed. And then to Lucy, "And I knew they'd love you. Can we go get some ice cream?"

"Sure." Darryl was in a hell of a mood.

And so they went for ice cream, during the consumption of which Raisa asked Lucy if the animal that ate her was the crow. "No," said Lucy, surprised. "It was Rikki."

"Who's Rikki?" the kid asked, causing Talba to get a great idea, which she bounced around her brain while Lucy explained.

"Hey," she said. "Can we voice-edit that tape?"

"Sure."

"Let's do this: Take out the place where Lucy says the title of 'Debut' and put in another word: 'Rikki'! And show Adele that version."

Lucy got it instantly. "Oh. My. God." was all she said.

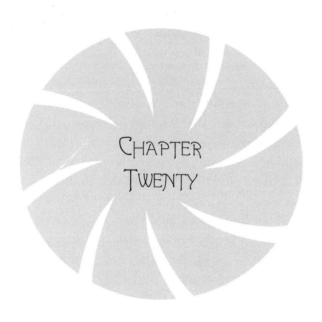

CHAPTER TWENTY

Fame, Talba thought, every now and then lived up to its press. All day Sunday Raisa hung on her like an acolyte, her status having magically changed from pariah to hero. But it wasn't the poetry—it was pure stardust. Those other people couldn't be wrong. Could they? She and Darryl took Raisa for a walk, then to a friend's house for a barbecue, where Raisa kept introducing her as "my friend, The Baroness— you know, the famous poet?" which was puzzling but cute to those unaware of her noble status.

Talba even got the kid to look at her Web site, which duly impressed her, and they held a viewing of the tape, everyone agreeing to edit out the poet with the bad words so Raisa could show it to her mom.

And then came Lucy's phone call: "They said I can keep Rikki! I showed the tape and everybody cried—even me! That is, everyone but Suzanne, and when they said, 'Who's Rikki?' I brought her out and Royce nearly fainted. You're right—he loves her. Suzanne pitched a fit, but I knew what to say, because you told me, and she stalked off. Mommo was laughing so hard! Swear to God. *Laughing.* And I gave her the book—I mean, *Life of Pi*—and now she's reading it and everything."

242

But still, Talba spent Monday in a fairly depressed state. She didn't have a clue what to do next, except talk to the big guy.

H ey, Eddie. Nice weekend?"
   Could have been better, he thought. "Well, we didn't go to Biloxi, if that's what you mean. What color are my bags?"

"Tan. You look rested."

"Too damn rested." Audrey had wanted to work in the garden and then she had been too tired for what he was in the mood for. "Angie came over. Everything's fine with her case—the DA dismissed the charges. By the way, this Champagne thing is taking up too much time. Weren't you supposed to renegotiate after ten or twelve hours? Ya musta put in thirty by now."

Ms. Wallis snapped her fingers. "Oh, darn. It slipped my mind."

"Could ya be serious for once?"

"Well, it did come up, but Kristin said to keep on it."

"Well, ya can't work it forever—it ain't ethical. There comes a time when ya've gone far enough. And we just got a pile of employment checks from a shipping company. And two new insurance cases. One's a black guy—I'm gon' need ya on that one." Before Ms. Wallis, he'd done it all alone. But a white guy in a black neighborhood was conspicuous even without a camera.

"Okay." She nodded shortly, not even interested. "I think I've got to admit defeat." She went through her LaGarde family adventures, which led off a long pier to nowhere—unless you really needed to know how crazy they all were. But so far as Eddie was concerned, for all they knew after all this work Buddy could be the victim of a random killer.

"They're all whack jobs," he said. "Too much information and not enough goddam conclusions."

" 'Scuse your French," Ms. Wallis said. He was getting so he hardly even bothered anymore.

"Look, why don't ya take some time, write the client report, and I'll look it over and see if I can think of anything else we can do. If we can't"—he sighed—"we gotta just tell Miss LaGarde we can't help her."

It occurred to him she was conferring with him a lot more than

243

usual on this one—that wasn't like Ms. Wallis. She was usually Miss Piss and Vinegar.

Write the client report. She wondered how she was going to explain the hours she'd spent interviewing the client's ex-husband and her parents. Finally, she put it under "research."

She wrote and then rewrote the damn report, gave it to Eddie, did about twenty employee checks, and went home to her mama.

She was at lunch on Tuesday—egg salad on wheat—when she got the call from Lucy. She was crying.

"Baby, what is it? Why aren't you in school?"

"Royce came and got me. Something happened to Suzanne, but I don't know what. Oh, God, I wish I were dead. Talba, they won't tell me what happened!"

What did you say to a fourteen-year-old who was dealing with a family catastrophe for the third time in a month? Her voice was shaky. "Suzanne?"

"Mommo's in her room, crying; and Royce went out. Oh, God, Talba, I think she's dead. Can't you find out what's going on? They won't tell me anything."

Dead. The word fell like a black glove on Talba's ears. How could Suzanne be dead? She was a young healthy woman.

"Did Royce say where he was going? Did he go to the hospital?"

"He didn't say anything. He just said there was a family emergency and brought me home, and he wouldn't say a word the whole way home. And Mommo came out and hugged me, and started crying so hard she couldn't talk. She just went back in her room and closed the door. By then Royce was gone."

"What's Royce's cell phone number?"

Lucy reeled it off to her.

"Okay. Do you have Brad Leitner's?"

"Just a minute."

Talba sat composing herself for a few minutes, trying to decide whom to call. She decided on Leitner.

"Brad, it's Talba Wallis. Lucy's hysterical and nobody's with her. What's happened?"

For once he was civil. "Omigod, that poor kid. Suzanne got killed. Royce went over to the funeral home."

Talba matched her voice to his: calm, polite. "What do you mean she got killed?"

"She was mugged on her way back to her car after her yoga class. Royce is a zombie."

"What *happened*, Brad?"

"Nobody knows. The police just showed up with the bad news. Her purse was gone and she was shot in the head."

"Oh, Jesus."

"Look, I'll go over to the house."

"What's your relationship with Lucy like?"

"It's good. Royce is crazy about her, so we've done lots of stuff to-gether, just the three of us. I like the kid."

"Brad, somebody's got to tell her what happened. She says Adele's in her room crying. Can you do it?"

"Hell!" And then, "All right. It's the least I can do for Royce."

"I'll come when I can." At least she didn't have to tell the kid herself.

But she was shaking nonetheless. Eddie would kill her for getting this involved in a case; she had to pull it together.

Finally, she went back in his office. "Eddie, there's been a develop-ment. We've lost another member of the Champagne family."

"Ya kiddin' me!"

"Suzanne got shot during a mugging."

"Who the devil's Suzanne?"

"The daughter-in-law—Royce's wife. I don't know what the hell to think."

Eddie's bags jiggled. "Pretty damn coincidental."

"Yeah." Talba chewed a cuticle, thinking. "Listen, I've got to go see Lucy. Nobody's with her. At least nobody who's *compes mentes*."

"Yeah," he said. "Yeah. I don't know what the hell that is, but take the rest of the day off. Do what ya have to do." Not a word about get-ting too involved.

But what to do once she got there? Talba called her mama and asked her for advice. "You get on over to that house right now and read the Bible with that girl."

"I can't. Lucy's a pagan."

"Sandra Wallis, you wash your mouth out with soap! She's just a kid. All kids are little heathens. Don't mean nothin'. You get on over there and read her the Twenty-third Psalm."

"Okay, Mama. You're right." She assumed the word "pagan" had a different resonance with Miz Clara than it did with Lucy. But her mama, as usual, had set her on the right path, however unwittingly. She got on over there.

Brad was there, and he'd told her. He'd also done something very smart—he'd called Kristin. And also Alberta, who was rocking Lucy in a grandmother's arms when Talba arrived. But the girl broke loose and turned to Talba, who took over babysitting duties. Kristin, for once, seemed withdrawn, though not hysterical—unlike Adele, she hadn't fallen apart. She'd assumed a grim, silent, can-do manner, efficient, though a little robotic. "I thought I could make some calls," she said, "since Adele can't function yet."

"She's still in her room?" Talba, holding Lucy, was talking over the girl's shoulder.

"Yes."

"Think we should call a doctor for her?"

"No. I'm fine." It was Adele herself, having come down the stairs in slippers, which seemed incongruous with her black dress. "I'll make the calls myself. Kristin, you order food and make tea." Kristin was out of there, Alberta on her heels. Adele held out a hand to Lucy. "Baby. Come here."

And the girl finally got to cry on her own grandmother's breast.

After a while, Talba said, "Luce? You okay for now?"

Lucy nodded, then burrowed deeper into Adele's skinny bosom.

"I'll be back," she promised, glad to be out of there. She went to police headquarters, where she found Skip Langdon on the phone at her desk. She held up a finger for Talba to wait, and when she'd finished her call, she said, "Your Grace. What can I do for you?" She sounded uncharacteristically tired, and she was even more untidy than usual.

The detective was six feet tall, blessed—or cursed—with hair so curly Talba could have been related to her, and she was maybe the world's worst dresser, partly because she could never seem to find pants long enough for her. She had on a white long-sleeved top—

something between a sweater and a T-shirt—with brown pants that probably weren't meant to hit her at the ankle, but did. Her white top had a spot of coffee on it. Her hair looked as if she'd been caught in a windstorm.

"I just heard Judge Champagne's daughter-in-law got killed. You know anything about it?" Without being asked, she sat in Langdon's interview chair.

"Yeah. Terrible—two in one family."

"Is it your case?"

"No. Why do you care?"

The last thing Talba wanted to mention was the fact that she'd been hired to mop up after the police. "You won't believe this—"

"Try me."

"I've gotten close to the family."

"You? Brutus and Judas all wrapped up in one? What the hell are you talking about?"

"I resent that. Brutus was a murderer—Judas is hard enough to live with. What I really meant is that I got close to the kid." Langdon had no children, but she was a virtual aunt to a girl about Lucy's age. Her expression softened a little.

"Poor kid. Two in one family."

"Think it's a coincidence?"

Langdon hit her with a hard stare, then gave it up and sighed. "Offhand, I'd say no."

"What kind of progress are you making on Buddy?"

"Why do you care, Baroness? I don't get it. And anyhow, you know I can't talk about an open case."

"Okay, forget Buddy—I was out of line. I'm here for the family. Can you give me details about Suzanne? Like, do the police have anyone in custody?"

"Nope. That much I can tell you. No witnesses so far."

"I was afraid of that," Talba said. "Suzanne was at odds with the rest of the family—did you know that?"

"More or less," Skip said wearily.

"And she was pregnant."

"Shit! How do you know?"

"She told me."

"You're getting around, aren't you, Your Grace? I smell a little rat here."

"Yeah, well, nothing wrong with your nose. But it's not my place to tell you about it." Meaning her own embarrassing status. "You'll have to ask the family. But I have a bad feeling about this."

Langdon gave her the stare-sigh routine again. "You think her death is connected to Buddy's?"

"Yes, somehow or other. I just don't know how."

"Okay. I'll take that as a tip. What else do you know about it?"

"I'm not sure, if you know what I mean. I know a lot about the family, but who knows at this point if any of it means anything?"

Langdon sighed without the stare. "Fair enough. What do you want from me?"

"Just don't let them treat it as a routine mugging, that's all."

"It's not routine; it's murder."

"You and I both know—"

"Let's not get into that, okay? She was the daughter-in-law of a prominent judge, however crooked. Also of a murder victim. Nobody's going to let it slide."

Talba stood. "Let me know if I can help you."

"*Can* you help me?"

"Maybe. Depends where this leads."

"Baroness. Listen to me—if you know anything, give it up."

Talba was slightly offended by her tone. "I will when I do, okay?"

"Immediately. I mean that."

"Yes, ma'am."

"And lose the 'ma'am' routine."

"Yes, ma'am," Talba said, and left. She'd gotten the last word, but she felt unsatisfied. She had what she came for—as much information as the cop was going to give her—but it wasn't going to make anyone feel any better.

There were a few things she could do to make Lucy feel better, though. She stopped at the F&F Botanica on Broad Street and bought a St. Expedite candle for swiftness in solving the case, plus an orange candle for healing. It might or might not be the right color, but it would probably do. Adele had had Kristin order food, so maybe it wasn't necessary, but she went home to fry some chicken and put together a salad just the same.

Miz Clara was already busy frying. "Figured you'd need somethin' for the family."

Her mother could be a pain, but on this case she'd been a peach. "Thanks, Mama. I really appreciate it. I'll make a salad."

"You read the Bible with that girl?"

"Yes'm. It helped her a lot." Thank God for Eddie's lying lessons.

"Hmmph. Probably didn't hurt you none either."

"No, ma'am." She freshened up, loaded her food, and drove back to the Garden District, where she found the kitchen full of women fussing over still more food, and the living room filling up with friends. Lucy was nowhere in evidence.

"She's upstairs," Adele said. "With the cat. Talba, thank you for that. I don't know how she'd have gotten through without it."

"I'll see how she is."

She found Lucy cuddled up with Rikki, staring blankly at the television, which was playing *Buffy* reruns—maybe a tape or DVD.

Talba sat on the bed and stroked the cat, not touching Lucy but trying to lend a little warmth. "I'm so sorry, sweetness."

"I didn't love her. I didn't even like her. I don't know why I feel like this."

" 'Cause you're human, that's why. She was here and now she's not, and it's not fair."

Lucy made a sound like a whimper.

Talba brought out her candles. "Look. You're a witch. Why don't we do a little magic?"

"I don't believe in magic," the girl snarled.

"Okay, then, I'll read you the Twenty-third Psalm."

"I don't believe in God, either."

Talba was irritated, making her wonder what kind of mother she'd make, but she kept her voice gentle. "Lucy, that's what everyone says when they've lost someone. You don't have to believe in God right now. But the beauty of magic is that you don't even have to believe in it—you just do it."

Lucy gave an ironic snort. "You sound like me. Thought you weren't a pagan."

"Maybe I'm not—but you know what they say about atheists in foxholes. Isn't that what we're in? How about a mourning ritual?"

249

"Naah. The funeral'll have that covered." She was getting interested.

"Healing, maybe?"

"No. But that foxhole thing—let's do protection. The rate people are getting killed, what we need is a warding."

And Talba realized for the first time that the girl was frightened. And that she was right. There was way too much violence in the air to ignore. She nodded. "Let's do it, whatever it is."

Lucy told her what a warding was: To do it right, they should walk around the house chanting and charging the building with the four elements, thus creating a circle of protection, and then they should paint pentagrams on the windows with ashes, for protection, having first banished all the old energy with brooms and shouts. But no way were they going to get away with any of that.

So they made a floor plan of the house and improvised. The girl explained first what they were going to do—cast a magic circle in which to work, call in the four directions and invoke protection deities (that one would have curled Miz Clara's hair, had she had any), so they could do a mini-banishing within what Lucy called the "sacred space," then, finally, cast a miniature protective circle around the floor plan. "We can use the St. Expedite candle to make it work fast," Talba offered.

"Naah." Lucy answered. "It works right away. Automatically." And then she changed her mind. "Forget it—can't hurt," she said.

The stage had to be set first, with candles and altar cloths and various artifacts representing the elements, after which they meditated for a moment before beginning. Her mind quiet, Talba got a great idea. Breaking the silence, she commanded, "Wait! What about if we drew a lifeboat around the floor plan?"

"Yeah! Let's put Rikki in it—like you-know-who."

Talba drew a boat that looked more like Noah's ark, except that it had only one animal, which sat on the bow with its paws over the side. And then Lucy cast the circle.

As they worked, Talba was once again impressed with the girl's stage presence and her focus, once she had something to focus on. When the ritual was done and they had celebrated with what Lucy called a "feast" (consisting in this case of chicken that Talba fetched from below and some water to represent wine), she was surprised at how calm she felt. No question, the magic had worked—if only to make them both feel better.

"I get it," Talba said. "The whole thing's about metaphor."

"Of course," Lucy said. "Why do you think I like it?"

CHAPTER TWENTY-ONE

The funeral was two days later. Talba had skipped Buddy's, due to temporary ostracization, but there was no missing this one.

It was held in a Catholic church, and it was a by-the-numbers service as far as Talba could see. No one spoke except the priest, who appeared not to have ever met Suzanne, whom he described as "a bright and innocent spirit" who would be missed by "all whose lives she touched." It seemed to Talba the last indignity of an undignified and undistinguished life to be "remembered" in front of God and everybody, as Miz Clara would say, by someone who'd never met the woman.

Talba made a mental note to tell Miz Clara and Darryl to please skip the church formalities if she went before them—a secular memorial, maybe with Lucy there to cast a circle, ought to do nicely.

Brad and his partner, who was definitely the guy in cutoffs at the Bacchus party (but who now wore a black shirt and pants) sat with the family. Talba didn't, though Alberta did. Kristin sat with her father and the woman to whom she referred as "Tootsie-pop," which must have galled her. She was dry-eyed, but Warren, to her surprise, actually wiped a tear at one point. What on Earth could that mean? The music, she decided. It always got to her, too.

Alberta was the only one of the Champagne family who actually wept, though Suzanne's parents, a short-haired, suburban-looking couple who seemed utterly bewildered, shed tears enough for everyone.

Lucy was stoic and expressionless in a black dress that looked awful on her. Redheads ought to wear brown, Talba thought, or some deep wine color. But Adele's taste had probably carried the day, and Lucy wouldn't have fought it.

Afterward, Talba dropped by the house, mostly to make sure her young friend wasn't coming apart. Lucy as usual had retreated to the solitude of her room and the comfort of her kitten. She'd changed to her torn jeans and a man's T-shirt, maybe one of Royce's.

Talba entered without knocking. "You two okay?"

"Oh, please. You don't have to talk to me like I'm a kid. 'Tiggers don't like funerals.'" She singsonged the Tigger part, mocking the sentiment. "But now I've been to two."

The kitten jumped off the bed and toddled over to sniff Talba's toes.

Lucy seemed eager to distract herself. "Hey, listen, I've got a present for Raisa—want to see?" She held up a tape, which she inserted into her VCR.

"Sure."

It was her own version of the poetry reading, the tape Darryl made, in which Raisa, predictably, figured as prominently as the poets. The surprising thing was that Rikki was in it, too—not actually in the scenes at Reggie and Chaz, but in new ones taped in Lucy's bedroom, which she had cut in. The kitten chased a ball, turned on her back and disemboweled a toy, sniffed and explored, groomed, and sometimes stared expectantly, after which the scene shifted back to the reading as if Rikki were watching it.

"Cool!" Talba exclaimed. "How'd you do that?"

Lucy shrugged. "I just intercut it."

Talba felt a strange quivering in her stomach, the beginning of an idea. "You intercut it? Can you do that with audiotape?"

"Sure, if you've got the patience. Why?"

"Just curious." But she couldn't wait to run her idea by Eddie. In her head, the whole case had just turned itself upside down.

M s. Wallis had on a suit today. It was a pantsuit, but she wore it with high heels, which she never wore to work, and she'd added jewelry for a change.

"Lookin' halfway professional," Eddie said, accepting the coffee she brought him. "What's the occasion?"

"Funeral clothes. Did you forget?"

"Oh, yeah—Suzanne. How'd it go?" He was big on funerals. The whole city was, for that matter, but Eddie particularly liked them on the theory that murderers never missed them, like pyromaniacs always went to fires. Of course, his theory had never actually borne fruit that you could take to court, but what the hell, it was still a good theory.

"Eddie, I've got an idea."

"Oh, Jesus. Here we go." He pushed his glasses down his nose.

"Can we go in the other room? I want to show you a tape."

They had a television in there, with a VCR hooked up for viewing surveillance tapes.

"Dammit. My leg hurts today." He had an old injury, but it wasn't bothering him. He just wanted to give her a hard time.

The room in question was actually more like a closet where they kept their surveillance equipment, the coffeemaker, and a little refrigerator. Ms. Wallis already had the tape set up along with a chair for Eddie. When he had made a sufficient production of limping in and settling himself, she proceeded to treat him to a recorded poetry reading interspersed with stupid cat tricks. Fortunately, he was only required to watch about ten minutes before she said, "See what she did with the cat? Fourteen years old."

He didn't get it. "What, ya think it should get an Academy Award or something? Anybody could do that. Oldest trick in the book."

"My point exactly." She turned off the tape. "And you could do it with audiotape."

"Yeah? So?"

"So, what if that recording on the marina phone was done that way? Suppose you got a word here and a word there from various voice mails Buddy left—or even called him and asked a leading question that required him to say stuff you wanted—or picked stuff up from Lucy's home movies—and you strung them together to say he was coming to the marina and the night watchman could go home? And then you recorded it and played it on the marina voice mail?"

He finally saw where she was going. "Yeah, I getcha. You'd just hook up the audio lines from the videotape onto an audiotape and press 'record.' There's even a counter on the videotape. You could figure out when the word starts and stop it when the word stops. Yeah. All there is to it. A child could do it. Let's go back to my office."

"I'm glad your leg's better," she said when they'd repotted.

He realized he'd forgotten to limp. "The exercise musta done me good. So whatcha sayin' is, maybe he never made that call. And if he never made that call, he wasn't planning to come to the marina."

"But maybe somebody was bringing him. What was left of him."

"Yeah." Eddie was taking it in. "Ya sayin' he coulda been killed somewhere else. Well, first thing's to call the night watchman and ax him what he thinks."

"May I do the honors? I've got his number programmed into my cell phone."

Of course she did. "Which ya just happen to have in ya pocket. Sure. Give him a holler." The only surprise was that she hadn't already done it.

She pulled out the phone and pressed a button, not even dialing. One day he was going to have to figure out how to do that. "Hey, Wesley. It's Talba Wallis."

And then, "Great, thanks. How're you?" Her manners were improving. "And how's Mary Ann?" Better still. Eddie'd probably have asked about the garden next, but he'd have bet his last dollar she wasn't going to.

"Listen, I was wondering something," she said. "Can you think back to that voice mail you got from Buddy? Yeah, that's right. The night he died. Was there anything strange about it? Uh-huh. Garbled. You mean you couldn't understand the words? Uh-huh. I see. Was the intonation strange? Ah. Yes. Okay, thanks a lot, I really appreciate it. Can you tell me again what he said?"

She made a writing motion, and Eddie put a pen in her hand. She wrote as she repeated the words. "'Hey, buddy, this is Buddy—I'm heading out there right now for a meeting and there's no need to stick around. You can go ahead and go home.' He didn't use your name? You sure about that?"

Eddie waited a while longer. "What?" he said when she rang off.

"There was static and background noise and the words seemed kind of halting—like maybe Buddy was drunk—but he wasn't slurring, more like he just wasn't paying attention. Then I asked that question about intonation and he said that was right—I mean, that was one thing that was wrong. Wesley hadn't thought of it before, but it just sounded kind of odd. I didn't press him—I didn't want to put ideas in his head. But no question, something was funny about it."

"So what's ya theory?" He was sure she had one.

"Well, maybe a family member killed him and Kristin suspects that. Maybe that's why she hired me. Listen, if this happened, it couldn't have been a stranger. It had to be someone with access to Buddy's voice, and someone who knew when Wesley went on rounds. That kind of narrows it down, don't you think?"

"I'll grant ya the first, but I don't know about the second. Maybe they were already at the marina with a cell phone, and they just watched till he was gone. And then phoned."

She thought about it. "Okay, yeah. That could have happened. But they had to know Wesley'd be there in the first place."

He shrugged. "Maybe," he said. "But they didn't use his name—maybe they just saw him. Still, ya got a point. But it's been awhile since then. How do we know Wesley remembered the message right?"

"I asked him about that. He said he has a fantastic memory for things like that, and anyhow, he's been over it a million times with the police, much closer to the time it happened. He's pretty sure he's not off by more than a word or two—and knowing Wesley, I'd trust him on that."

"If ya say so—sounds like a pretty smart guy. So if somebody did it, then who? Did Suzanne have a motive?"

"To kill Buddy? I saw him hit on her once. Maybe he went too far and they had a fight, and they . . . oh, you know."

"Or maybe Royce found out and *he* fought with Big Daddy."

"Big Daddy. That's funny—that's my nickname for him. Okay. But either way, what about Suzanne? Why kill her?"

"Two possible motives. Revenge or to keep her quiet."

"Mmm." She chewed a fingernail, one of her most annoying habits. "I never quite buy revenge unless it's the mob."

"Well, ya do have a mob connection goin'."

The right side of her mouth went up in rejection. "Too far removed. But I'll tell you one thing. That tape thing would have taken time and patience. And brains. The only two in this outfit who seem to me to have brains enough to do something like that are Adele and Lucy. And Lucy's out."

"Maybe out on the murder. But she could have helped with the tape—to protect someone else. Maybe that's part of what's bothering her."

"As if she hasn't already got enough trouble."

Eddie could actually think of a scenario that made sense. "Ms. Wallis. Could ya precious Buddy have been an abuser?"

Shock showed in her face, and he couldn't help feeling gratified. For once, he'd thought of something before she had. "S'pose he gropes Lucy—or worse—and Adele catches him and shoots him."

"Then Lucy helps her makes the tape—to save her grandma. Jesus! That's horrible. Omigod! And everyone knows—but Suzanne threatens to cave and go to the police. So then they whack her. The whole family could be in on it."

"Naah. Ya lettin' your imagination run away with ya. Buddy coulda been anywhere when he was shot."

Eileen Fisher popped her head in. "Hey, Talba, ya got a call. Kristin LaGarde."

"I'll take it in my office. Thanks, Eddie."

For what? he wondered, thinking theories were lots of fun, but Wesley had erased the voice mail—there was absolutely no way to prove it hadn't been Buddy talking.

"Talba. I'm scared." Kristin sounded shaky, not a way Talba'd ever have described her.

"What is it?"

"There's a gun in my car." Her voice was shrill, the high-pitched keen that signals hysteria.

"What do you mean there's a gun in your car?" Talba couldn't figure out why she was so frightened. Was someone holding it on her?

"I'm on my way over. I'm almost there." She hung up, but Talba rang her back.

"Kristin. Are you alone?"

"Yes."

"Don't touch the gun, okay?"

In another ten minutes, the client clacked into the office dressed in the dark green suit she'd worn to the funeral, one with a built-in belt that fastened with a satin bow, the tiny skirt cut some clever way that made the hem seemed to flutter. But there was a run in her pantyhose and her hair was disarrayed, as if she'd been running her hands through it.

"Thank God you were here. I'm scared to death." She looked it. Her skin was custard-colored.

"Let me get you some water," Talba said, automatically moving toward the office door. But glancing again at her client, she realized water might not be enough. She stopped in alarm. "Kristin? Hang in there, baby. Do you need to lower your head? Feeling faint?"

Kristin didn't need any more encouragement. She leaned her forehead on Talba's desk, and when Talba returned with the water, she raised it, looking slightly pinker. "Jesus. I don't know how I got here."

"Take deep breaths."

But Kristin shook her head. "No, I'm okay. I'd rather talk. Talba, what's going on?"

Remembering Angie, Talba had thoughts on the subject. She said, "Can you start from the beginning?"

"I think so." Kristin paused for breath, finally drank some water. "After I left the Champagnes', I had to go out to the East to see somebody on business." New Orleans East, she meant. "And since I don't know that neighborhood, I opened my glove compartment to look for a map. And there was a gun there."

"Whose gun?"

"Not mine. That's all I know."

"Do you think someone planted it?"

"How else would it get there?"

"Okay, then, who had access to your car?"

"Nobody. I never, ever leave it unlocked."

Talba sighed. "Nobody? Did you give someone a ride and leave them alone?"

"No. Nobody's been in it but me. How could this *happen?*"

"Do you keep an extra key anywhere?"

"I never lock myself out."

She wouldn't, Talba thought. "All right, then. Does anyone else have a key?"

"No. Why would—" She stopped in midsentence. "Well, my dad does. He gave me the car and insisted on keeping a key in case I did lock myself out." She tried out an indulgent smile. "You know how you're never grown up to your parents?"

LaGarde. The same LaGarde who didn't mind assassinating his daughter's character to a perfect stranger. Talba's stomach flipped over, but she knew she had to keep her face and voice steady. How to approach this?

But Kristin said, "Okay, I know what you're thinking—I can tell by your face."

Talba smiled, wishing she had Eddie's poker puss. "And here I thought I was hiding it. Okay. Let's get into it. Just for the moment, let's assume that whoever put that gun in your car is the person who killed Buddy—and maybe Suzanne. Any chance your father—"

"*Suzanne?* I never thought of that."

"You never thought the two murders might be connected?"

"No. Of course *that* occurred to me. I never thought . . . my dad . . ."

Figuring she was trying to work something out in her head, Talba gave her a minute. Finally, Kristin said, "Suzanne and Dad were always flirting. I wonder if they could have been having an affair."

"You tell me."

"Buddy and I used to talk about it. We always kind of suspected it."

"So what's the part you never thought of?"

"Well—is that a reason for killing her?" Kristin lowered her head so that her hair hung upside down, ran her fingers through it, and raised her head again, brushing it back as she did.

"Did that clear your head?" Talba asked, thinking she sounded like Eddie, talking to her.

"Nervous gesture." She offered a weak smile. "Look. Forget that idea. My dad wouldn't hurt a fly."

Talba doubted it, but she kept her mouth shut.

"What the hell am I supposed to do about this?" Kristin wailed.

"Have you touched the gun?"

"A little. I felt it when I opened the glove compartment."

"I suppose you couldn't tell whether it's been fired or not?"

"Are you kidding? I don't know anything about guns. I just closed up the glove compartment and called you."

"So the gun's still there."

"I locked the car."

"Look, if this is a setup, it's not going to end here." Someone, she thought, had to tip the cops to complete it. "The only advice I can give you is to take the gun immediately to Langdon—the cop who's handling Buddy's case."

Kristin reared back, sucked in air. "A setup? I thought . . ."

"What? What did you think?"

"I thought . . . someone wanted me to kill myself."

Talba was shocked. "Who, Kristin? Why the hell would you think that?"

"I don't know who." Her voice was barely audible. "I just . . . couldn't think of another reason for it."

"All right. Let's phone Langdon." *Before someone else does.*

Kristin nodded assent.

Talba called the cop's pager, thinking that might be the most direct way, and then got Kristin more water while they waited for a call back. When it came, Langdon was impatient. "What's up, Baroness?"

"I've got something for you."

"Well, what?"

Talba wasn't too sure how to say it. "A gun."

"Oh, shit! I might have known."

"What are you talking about?"

"Forget it. Just tell me how you got it, and where you are."

"Look, I know you're in a hurry, but let me guess—right now, you're acting on a tip, aren't you? About a gun in the Champagne case."

260

"What makes you think that?"

"I've got a hysterical client who just found a gun in her car."

"And who might your client be?"

"Kristin LaGarde. We're in my office."

"Well, I'm in hers. Stay there. I'm on my way."

CHAPTER
TWENTY-TWO

Langdon was by herself, but she more or less made two of Kristin. She wore two-inch boots, which made her two inches taller than her six feet, and her nubby tweed blazer added pounds she didn't need. Her black slacks didn't match the blazer, and looked as if she'd slept in them. Talba was amused, watching the petite, perfectly groomed blonde give her a mental makeover. Kristin's expression was a virtual sneer. Clearly, she thought herself a superior race. Her composure returned almost immediately.

"Hello, Detective," she said, with a confidence she hadn't displayed before.

"Hello, Miss LaGarde."

"You two know each other?" Talba asked.

"Oh, yes." Langdon's voice indicated she regretted it.

They must have met on Buddy's case. And hated each other. "May I sit down, Your Grace?" Langdon didn't wait for an answer, and didn't waste time on pleasantries. She said to Kristin, "I understand you found a gun in your car."

Kristin told the same story she'd told Talba, and then the three of them went to Kristin's car to see if the gun was still there, and Langdon took it and Kristin back to Headquarters to give a statement. That alarmed Talba. It seemed a bit much for the situation, but there wasn't exactly a way to horn in. All she could do was wait awhile and then pay Langdon a call.

She waited till Kristin phoned to say she'd been set free.

"I've been expecting you," Langdon said. "Why didn't you tell me you were working for that woman?"

"Couldn't. Confidentiality." Technically she wasn't bound by it this time—she was just embarrassed to say she'd been working Langdon's case. "Did Kristin tell you about it?"

"Uh-huh."

"Okay, look, I'm an idiot. The great Skip Langdon can't solve a case, nobody can. I just thought I ought to do *something*, that's all."

Langdon grinned. "Take it easy, Baroness. I can use all the help I can get. Have a seat. You've got something for me, right? Otherwise, you wouldn't be here."

Talba knew perfectly well how Langdon worked—had already made the decision to give something up. "Maybe," she said. "A thought or two. Who phoned in the tip?"

Langdon shrugged. "A whisperer." Meaning the caller could be either sex. "Pay phone."

"I'm curious. Did Kristin say anything about her father?"

"No. Why?"

"She told me he had a key to her car—she tell you that?"

Langdon sat straight up and gave Talba a look clearly meant for Kristin. "Goddammit, no! She said she'd left it unlocked on the street one day. What's up with Daddy dear?"

"Couldn't say. But he took me to lunch and filled my ear full of poison about her."

"Her own father?"

Talba shrugged.

"Well, if the gun's registered to him, we'll know soon enough."

"The question is," Talba said, "was it the gun used in either Buddy's or Suzanne's shootings?"

"Don't know yet."

"But you probably do know whether the same gun was used in both of them."

"Yeah. I know. Why?" The cop barely paused, unable to wait for an answer. "She's LaGarde's *daughter*—why would he plant a gun on her?"

"He told me she was a manipulator. But maybe he was setting the scene for a setup. Kristin mention she thought he was having an affair with Suzanne?"

"Christ, no!"

"Quite the dutiful little daughter, isn't she? Maybe you ought to ask LaGarde. By the way, was Suzanne really pregnant—or was that just some story of hers?"

Langdon had evidently grown tired of being told how to do her job. "What was that you had for me?"

"I've already given you two things—LaGarde had a key and he went out of his way to trash his daughter. What do you have for me? Same gun or not?"

"Come on. More. And make it good."

"I don't know if it's good," Talba said honestly. "It's just speculation. But I've got some reason to think it might have happened—and if it did, it changes a lot."

Langdon sighed. "Dammit, Baroness. How do you always get around me? Yes. Same gun."

"I thought so."

The phone rang, and Langdon talked. She came back saying, "Great. The gun's not registered. But then, neither are half the guns in this state. So what's your big theory?"

Talba told her the tape idea, along with Wesley Burrell's story, ending up with, "What do you think?"

"I think it's a thought."

"I thought I was being a big help."

"Well, you told Kristin she had to bring the gun in. That was a help." She shook her head. "I don't know about that woman."

"What's wrong with her? Lucy loves her; so does Adele."

"She's a parakeet."

Talba giggled. She'd coined the term herself—in a poem about skinny Uptown women. "Don't be a size-ist, Skip."

"Bad things come in little packages."

Talba left feeling as if she'd somehow dodged a bullet—Langdon had been unexpectedly gracious about her hubris in tagging after her on a murder case. But then why shouldn't she be? She was the expert. If it made Talba feel silly, it was her problem.

The tape thing bothered her. If there was anything there, there ought to be some way to prove it. Maybe there was something on Lucy's Bacchus tape—words that Wesley might remember, that someone could have cut out and rerecorded.

The only version she'd seen was the one edited for Raisa, which focused mostly on the child. *I wonder,* she thought, and called Lucy before she talked herself out of it.

"Hey, Luce, how're you doing?"

"Tired. I just took a nap and the damned nightmares woke me up."

"I'm sorry, baby. You're seeing a shrink, right?"

"Oh, please. Let's not go *there.*"

"Listen, I need a favor. How is it over there?"

"Quiet. Royce is up in his room, drunk. Just about everybody's left. Mommo's probably still downstairs with whoever's left."

"Can you get something to me without anyone knowing?"

"Why?"

"I told you. I need a favor. I want to see the tape you made the night of the Bacchus party. Not the one for Raisa—I need the unedited version. And I don't think we can look at it there."

"Why?" she asked again.

"Just a thought. Nothing big. Indulge me, okay?"

"Where are you going to go look at it?"

"My office—why?"

"Let me go with you—I need to get out of here."

Thinking about it, Talba didn't see a reason why not. "Okay. Tell Adele I'm taking you to dinner."

"No way she'll go for it. Call me when you get here and I'll sneak out the back door."

Talba sighed. But she knew Lucy would be safer with her than anywhere else. "Just leave a note, okay? So they don't worry. And say the thing about dinner—don't say what we're doing."

"Why not?"

"Because that's how P.I.s work." Once again, she questioned her capacity for motherhood. All those damned "whys."

It was nearly six and the office was dark when they got there, Eddie and Eileen having long ago left for the day. "Sorry," Talba said, "we'll have to look at it in the back room. The accommodations aren't that good, and the equipment's worse."

"That's cool." Lucy was pale and looked tired. Talba wasn't sure this was the greatest thing to be doing, but she was committed. She got the kid a soda and put the tape in to play.

Lucy had caught a lot of things Talba hadn't seen, moments frozen in time, made more poignant by later events. In her role as serving wench, she couldn't just stand back and look—Lucy could, and she did, concentrating on family members.

Not knowing who he was throughout most of the evening, Talba hadn't even noticed Warren LaGarde. But it wasn't LaGarde who caught her eye—it was Suzanne; Suzanne dogging his every step, tracking him with her eyes. Once, he brought her a drink and spent a few minutes. When he left, she stared after him as if her heart was breaking. Kristin, she thought, could have been right about the affair.

And the words she wanted were there in spades—so openly there it spooked her.

She turned up the volume when they came to the part where Buddy said, *"Now that I have your attention."* She remembered how much it had annoyed her.

Next, he said, *"I just wanted to welcome y'all all here and let you know that Zulu came early this year. Look what I got!"* Here, he held up the coconut with KRISTIN written on it and continued:

"Looks like this is for my good friend, Kristin LaGarde. Honey, would you come here and get your present?"

"Buddy, you shouldn't have," Kristin answered, and he said,

"Hey, let's make sure everybody's here—Lucy, where are ya? Royce and Suzanne?"

"And there's Adele over there. Come here, y'all, and check this out. Lucy, ya got ya camera on?" He turned back to Kristin. *"It's a magic coconut, honey; it opens up like a box. . . . You've got to twist it."*

She got it open, and Buddy said, *"How ya like that?"* Then, *"Kristin LaGarde, will you be my wife?"*

Kristin had squeaked, *"I can't believe it! You mean it, Buddy?"*

"Never meant anything more, sweetheart," he answered. *"It's a cold world out there. I finally found what makes a house a home and I gotta make sure she's gon' stick around. By the way, you accept, or what?"*

Talba looked at her notes on the message to Burrell and checked the words *ain't no need to, out there, home, have to, you, stick around,* and *I'm.*

"Okay, folks! We got a meetin' of the minds, and we're headin' for a weddin'! Want to try the ring on?"

These words leaped out at Talba:

"meeting"

"for a"

and *"heading"*

Then there was Buddy's horrible social faux pas: *"Does this mean we can go on ahead and do it now? How 'bout if ya quit your grinnin' and drop your linen—right about now?"*

Talba wrote *go on ahead* and *right now.*

"Lucy, where are ya?" Buddy said. *"Let's get everybody up here. Hey, Adele, Royce, Suzanne, let's pose for our first official family video."*

"Hey," was good, as in *"Hey, buddy."* The tape artist could have picked up *"This is Buddy"* from Buddy's own voice mail, and reused the word *"Buddy"* in *"Hey, buddy."*

She had almost the whole thing: "Hey, buddy, this is Buddy. I'm heading out there right now for a meeting and there's no need to stick around. You can go on ahead and go home."

She didn't see *and*; there had to be an *and* in there somewhere. She replayed it again and found it: *"and I have to make sure."*

And there it was: Maybe not verbatim, but easily close. She had to hand it to Wesley.

Next came Lucy's impromptu interview, but she didn't need it. The killer had taken almost everything from the previous section. She turned the tape off.

"What was up with that?" Lucy asked.

"Tell ya later, agitator."

"You are such a cornball."

"You hungry?"

"I could use a burger."

"I know a place that makes burgers *and* milk shakes."

"Getouttahere."

"Would I kid about something about that? Real, old-fashioned milk shakes." Talba had a slightly ulterior motive in spending a little more time with the kid—a vague idea that she ought to talk to Lucy about her fears. "Mind if I keep the tape for a while?" she asked.

"Sure, why not?"

"I'll just be a sec." And she went to copy it.

She took the kid to Huey's Diner, which occupied the site of the old Metro Bistro, once one of Talba's favorite eateries, a good restaurant that had come and gone. When she been served a soggy salad and Lucy had her burger, she began her meddling. "Lucy," she said, "would it help to talk about your nightmares?"

"Uh-uh. Shrink's got that covered. He says I'm just scared and it's only natural."

"Is it always the same dream?"

Lucy stopped eating. "How'd you know that?"

"Because so often it is. What do you dream?"

The girl put the burger down. "I dream there's someone in my room—and I'm scared to death, because he's about to get me."

Talba didn't like that—and yet she was halfway expecting it. "'He'?" she asked.

"I don't know. I think so. It feels like a 'he.'"

"I wonder if it could be about something real."

"I don't see how."

"Well, maybe someone *was* in your room sometime."

"Like maybe I got molested or something? You sound like Dr. Watson."

"That's his name? Dr. Watson?"

The girl giggled. "Don't think I ever miss a chance to say 'elementary' to him."

"So, *were* you molested?"

"Are you kidding? I'd remember, believe me. Besides . . . who'd want me?"

"Oh, Luce, you idiot! Look, was someone in your room or not?"

The girl's face grew dark. Slowly, she nodded. Knowing she was busted. "I think so. But they didn't hurt me. I'd know."

"When?"

"Now why'd you ask that?"

" 'Why this, why that'—what's up with all the whys?"

"Okay, okay, take it easy. I just asked because it was kind of strange timing—it was the night my father died."

"Was that your first nightmare or did it really happen?"

"It's just a coincidence," she said crossly, draining her milk shake with a sucking sound.

Right, Talba thought. *And I know what they wanted.*

She steered the conversation on to other things, and when she dropped the kid off, reminded her not to tell anyone the real reason for the outing.

Chapter
Twenty-three

She called Langdon first thing in the morning, but got no answer, not even when she paged her. Next she tried Warren LaGarde, but his voice mail said he wasn't in. There was only one person she hadn't talked to in the whole dysfunctional greater family unit, and now seemed like the perfect time.

She had LaGarde's address from her files and the name of his current wife, Melissa, whom she spent half an hour backgrounding. Melissa had been a store clerk before Warren met her, in a shop that sold women's underwear. He'd probably gone to buy a gift for another tootsie-pop and switched loyalties. But she wasn't just a saleswoman. Oh, no. Every trophy wife must have a career of sorts and Melissa had one—she was a set designer, not something that was likely to keep her in designer clothing. So she did decorative painting as well—faux finishes and stencils, mostly for restaurants. Talba called the house with a pretext to find out where she was working, but, happily, the maid said she was home. Talba hung up while the woman went to find her, and drove to the LaGarde home.

It was out in old Metairie, a suburb that was home to new money—

and some old as well—but this house was new construction, evidently built on the site of a much smaller teardown, judging by the small size of the yard. Melissa flung open the door before she could ring, wearing jeans and a chambray shirt. "Oh! I thought you might be Warren."

Talba gave her a reassuring smile. "I'm Talba Wallis and—"

"I know who you are. You're that P.I. who's working for Kristin."

So much for the lie she'd so carefully constructed. She tried another one. "Kristin's terribly worried about her dad. He's not at work and she didn't—I mean—"

"She didn't want to call here because we hate each other." Tootsie-pop was sharper than she'd thought.

"Nonetheless, she is worried."

"Go ask your cop friend about him. Warren says you're in bed with the mighty Skip Langdon."

Talba tried an ingenuous smile. "She's not answering my calls. May I come in? Maybe she'll answer her page."

Melissa hesitated.

Talba said, "Langdon's been here about a gun, right? And Warren's with her. Maybe I can shed some light."

Reluctantly, Melissa stepped aside to let her in, revealing a buff marble foyer hung with a brass chandelier. The living room had been painted a silvery blue color, and finished with something shiny that cracked artfully in places, so that it looked as if it had been varnished so long ago that the varnish was breaking down. It was probably Melissa's own work, and Talba liked it. The furnishings were contemporary, in a way that made Talba realize her own prejudice against new furniture stemmed from an unfamiliarity with the really good stuff, clean and simple in a way that made her want to rethink her own love of the flamboyant and cluttered. A sofa was covered in warm gray-blue linen piped with midnight blue, and two chairs were covered in tan linen piped with the same midnight color. Salmon throw pillows accented the neutrals. Talba would have gone with an oriental rug, but sisal carpeting covered the floor, probably so as not to detract from the fine collection of contemporary art that hung on the walls. Talba recognized a couple of the artists—Katharine White and Allison Stewart—whose work she could only dream of affording. The LaGardes had good taste—or maybe their decorator did. Or maybe Warren bought the art for his hotels and let some of it spill into his house. It was that, she decided. She didn't want to think too well of these people.

"Beautiful art collection," she said, but Melissa didn't take the bait. She sat down and motioned Talba to do so as well.

"What's happening, Miss Wallis?"

"The police think they have some evidence against your husband—something that ties him to Buddy Champagne's murder."

"That's ridiculous. And they were just awful. They came here first thing this morning and asked about a gun—after he'd gone to work. Well, sure we've got a gun—everybody does. It's not safe not to anymore. So I went to Buddy's desk to show them, and it wasn't there. Then *they* showed it to *me*—bastards had it all the time. Is that even ethical?"

"Mmm. Mm," Talba said, thinking that at least Melissa was innocent, or she wouldn't have been so stupid.

"I didn't want to lie—I mean, they were going to find out anyway, right?—so I said, sure, that was it, and the next thing you know, they hauled Warren down to Headquarters. His assistant called and told me. Now tell me something—how'd they get that gun?"

"It must have been some place it wasn't supposed to be." And it must have matched the ballistics report on one or both of the victims, Talba figured, or they might not have bothered. That would also be why they'd waited till morning—to get the report.

"Listen, you said maybe you could shed some light. What do you know that I should know?"

She fell back on one of Eddie's maxims—when you don't want to answer a question, ask one yourself. "What does your husband say about it?"

"I haven't talked to him. I'm waiting for him to call me."

"Don't wait," she said. "Get him a lawyer." Though he'd probably taken care of that himself. She stood up.

"That's what you came to tell me?"

"I told you—his daughter's worried. And after what you've told me, I think there's reason to be." She was dying to ask if LaGarde was having an affair with Suzanne, but she just couldn't bring herself to go there. This woman had enough trouble as it was.

W hat now, Ms. Wallis?"
Eddie pretended impatience, but he was actually enjoying his new role—in this case, he thought of himself as a sort of all-seeing Nero Wolfe character, with Ms. Wallis as Archie Goodwin.

"Got another tape for you."

So once again, he had to haul himself to the little coffee room and watch an amateur video. She pointed out the words to him, the same ones Wesley Burrell had heard on the marina tape. And then she told him about her visit to Melissa LaGarde, aka "Tootsie-pop." And finally, she got to the good part—the part where she asked the master for his pearls of wisdom.

"I see whatcha sayin'," he said. "That bastard LaGarde set his own daughter up. But I got a problem with it, Ms. Wallis. How the hell did he get the tape?"

She was swinging her leg with impatience. "He took the key to Buddy's house off Kristin's key chain. She must have had one."

Eddie measured off a chunk of air with his hands. "Well, if he got it off her key chain, anybody coulda. I thought the whole point was, he already had a key to the car."

That stopped her. "Oh. Yeah."

"Or maybe," he said, "he didn't need a key. Maybe someone in the house got the tape for him."

"Suzanne!" she said, as if it meant something. "Eddie, you're a genius."

He was irritated. "What's Suzanne go to do with the price of tea?"

"Kristin thinks her father was involved with her—and by the way, Suzanne was pregnant. Did you see the way she dogged him on the tape?"

He hadn't. So he had to watch the whole damn thing again. It was possible, about the affair. And the words from the tape were way too similar to the message at the marina.

"Ya want my advice?" he said. "Get out now. Take that tape to the cops, finish ya client report, and collect ya money."

A s it happened, that was the way she saw it, too. The thing had a lot of holes in it, but the fact was, she *had* turned the case on its ear—

or would have once she delivered the tape. That ought to be worth paying her for. And so what if it wasn't? There was nowhere to go from here. Let Skip Langdon figure it out.

She went back, finished the client report, copied the tape, and took the copy to Langdon, enduring along the way a lecture about fingerprints, which indeed she hadn't been careful about. On the other hand, she pointed out, any number of people might have handled the thing, but that didn't calm Langdon down any.

Finally she called the client and asked to see her that night, the time being well after five already.

"I want to see you too," Kristin said ominously. "Come now if you can."

Talba could.

Kristin had changed to a pair of capris, and she looked a little haggard. She'd slicked her hair into a ponytail, exposing ears that stuck out, an unexpected flaw. She was flushed with anger. "Come in and talk to me. What the hell did you mean, telling the cops what I told you about Daddy?"

For a woman in her thirties, Kristin had amassed quite a lot of nice stuff, including some paintings as good as her father's. She had a Juan Laredo and a Chris Clark, two more artists Talba couldn't afford. She figured these, too, were borrowed from the hotel collections.

"Nice house," Talba said, "I see art collecting runs in the family."

Kristin shrugged. "It's a dump." A dump a lot of people would have killed for.

Aside from the art, the house was way too decorated, too formal for Talba's taste, and a bit on the impersonal side, but the pieces were good—or looked good to Talba—except for an antique, high-armed, wood-framed sofa that would never permit snuggling down with a good book. Kristin had a lot of silver that might be real. Talba tossed out a little bait. "Those are beautiful candelabra."

Kristin gave an impatient toss of her head. "I collect antique silver." Right. Real. And then, without a pause, "What the hell did you mean implicating my daddy?"

"I thought you two didn't get along?"

"He's my father, goddammit!"

"And this is a murder case. Can't you get it through your head that whoever put that gun in your car set you up? And it was your father's gun. Does that mean anything to you? Anyhow, how could I know you hadn't told them about the key?"

"I suppose you told them about Suzanne too."

"Kristin, for God's sake, drop it. Do you realize how serious this thing is? Hear this: Your dad's gun was probably used in two murders. If he's innocent, he'll probably have an alibi."

She brightened. "He does." She slapped her forehead. "How could I be so stupid? He was with me."

"The night of Buddy's murder he was with you?"

"The day Suzanne was killed. He and I had lunch together."

"Oh. Well, tell the cops then. Meanwhile, I came to let you know I've gone about as far as I can go on this. I didn't solve it, but I did make a breakthrough."

"What? Getting my father arrested? Thank you very much, that's not what I had in mind."

"He's arrested? They've arrested him?"

"Well, if they don't, it won't be any thanks to you. What's this great breakthrough?" She was sitting on the unappealing sofa with her legs folded, bare feet peeking daintily out from under her backside.

"I'm pretty sure Buddy never called the marina that night, which means he wasn't killed there."

"What?" She uncoiled her body. "I never knew about that call."

"It's all in the client report. The night watchman says he called to say go home, but the words on the tape came from somewhere else."

"Where else? What are you talking about?" She grabbed Talba's wrist.

Talba hadn't expected this reaction—Kristin seemed near hysteria—but it occurred to her that she should have. This was a woman whose fiancé had died, and whose father apparently had tried to frame her for it. She couldn't tell her the evidence was a tape from her own engagement party. Let Langdon do it.

"I've said too much already. I can't really go into it now."

"Give me the client report."

"I'm sorry; I didn't bring it." It was safe in her bag. "I'll have to mail it to you."

"Uh-uh. No, you don't. You've got it in that tote, don't you? Give it to me." She looked ready to grab the bag, and Talba was in no mood to fight.

"Look," she said. "I took this case because I felt bad about deceiving the family. Now I've done more damage, and I feel horrible about it. I wouldn't have upset you like this for the world. Can't I do something for you? Let me get you a drink, or a cup of tea or something."

"How dare you! What right have you to the moral high ground, you little bitch? Who the hell do you think you are, with that black baroness routine? I've got something to tell you, your fucking grace—you're just a two-bit little lowlife and you know damn well you took the case for the money. I'm not giving you a dime until I get that report."

If Talba had one hard and fast rule, it was this: Never work for people who insult you, no matter how upset they are at the time. Walk away the minute it happens.

"I'm sorry you feel that way," she said, and rose. "This one's on the house."

"Give me that report!"

"I'm sorry." Talba turned to go, but she felt a hand grab her shoulder and start to wrench at the bag.

She felt her heart speed up, her hands begin to shake. She was having an adrenaline rush. This wasn't good. Talba knew herself too well not to be frightened. When the fight-or-flight response set in, it took flight mode with her. She withdrew mentally, like a turtle tucking its head in its shell. She even had a word for it: She called it "turtling out"—had called it that all her life. Knew exactly what it was. Knew she couldn't think on her feet and she might as well not try. This was way, way out of hand.

Her breath was so uneven, she could barely speak. "Look, I'll get it for you if you'll let me go," she rasped. "It's in the car."

Kristin dropped her hand. Thank God, Talba thought, and turned to face the other woman. At least this way she couldn't be stabbed in the back. "Okay?" she asked, breath still coming hard.

But it wasn't okay. Kristin's fury contorted her tiny triangular face so badly she resembled a gargoyle with protruding ears. "Give me the bag."

It was a weird thing. Kristin couldn't have stood more than five-three nor weighed more than a hundred pounds, but at the moment, she looked six feet tall. It was like she'd stuck a bicycle pump in her mouth and blown herself up.

Talba eased the bag off her shoulder, and opened it to show nothing but her purse—a much smaller bag—and the bound client report. "Look, you're right. It's your property. I could see you were upset—but I didn't realize how upset. I was just trying to save your feelings. Go ahead and take the report."

Kristin's hand crept into the bag. As soon as her fingers had closed around it and begun to slide it out, Talba jerked the bag back, turned quickly, grabbed the doorknob, ripped open the door, and tore up the sidewalk.

When Talba was in the car, doors locked, she stared back at the house. The front door was now closed; there was no sign of pursuit, but maybe her client had gone to get a gun—at this point, Talba wouldn't have put anything past her. She needed to get her breath, but she also needed to get out of there. Hands shaking, heart pounding, fighting for breath, she turned on the ignition and eased the car around the corner, where she stopped, turned out the lights, and let herself recover, breathing deep into her belly, cursing herself for a coward.

It's just a physical response, she told herself. *It doesn't make you a bad person.*

And in fact, when she thought back on it, there really wasn't anything she would have done differently, even if she hadn't lost control of her faculties. Kicked the client in the teeth? Not an option. Wrestled her for the bag? What was the point? Of course, she could have done without the ignominious retreat—that one made her cringe—but mostly it was the way she felt that seemed so dishonorable.

The thing was—she could see it now—she'd made her mistake while she was still *compes mentes*. She should have just surrendered the damned report in the first place. She'd withheld it out of kindness, and then, after saying she didn't have it, she didn't want to admit she did. Pride: a deadly sin.

On the other hand, if the client hadn't turned out to be a maniac, it would have been fine.

Her heart rate was slowing, her breath returning to normal while her mind raced, sifting through the disturbing elements, making sense of them. She was almost good to go when Kristin's white Lexus sped past the intersection where Talba was parked. Unfortunately, she was turned the other way—she'd only seen it in the rearview mirror.

But, damn, it sure looked like her car.

Without hesitation, she turned around to follow, but it was too late. The car was nowhere in sight. Still, if it really was Kristin's car, this shed a new light on things. She drove by the camelback to make sure, and just as she was passing—sure enough, no Lexus—her cell phone set her nerve endings on end. The caller ID said it was the lady herself, which was even more scary.

Half expecting a death threat, she iced up her voice and answered. "Hello, Kristin."

"Omigod, Talba, are you still speaking to me?" The old Kristin. Talba relaxed, but kept her voice below freezing.

"You want to tell me what happened back there?"

"Listen, all I want to do is apologize. I think I went crazy for a minute there."

"Is that what it was? That 'bitch' part kind of got to me. Oh, and the 'two-bit little lowlife' thing—been watching a lot of *cinema noir?*"

"Have I been *what?* Oh, I see what you mean." She giggled self-consciously. "Okay, yeah. That was a little on the *Maltese Falcon* side. You know I didn't mean it, don't you? I was just upset. I wanted to apologize before you completely wrote me off. By the way, of course I'm going to pay you. I just thought I'd die if I didn't see that report."

"Want to talk about it? I can come back." Testing the water.

"Can't. I'm in the car. I got so upset I had to take a ride."

"Okay, forget about it. Like I said, the job's on the house."

"But you put in all that work."

"Not important. Let's just agree to disagree, as my mama likes to say."

"Talba, don't be that way! Look, I'll send you a check tomorrow."

"And I'll send it back," Talba said coolly. She pressed "end."

The phone rang again, but she ignored it, started seething again, and mentally replayed both encounters in her head, indulging herself in *l'esprit de l'escalier,* or whatever the phrase was that meant thinking of a witty retort too late. Except in this version, she didn't think up snappy answers—she beat the crap out of the bitch.

CHAPTER
TWENTY-FOUR

Eddie was away the next day, on a job in Terrebonne Parish, so she didn't even have the pleasure of a morning chat. And she was dying for one. She'd awakened with a new perspective. She had to tell Langdon about it, but she wanted to talk to Eddie first.

She'd done a lot of thinking about the night before, and she was halfway expecting a call, but she wanted to talk to Warren LaGarde first. To her surprise, he answered her call without any special ruses or pleas. "What can I do for you, Miss Wallis?"

"I was thinking about that talk we had. Mind if I ask you a question? Does Kristin's job involve any work with video cameras?"

"Sure. She makes tapes of the properties she wants to buy, and shows them to the rest of us. She's pretty good. Why did you need to know?"

"Can I let you know later?" She hung up before he could answer. Her suspicions were getting stronger—so much so that the back of her neck was sweating. If she were right, she should be hearing from Kristin very soon.

The call came on her cell phone right on schedule, about nine-thirty A.M. "Good morning, Miss LaGarde."

"You still mad?"

"Not at all. What can I do for you?"

"I was wondering about that tape you mentioned—can I ask where you got it?"

"Sure. It's a free country."

"Talba, don't *be* that way!"

"Where I got it is confidential." *And so is where I have it.*

School had been in session for an hour and a half, enough time to ransack Lucy's room for it. She figured that was why the call had come when it did.

"This client report seems very incomplete without it. I really don't see how you can expect to be paid until I have the result of your investigation."

"It's evidence, Kristin. I'm taking it to the cops."

"I'll be happy to do that for you," Kristin chirped. "Why don't I come by and get it?"

Talba really couldn't believe this woman. In movies, the bad guys were always diabolically clever. This little idiot—who she now thought had probably killed two people—thought she could waltz off with a vital piece of evidence, just by asking for it.

"Surely," she said, "you jest."

There was a long silence. Finally, Kristin said, "Listen, I read the client report and you really did a great job for me. I was thinking maybe a bonus."

This was starting to be fun. "How much were you thinking?" she asked.

"Oh, say, ten thousand. For the *complete* report, that is."

"Thirty," Talba replied.

Kristin got right into negotiating. "Twenty-five."

"Done."

"Done? You'll turn over the tape."

"Hey, for twenty-five large, I'd turn over Eddie."

"Who's Eddie?"

"The guy who's got the combination to the safe. Where the *complete* report is."

"Has this Eddie person seen it?"

And at that moment, it dawned on Talba that this little silver-spoon maniac, this insignificant, undersized, dressed-for-success premature black widow, might very well intend to kill her. Probably thought it was going to be as easy as framing her own father for murder. "No, of course not," she said. "We all keep things in the safe from time to time. He doesn't even know what it is. I just have to wait for him to come back and get it out for me."

"And when are you expecting him?"

"Listen, about that twenty-five. It'll have to be in cash."

"Agreed."

"Well, you've got to get it, right?"

"No, I, uh, I have it with me."

"You have access to twenty-five and you offered me ten? If you've got that, you've probably got fifty."

"No!" Kristin seemed to be casting about for what to say next. She settled on, "Twenty-five max."

"It just went up to thirty-five." Talba figured it didn't matter how much she asked for, because she'd long since realized no money was going to change hands. (Well, it might, briefly—but Kristin would take it back once she had the tape.)

"I don't have it." Kristin said.

"Well, then, get it. I need time to get the combination, anyhow." She hung up. Kristin called back.

Let her stew, Talba thought, and called her favorite cop. "Langdon. 911. I need you immediately. With lots of Kevlar—and maybe the TAC squad."

Langdon sighed. "Good morning to you too, Baroness. You want to start at the beginning?"

"You know that tape I brought you yesterday? Kristin LaGarde just offered to buy it for thirty-five thousand dollars, give or take."

"What do you mean 'give or take'?"

"We're still bargaining. Hang on, my other phone's ringing." The office phone. She activated the speaker feature, hoping Langdon could hear and Kristin wouldn't notice. "Hello, Kristin," she said. "I just got Eddie on the phone. He's coming back at noon. Are we on?"

"I'm on my way."

"With the thirty-five K, I hope."

"Certainly. Look, Baroness, can you just bring it downstairs? We

281

don't want Eddie knowing—I mean, then you'd have to split the money, right?"

Talba thought at the time it would have been hilarious if this had really been the game Kristin seemed to think it was. (Though later, it occurred to her that she should have paid better attention to that little gambit.) "Don't worry about Eddie," she said. "I told him he had to come back to sign a check. He was furious because he has a lunch date at twelve o'clock, and now he'll be late. Believe me, he'll be here five minutes, max. See you at—I don't know—twelve-fifteen?"

"I'll be there. Just be sure he's gone."

She got back to Langdon, who said, "I can't believe I just heard what I think I heard."

"Listen up, Skip." Talba outlined her night's adventures, and then said, "What do you make of it?"

"I knew that woman was poison."

"What I thought was, we set up a surveillance camera—you can watch the whole transaction—"

"What? Watch her shoot you? How do you know that's not what she's planning?"

"Oh, I do think she's planning it. But she won't do it till after she makes sure it's the right tape. So you wait in the little coffee room where we have the VCR, and when we come in, you arrest her."

"Baroness, are you crazy? Arrest her for what? Overpaying her bill?"

"Okay, you don't arrest her yet. You take her down to Headquarters and apply rubber hoses, or whatever you do. And then you arrest her."

"Watch your mouth, okay? And no. I can't do that. And you can't do that. It's too dangerous."

Talba took a deep breath. She'd known the cop was going to say that. "You're forbidding me to meet a client in my own office? *You* can't do that. Look, I'm asking for police protection. Should I just hire a private security firm or do you want in on this?"

"Police protection."

"Let's try it another way. I've got a client coming into my office that I don't trust. Maybe you could be here as a friend, make sure nothing happens."

Langdon sighed, the sound rasping heavily over the wire. "I never used to do that."

"What?"

"Sigh. I never used to sigh. I counted three gray hairs this morning, and I've got big bags under my eyes. I never had either one till I met you."

"Yeah, Eddie complains, too."

"Not half as much as he's about to. He'll probably fire you, you know that, don't you?"

Talba hadn't thought of that. The trauma center at Charity, yes. But not Eddie firing her. And then the reality of it hit her. "It's too late. I've already made the date."

"Well, unmake it."

"I'm doing it."

"*Goddammit*, Talba! You make sure that office is empty, okay? I'll be there in fifteen minutes."

"Don't forget the Kevlar. And maybe a riot helmet."

While she waited for the cop, she asked Eileen Fisher if she could please take her lunch break at eleven-thirty, and then she put together a plan—not that Langdon wouldn't arrive with one of her own, but they could always argue.

The cop did bring Kevlar—and another cop. Backup. Good. She was first aware of their presence when she heard a man's voice saying, "Hi, the Baroness in?" It sounded like Adam Abasolo.

And Eileen Fisher saying, "Sure. I'll get her. Just be a second." Very friendly for Eileen.

"I'm coming, Eileen," Talba said, and by the time she got there, Langdon was already ordering her to get out and stay out till further notice, which miffed her. It miffed Talba as well.

"Some people can be so rude," she said. "Eileen, don't you have a wedding to go to? Why don't you take the rest of the day off and go buy a wedding present."

"I already ordered one online."

"Well, get some dancing shoes, then. This woman's a cop and she has no manners. Skip, maybe you need to apologize."

"Omigod!" Eileen cried. "You're Skip Langdon! Talba, for shame— *nobody* talks to Skip Langdon like that." What was up with Eileen?

Abasolo, probably. He was famous for his crowd-pleasing looks (so long as the crowd was female)—tall, wiry, with black hair and blue eyes. He looked a little like a movie star and a little like a thug, thus appealing to the bad-boy yen that apparently afflicted even Eileen Fisher. Not Talba's type, but easy on the orbs.

Langdon laughed. "Well, Her Grace is the only one. But she's right—I was out of line. We need you out of here for your own safety."

"Does Uncle Eddie know about this?" Eileen was rattled. Hardly anyone knew Eddie was her uncle.

"Eileen, don't *worry* about it." Talba said. "We haven't got much time. Look, call him, okay? Tell him something's going down in here and not to come back without calling."

Having a task seemed to please the girl. "Okay, then. I'm outta here." And she was.

"This better be good, Baroness," Langdon said. "You're tying up important brass here." Abasolo was a lieutenant. "Now here's what we're gonna do." And she outlined a plan that was startlingly similar to Talba's own.

By eleven-forty-five, Talba had tucked herself into a Kevlar vest, which did nothing for the way her blouse fit, and they had the camera set up, with Skip in the little closet-room to watch the monitor, and Abasolo in Eddie's office as backup.

Kristin was early. She strolled in about five after twelve, kitten heels clacking. Talba came out to meet her, noticing that she was carrying a purse and a briefcase. "Hi," Talba said. "The money in there?"

"You're awfully eager, aren't you?" Kristin was smirking, a new look for her.

"Come on in my office—in case anyone comes back."

"You guaranteed me nobody'd be here."

"And nobody will be. Let's just be safe." She let the little heels clack ahead of her—one of Skip's admonitions had been never to turn her back on the woman.

Once there, she said, "Okay, it's like that first time. Let me have the two bags."

"Why?" Kristin seemed surprised. "Oh. To check for a gun, you mean." She shrugged and handed over the bags. "Go ahead." Talba breathed again. An ankle holster wasn't possible—Kristin's miniskirt couldn't hide one. But she was wearing a suit jacket—a shoulder holster was. And the jacket had pockets. "Let me see your jacket."

Kristin handed over the garment, which Talba patted after first noting that not only wasn't Kristin wearing a shoulder holster, her knit top fit too tight to conceal anything but a pair of nipples, and it wasn't doing such a great job of that. Kristin caught Talba mentally frisking her. "You really don't trust me, do you?"

"I know it might come as a shock to you, but a lot of people would do anything to hang onto thirty-five thousand dollars." Talba opened the small purse, which contained nothing but a Gucci wallet, checkbook, cosmetics, and keys, and then opened the briefcase. It was full of cash, tied in neat bundles, like in the movies.

"Do you want to count it?"

"No. It looks all right."

"Go ahead, why don't you?"

Talba didn't like that. Why should Kristin want her to count it? Anyway, counting it wasn't in the plan. This was supposed to be quick and dirty. "No, thanks." She opened her desk drawer and pulled out an unlabeled (and illegal) tape of *Home Alone* that she'd made for Raisa. "Here's the tape of the Bacchus party," she said, identifying it fully for the surveillance tape. "A pleasure doing business with you."

"Hold it. How do I know this is really it?" Absolutely as predicted. Talba shrugged. "Let's go watch it."

That was the signal. The way the cop plan differed from hers was this: Instead of Talba marching Kristin into the coffee room, it called for Abasolo to step across the hall and Langdon to step down the hall—right behind him—and start asking embarrassing questions. Meanwhile, the camera was still running—Talba didn't know if it was something you could use in court, but at the very least, it ought to be lots of fun to see Kristin's reaction to it.

But it didn't work that way. What happened was, Talba did indeed hear footsteps in the hall, but they were coming from the wrong direction. Then she heard Abasolo step out of Eddie's office and say, "Police. Freeze or I'll blow your head off."

There was a fourth person in the office.

Talba and Kristin both froze, but apparently the intruder didn't. Someone fired two shots in rapid succession, and someone went down—more than one person from the sound of it. *Skip?* Talba thought. *Abasolo* and *Skip?*

Kristin whirled. Talba started around the desk, but by the time she got there, the other woman had done a three-sixty (or technically, two one-eighties), and she was coming at her, elbows bent, palms out, ready to shove. Talba registered that much before the elbows straightened and she took a blow in the chest, which knocked her backward. She struggled to get her balance. Her adversary kept coming.

Later, she thought that she should have heard Skip running, heard her radioing for help, but at the time, amazingly, she was in the zone. Not turtling out; right there. Not exactly on top of her game, but fully focused on trying to think of what the hell to do. You kick a man in the groin—what do you do with a woman? She had once read one of those Internet warning things about how not to attract rapists, and the very first thing to do (after staying out of parking garages) was never wear a ponytail, because they were easy to grab. Kristin wasn't wearing one, but she had plenty of hair to pull. Talba grabbed for some.

Kristin jerked her head back, but she threw a fist at Talba's chest. It probably would have hurt a lot worse without the vest, but it was still no day at the beach.

More Internet self-defense methods were coming to her, something about elbows. She threw her right one at Kristin's boobs, and that was better. "Uuuuuhhhh," the woman said, and teetered on her itty-bitty heels. But she was still standing. "Down!" Talba shouted. "Down, goddammit!" She kicked at Kristin's knees, but the other woman kicked back, with those nasty little heels. She was no Jackie Chan, but you still couldn't get close to her with that going on. Her hand snaked out, but not at Talba—at Talba's desk. It came up with a pen in it.

Talba knew from the Internet what she was going to do with that—she was going to go for the eyes. Only one thing to do. She closed them.

Closed them, lowered her head, and butted like a billy goat, catching her assailant full in the face. That did the trick—she could see flowered turquoise panties as Kristin went over backward. And then the woman's legs hit the floor, revealing a no longer beautiful face. If Talba wasn't mistaken, the lovely Miss LaGarde was going to need rhinoplasty to look her best in court.

"You bitch!" Kristin screamed, one hand gingerly touching her battered face.

She heard pounding footsteps, and Skip skidded into the office, barely stopping before she fell over the fallen former angel face. Shooting a quick look at Talba, who was rubbing the top of her head, she flipped Kristin over and cuffed her. Standing up, she barked, "You all right?" somewhere in Talba's direction.

"No!" Kristin screamed. "Call an ambulance."

"Thank God," Talba said to Skip. "Is Adam okay?"

Skip didn't answer. Instead, she rushed back to the hall, Talba following. She saw immediately why Skip had skidded—the floor and much of the walls were slick with blood—arterial blood, it seemed, from the looks of what was going on on the floor. Abasolo was bent over a man, applying pressure to his thigh, and Skip radioed for help, then took over as he ripped off his belt, to try to tie it into a tourniquet. The man was moaning in agony, his face turned away. Talba had to step around the whole grisly tableau to see that it was Royce Champagne.

Chapter Twenty-five

At Langdon's insistence, Talba went with the three of them to the hospital, ostensibly to make sure she wasn't seriously hurt—though she knew perfectly well she wasn't. But she *was* shaking and cold, utterly wrung out—the shock, Langdon said, the adrenaline crash. She was amazed at the "a" word—for once, adrenaline had been her friend. And now that she thought of it, this wasn't the first tight spot she'd fought her way out of. The turtle mechanism seemed to go off when she was blindsided—the surprise set off her imagination, and that stopped all motion. But she'd gone into this thing with her eyes open.

Also, the danger was real, not something in her head. The body had responded as it was programmed to do, as it did when soldiers went to war. She didn't try to figure it out. She made herself stop thinking about it.

Kristin must have gone out to meet Royce last night. It was probably his idea for her to call Talba with an ass-covering apology. Why had Talba believed that just-out-for-a-ride story? Then there was the suggestion that she bring the tape downstairs—what was Kristin going to do, shoot her from the car? No, someone else was going to grab her, or maybe follow her back to her office and kill her there.

Hindsight. Even Langdon had missed that one.

On the other hand, Kristin and *Royce*? On the face of it, it made no sense at all.

But it started to fall into place if you considered the economic possibilities of such an alliance. (And Kristin's well-known wandering eye.) She was a woman who was heavy into economic possibilities. Talba thought about her Lexus, her antique silver, her art collection; her dismissal of her nice house as a dump. She must have been counting the minutes till she could get her hands on the Champagne mansion. Then there was the disrespect she got from her father the boss. Getting rid of Daddy was probably even more appealing than shedding Buddy.

While Talba waited her turn in the emergency room, she pried Abasolo's story out of him: Royce had come in with a gun, Abasolo had warned him, Royce had raised the gun, both had fired, and the Kevlar vest had come in handy. Abasolo had a nasty bruise on his chest (or so he said—he didn't offer to show her), but no holes in it. Royce, on the other hand, had a crater in his thigh.

Abasolo had shouted that he was all right (Talba hadn't heard this, but she took his word for it), and Skip, running out of the coffee room, peeled off her jacket and threw it to him on the way to help Talba. Abasolo held it tight on Royce's wound till Skip could check on Talba, cuff Kristin, and return to help him. About thirty seconds' worth of action, and damn good police work, in Talba's opinion.

Meanwhile, Kristin maintained that she was only paying for a job well done and had jumped Talba because she thought the P.I. had set some trap for her that involved gun-toting thugs. Royce, she suggested, was in it with Talba. They were planning to kill her and/or frame her for two murders, she wasn't sure which. Eventually, her lawyer turned up to tell her to zip her lip, but the cops now had a nice story to run by Royce, who hollered "Bitch!" and even ruder epithets—and spat out his own version—before his own lawyer slapped duct tape over *his* mouth.

Talba spent a few hours at Headquarters, but between tête-à-têtes with Langdon and Abasolo, she at least had time to call Eileen Fisher about a cleanup crew.

And she called Eddie: "EdDEE. Ever see *Gunfight at the OK Corral?*"

"I'm hangin' up. Right now."

"Just don't go back to the office today, okay? I know you can't stand the sight of blood."

Maybe, she thought on signing off, there'd been a better way to handle that. So she called Angie, reeled off her yarn, and asked her to pour oil on the waters. After that, she returned the twenty-seven calls she'd logged from Jane Storey, but only to say she couldn't say anything, but to treat her nicely in tomorrow's paper and Jane would get her reward when the details shook out.

It took a while longer, but Talba finally got a chance to talk to Langdon alone. Quite simply, it seemed that Royce and Kristin turned on each other. The way Skip told it, they both produced more or less the same story. "He said, she said," Skip sighed. "See, Royce says he was a happily married man, but somehow Kristin managed to seduce him—just once, of course—and after that, she just couldn't leave him alone, no matter how much he resisted her unwelcome advances."

Talba smiled. "It could happen to anybody, right?"

"Poor little Royce," Skip said. "Well, one night he's minding his own business and Kristin gets in a drunken brawl with Buddy, and naturally Royce comes running downstairs to see what's going on. You can just imagine his horror and grief at the sight of his own father dead on the library floor, having been beaned by his sweetie with a marble statue."

"One of those damned blackamoors," Talba said.

"Yeah. Figure of a guy in a turban."

"Buddy had two—Adele was kind of embarrassed by them."

"Ugly damn things," Skip said. "Well, the evil Kristin coerces him into helping him disguise the murder by saying if he didn't, she'd wake up the household and accuse *him* of it."

"What'd she tell him the argument was all about?"

"Buddy's obsessive jealousy. So Royce reluctantly agrees, and they hatch a plan. First they lift the Bacchus tape from Lucy's room, and make a phony tape for Wesley Burrell. Then they load Buddy in the trunk and Kristin steals Daddy's gun—"

"Hold it—how do they do that?"

"Kristin has a key to Daddy's house and she knows the alarm code. So they get the key, drive to the marina, put Buddy in the boat, and take it out far enough so no one hears the shot—or at least they hear it from a distance—and Kristin shoots her own fiancé in the head to cover up what really happened. You following so far?"

Talba nodded, riveted.

"Well, that's it. You buying it?"

"It fits with the facts, anyhow. But what about Suzanne? Kristin killed her, too?"

"*Oh*, yeah. Must have, anyhow. Royce wouldn't know a damn thing about that, and Kristin still had the gun."

"The motive being?"

Skip heaved her shoulders in a big fake shrug. "Royce wouldn't know, but it must have been jealousy because Kristin was so obsessed with him. So he had to stand by and see his own wife murdered and couldn't even go to the cops because of his completely understandable part in the cover-up of Buddy's murder."

"Oh, boy. In that case, what was he doing in my office?"

"Well, he had to try to help recover the tape because it incriminated him, even though he was completely innocent."

"Right. That sure explains the gun."

"Oh, that. Well, Kristin explained how dangerous you are, being a blackmailer and all, and he fired because he'd encountered a strange man holding a gun on him. Wouldn't anyone?"

"Good enough lawyer, a jury might buy it."

"But you forget, if the DA buys that scenario, Kristin's the one on trial, and naturally she'd have to testify in her own defense."

"Okay. Hit me with the 'she said.' "

"Would you believe it? It's practically the same story, only in reverse. See, even though she was deeply devoted to Buddy, Royce seduced *her* (really, just once)—"

"Could happen to anybody."

"Uh-huh. And after that he just couldn't leave her alone, no matter how much she resisted his unwelcome advances. So finally, unbeknownst to her, Royce goes to his father and says the two of them are in love, but Buddy, of course, rightly refuses to believe him, and a fight breaks out, which ends with Royce killing him with the very same

291

marble statue he said *Kristin* killed him with. She figures he must have somehow stolen her key to her father's house, lifted the gun, moved the body to the marina all by himself, and shot his dad to obscure the evidence, after first making the tape. She figures all this out, but she figures I won't, so that's why she hires you—so he'll get his just deserts."

"But she doesn't tell me anything about her suspicions."

"Right. But then later Royce kills Suzanne because somehow she must have found out, after which Kristin finds the gun in her car and gets scared because she knows he planted it."

"But she still doesn't mention any of this to anybody."

"Right. Must have had a lot of faith in you, Baroness, knowing you'd somehow get to the bottom of it, not having a clue where you were going."

"But then I figure out about the tape and *she* tries to buy it back. How does she explain that? Not to mention the fact that Royce turns up in my office with a gun."

"Well, see, she gets brave and confronts Royce all by her sweet self, and he coerces her into getting the tape for him. Says he'll kill her if she doesn't, and she knows how dangerous he is, because by now he's pretty much admitted to all the rest of it—"

"Uh-huh."

"And she had no idea he was going to follow her into the office. Why, he was probably going to kill *her*."

"*And* me."

Skip slapped her hands together and folded them, seemingly in conclusion. "That's her theory."

"What's yours?"

"No way they weren't in it together. The main question is, who actually killed Buddy? No prints on the statue, naturally."

"Well, I've got another couple of questions. Why hire me, and why turn in the gun?"

"Okay, what's *your* theory?"

"I think they always meant to frame LaGarde—only they needed me to make it work. They couldn't manipulate you, but they thought they could lead me right to LaGarde. So they let me spin my wheels, then they plant the gun, and the idea was, I turn it in, then he goes to prison, and Kristin takes over the business. And Royce inherits his half of his mother's money. When Buddy died, the money probably passed to Lucy and Royce. I already know the house did."

Skip nodded. "Right on that count. Celeste had a trust that matured before she died, and Buddy got the money."

"So if they were in it together, Royce and Kristin could get married and they'd be in control of two major fortunes."

"Yeah, that's what I think, too."

"Only thing was, they thought they needed me to poke around enough to set LaGarde up. Probably thought I couldn't detect my way out of a broom closet, but then I found the tape, and they panicked."

"We're on the same page, Baroness. Just give me a few more days."

So what do you think, Eddie?" Ms. Wallis asked.

Eddie had had to forgive her for the OK Corral. Sure, it messed up his office, and, well, yes, it was kind of stupid and dangerous. But it did show ingenuity. Not to mention the fact that it had worked.

But the best part, in his opinion, was the way she'd folded the cops into her scheme to trap Kristin. She'd gotten around them. He liked that. He wondered if he'd have had the guts to do it himself.

"What I think," he said, "if either of those two birds tried to apply for a job as a White House spin doctor, they'd be laughed right out of the place. And nobody, but *nobody* can come up with dumber lies than the jokers in the West Wing."

"Yeah. They need lying lessons from the master."

"Uh-uh," said Eddie. "They need about a hundred years in maximum security. Or worse. But I still don't see why they bothered to shoot Buddy. The whole idea was to cover up who killed him—all they had to do was make the tape and move the body."

"That was to frame LaGarde. One or the other of them must have thought of it right at the get-go. Buddy had a gun in his night table; I found it when I was working there. They could have used that and made it look like suicide if that was what they were after."

"Oh. What do you bet that explains the second gun? The one Royce had when he came to the office?"

Ms. Wallis snapped her fingers. "Eddie, you're a genius."

"Uh-huh. Talked to LaGarde yet?"

"Oh, sure. And he cleared up a couple of big things for me. When Kristin came in with the gun yarn, she seemed really, really upset—pale, shaky, the whole thing—like she was about to faint. Absolutely took me in. I told her dad she sure was a good actress, and he said when she was a little kid, she used to drink salt water and throw up to create that little effect."

"The woman's got a screw loose."

"Her dad's an expert on that one. He just had to mention he tried to warn me, which, by the way, would have worked against him if those two had succeeded. He's not even paying for Kristin's lawyer."

"Well, that's pretty cold. He *is* her father."

"Yeah, but she did try to set him up. The whole idea was to get rid of him and take over his business."

Eddie shifted, uncomfortable with such a pat explanation. "Yeah, but he knew she was a sociopath, and he'd have to know she set him up—no way would he sign it over to her. I never really got why he kept her on the payroll, anyhow."

A canary-feathers look came over her face. She'd figured it out, of course. "He had to. That was the other thing I asked him about. It was all in Grandpa's will—you remember the whole LaGarde empire started with Warren's daddy. She was to go to work for the company and learn the business, and after Warren's death—or if anything ever happened so that he couldn't run the business—Kristin took it over. And once she had control of it, that would have been all she wrote—she'd have stolen every dime he and Tootsie-pop ever had. That's the real reason they hired me—they *really* needed to put him away. Sure, the police might have done it, but they could steer their humble employee in the right direction."

"Or thought they could."

She acknowledged his vote of confidence with a pseudosalute. "And the fact that Kristin hired a P.I. made her look above reproach. She gave the game away herself—by freaking out when I told her about the tape. But if it had worked, she and Royce would have walked away with the entire LaGarde empire and half of whatever Buddy left—which was considerable, by the way, even if you don't count that Creole Versailles they've got over there, which would probably go for about six million by itself."

"Well, how about Lucy and Adele? How were they were going to screw them out of the rest of the Reedy money?"

"Gives me goose bumps just to think about it. Where were these people going to stop?"

Eddie said, "They really were an item, then? Kristin and Royce?"

Ms. Wallis laughed. He had meant it ironically, and she took it as such, which pleased him. "It was all about greed," she said. "Every bit of it. If we can extrapolate from what the ex-husband said, La-Garde foisted her off on Buddy to get what he wanted from a crooked judge, but he had no idea she'd try to marry him. Know what La-Garde told me? He asked her why, and she said, 'I like the house.' I'll just bet she did. I've been to *her* house—that woman is into possessions in a big way. I'll bet she couldn't wait to get that monster for herself and turn it into the Hearst Castle South. Meanwhile, she gets involved with Royce—she's got a history of that kind of thing—and then . . ."

"Yeah? What next?"

"I don't know how far it went. But I think she did it just because she could."

"Kind of like Bill Clinton."

Ms. Wallis nodded. "I think she would have dumped Royce once she was married to Buddy and turfed him right out of the castle. But then— here's the one thing we know for sure: One of them killed Buddy in a fight in his own house. So she must have gone to Plan B."

Eddie said, "The question is, which twin has the Toni?"

"Huh?" Ms. Wallis asked. "What does that mean?"

"Ms. Wallis, Ms. Wallis. I forget how young ya are. What it ain't is some hip-hop lyric. Know what home perms are?"

"I think they still have them."

"It's from an old perm ad. Wonder if Langdon'll be able to charge either one of them."

"She will, or she'll die trying."

It took a few days, but one morning Talba got the call from Jane Storey: "It's Royce."

"Meaning?"

"Royce Champagne has been charged with the murder of his father. FYI and all. Thought you'd want to know."

"Oh, yeah? What's the reasoning?"

"They've got a witness, but they're not saying who it is."

"Oh." It could be only one of two people.

"But get this," Jane said. "They've both been charged in Suzanne's murder."

"Both? How could that be?"

"I'm still working on it."

CHAPTER TWENTY-SIX

Talba took a ride out to the Champagne house, where she found Adele working in the garden, wearing jeans for once.

"Hi."

Adele stood up, brushing off her hands. "They've charged my grandson—you heard?"

"I hear they have a witness. I'm just hoping her name doesn't start with 'L.'"

"Thank God Lucy didn't wake up that night—at least she's saying she didn't. Come in, why don't you. I've got some iced tea made."

They drank the tea in the sun room. Adele looked smaller, older, and a whole lot sadder. The lines from her mouth to her chin reminded Talba of a marionette. She couldn't remember noticing that before. "I couldn't get past Suzanne," Adele said. "Yes, he's my grandson, but my God! He killed his own wife!"

Not to mention his father, Talba thought.

"Buddy. Jesus. Anybody might have killed him. Had all of Celeste's money, and still sold himself for hams. The man was bent, that's all. He enjoyed being a crook."

Talba had thought a lot about that. "Some kind of power thing," she mused.

"Oh, yeah. Buddy loved to play the big man. Listen, I heard the argument they had. I wanted to kill him myself. It wasn't anything to do with Kristin. That was Royce's story to the cops, but it wasn't *anything* like that. He was so shamed by his own father, he wouldn't even tell them why he killed him."

"What happened, Adele?"

"You know how big this house is." She flung out an arm to illustrate. "You can't hear anything from one room to another. That's why I'm hoping and praying Lucy really did sleep through it. I was awake when it happened. I came downstairs for a nightcap and heard them arguing in the library. You know what it was about? Buddy's damned greed. That was all in the world there was to it. Royce was furious that he'd cheated those poor shrimpers—specifically that Cheramie man. He was trying to get him to pay 'em and shut down that goddam loser of a marina. Then Buddy started yelling at him—berating him for being a failure. Jesus, I was mad! I wouldn't treat a roach the way he treated that boy. I was tempted to go in there and smack him down myself. But what I did was fix myself a bourbon and water, and go back upstairs. With the rest of the bottle."

"You didn't actually see the murder?"

"Oh, God, no. That's how I rationalized not saying anything. Buddy could have gone out after the argument, you know? I didn't *know* Royce did it. But then when that message thing came out, I couldn't keep quiet anymore. Anyhow, that night I had my drink, and then another, and I read for a while. And then I did hear someone on the second floor. I thought it was Lucy going to the bathroom, but it must have been Royce getting the tape. Anyhow, at the time, I didn't think much about it. I just had yet another drink and went beddy-bye. Slept very damn soundly, I might add."

"You never heard Buddy fall?" It seemed to Talba the house might have shaken a bit.

She shook her head. "Absolutely not. But he was probably sitting down at the time. He probably *didn't* fall. Royce probably got to the end of his rope and threw the blackamoor at him in a rage. But he must have calmed down and realized all he'd have had to do to cover it up would be wipe his prints off the statue, make the tape, and get someone to help him move the body. But he wouldn't have known how to make the tape himself. That's why he must have called Kristin." She winced. "That and the fact that he thought he could trust her because he was screwing her. He and Kristin could easily have gotten Buddy out of there, and no one the wiser."

"But someone was, apparently."

For a moment, Adele looked puzzled. "Oh. You mean Suzanne. I guess she woke up. Or somehow figured it out. Or maybe Royce was fool enough to think if he killed her, that psychopath Kristin really would have married him, the idiot." She pulled a tissue from her pocket and dabbed at her eye. "Goddammit, he never had a chance."

Privately, Talba disagreed. He'd had at least two chances to keep blood off his hands and he'd blown them both. "Why," she said, "do you think *he* killed Suzanne? Kristin could have done it—she was the one who ended up with LaGarde's gun. Maybe he gave it back to her after they shot Buddy."

Adele sighed. "She has an excellent alibi."

Talba remembered that Kristin had offered to alibi LaGarde when the heat was on him. "Not her father," she said.

"No. People in her office. Clients. She was in the office all day— had meetings straight through. Oh, yes. Little Kristin looked after herself."

"So did Royce really try to frame her—with the gun?"

"*Hell*, no! He was a fool to the very end. It was the bitch's idea to frame her dad. Royce killed Suzanne and gave the gun back to her, poor trusting idiot."

"But how do you *know* that?"

"I know what my grandson told me," she snapped. "Kristin thought that alibi thing would protect her. She didn't count on a conspiracy charge." She paused and then put all the venom she possessed into what she said next. "Idiot!"

It seemed to be Adele's favorite word of the day.

Her conjectures about the murder seemed far too well thought out to be theory only. Talba suspected that Royce had told her the story before Suzanne was killed, and counted on her silence on that one also. She was still confused about one thing, but she didn't quite know how to ask it. "So they plan the setup together, but who actually fired the shot to make it work?"

"Are you kidding? That bitch Kristin. Royce could never do a cold thing like that."

Her faith in her grandson was touching, but Talba tended to agree with her. Kristin was definitely the cooler of the two customers. She finally asked the main thing she'd come to find out. "How's Lucy?"

"Terrible. Refuses to see Dr. Watson any more. Hates him. Hates me."

"She's not answering my calls, either."

"Hates the world." Adele shook her head, apparently to shut out anything and everything. She'd begun weeping, and got up to find more tissues.

Talba took the hint and left, but she had a tiny bit of a plan—there was one thing she might be able to do for Lucy. She called Cindy Lou Wootten, a psychologist she knew who sometimes consulted with the police department, and asked for a name.

"Let me call Skip," Wootten said. "She knows somebody."

"Skip? How would she know a kid shrink?"

"Trust me—she does. I'll get back to you."

The name she got from Langdon was Joanne Leydecker, known to one and all as "Boo." "I've already called her," Langdon said. "She'll meet the kid. How you arrange it is up to you."

"Boo? That's a name?"

"B-o-o."

"Tell me about her."

"The short version is, she's a woman who's had a lot of trouble. She's also a great shrink. I went to her myself."

"But this is for a kid."

"Well, she specializes in kids now. She has an adopted son who's also had it hard and somehow, they ended up with each other. Trust me, nobody in Louisiana but this woman can understand what Lucy's been through. If Lucy likes her—and she will—she's the right person. But it's going to be up to you to get them together."

"So what's the story, Skip?"

"It's not up to me to tell it."

Two weeks later, at Reggie and Chaz, Princess Lucy returned for her sophomore performance. Raisa and Darryl were there, and so was Boo Leydecker. Lemon Blancaneaux was the emcee. Serenity Prayer Jones was too drunk to read, but the Baroness did (though her introduction was somewhat longer than her poem). She was dressed uncharacteristically in black, with a red scarf tied round her head.

"I didn't title this one," she said, "because I thought I'd let you decide what it's about. Could be life itself maybe, or your best friend—it could be any kind of betrayal. Hope it's not your husband, though. 'Haiku.'"

Haiku
A kiss before it
Rips a nasty line of blood
From your fine smooth skin.

She ended with her usual line, "The Baroness myself thanks you." And, as always, she curtsied, but this time she didn't get her usual appreciation. The audience seemed more or less stunned.

Lemon came back onstage. "Hey, Baroness, what's up with that shit? That was cold."

"Oh, come on, Lemon. It was only a little *trickle* of blood. Haven't you ever had a cat? Know how they jump out of your lap and scratch your hand in the process?"

"*That's* about a cat?"

"If you like," said the Baroness. "Go put a Band-Aid on it."

"I'm gon' have to put a Band-Aid on this *show*," Lemon said. "I'm the one bleedin' over here. Bet a fourteen-year-old kid could do better than that. Okay, y'all, let's all welcome, for the second time at Reggie and Chaz, that poetic prodigy, the teenage mistress of metaphor and mystery—the Princess *Lucy!*"

Lucy was dressed in a short, kiltlike skirt with little pleats, a navy zip-front hooded sweater, and black canvas boots, each of which was decorated with a cat's skull (ears miraculously intact) and a pair of crossbones. She had lost still more weight, which would have been becoming if she hadn't been so pale, and even that might have been dramatic if not for the sprinkling of zits on her fair skin. She looked like what she was—a kid going through a hell of a time. "That was *so* transparent, Talba," she said. "But a Band-Aid's not gonna do it—I think I need a full body cast. Don't y'all worry about it, though—it's just that teenage angst thang. This is a little thing called 'Santana.'"

Before she started to read, Raisa's whisper could be heard in the silence: "What's that mean, Daddy?"

"Later," Darryl whispered, and Lucy said again:

Santana
I turn East, hoping for dawn
And instead hear the rumble
That signals winds of change,
That roar and tear,
Cold and furious
Through the chaotic quiet.

Uh-uh. No way.

I'm going South—
Where the sun burns and blinds
But dries my tears
As it warms my frozen marrow
And thaws my fury
And unleashes it,
Searing through hide to naked bone.

Raw and ragged, I flee West

Into the rain, which pelts, relentless,
Till I am in above my head.
The water soothes.
It calms.
It rinses Yesterday.
It rushes and cascades
Like love itself
And it drowns hope
And then recedes
And I see that it has worn away

P.I. on a Hot Tin Roof

The stone that took
A billion years to build
And nothing is left

Except the solid wall of North.

I walk into the mountains
And I see the stones
The wild cascades have missed,
Outcroppings of a thousand ranges
That cannot be blown away
Or burned
Or worn down smooth—
A plain of desolation that
Might hold my weight.

But these new rocks are hard and sharp
And bruise and beat and tear.
I want the winds again.
I want the East!
I CRAVE SANTANA!
But I am like that Irish falcon,
Turning and turning—
Nor knowing where to turn.

Lucy stopped and curtsied, ever so sweetly. "The Princess myself thanks you."

She got the applause that usually went to the Baroness. Lemon took the stage again and said, "Hey! What y'all think of that? Young lady been readin' Yeats! Prayer, you and everybody else better wake up and start writin'—we finally got a *literate* poet up here. Stealin' all y'all's thunder. Only fourteen, ladies and gentlemen—the Princess *Lucy!*"

More applause. Lemon seemed to have taken a shine to her.

Lucy was radiant. She turned to Boo, whom she had barely met before the reading. "Whatcha think, shrink? Am I crazy or what?"

"What do *you* think—are you?"

"Right. Just like all of them—always asking questions."

"Well, you asked me a *dumb* question. You know the answer. You really want to know what I think?"

"Not especially."

"Well, I'm going to tell you anyhow. I think we should go South—that is, if you want to work with me."

"South?"

"That's where the energy is—all that lovely anger. Besides, you're a redhead. Lots of fire there. Slouch on over at six Tuesday. You've gotta get out of that widening gyre."

"Daddy," Raisa asked, "what's 'santana' mean?"

"I don't know. Something like nirvana, Luce?"

"It's a warm breeze," the girl said.

"Or a hot wind," Talba added, "depending on how you look at it."